LAST
NIGHT

ALSO BY KERRY WILKINSON

Down Among the Dead Men
No Place Like Home
Watched
Ten Birthdays
Two Sisters
The Girl Who Came Back

THE JESSICA DANIEL SERIES
The Killer Inside (also known as *Locked In*)
Vigilante
The Woman in Black
Think of the Children
Playing with Fire
The Missing Dead (also known as *Thicker Than Water*)
Behind Closed Doors
Crossing the Line
Scarred for Life
For Richer, For Poorer
Nothing but Trouble

SHORT STORIES
January
February
March
April

THE ANDREW HUNTER SERIES
Something Wicked
Something Hidden

SILVER BLACKTHORN SERIES
Reckoning
Renegade
Resurgence

LAST NIGHT

KERRY WILKINSON

Published by Bookouture in 2018

An imprint of StoryFire Ltd.

Carmelite House
50 Victoria Embankment
London EC4Y 0DZ

www.bookouture.com

ISBN: 978-1-78681-424-1
eBook ISBN: 978-1-78681-423-4

ONE

- TUESDAY -

There's blood on my windscreen.

It's in the corner, a few speckled spots and then a thicker pool towards the bottom.

This is definitely a dream; there can't be any question about that. There's a hazy grey around the edges of my vision; that blinking, fuzzy sense that everything in front of me is a bewildering construct of my imagination.

The only thing that tells me it's not is when I yawn. It's a big one: head back, neck cricked, jaw dislocating, eyes streaming – the works. The type of thing that grips a person and doesn't let go until there have been multiple follow-ups and apologies, combined with the rapid flapping of hands.

Sorry, I'm not bored of you – I'm yawning because I was up early this morning. It's been a long day.

That sort of thing.

People don't yawn in dreams. I don't think I ever have. Dreaming is for flying and fantasising; reality is the mundanity of yawning.

Then there's the unflinching stare of the clock. The greeny-grey LED figures beam through the fog of darkness, relentlessly insisting it is 02:41. Then, unexpectedly, 02:42.

That's another sign. Dreams don't pass in individual minutes, they move with dizzying speed; jumping from place to place, time to time. They're everything and nothing all at the same time.

They don't tick by minute to minute.

But if I'm not dreaming, then how to explain what I am seeing?

There's a steering wheel, the digital clock, a windscreen. The inside of a car, obviously. An air freshener is jammed into the vent by the window with a grubby chamois stuffed into the well of the driver's door.

My car – although it takes me a few seconds to figure that out. Everything feels a bit slow, even my thoughts. Like a phone call from a far-flung country in the old days where someone would speak and the voice would sound a few seconds later.

It's definitely my car, though. A third-hand Kia that has a dent in the rear bumper from where I mistook a concrete pillar for a parking space.

Easy mistake to make.

I'm in my car at 02:42 and it's dark. Of course it is. I can't see much beyond the windscreen. The glass is misty and damp with a thin sheen of condensation tickling the outside.

When I try to sit up straighter, I realise the seat belt is across me and I'm strapped in. The overhead light is on.

It's such a familiar scene and yet so unclear. I get into my car day after day without thinking. Press the button on the fob, driver's door open, bag behind the driver's seat, slide inside, key in the ignition, handbrake down, and go. Like a reflex.

This is wrong. Everything's in place physically: from the half-eaten bag of M&Ms by the handbrake to the sunglasses tossed haphazardly into the space between the gearstick and the cigarette lighter.

The problem is that I have no idea why I'm in my car at what is now 02:43, let alone where I am. It hurts when I try to think, as if there's something inside my head fighting against me.

I'm not sure if it's that thought or the actual cold that brings goosebumps to my arms.

The key is in the ignition. It's when I go to turn it that I realise the condensation towards the bottom of the windscreen isn't water at all. It's darker and thicker.

It was the first thing I saw when I woke up but I'd somehow forgotten.

Blood.

Before I know it, I've opened the door and I'm leaning over the bonnet to get a better look. So many things occur to me at the same time that it's difficult to take it all in. The ground is mushy and soft: a field with a slight peppering of grass or plant. I can see that because of the light from the moon. It's far from full, a sort of apologetic excuse for a crescent, but it's bright enough to spill white across the field, even through the speckling of clouds. There's a hedge shrouded in darkness behind me, with an obvious gap of flattened space where the car has come through.

Then there's the blood.

There are a few splashes on the windscreen but much more spotted across the silver bonnet. It is a shiny black in the moonlight, slick and smooth like oil. The merest hint of crimson gives away the truth. There's more on the front of the car, spattered across the paintwork and drizzled onto the grill.

Trying to force the memory only creates a fizzing stab of pain near my temple. The familiar prickle from my age-old scar is there when I run my fingers across it. There's something hypnotic about the sensation and I don't dare to think of the number of hours I've spent absent-mindedly running my fingers along the raised zigzag of flesh. I barely remember a time when it wasn't there.

At first I wonder if it's my blood. I pat my chest and abdomen, dig my fingers into my hair – but there's nothing. I'm not in any particular pain, either. Only that dull, thumping confusion.

The car – *my* car – must have hit a deer, something like that. I remember it happening to the woman who lived across the road until a few years ago. Sophie or Sonia. One of those shorter names.

She was heading home from her weekly big shop. One minute she was driving along the dual carriageway, the next a deer had hurtled out from the bushes. There was only going to be one winner – and it wasn't the poor animal. There was a thud and a squeal, then Sophie or Sonia's car slalomed across the highway before slamming into a crash barrier. She woke up in hospital. I suppose Sophie or Sonia wasn't a winner, either. It took her almost six months to get behind the wheel again. I once found her sitting in the driver's seat on her own driveway, too frightened to turn the engine on.

That must have been what happened here. I was driving… somewhere… hit a deer and careered through the hedge into this field. That explains the blood. What it *doesn't* explain is the gaping hole in my memory.

Holes.

I remember bits and pieces. There was the hotel bed. It was harder than I'm used to, like sleeping on the floor. The sheets were tucked tightly, like they always are in hotels, as if they're trying to stop people from getting inside.

I was in bed and now I'm here. From there to this.

I do a lap of the car and feel groggy, like the morning after a night on the razz. My mouth is dry but I don't remember drinking that much. I used to pride myself on not getting hangovers when I was in my twenties, but now, at forty-one, it's all too much. Not only are hangovers barely a couple of drinks away, but they last entire weekends. It's not worth it any longer. I wouldn't have had more than a glass or two. That's not me.

Once around the car and there's no sign of a deer.

I do a second lap just in case I missed something and then head unsteadily towards the hedge.

I'm in my work uniform: smart skirt, blouse, jacket – and the flat shoes I keep in my bag that I switch out with my heels as and when I'm meeting a client. It's what I would have been wearing at the hotel before going to bed.

My shoes are thin, more for comfort than practicality. They slurp and slide across the soft marshland. At least I'm not sinking into the ground.

A road is on the other side of the hedge. It's crumbling and narrow, barely wide enough for two cars – a typical country lane. I could be pretty much anywhere in rural Britain. I navigate a shallow ditch and then walk up and down the road, looking for any trace of a deer.

Nothing.

No skid marks, no trail of blood, no anything.

There's not even the hum of night-time traffic in the background, let alone street lights. It feels like I'm, well… nowhere.

After a few fruitless minutes, I walk back to the gap in the hedge – which is the only spot where I can see tyre marks. There's a slim bump of a ditch with dents in the soil from where the car left the road. From there is a direct trail to the car in the field.

No deer though. No badger or fox. Not even a rabbit.

Even if the car had hit an animal that had survived and run off, there would surely be blood – but the only place I can see it is on the windscreen and bonnet.

I stand at the side of the driver's door turning in a circle, trying to figure it out. It's cool but not cold, a gentle breeze licking across the seemingly endless field. All I can see in the distance is the dark.

Back in the car and I find my bag behind the driver's seat. It's where I always leave it. Everything is as it should be. Except that the car is covered in blood and in a field, obviously.

There was a time when I was scared of driving. I wasn't as bad as Sophie or Sonia across the road, but, for a while, I'd avoid motorways, preferring quieter roads with slower speed limits. I always gave way, stopped at amber lights, never broke the speed limits. It was such a long time ago that I'd largely forgotten that feeling of fear when it came to cars.

The two things went together whenever I got into the driver's seat.

A key in the ignition meant a fleeting tingle of anxiety. That was when I was a teenager – another time, another person – but it's there again now, niggling at the back of my mind.

I blink the sensation away – and find my phone in my bag, where it should be. I'm ready to use the maps app to figure out where I am, but there are already notifications waiting for me. The bright white of the screen burns through the gloom and it takes me a few seconds to take in the words.

There's a missed call from Dan, which is strange, as he never usually calls. My husband isn't a big talker, not when it comes to me. Texts are another thing – and he's sent one of those.

Olivia didn't come home tonight. Did she text you? Call if you want. Don't worry about the time. I won't silence my phone.

It's typical Dan. Complete sentences and full stops, even in texts. There's the passive aggression as well – 'if you want' – as if our daughter not coming home is something that wouldn't concern me.

He sent it a little before eleven, by which time Olivia should have definitely been home from work. She's eighteen, so old enough to stay out for the night – but she does usually let us know if she's not coming home.

I read the text again, focusing on the 'if you want'. I can imagine him saying it in that casual, off-the-cuff way that he does, as if it means nothing – even though he'll throw it back in my face if we argue. *When* we argue.

If you want.

Yeah, I bloody *do* want, actually.

Let's see if you *want* to be called at three in the morning.

Dan answers his phone before it can ring a second time. I wasn't expecting that. He sounds awake and alert, no hint of a yawn, despite the time. He doesn't bother with a 'hi', going straight in with, 'I wondered if you'd call.'

'Only just got your message,' I reply – which is more or less true.

'Let me check her room. Hang on.'

There's a muffled thump and then a stunted silence. I press back into the driver's seat and hug an arm across myself. It's starting to feel cold. I check myself in the mirror but there are no scrapes or scuffs on my face. A minute or so later and Dan is back.

'Liv's not home,' he says. 'Did she text you?'

'Nothing. Did she go to work as normal?'

'I guess so. I was at work and then the gym. I've not seen her since this morning. Rahul would've called if she hadn't made it, though.'

That's true enough. Olivia's boss has called in the past when she didn't show up. That was back in the old days – three months ago – when Liv wasn't as reliable as she has been recently. A few months can feel like ice ages when it comes to living with teenagers.

'She seemed fine this morning,' I reply, knowing that 'fine' involved her hardly saying anything and then grunting her way back to her bedroom with a bottle of water.

Perhaps it's because I'm in a field in the middle of the night but it doesn't feel as if I should be too concerned about Olivia. She's at that age where a drink with friends can turn into more than one, which then becomes sleeping on someone's sofa. Slightly concerned parents can easily be forgotten. I was the same at her age – *worse* – and we didn't have mobile phones back then.

Dan hums to himself, thinking it over. 'I'm sure she's fine,' he concludes.

'I'm sure, too.'

'I thought you'd want to know.'

'That's very considerate. Thank you for telling me.'

There's a silence as we each think over the forced politeness. We can do this when we want. We're actually pretty good at it.

Dan continues to say nothing, which, in itself, says plenty.

'Is there something else?' I ask.

'No… well, perhaps. Did you move my gym fob? I couldn't find it earlier. I had to get a temporary one.'

It's typical really. I'm away for the night, our daughter is AWOL, and Dan's worried about the gym.

'I don't remember seeing it around,' I reply. 'Did you try the kitchen drawer?'

I'm good sometimes. He's not the only one that can do passive aggression. The kitchen drawer is where we keep all those types of things. Old and new keys, emergency money, receipts, coupons, lottery tickets. It's an emporium of everything. It's exactly where his gym fob would have been; the first place he would have looked.

I can sense the annoyance in his voice when he replies. 'I tried there,' he says. 'Checked my pockets, my car…'

He tails off but I've had my moment of satisfaction.

'Hopefully I'll find it in the morning,' he concludes. 'I'll see you tomorrow.'

Without waiting for a goodbye, let alone offering one of his own, he's gone. I stab the phone screen twice to make sure it's not that I've lost reception. It's not – it's that he'd had enough of talking to me. It occurs to me that the only reason he called and texted was because of his misplaced fob, nothing to do with Olivia at all.

I drop the phone into the well on the side of the door and, from nowhere, have a moment of clarity, grabbing the chamois from the driver's door and heading back into the night air. I wipe as much of the blood as I can from the windscreen and bonnet but, even in the grim light, it's a poor job. I've done more smearing than I have cleaning. It'll have to do for now.

It's only when I'm back inside the car, fingers touching the key, that I realise the one thing that should have been obvious.

If the blood doesn't belong to an animal, then maybe it belongs to a person.

TWO

The ripple of doubt makes me shiver. It can't be a person. It just *can't*. Besides, I walked around the car, I checked the verges and the road. It's not simply that there's no sign of a wounded or dead animal, there's no sign of anything – or anyone.

The car starts first time, the headlights switching on automatically and flaring deep into the distance, only to be swallowed by the murky shadows. I clip in my seat belt once more and then press gently on the accelerator, listening to the engine rev as it fights against the handbrake. It sounds as if everything's working. Not that I know anything about cars. 'It sounds fine', or 'it looks fine' generally does me.

I let the car idle for a moment, then softly release the handbrake while whispering a quiet, 'Come on.'

The ground is soft but not overly muddy, though I'm sure there's a chance the car could get stuck. I have no idea if someone's supposed to go quickly or slowly in order to avoid being marooned. I opt for slow, easing the car backwards.

'That's it,' I say quietly, urging the vehicle on. 'Just like that.'

The engine purrs smoothly as the tyres grip. The car bumps up, then down, as it carefully manoeuvres over the uneven ground. I'm closing in on the flattened hedge in the rear-view mirror when there's a gurgle from somewhere underneath. It feels as if I'm moving sideways and there's a gloopy glug, then the car jolts upwards, shooting over a bump and creaking before I ease off the accelerator.

'C'mon,' I whisper. 'Do it for me. I'll give you a nice clean in the morning.'

I try again, a little more forceful on the accelerator this time, and the car shunts up and down like an old wooden roller-coaster cart. I'm momentarily bounced around in my seat and then the car slaloms into an abrupt descent. The verge is shallow and there's a fleeting, fearful second where I'm convinced I'm going to be trapped. It only lasts for a blink. The moment the rear wheels touch the tarmac of the road, the car zips back, temporarily out of control until I spin the steering wheel and find myself staring down the shadowed country road, out of breath. The headlights beam into the distance but all I can see is tarmac and the leafy, silhouettes of hedges on either side.

And, breathe…

The maps app really has got me in the middle of nowhere. There's green on either side for miles, no sign of anything even close to civilisation until I zoom out. I was in the Grand Ol' Royal hotel south of Birmingham, not far from Royal Leamington Spa. Now, somehow, I'm around twenty miles closer to my home in Lincolnshire. Depending on the speed limits and route, that's at least thirty minutes lost. I suppose I was driving – who else could have been – but all I have is one gaping dark hole.

I spend a few seconds zooming in and out of the map, looking around the local villages, wondering if I've ever been in the area. It's easy to conclude that this spot is so far out of the way that, unless someone lives here, *no one* would voluntarily be in these parts. Not unless there are some rural pubs serving mountainous Sunday roasts, of course. That's about the only reason anyone I know ever visits the countryside.

The engine is quietly idling and I wonder if I should call the AA. The membership card is in my bag, the number stored on my phone. They'd get me home safely, but what about the questions? How could I explain away the smeared blood, or the gap in the hedge? They'd probably call the police. I'd be breathalysed at the very least, possibly charged with careless or dangerous driving. They'd ask question after question and I don't know the answers myself.

As I pull away carefully, I keep an eye on the verges, hoping there's something that might explain at least part of what has happened. As before, there is no sign of an animal, or anything even close. The most interesting thing is an abandoned traffic cone, caked with muck, that's been dumped further along the hedge.

If I *had* hit something, it's hidden by the night.

If, I tell myself. *If* I hit something. Some*thing*, not some*one*.

Ignoring the obvious is the only thing I can do for now. It's not like there was a freak rain-storm of blood; the splashes must have come from somewhere.

After a mile or so, I decide that the car's fine and there's no point in driving so slowly. Whenever I reach a junction – which isn't often – I check the phone in my lap to make sure I'm going the right way. It's after fifteen minutes or so when I realise that 'right' way is the route home, not the way back to the hotel. I'm on autopilot, searching for some sense of normality among this madness.

Concentrating on anything feels like hard work. The road blurs and it's only the frequent bumps of potholes that keep me even close to alert. My reactions remain sluggish and it's almost as if I'm watching myself drive, rather than being the actual driver. Perhaps this was the problem in the first place? I left the hotel for some reason, started driving home, got lost, and fell asleep at the wheel.

There are stories like that in the news all the time. A lorry driver swerves off the motorway after falling asleep. That would explain waking up in the field, even if it doesn't clarify why I left the hotel or why there is blood on the windscreen.

Perhaps I bumped my head at some point, which explains the amnesia.

Or, I assume it does. When it comes to memory loss, my only knowledge – if it can be called that – comes from ludicrous soap plots and stupid movies. Amnesia is a staple.

It hurts every time I try to force the memory – and there are only flashes. I remember the beech wood of the hotel bar, the row of wine glasses above my head. There's the carpeted, wide staircase that felt so illustrious. The hard bed, the tightly tucked covers.

After a while, the B-roads link onto the A-roads – and then it's not long until I start to recognise landmarks. There's a petrol station I've stopped at a couple of times. The interior lights are off, though the price board is lit up like a capitalistic Christmas tree. Another mile and there's the pub where Dan and I once came for lunch many years ago. It's boarded up now, left for the rats or the developers, whichever gets to it first. There are two skips in the car park and the only indication of its previous life is the faded name board facing the road. It was packed when we stopped. There used to be a carvery and even the walls smelled of meaty gravy. I wonder why we never returned, then it occurs to me that I'm still thirty miles or so from home and it was probably a decade ago anyway. Perhaps longer. It's passed in a blink. Olivia would have been young but I don't remember her being with us. She might have been at hockey practice, or at a dance show. That was back when she had hobbies. It's hard to remember specifics and a long time since Dan and I used to drive aimlessly, looking for somewhere new to eat.

Perhaps it was my naïvety but the world felt simpler then.

The rows of street lights have taken hold now, eating away at my sluggishness. The A-roads are now the suburbs, with sprinkled red-brick housing estates. I slow for a zebra crossing, even though there's nobody waiting. I'm stabbed by the thought that perhaps I shouldn't be driving. There's a play park off to the side, a multicoloured climbing frame plonked on that soft black matting they have nowadays. There are swings and a roundabout and imagining the children who might play here during the day is straightforward enough. What if I have that thing where people fall asleep for no reason? I could be a danger to those kids, a danger to myself.

I wonder why I'm only thinking of this now.

If other people found themselves in that field, would they have acted differently?

I let the window down a centimetre or two for a token bit of fresh air. Something to keep me awake.

The housing estates have become rows of shops, though nothing is open. The shutters are down across the front of the betting holes but lights are on inside the giant Lidl. I keep going, sticking to the speed limit, though edging through a nonsensical red light that's giving priority to traffic that isn't there at this time of the morning.

My heart rate quickens when I see the first car since I hit the street lights. A battered dark blue Vauxhall cruises towards me on the other side of the road and I feel sure the driver knows I'm guilty of something. My fingers are trembling on the steering wheel as my gaze drifts towards the other driver. It's a young woman, twenty or so. I'm guessing she'll be on her way home after a late shift in a factory or something similar. I feel sure she'll notice a patch of blood on my car but her eyes are fixed on the road ahead.

Probably where mine should be.

Ten minutes more and I'm pulling into our street. There's not much I can say for it, other than it's normal. Cars are parked intermittently and there are rows of semi-detacheds on either side. There are small patches of green outside each house, with tarmacked driveways leading to individual garages. It could be any street in any part of the country. When people think of Britain, they usually think of cobbles and red postboxes – but, for most, *this* is the United Kingdom. We're cookie-cutter houses, with plastic wheelie bins and recycling boxes on the pavement outside.

The clock reads 04:39 when I pull onto the driveway. Dan has set up a gadget in each of our cars that makes the garage door open automatically when we approach. The gears grind and boom as I wait, like a jet liner taking off. I'm convinced it'll wake the neighbours but, when I'm parked safely inside, I instantly forget about anyone else. My fingers throb from where I've been gripping the steering wheel so firmly and my shoulders are tight and sore.

Despite the madness of circumstance, I'm home.

The car looks far worse in the bright overhead light of the garage.

In the bluey-white glow from the moon, I knew I'd done a poor job of cleaning away the blood from the bonnet – and can now see how I've only succeeded in smearing the red into the silver paint. There are spots where it looks like a faded tie-dye job. It's almost hypnotic. It could be some sort of Turner Prize nonsense, some abstract image of gore – except I did this.

For the first time, I wonder why there's no damage. In my confused, flustered state, I'd somehow missed it. If I did hit something, then why is the car unaffected? There are no dents in the front bumper, nothing other than blood swirls on the bonnet – and the windscreen is not cracked. Would it be possible to hit something and cause that much blood loss, and yet not damage the car?

I have little time to dwell because, as I'm about to dig out a bucket and sponge, the door that leads into the house opens with a resounding click.

THREE

The route from house to garage involves a double door, with a slim one-step porch in between. It's instinct, perhaps self-preservation, but I lunge for the garage light switch and plunge the room into darkness. At the same moment, Dan's silhouette appears in the doorway. He's haloed by the light behind; his slim waist and wide, muscled shoulders striking in their athleticism. I'm not used to his new physique.

'Rose?' he says, unsure of himself.

I step towards him, stopping him coming down the stairs into the garage. He takes the hint, shifting back into the light of the porch. He's wearing lounge pants and a loose shirt but they're uncrumpled and it doesn't look like he's been in bed anytime recently.

'Are you okay?' he asks.

'Bit tired, that's all.'

I can see him clearly but I doubt he can see me, not with the darkness of the garage behind. I'm on the top step, an arm's length from him, close enough to see his pupils expanding and narrowing as they try to adjust to the light.

'Why'd you drive home at this time?' he asks, perfectly reasonably.

'The hotel bed was too uncomfortable. I was awake anyway, then I saw your text. I figured I could get a few hours' sleep at home before work later.'

The lie comes so easily that it leaves me a tiny bit wary of myself. Everyone lies: 'That shirt looks fine,' 'Your daughter's a really good singer,' 'No, I don't mind staying at work for an extra hour.' They're white lies to save someone's feelings, or to maintain a social norm. This feels bigger and yet the words are out of my mouth before I've even processed them.

I take another step forward and Dan moves with me, backing through the second door into our kitchen. There's a dim light glowing through from the living room, not enough for either of us to properly see one another. We're silhouettes in the murk.

'Did you check out from the hotel?' he asks.

'Yes. Some poor sod was on the night shift. He seemed a bit confused.'

Another effortless lie.

'How'd the meeting go?'

I'm surprised he remembered why I was away. I was meeting a client, hoping to make a sale – and the offer of a free hotel at the end of it was too much to turn down. I could've driven back, of course, but that would have only meant a restless night in bed with Dan, each of us trying not to cross the invisible wall down the centre of our mattress.

'Fine,' I reply, even though it definitely wasn't.

One lie feeds into the next in the same way that one truth would lead into another. It's not like he really wants to know the answer anyway. It's been quite a while since we spent the evenings telling each other about our respective days. It's all small talk now. Good day at work? What did you have for lunch? That sort of thing.

'Is Liv back?' I ask.

'No. I'm sure she's fine.'

At least we're sticking to that line of answering.

He doesn't sound as reassuring as I'd want him to be. The safety of a child should be definitive. She's *definitely* safe.

'I'm sure she is, too,' I reply.

He nods shortly and there's a moment in which I wonder if we're thinking the same thing. On the same wavelength, for once. Whatever's happened between us, she's still our daughter.

'I suppose she *is* eighteen,' he adds.

'Did you try calling her?'

'No answer.'

This is the first time in two years that Olivia has failed to let us know she's staying out. Sometimes the text comes late – and oftentimes it's short and to the point – but it's always there. She was sixteen and I was the typical panicked parent back then. Dan was the cool head. 'She'll be fine,' he cooed – and she was. To a point. She was drunk on cider, probably high on something too, though she always denied it. One of her friends called Dan in the end, asking if he could pick Olivia up because she wasn't feeling well. It was five in the morning and I'd barely slept. We grounded her, because that's something you can do – *just* – when your child is sixteen and underage. At eighteen, you can only ask for a bit of courtesy.

Dan yawns but there's something odd about it, as if he's pretending. His hand covers his mouth before he starts and there's no squinting tiredness to him afterwards.

'I'm going to go back to bed,' he says, 'get another hour before I have to be up for school. Can't have the kids looking more awake than me.'

He chuckles at his own joke and heads for the stairs, not waiting for a reply. He's a deputy headteacher, so he has a point – although he's never been one of those parents whose heads can't hit the pillow until our child is home.

It's only when he gets to the bottom of the stairs, directly underneath the light, when I notice the smudge of dirt on his wrist. Dan's not quite a neat freak and certainly not a germaphobe – but he likes things to be in their place and is the sort to religiously wash hands before meals.

'What's on your wrist?' I ask.

He spins, looking at me and then down to himself. He rubs the mark, only succeeding in spreading whatever it is.

'I was unblocking the kitchen sink earlier, probably that.'

He shrugs and then he's gone, not bothering to ask if I'm going to follow.

I call after him to say that I'll be up in a bit but it's meaningless. Our bed sharing is more to do with habit than anything else.

The kitchen counter is a good place to lean as I listen to him padding around upstairs. He heads to the bathroom first and the water runs, then he's off to the bedroom. There are a couple of dull thumps and then quiet. I think about calling Olivia myself, perhaps firing off a text to check she's all right, but she won't appreciate it if she is asleep on someone's sofa. She probably won't hear or see it anyway, then she'll get annoyed I was harassing her. I figure I'll give it an hour.

Back in the garage and I try to work as quickly as I can. There's a tap that Dan installed, along with a plug in the centre of the garage floor. His thinking was that it would be easier to wash our cars in the winter if we didn't have to stand out in the cold. His BMW is spotless next to mine, as ever. His car is an extension of him.

I fill a bucket with water and washing-up liquid, but there's even more blood than I thought. It's not just on the bonnet, lower windscreen and grill, it's drizzled down towards the front wheels. There's mud, too. Lots of it, dried and caked. It clings to the underside of the wheel arches like a leech latched onto flesh. I hate cleaning cars at the best of times. For Dan, it's therapeutic. He'll spend a few hours in here clearing his thoughts – or so he says – while shining his car. I don't think that's a euphemism. Either way, I prefer to pay a few quid to stick mine through the car wash next to the local Tesco. Can't really show up with a tenner and a blood-covered car, though.

The first two soapy buckets of water quickly turn a reddish sort of black and disappear down the drain, but I am beginning to get somewhere. The crusts of mud and filth recede, along with any trace of what I've done. Or might have done.

When my back starts to ache and my fingers are wrinkled and white, I realise an hour has passed. It's almost six in the morning and the world will be waking again soon. Dan will be back downstairs.

Now the fog has started to clear, I feel surprisingly awake. It'll be adrenaline, something like that, but it's like I've had a full and comfortable night of sleep. Those nights where the head hits the pillow and the next thing anyone knows, the sun is up. I'm sure it shouldn't be like this.

The final bucket of water disappears into the drain; the soapy, filthy suds spinning until there are only a few dregs clinging to the concrete. If I didn't know better, I could have imagined it all. My car is about as clean as it gets. It's nowhere near as shiny as Dan's, but the traces of last night have gone.

It's only when I step away to examine my handiwork that the phrase slips into my mind. 'Tampering with evidence' – that's what it's called. It's what they write in the news reports, what the presenters say on *Crimewatch*. 'Police have charged Mr So-and-so for tampering with evidence'.

Is that what I've done?

I tell myself that it's not. That's not the sort of person I am, and yet, here it is. I've acted clinically, barely thinking at all. Act first, think later.

But there wasn't a crime scene. Was there? If I hit something, then where's the damage to the car? Where's the animal – or person – from which the blood came? I looked, I really did. A person can only tamper with evidence if there's been a crime – and there hasn't.

I have to tell myself that.

There's little point in going to bed now and I don't feel tired anyway.

I head through the house into the kitchen. Olivia's energy drinks are in the fridge. The ones that are ninety per cent sugar and called things like 'Carnage' and 'Assault'. She knows I don't approve – what reasonable parent would? – but it is what it is. She could be using worse things to get that buzz.

I think about having one, but my own addiction is a little more acceptable. I fill the coffee machine with granules and water, setting it to fizz and pop as I curl up on the sofa in the living room.

Unsurprisingly, my phone is on its last legs battery-wise. The modern ones are more addicted to power sockets than Olivia is to her energy drinks. I plug it in and then text her, keeping it straightforward and without accusation.

Hope u had a good night. Let me know if u want picking up from somewhere

There's only one thing more valuable to teenagers than money – and that's free lifts. Olivia failed her driving test a month ago and hasn't rebooked it. Part of that is for financial reasons, but it's mainly because she hasn't handled the rejection well. The reason she failed was, of course, because of the examiner. He gave her confusing instructions, he wanted her to fail, he'd hit his quota for the day. Those sorts of things. There was little point in asking for specifics of what happened because it would be taken as implicit criticism that the reason she failed was something *she* did, as opposed to a crooked tester.

I scroll through our recent texts, hoping a new one will appear. A minute or so passes and there's no reply, so I switch to the web browser instead and get back to my own predicament. I search for terms like 'hit-and-run', checking the Twitter feeds of the local police forces. No matter how many times I tell myself I couldn't have hit something, some*one*, there's that niggling voice at the back of my mind.

There's nothing of any particular interest to find. A lorry driver was stopped on the motorway for his vehicle being too heavy;

someone else arrested for drink-driving. That's it. An uneventful night in the real world – certainly no reports of anyone found in a ditch. I want reassurance, but it's early yet.

The problem is that, as I press back onto the sofa, those three words keep spinning around my mind.

Tampering with evidence.

FOUR

I jolt awake at the sound of something clanking onto the granite worktop in the kitchen. For a moment, I'm back in that field, confused and unsure where I am. It takes a second for me to realise I've fallen asleep on the sofa. My phone is on my lap, light creeping through the blinds from outside.

Dan is in the kitchen, opening and closing the fridge noisily. I wonder if he's doing it on purpose. He must've walked past me sleeping on the sofa and said nothing. The tiredness is blinked away and I stretch high, my shoulders and neck clicking with grim satisfaction.

Most of our ground floor is open-plan and I continue watching as he mixes some powder into a protein mixer bottle. He shakes it up and then peers closely at the greeny-grey gloop, before popping the cap on the top and glugging down a mouthful. He's in shorts and a tight, athletic T-shirt, with a large holdall bag on the counter.

'Didn't wake you, did I?' he asks.

'I need to get moving anyway.'

As he takes another mouthful, I check my phone quickly. There's nothing from Olivia.

'Did you hear from her?' I ask.

'She says she's fine.' He speaks with an invisible shrug.

'Oh.'

The word slips out unguarded. I check my phone once more but there's definitely no reply. Olivia always was a daddy's girl and it's hard not to take it personally that she's chosen to tell her father she's fine instead of me.

'She says she fell asleep and forgot to text,' Dan adds. 'No harm done. She'll be home later this morning.'

'Right.'

'I found my gym fob, by the way. I'm off for a quick hour before school.'

'Right.'

I'm a broken record.

Dan bobs awkwardly from one foot to the other as he loops his bag onto his shoulders. 'I'll see you later, then.'

'Okay.'

Neither of us make an effort to cross the room to say goodbye, let alone exchange a kiss or a hug, so that's that. It's been a long time since we did anything other than offer vague wishes of good days and the like. I can't remember if it was him or me who stopped first. I can't even remember when it happened. We always used to make sure we said a proper goodbye. It was our thing: regardless of what we had going on in our lives, at home or work, we'd find a minute or two to offer a decent farewell. Then, one day, we stopped. It's a slippery slope after that – and we've been hurtling down that hill at ridiculous speed.

Dan takes another mouthful of his godforsaken vomit in a cup and then heads to the garage, whistling something out of tune.

He has become anything but a typical deputy headteacher. When I was at school a long time ago, the men in charge – for it was always men – were strict grey-haired or balding old-timers. Dan's in his early forties and the gym is his midlife crisis. For some, it's motorbikes or cars, travelling or women. With Dan, it's running, weights, and those protein shakes. It's measuring out his meals, chronicling every fitness session to see if he's improving. It's organised races and crack-of-dawn departures. I thought it might be a phase but that was eighteen months ago and, if anything, he's more obsessed now. He exercises every day, sometimes twice a day. He did one of those Tough Mudder events the other month, heaving himself over barriers through the sodden earth for no reason other than to prove that he could. He's done 10ks and the Great North Run; next he's talking about entering the ballot to run the London Marathon. If he misses out on that, he said he might try Amsterdam or somewhere else.

Jealousy is the wrong word. I'm not *jealous* of him, but I suppose there is a part of me that admires the changes he's made. He had a goal and he stuck at it – and that's something I grudgingly respect. Grudgingly because I've been left behind. His previous doughy physique is now taut and lean, not that I go anywhere near it. I'm not sure when we stopped doing that, either. Our waistlines were growing old together, but now he is going backwards, leaving me by myself. I know I shouldn't, but I resent him for that.

He does all that as well as continue to work his way up through the education system. It's all cuts this and academy that nowadays. Government targets here, league tables there. Despite all that, he's thriving in a career he enjoys.

I probably resent that, too.

The garage doors grind open and then closed, leaving me alone in what suddenly feels like a very empty house.

With the room to myself, I check the news websites again. After that, it's the police feeds – but there's no mention of a hit-and-run. It's still early, not long after seven, but would some sort of incident be there by now?

It's almost as if the garage is calling me and I head through the double doors and down the stairs until I'm staring at my car, hoping it'll somehow give me answers. There are none, of course. The car is swabbed clean of anything incriminating.

Tampering with evidence.

In the daylight, last night feels like a weird dream. It's only the fact I'm here instead of a hundred miles away from where I'm supposed to be that's wrong.

I suppose that's a good place to start.

I'd never heard of The Grand Ol' Royal Hotel before Graham offered to put me up there for the night. My boss is hardly known for his generosity, which was another reason not to turn him down when a meeting with a potential new client was arranged there.

I fiddle around with my phone's calendar until I find the details – and then I dial.

It's one of those annoying systems that every business seems to have nowadays. Press one for reservations, press two for the spa, press three to kick the crap out of the person who invented these automated messages. Talking to another person is too much of a chore, even though they apparently 'value your call'. If you value it so much, try answering the damned phone!

I jab a series of numbers until the line eventually rings again and then there's the voice of a youngish man who sounds far too sprightly for this time of the morning. He tells me I'm through to the front desk.

I can hear his fingers clacking on a keyboard as I tell him my name, explaining that I had to leave in a hurry.

'I wanted to make sure everything was all right with the checkout,' I add.

There's a pause and I can hear my heart beating. It feels important.

'Everything's fine, Ms Denton,' he replies. 'I can mark you as checked out on our system.'

'So I hadn't checked out before?'

Another pause, a bit longer than the previous one. He must be wondering if I'm a nutter.

'No, but, as I say, I can mark you as checked out now. Thank you for your call – most guests wouldn't do so. It's very highly appreciated.'

I wait for a 'but', though there is none, so all I can do is hang up. I suppose it clears up one thing – whenever I left the hotel, I simply left. No fuss about checking out. My overnight bag containing my belongings was in the back of the car, so I must have taken that with me. I don't think I even unpacked.

If the hotel is a dead end, then I suppose that new client is another place to start. He's stored in my phone under 'Luke', but there's no answer when I call. There is a lot I don't recall about last night – but I *do* remember his final text and it's still there on my phone anyway.

Sry. Things got out of control and I'm not going to make it. Will hv 2 rearrange 4 another time

After driving a hundred miles and checking into a hotel for an evening meeting, it's fair to say I wasn't best pleased. Still, he *could* turn out to be a client at some point, so there's little point in being anything other than perfectly polite. My previous reply from last night was:

No worries. These things happen.

That got no reply, so I tap out:

Hope everything is well from last night. When would you like to try again?

It's professional and to the point. Really, I'd like to tell him what I think of his late notice. I was sitting in the hotel bar when his text arrived. My real concern is my boss, Graham. He said

I can claim expenses for the hotel room but he'll be expecting a sale.

It really has come to something when one of the highlights of my week is being able to claim something on expenses.

I give the car a final once-over and then head back into the house. Another web search for hit-and-runs proves fruitless and the part of me that believes this is all a strange, unexplained misunderstanding is starting to swell.

Graham isn't expecting me at work until late morning but it can't do any harm to get in early, especially as I have no sale to show for myself. I retrieve my overnight bag from the back of the car and unpack, then take time checking myself over properly in the mirror in case the blood could have somehow come from me. There's nothing, of course. No little cuts, no unexplained bruises. I knew there wouldn't be.

The shower makes everything feel better, the water pummelling and pounding, washing away my indiscretions – the ones I know of, and, hopefully, the ones I don't.

There are two types of people in the world: those who attack a problem and those who try to ignore it. I've often fallen into that second category, hoping things will go away rather than making myself do something about it. I guess that's why things between Dan and myself have got so bad. Neither of us particularly wanted to address the obvious and now it is probably too late.

I towel myself dry, making one final check that there are no marks or scrapes I could be missing. Still nothing. I blow-dry my hair and then dress for work, before sending one more text to Olivia, saying I'll see her later.

There's no reply – and also no response from Luke. I'm a pariah.

It's only when I'm checking I have everything before I head out that I realise I'm missing my work swipe pass. It's the shape and size of a credit card – and I usually keep it attached to my keys. Ironically, I detached it because I didn't want to lose it at the hotel.

Losing it is probably my own fault for that cheeky remark towards Dan when he asked about his missing gym fob. I left it in the kitchen drawer yesterday before leaving for the hotel... or at least I thought I did. It isn't there now. I even empty the entire drawer onto the countertop.

There's far more junk inside than even I thought. Long-expired coupons for restaurants, keys for the old shed we got rid of years ago, endless receipts for goods we threw away. There's a bit of emergency money, old shopping lists. Everything except for my work pass.

As I slide everything back inside, that niggling devil at the back of my mind only has one conclusion. It's Dan – he's messing with me.

FIVE

Except Dan was missing his fob, too. Is that a coincidence? He said he'd found it but didn't say where – and I wasn't bothered enough to ask. I glance towards the back door and then through the house towards the front, as if wondering if we've had a break-in. It's nonsense, of course. If someone broke in, they'd be interested in more than Dan's gym fob and my work pass. The more obvious conclusion is that I can't have left the pass in the drawer. I must have put it somewhere else. Ageing is a terrible thing. It starts with that extra half-a-second to remember a name and only gets worse from there. Next, it's an hour-and-a-half lost trying to remember where a pair of shoes have been left. That or my work pass. Let's not get into waking up in the middle of a field.

I take a moment to sit on the sofa and try to actually think about where it might be. Those thoughts are distracted by the sound of the front door banging open and clattering into the wall. There's a gust of wind and then stomping feet.

Olivia.

The mother inside me that definitely isn't *my* mother bristles at the slamming door and loud footsteps. I've tried to stop myself from making these small digs, from causing these arguments about nothing, but it's almost automatic. If we're going to fall out, it should at least be about things that matter, not feet and doors.

Olivia lurches in from the hallway, Doc Martens scuffing across the wooden floor. When she gets into the kitchen, she stops dead, noticing I'm home. She stands straighter, as if challenging me to say something. I wonder if she was waiting for my text about seeing her later before she entered the house. She might have been around the corner anticipating an empty house.

She's wearing a tight leather jacket with a tartan skirt and ripped tights. We've had the 'you're-not-going-out-in-that' arguments years before and I suppose I'm used to it now. Clothes are one thing, but it was the nose piercing that really set us at each other's throats. She was only sixteen when she had the ring put through her septum. It was perfectly legal, of course, but the first I knew of it was when I saw it. It's hard to argue back when she says it's her body and she can do what she wants with it. What is there to say? '*Yeah, but I kinda made it*'?' Instead, I said she'd struggle to get a job which, it's fair to say, didn't particularly appeal to a sixteen-year-old.

'Good night?' I ask, forcing a cheerfulness I don't feel.

'Salright.'

The words slice together into one and then Olivia scuffs across to the other sofa, dumping her badge-covered backpack on one cushion and flopping into the other. She digs deep into the bottom of the bag for a tangled phone lead and then, having set the device to charge, begins to thumb away at the screen.

I want to say, 'Oh, so your phone *does* work?' but can only hear those words in my mother's voice.

Olivia's fingers flash frenetically across the screen and then she holds a hand to her head, and sighs.

'Anything I can help with?' I ask.

She angles her head a tiny amount, just enough so that she can stare crookedly at me. I've seen the scowl numerous times in the past few years and it can mean anything from she missed a bus to the world is actually ending. The Four Horseman could be coming down our road as we sit here, or her hair straighteners have stopped working.

I wait, knowing full well that the wrong word now will get me nowhere.

She looks back to her phone before finally speaking. 'I can't get hold of Ty,' she says.

That explains it. Tyler is the boyfriend.

'He's not replying to my texts and his dad says he's not been home since Friday.'

Not replying to texts? Oh, the irony, daughter.

'Isn't that normal for him?' I reply.

Another sideways scowl and so I quickly add: 'I'm not having a go.'

'I've tried Nicky and Will – but they've not seen him. Neither's Dele or Gadge.'

There was a time when I knew all of Olivia's friends but that was when she'd happily have birthday parties at the house with party bags and cake for everyone. It was a long time ago but those were happy days. Dan and I were getting along and Olivia was still our little girl. Now, of the four names she's mentioned, I think I know one – and I'm not even sure about that. I hope to everything that's holy that 'Gadge' is not some lad's real name.

'When was the last time you saw him?' I ask.

She sighs and her entire body slumps. 'Saturday night.'

Her eyes narrow momentarily and then she turns back to her phone. There was an accusation in that stare but I'm really trying not to argue.

'How's the café?' I ask.

'It's work. What do you think?'

'I don't know. Rahul seemed pleased with you the last time I saw him.'

'Yeah.'

Olivia is all elbows and knees as she hugs her legs to her chest, peering around her legs to continue using her phone.

I try a different approach: 'What about the accountancy lessons with Ellie?'

She rolls her eyes. 'They're fine.'

The worst thing about my relationship with Olivia is that I know it's not that different from the one I had with my mother when I was the same age.

'What are your plans for today…?'

A shrug. 'Try to find Ty.'

I leave it a moment, not wanting to jump on her. 'He has done this before, though…'

She looks up, frowns, looks down.

I suspect that, deep down, this is the fact that's annoying Olivia the most. Her boyfriend *has* done this before. It's fair to say his relationship with his father isn't the best and he's disappeared for days at a time on at least two occasions that I know of. Then there's Olivia and Tyler's relationship in itself. They're one of *those* couples. Everybody knows one, especially at that age. They break up and make up incessantly, falling out and arguing over petty things and then getting back together days later.

When they first broke up, I was stupid and naïve in assuring her it was all for the best; that she could do better, and so on. Three days later and they were back together. I know she told him what I said because he was brazen enough to tell me to my face that he was definitely good enough for my daughter.

Even though they've broken up at least three times since, I've not made the same mistake.

There's a part of me, that I'd like to think is small, which hopes he doesn't come back. The truth is he's *not* good enough for her.

'Have you heard from him at all since Saturday?' I ask.

'I already said.'

'You said you'd not *seen* him since Saturday…' I tail off, immediately regretting firing straight back.

She spins to face me, knocking her phone onto the floor in the process.

Olivia's top lip has curled in fury. 'And whose fault is that?'

'What do you mean?'

'You're the one that argued with him. You made him run away.'

'I really didn't.'

'I was right here, Mum! I heard you.'

'All I said was that I wasn't going to lend *you* money if you were going to give it straight to him.'

She bends to scoop her phone from the floor, checking the already cracked screen as she shakes her head. Her hair is baby pink at the moment, having gone through the full rainbow in recent times. She tugs at the short curl that's come from tucking it behind her ears. Dan always says she's her mother's daughter – and there's a certain amount of truth to that. As much as Tyler and Olivia antagonise one another, the same is true of me and her. When it comes to looks, however, Olivia is her father's daughter. They share the same high, angled cheekbones that are topped off by big brown eyes. Though I'd like to pretend it isn't true, there are times when I'm jealous of how little she looks like me.

Olivia is on a roll now: 'You called him a scrounger.'

'No I didn't.'

'Last week you did.'

'I thought we were talking about Saturday?'

'We were – but it's the whole thing, Mum. You're always having a go. No wonder he's run off.'

'All I did was ask him how the job-hunting was going…'

I tail off because I know she sees straight through it. Anyone would. I might have been annoyed at Dan's passive aggression but I can hold my own as well.

Olivia throws her hands up. 'You know he's got a bad knee.'

I bite my lip because we've been over this numerous times. Whether or not Tyler has a bad knee – and I have my doubts – the fact is that he's five years older than Olivia and has never had a job. She works evenings in a café to earn her own money and, from what I can tell, much of it is spent *by* him or *on* him. Olivia doesn't see it, of course. She's in love and, for her, this is what that means.

The one thing I do know is that I've heard more than enough about Tyler's alleged bad knee. In his own words, he 'totally ballsed it up' playing football when he was fifteen. Quite why that's stopped him doing any work whatsoever is unclear. What's also unclear is the lack of a doctor's note reinforcing his own rigorous medical opinion. Given Tyler's lack of qualifications, job, or experience, I'm not convinced he's qualified to practise medicine. Pointing out that sitting around playing Xbox all day means he could sit around an office all day didn't go down well with either him or Olivia on Saturday.

Dan told me I should lay off and I know he's right – but watching a daughter repeat your own mistakes isn't easy.

'Have you seen my work pass?' I ask, getting to my feet.

Olivia doesn't look up. 'No.'

'I thought I'd left it—'

She launches herself to her feet, grabbing the charger from the socket and hauling the bag to her chest. 'I said I hadn't seen it. You're not bothered about Ty, why should I care about your pass?'

There's no time to reply because, in a few strides, she's already across the room.

'Liv,' I call, but it's too late. Her Doc Martens stomp across the floor, the front door slams into the wall and then back into the frame. Her abrupt departure echoes through the house, booming and bouncing to emphasise my failure as a parent.

I breathe in deeply through my nose, holding it and then slowly letting it out. My eyes are closed and I know I'm talking to the empty house but I need to get the words out.

'Your father and I need to talk to you,' I say. 'It's important.'

SIX

I know Natasha can see me through the glass. I'm knocking on the door of my work and she's across the office, half-turned in her seat, aware I'm here but doing nothing to let me in.

After a third knock, I give a chummy wave that kills a tiny bit of my soul. I mouth the word 'hi' and smile, hoping she'll get off her sodding arse and let me into the damn building. This time, she spins fully around in her seat, offering the dampest of watery smiles; the type of expression that has a big fat middle finger directly behind it. She motions towards the door with her hand, pointing at me, then at her own chest. I nod, maintaining my smile.

Yes, I do need letting in, you massive cow.

Natasha is barefoot, her skyscraper overpriced Italian heels placed neatly under her desk. She only ever wears them from her car to the office and back each day – unless she has a meeting with Graham, of course.

She takes her time drifting across the office, showing off her shiny, waxed legs in case any of the lads are looking in her direction. When she gets to the door, she points to the scanner to the side.

'Forgot your pass?' she asks, the forced sweetness of her voice muffled by the door.

What do you think?

I nod and she finally presses the release button on the inside to unlock the door. I thank her and she gives me a look as if she's just donated me a bloody kidney.

She starts off back to her desk. 'You're late today,' she says over her shoulder.

'Graham approved it,' I reply.

'That's nice. Did you have a lie-in?'

'I was working away.'

The smirkiest of smirks: 'Right.'

Natasha and I are both IT sales reps. The thing with telling people my job title is that their eyes instantly glaze over. It sounds boring and, in all honesty, it *is* boring. It's one of those careers a person falls into. No child dreams of growing up to sell computer networks from one company to another.

If the other person does show any degree of interest in my job title, the next question is along the lines of, 'You must know plenty about computers?' – and that's when any explanation really does become a chore. I know an awful lot about one *specific* network system and how it integrates into a company's framework. Even that sounds dull. When it comes to that one and only system, I can tell other people about its intricacies, what it can and can't do, how it can help a company with its business, how users can be trained. And so on. It's like being a butcher and knowing one hell of a lot about pork sausages but very little about beef.

What it does do is pay the bills. It also gave me something to do after Olivia was old enough to start school. I've been doing it for nearly thirteen years and I know I'll almost certainly be doing something similar until I can afford not to.

I think that's probably why I don't like Natasha. For a start, she has almost two decades on me. This is a beginning for her, a first job after college. This will be the finish for me. It wouldn't be so bad if she wasn't so bloody obvious about knowing that. She's the sort who puts every aspect of her life on Facebook or Instagram. It's all 'post-run selfie' or 'night in with my baby', accompanied by a picture of her with her handbag dog. I know all this not because we're friends online or anything like that, but because I'm something of a stalker. It's hard not to look and I dread the day she ups her privacy settings. I'm living vicariously through her.

My desk is opposite Natasha's and we're separated by a cloth-covered piece of plywood. Natasha sits next to Claire, who's nice enough – if a little quiet – and then there are three men who spend more time out of the office than in it.

When I get to my desk, there's a Post-it note pinned to the monitor with 'See Graham' scrawled in felt-tip.

'Oh, yeah,' Natasha says. She's twirling a strand from her blonde fringe. 'You've got to see Graham.'

I'm not even sitting and pluck the note from the screen, holding it up.

'Thanks,' I tell her.

'You're welcome.'

There are times when I wonder how many of the interactions I have with people are false. My entire job is about talking up the functions of an IT system to try to make money. I fudge the awkward questions and overplay benefits. I'm frequently on eggshells with Dan and Olivia at home, pretending all is well – and then, even in the office, I never tell Natasha what I think of her. It'd mean too much of admitting what I think of myself. Most of what I do involves being fake-nice to people.

Graham's office is a little down the hall, separated from the rest of us. I knock on the door and wait a few seconds until he calls for me to enter. He always leaves it a few seconds; perhaps making whoever's outside worry a little more, perhaps clearing whatever's on his monitor. I know which of the two I think is true.

He's a very sweaty man, always has been, and – probably because of that – the air-conditioning in his office is always cranked up to levels that would have Greenpeace up in arms. On top of his stocky shoulders is a big bald egg and I've never been sure it's through choice or premature hair loss. He's forty-three, two years older than me, but a person would never guess it from looking at him. He's got that red-faced fifty-going-on-sixty-thing going for him.

Graham nods at the seat opposite his own and the chair squeaks noisily as I slide onto it.

'How was the meeting?' he asks gruffly.

'The client didn't show.'

He tilts his head sideways, examining me with closed lips as if wondering if I'm lying. 'He didn't show?'

'I got a couple of texts through the evening. He was running late, then said he was stuck in traffic, then he said he couldn't make it.'

I get my phone out to show him, but Graham bats the evidence away without looking at it.

'So I've got to pay for your night in a hotel and there's not even a sale to show for it?'

'I'm trying to rearrange.'

'What was his name again?'

'Luke.'

Graham taps the mouse on his desk and stares at his screen, scrolling and clicking until he's found what I presume is the email I forwarded him for the hotel booking.

'Remind me again why I'm paying for a hotel stay?'

'Luke suggested meeting in the middle. He was coming up from Cheltenham but said he was too busy during the day. I said I'd go to him but had something in Birmingham last night. It was a compromise.'

I don't add, 'It was your idea to put it on expenses'.

Graham hmms as if this is somehow suspicious when it's actually the norm. Our office is in Lincolnshire, which is, to say the least, out of the way. Few clients come here, so us reps go to them.

He presses back into his luxurious leather chair and purses his lips, glancing towards the certificates on the wall. His office is a shrine to himself. There are diplomas showing off his qualifications, which, from what I can gather, involved attending various weekend conferences. Those type of events in which everyone gets a prize – as long as they pre-pay for it. There are enlarged photos of him with clients that have been framed and mounted, as if they contain someone who's actually famous.

'I'll try calling him,' I say.

'You do that. In the meantime, I've set you up an appointment for later.'

'Oh.'

His eyebrows raise at the surprise in my voice. It's rare that Graham sets up anyone other than Natasha with appointments. He's her favourite, for what I assume are two very good pushed-up reasons. 'I'm throwing you a bone here,' he adds.

'I know. I didn't mean it like that. Thank you.'

He passes me a Post-it note, with the name 'DECLAN IRONS' and a phone number. That's followed by a second note with an address. Graham likes his Post-it notes. If I ever went to his house, I wouldn't be surprised to see the living room wallpapered with sticky yellow squares of paper.

The 'bone' he's throwing is that Natasha picked up a massive new contract last week. Before that, her sales figures weren't that impressive. The blokes always do okay and Claire ticks by. It's not quite official, but it might as well be – I am the weakest salesperson in the office. I console myself by imagining Natasha picking up that contract while on her knees, but I know it's not true. Her success is hers and my failure is all my own.

Graham tells me he'll forward the rest of the details in an email and then I stand, assuming that's it. I feel like a naughty schoolgirl waiting to be dismissed from the headmaster's office. Graham is looking at his screen, apparently oblivious.

'Shall I go…?' I ask.

He tuts. 'How many years have we worked together now, Rose?'

I make a point of counting on my fingers, as if the number isn't imprinted on my mind. 'Nearly thirteen.'

'Right. You're my longest-serving rep. Others have come and gone. Rats deserting a state-of-the-art cruise liner. I appreciate your loyalty, but that is something that has to work both ways…'

He stares me directly in the eyes and there's a moment in which I wonder if he's trying it on. His neck bulges against his tie, the top button of his shirt clinging on for dear life. He isn't my type at all – and never has been. He divorced a couple of years ago and there were always rumours that he was having an affair with his PA. She left and wasn't replaced – but I don't know for certain. There are always rumours like that in places like this. Offices run on tea, biscuits and gossip about who's shagging who.

What I do know is that Graham tried it on with me four or five years ago when he *was* married. We were away at a weekend conference and he'd been drinking for eight straight hours. He bought me a drink and then put a hand on my knee, saying he'd always found me 'intoxicating' – whatever that meant. He was unquestionably intoxicat*ed*. I turned him down politely and, ever since, he's acted like it never happened. Or, almost. Before that, any small workplace failures on my part were accepted and not spoken of. Ever since, I've been questioned on every hiccup.

It's when he jabs at his screen that I realise I've completely misread him.

'I'm getting CVs every day,' he says.

There's nothing cryptic about it: he could replace me with someone younger who'll work for less money. Our salaries are bumped up with performance-related bonuses – but I'm likely on the highest base rate, simply because of how long I've worked in the office. I also get more holidays than anyone other than Graham. He's happy for all that to continue – as long as I keep selling.

'I'm trying,' I reply.

There's a moment where I think he'll offer a sarcastic 'try harder' – but he doesn't. Instead, he nods at the Post-it note in my hand. 'That Declan sounds keen.'

Perhaps I'm expecting it because of my own insincerity around people, but there's no punchline. It takes me a second to realise he's being nice.

'Thank you. I appreciate it.'

He's expressionless as he turns back to his monitor. I think – perhaps hope – that he wants me to do well.

After closing his door, I wait in the hallway for a moment. I'm not ready to face Natasha and the others yet, so I try calling Luke. There's a gap of a few seconds, a plip, and then nothing. It doesn't even ring, let alone go to voicemail. I can't remember if this is what happens when a phone is turned off, or if someone has no reception. Either way, I tap out another text message.

Hi. Me again. Hope everything is well with you. Did you want to reschedule? I can call if you prefer?

I read it through twice and then press send.

Back in the main office and I skim through the emails Luke sent last week. We never spoke on the phone, let alone met. Everything was set up through emails and texts. When I did try to call, there was no answer and he texted a minute or so later to say he was in a meeting.

None of this is necessarily unusual. At least part of the job is – or perhaps *was* – travelling the country and having late nights in bars, hotels and restaurants. The twenty-first century is the age that face-to-face everything died.

Luke's emails read perfectly true. He works at a medium-sized cleaning firm that is hoping to become a large cleaning firm. They want to take all the ordering and finance onto a better system with external hosting that can be accessed remotely from phones and the like. It's the type of thing my company sells.

I click the link at the bottom of his email and it takes me to the cleaning company's website. It's perhaps a bit bare but there's nothing unusual that I can see. That is until I click the contact button – which only brings me to a webform. There's a box in which to type a name, another for email address, and a final one to leave a message. There is no specific email address or phone number to use… which is certainly odd for a company trying to drum up business. I hadn't checked the link before because there was no need – I already had Luke's name and contact details.

The tingle at the back of my thoughts starts to ring louder.

It doesn't make me feel any better when I hear Natasha snorting with laughter on the other side of the divide between our desks. I'd normally let it go but instead push myself up so I can see over the separator.

'You all right?' I ask.

She's grinning wide, looking at her phone. 'Fine, thanks.'

'What's funny?' I ask.

She waves a dismissive hand. 'Oh, nothing. You wouldn't get it.'

I hover there for a moment, before taking my seat to stop embarrassing myself. Natasha continues to giggle as I find myself clicking on the web browser. My first search is thankfully fruitless. There have been no reported hit-and-runs anywhere close to the area where I woke up last night. I check the websites and Twitter feeds from a few of the neighbouring police forces just in case, but there's still nothing.

There's unquestionable relief, those three words – 'tampering with evidence' – starting to fade when my breath is taken by the scrolling news strap on the police site.

Someone from the nearest town to where I awoke is missing. His name's Tom Leonard, a teenager who went to work and hasn't been seen since. There's a picture of him in a running vest and a few lines saying that he's a keen amateur athlete. He's nineteen with short dark hair and the merest hint of stubble. He's smiling, happy, a normal kid. He has the whole of his life ahead of him.

The real kicker is in the final line, however: *Tom Leonard worked at the Grand Ol' Royal Hotel.*

SEVEN

The only thing that doesn't stop me leaping from my chair is that Tom Leonard went missing before I'd even checked into the hotel. He was due at work yesterday morning – and I didn't get there until late afternoon. I keep reading the name of the hotel, wondering if there might be two. There isn't, of course. There's not even a second hotel with a similar name.

I stare at Tom's photo, wondering if I know him from some-where – but he has one of those faces that could be anyone's. His hair is slightly curly, his ears perhaps a little large – but it's nothing unusual. We live a hundred miles apart, so he won't be one of Olivia's friends, either.

Something happened at the hotel on that day, though. I was there and then I wasn't. Tom Leonard was *supposed* to be there – but he wasn't.

For now, there's only one thing for it – and that's a cup of tea. I stand, waggling my mug and asking if anyone else in the office wants one. There's a succession of shaken heads, so I nip to the small kitchen myself. It's not really a kitchen, of course. The office isn't big enough for that. It's in the corner of the main area and more of a sideboard with a fridge underneath. The kettle hums but the only other noise in the office is the tapping of keyboards and Natasha quietly talking to Claire. There's a moment in which the pair of them glance at me and then quickly turn away when they realise I'm facing their direction.

I might be watching – but I also feel watched.

It's hard not to see conspiracies everywhere. Luke – if that is his real name – messing me around; Graham wanting to fire me; Dan moving my things; Natasha talking about me behind my back.

Or perhaps I'm looking to blame everyone else for my own failings?

I know I've been doing this job for too long. I'm going through the motions, caring about little other than the salary at the end of the month. It's all about the money and nothing to do with a challenge. Sometimes, I think I should take some sort of online course, or perhaps quit and force myself to try a different career. If things were better with Dan, I probably would.

The kettle is still bubbling when I check my phone again. Luke hasn't replied to my text, so I try calling. Once again there's a pause and then nothing. No voicemail. Natasha giggles for seemingly no reason again and I wonder if it could be her. She set up a fake email and fake website, got hold of a pay-and-go SIM card and then… I don't know. I end up wasting a few hours and look a bit stupid – but how does that benefit her?

I'm only a couple of sips into my tea when the yawns begin. I've not slept since waking up in the car a little after half-past-two – and it's catching up to me. I sit at my desk, hiding behind the divider and trying to stifle the yawns. It's the sort of tiredness that infects every part of a person, where the arms and legs feel floppy and useless. My eyes water and I find myself pinching the loose skin on the back of my hand to try to keep myself alert.

'You all right over there?'

Natasha's chirpy voice is loud enough that everyone else in the room can hear.

I tell her I'm fine and try to focus on Graham's email. He's forwarded the whole chain and it seems as if he and Declan have been going back and forth for a couple of weeks. I'm meeting the potential client at his office on a trading estate thirty miles or so away. I've got about three hours to sort myself out. I've never been there before but it all checks out, which is one step up from Luke and his cleaning company.

I was in earlier than I was supposed to be and figure no one will miss me. I tap Declan's number into my phone, store the address in the maps app – and then tell everyone I'll see them tomorrow.

Despite the tiredness from before, being in the car has woken me up again. The vents are blowing cool air and the radio is chirping with cosy local DJ voices and eighties pop hits. It's when I reach the country roads that the twinge of anxiety returns. The hedges are tall, lining both sides of the lanes; and there are overgrown trees with branches dangling low, obscuring the signs. Everything's in shadow, so dark in places that it's like night.

I really don't like these roads in the dark.

I turn the radio up louder, trying to focus on the voices of a man and a woman jabbering on about what they're going to be up to that night. It doesn't sound like much. One of them is going running, the other taking their kids to some football match.

My phone is acting as a satnav, telling me there's another seven miles until I turn off these roads.

It's a *long* seven miles. At one point, there's a car coming towards me on the too-narrow carriageway. There's only room for a car and a half, with frequent pull-in points. The driver is a young lad talking on his phone, not paying attention. He's in the centre of the road and looks up when I beep my horn, swerving towards the verge, staring daggers as he continues to hold the phone to his ear. We avoid each other by barely centimetres.

Another half-mile and I think I see a fox off to the side. It's skulking in the shadows, nose to the ground, looking for prey. There's a flash of white and auburn but, when I get closer, there's nothing – and I wonder if I imagined the entire thing.

When I finally get back into civilisation – street lights, shop-fronts and, most importantly, people – it's as if a weight has been lifted. The gasp of relief makes me realise I've been holding my breath intermittently. A red traffic light gives me a moment to compose myself to such a degree that it's only the irritated beep of the car behind that makes me notice the light has gone green.

My phone directs me around a series of roundabouts until I'm in a concrete paradise. There are vast warehouses next to barely filled car parks. A crumbling, steepling chimney that's a relic of a different age sits in the distance and there's sign after sign warning of lorries that might be turning.

It's the exact opposite of those country roads: flat open and grey – but this is equally as British. A vast expanse of factories and companies; anonymous and ignored.

Declan's office is on a rank of five single-storey glass-fronted offices. Of the five, four have a 'To Let' sign – and it's only the one on the end that has lights illuminating the inside. When I pull into the parking space outside, a man is standing on the kerb, talking into his phone. After clocking the car, he hangs up, waiting for me to get out, and then introduces himself as 'Call Me Declan'.

He's in his early twenties, wearing a tight-fitting suit with spiky dark hair. He's fit and his face is a little shiny; one of those blokes who spend a good hour in front of the mirror each morning. We exchange the usual niceties, 'How was the traffic?' 'Aren't those roadworks a nightmare?' 'Did you hear it's likely to rain later in the week?' – that sort of thing. It's more autopilot stuff. Almost everyone has this meaningless drivel nailed down that it's strange when this isn't the pattern.

The office is a wide, open space that is filled with two desks and computers at the front, and piles of boxes at the back. The floor is bare concrete and there's a loose electrical wire hanging from a switch off to the side. It makes our office look luxurious.

Declan explains he and a business partner have only just moved in. Previously, they were working out of bedrooms and garages. The company sells nutrition and fitness products via the internet. Things are starting to pick up, but to such a degree that they're becoming overwhelmed. They need IT infrastructure and then more employees. It all sounds very familiar.

He's one of those people that forces eye contact a little too much. It isn't simply a friendly thing; it goes beyond that. Every sentence feels as if it's being vehemently shoved into my brain. His handshake was firm and needlessly forceful. I suspect he's been on one of those weekend courses about management and assertiveness. The type of thing Graham loves that gives a certificate to everyone at the end.

'This is just the start,' Declan says, turning in a half-circle to show off the barren space.

I tell him about our services and he seems keen, though he doesn't interrupt to ask any follow-up questions. He's a bit like a nodding dog, enthusiastically bobbing along with everything I say, still holding my gaze. It's hard to read him and I'm unsure if this means he's not that interested, or if he doesn't understand everything I'm saying.

I ask if he has any questions and he does that horrific finger-point gun thing: 'We do need everything to work twenty-four-seven,' he says.

'We offer full round-the-clock service,' I reply. 'Everything is guaranteed to work all day, every day. If there are any issues, we have twenty-four-hour off-site support, or remote engineers who can be on-site within ninety minutes. It's usually quicker than that.'

His eyes narrow. He has really long, dark eyelashes and it's hard to figure out if they're natural or if he wears some sort of mascara. 'You do know what twenty-four-seven means, don't you?' he adds.

I stare back at him, wondering if I've missed a joke. I haven't: He's serious.

'I understand,' I tell him. 'Our services are twenty-four-seven.'

Declan eyes me for a moment longer, apparently unconvinced, and then turns away, nodding. He walks himself in a circle, his shiny shoes clip-clopping on the hard floor.

'What about the price?' he asks – this time not looking at me.

I tell him about our standard package, as well as the first-month discount, or a bulk support package where he could pay for a full year up front. All the while, he continues pacing and I'm not sure if he's listening. He picks at his fingernail and brushes away non-existent strands of hair from his face.

After a standard start, it's all gone a bit odd and I'm not sure what I'm missing. Potential customers usually haggle over price but he doesn't seem too bothered. There are always follow-up questions as well, mainly to do with how our service can be tailored specifically for their company. It's expected and perfectly normal – except there's none of that here.

There's an awkward silence when I finish talking, with Declan standing and staring through the glass front to the nearly empty car park beyond.

'How does that sound?' I ask.

He spins and reaches into an inside pocket, removing a light-grey business card which he passes across. I exchange it for one of my own, slipping his into the pocket of my jacket. He examines mine to such a degree that I wonder if there's an errant spelling mistake. I've had them for years and never noticed anything before but he's staring unwaveringly at the card in his palm.

'Rose Denton,' he says. 'Is that short for Rosemary?'

'No,' I reply, slightly surprised given that he'd shown no interest in me until now. 'It was only ever Rose on my birth certificate.'

'It's a nice name.'

'Thank you.'

He's staring me up and down once more.

'I'll have to talk to my partner and then I'll be in contact,' Declan adds. 'Should I touch base directly with you, or that Graham bloke?'

I force myself not to cringe at 'touch base'. He'll be 'reaching out' next.

'Either,' I reply. 'But I'll probably be able to get back to you quicker.'

Declan stretches out his hand and we shake. His grip is once again overly firm, but this time, when I motion to pull away, he holds onto me. It's only a fraction of a second, but there's steel in his eyes when he does so. I've been meeting men and women in various corners of the country for years. It's often one-on-one, away from the public's glare, but this is the first time in a long time that I've felt genuinely vulnerable.

And then, as quickly as the panic arrives, it's gone again when Declan releases me.

'I'll be in contact,' he says.

I instinctively pull my jacket tighter, unable to hide that he's flustered me. He smirks, knowing what he's done – and then I head for the door.

EIGHT

As I start my car, I can sense Declan watching me through the glass of his office. The glare is too intense and I can't actually *see* him – but I can feel his stare. I pull out of the car park as quickly as I can, keeping an eye on the rear-view mirror as I head off the estate. Nobody is following and I make a quick decision, turning off a roundabout without indicating and rolling to a stop behind a giant skip.

I'm out of view from the road and switch the engine off, taking a few breaths to try to compose myself. It's hard to square precisely what happened. Was Declan being weird, or is it me? Did I read things the wrong way?

After a couple of minutes, I check my phone – no messages – and then text Graham to say that Declan sounded keen and should be in contact soon. It's a bit of a stretch. I wait for the 'sent' notice and then continue holding the device in case Graham fires back. He does sometimes, but it's hard to read his habits. Sometimes I'll wake up to find that he's sent a series of texts at three in the morning; other times he'll go a day or more without acknowledging an email.

A minute or two passes without reply, so I switch to maps. I'm about to set the destination for home – there's little point in returning to the office – when I have another idea instead. There are still a few more hours of daylight, so I follow the directions, weaving my way off the trading estate, through a run-down town centre, onto a dual carriageway.

I never used to be a particularly anxious person, but, when I turn off the main road back onto the twisty-turny shadowed-shrouded lanes, it feels as if someone is pressing on my chest. I find myself counting my breaths, but it never feels as if there's enough oxygen. Olivia was tested for asthma a few years ago and was given an inhaler. The doctor said it might be more anxiety-related as opposed to physiology. Olivia has never asked to return to the doctor since, but the things she used to complain of – the tightness of her chest, the shortness of breath – is exactly what I'm feeling.

It's hard to keep going but I do so anyway. It's more than an hour of feeling as if everything is on top of me. The roads all look the same and it's only when my phone says I've arrived that I pull into one of the passing places and notice the gap in the hedge a little down the lane. As I walk along the verge, the daylight makes everything seem less serious, but there's a morbid familiarity, too. In clearer light, the muddy tyre tracks are zigzagged across the disintegrating tarmac from where I reversed out. The hedge is thin, with wiry twig-like bristles and few leaves. Of all the spots in the immediate area, this is perhaps the only one through which I could have accelerated safely. The verges are deeper in other spots – especially on the opposite side of the road – and the hedges are thicker even a few metres down. If I'd slammed into one of those, chances are I might not have got through to the field on the other side. The car would have been embedded among the branches, likely stuck until a tow truck arrived to drag me out. Then there would have been breath tests, police, and endless questions. If I *was* lucky, I don't feel it.

The déjà vu prickles the backs of my ears; a ghostly apparition whispering mischief.

'You all right there?'

The male voice makes me jump as I turn away from looking at the gap in the hedge, coming face-to-face with a man with a thick grey beard.

'Can I help?' he adds. His accent is as abundant as his beard and it takes me a second to decipher what he's said.

'I was a bit lost and I noticed the, er…'

I find myself pointing at the gap in the hedge.

'Happened last night,' he replies. 'Some bugger going too fast.'

'You make it sound like it happens a lot.'

He snorts through his nose. 'Aye. It bloody does. At least once a month. Usually some kids. Then they wonder why their insurance is so high.' There's a hole in his body warmer near the belly and he reaches through the material to give himself a good scratch.

I'm not sure if I feel better or worse at this fact. 'Is this your field?' I ask.

He nods, pointing to either side of the road. 'And that lot,' he replies. 'What brings you out this way?'

The man turns to look at my cleanish car and it's unmistakeably out of place in the middle of nowhere.

'I'm lost,' I say. 'I'm on my way to, er…' My mind races but the only thing I can come up with is the name of the hotel. '… the Grand Ol' Royal hotel,' I add.

He shakes his head: 'Never heard of it.'

I show him my phone. 'I'm following directions but I can't work out if I've gone wrong.'

'Those things are bloody clever nowadays. I stream all my music while I'm out in the fields.'

When I laugh with surprise, he joins in.

'Aye. Betcha didn't expect that.'

My poker face is awful: 'I guess not.' I point towards the gap in the hedge. 'What happens now? Do you fix it up again?'

A shake of the head. 'No point. It's always the same spot.'

'Why?'

He points to a kink in the road a little further along. 'They take that bend too fast. Was in the news a few weeks ago. Had some fella here with a camera taking photos. Not done any good, has it?'

'No…'

I wonder if that's what I did. In my sleepy, confused state. I was racing home, took the corner too quickly and then woke up in the farmer's field. It still doesn't explain why I was travelling on *these* roads. It's far from the direct route home.

'Mud on the road don't help,' he adds. 'But what am I s'posed to do? I need to get my tractor round and about.'

He's right about that, too. There are narrow tyre tracks coming away from the gap – the ones I made – but, further along, most of the surface is covered with a thicker padding of muck. It seems so straightforward now he points it all out. It could happen to anyone. I'm not special at all, perhaps not even that unlucky.

'Hope you find your hotel,' the man adds. When I turn back to him, he's already a couple of paces away, heading towards a wide metal gate to the side of my car. I watch him disappear over the top into the field beyond and then there's only the distant fluttering of the breeze. It's so silent that there's a moment in which I wonder whether the man existed at all. He came from nowhere and then disappeared back there as well.

I walk along the verge until I'm at the mud on the road. It's thicker than it looked from further away, packed tight from the weight of vehicles bumping over the top. I'm almost ready to convince myself that I simply slid off the road in the way many others appear to have done so when the truth comes punching back. It doesn't explain the blood. I move slowly along the edge of the road, checking the edges for any sign of an animal I might have hit. After searching one side of the road, I double back and look along the other.

There's nothing.

There was no sign of anything last night and the same is true now.

When I return to my car, I sit in silence for a moment or two but nothing feels any clearer in my mind. There's a part of me for which this all feels like a dream – but the physical evidence is there. Or *was* there. I got rid of most of it.

I turn the radio up and follow the directions of my phone until I'm back on the dual carriageway once more. Traffic is busier as rush hour approaches and it's easier to focus on the bumper in front and simply follow, rather than have to think too much about where I'm going. That's all well and good but I'm so absorbed in my thoughts that I almost miss the exit that will take me back to North Melbury.

Our little corner of the world is slightly too big to be called a village but probably too small to be a town. It sits in Lincolnshire and is where I've always lived. There's a stream, a small High Street and a swathe of green around the outskirts. At one time, it felt so important, as if the centre of everything went on outside my front door. Now I wonder if I've wasted my life by rarely spending more than a few days at a time outside the Britain In Bloom signs that surround the boundary. Dan's midlife crisis is fitness and firming up his body and I wonder if this is mine. That wanderlust and sense of missing out. The realisation that I can never go back and change things. This is the life I've built.

I drive along the High Street, remembering how much of it has changed over the years. The bakery used to be independent, where the owner knew people's names and took weekly orders for various things. Now it's a Gregg's. The café on the corner was once run by Mrs Griggs. The creaky, wooden furniture inside smelled of exotic teas – or they were at least exotic to me as a little girl. My mum would take me there in the school holidays and it was something of a day out. It's a Starbuck's now. I'm never quite sure if we've lost something or gained it. I don't even know if it matters but it's something I think about too much. A melancholic sense of sadness for something about which I don't have any overly strong feelings.

It's not long until I'm on our street. I wait for the garage to open itself and then pull inside. Dan's car isn't there, but then he spends longer and longer away from the house – not that I blame him.

When I get into the main part of the house, the first thing I notice is the draught. I wonder if it's just me, if the chill is a leftover sense of bewilderment and confusion.

It's not.

As soon as I move around the kitchen counter, I can see where the breeze is coming from. There's glass on the kitchen floor, sprinkled and splintered from the shattered window above the door handle.

Someone has broken in.

NINE

'Hello…?'

My voice echoes around the walls, bouncing the final 'oh-oh-oh-oh' back to me with haunting despondency. There's no reply. The house feels cool; devoid not only of people but as if nobody's been home in a long time.

'Anyone there?' The quiver in my voice betrays an undercurrent of apprehension.

Nothing.

'Liv? You home?'

I edge backwards, avoiding the glass as I head for the stairs, repeating Olivia's name from the bottom. Again there's no reply – it's only me here.

It's been a really long sixteen or seventeen hours since waking up in that field and the exhaustion hits me all together. I lean on the kitchen counter, closing my eyes and battling a yawn. I fumble through my thoughts, trying to remember what I'm supposed to do. I've already pressed the second '9' on my phone, when I realise 999 is meant to be for emergencies. As I stare at the broken glass, I'm second-guessing myself. Am I in imminent danger? Will I be wasting someone's time? There are those adverts in which someone's in desperate need of an ambulance – but the emergency call is delayed because of someone phoning up to complain about whoever got voted off *X Factor* or *Strictly* that week. The thoughts clutter together and I have to force myself to Google the non-emergency number because 101 has somehow eluded me.

The call handler is kindly and polite with the exact type of soothing authority that I think I need to hear. She first asks if I'm all right and it's only at that when I hear the crack in my own voice as I assure her – waveringly – that I am.

She asks if there's anything missing and there's a strange moment in which I wonder why it never occurred to me that something might be. I fumble my words embarrassingly and look across to the living room. The television is on the cherry-wood unit, where it always is. I apologise to the handler for taking my time and check the drawers underneath the television. The laptop and iPad are both there, where Dan or I left them. Not that any of it is particularly valuable to a burglar, but the mixer, coffee machine and microwave are all present and correct in the kitchen. A silly thought flutters across my mind of a thief trying to sell a food mixer on the streets of North Melbury to fund some sort of drug habit. It's ridiculous and I'm not sure where the idea came from but I have to suppress the smile when I tell the handler that everything seems to be where it was.

She is reassuring and gives me a crime reference number, saying that I can pass it on to my insurance company.

'Is that it?' I ask. 'Isn't somebody coming out?'

'I'm afraid there are no free officers,' the voice replies. She sounds genuinely apologetic.

'Don't you normally send someone out to check for DNA, or fingerprints, or something…?'

I wonder if I've seen too many TV cop shows but it doesn't seem like too much to ask for.

'No one is available until morning, I'm afraid.'

She goes on to say that I should take photographs of everything – but that's it. Nobody is coming to look for clues. I could kick off and bang on about paying taxes and the like, but there's no fight in me. There would be no point anyway – this woman is only doing her job. She can't decide how many officers are available at any given time. This is the age in which we live: cuts, austerity, not enough ambulances and break-ins for which the best a victim can hope for is a reference number to give to the insurance company. I wonder if it would have been different if I said things *were* missing. Bit late now.

I say goodbye and tread carefully around the glass, checking the back door to find that it's unlocked. The spare key is still in the kitchen drawer with the rest of our junk and I can't believe anyone would be capable of stretching through the glass to reach the drawer and key. It's near – but it's not *that* near.

Except that the door *is* unlocked. Did either Dan, Olivia or myself leave it like that? We do pop in and out to put things in the bin, so it's possible. Unlikely, but possible.

I move around the house, checking drawers and cupboards. My most expensive jewellery – which isn't worth much – is still at the back of the bottom drawer in the bedroom. Not that I'm a cliché, or anything. I poke my head around Olivia's door, taking in the bomb site and figuring it'd probably look a bit cleaner if someone *had* broken in. At least the intruder would have picked out anything valuable, meaning some degree of sorting would have happened. As it is, her floor is littered with clothes, shoes, cables and who knows what else. I don't dwell.

Downstairs and the keepsakes with no particular value are fine. There is the official photograph from the day Dan and I were married pinned to the wall; with plenty more pictures of Olivia growing up. I take a moment to brush dust from the frames, remembering the happy times on beach holidays. She's there with her father, each licking an ice cream; then in another photo with me riding the donkeys at Blackpool. She's on the London Eye, pointing at Parliament, riding a canal boat somewhere I can't remember – and so on. Each photo has her a little older than the last until everything stops in her mid-teens.

I check the drawer that contains our birth certificates, passports and the like – but they're all present, too. The more I look, the less I see. What would be the point in breaking in to steal nothing?

And if nothing has been taken, then why break the window? There's no easy way into our back garden, except for climbing a fence and dropping down. Someone would surely be more likely to break in through the garage?

The last place I check properly is the drawer near the back door. There are small shards of glass on the floor and I wince at the crunch under my feet as I try – and fail – to manoeuvre around the remnants of the windowpane.

As well as the back-door key, the drawer is full of the same junk I looked at earlier. Other random keys, receipts, coupons, lottery tickets. The stuff neither Dan or I can be bothered to throw out. I empty it all onto the kitchen counter for the second time that day and notice that the emergency money has gone. There's normally two twenties and a ten-pound note and I'm certain it was there a few hours ago. It could be Olivia who took it, of course – except that she never has in the past. She's many things but I don't think a thief is one of them.

I pick through all the scraps of paper, piling and replacing them in the drawer until I'm certain the money has gone. Is this what the break-in was about? Fifty quid? It's not much compared to the expensive electrical items that have been left – and it's a lot of effort. That said, I don't know much about drugs. I've read that most crime is drug-related in one way or another, so perhaps two twenty-pound notes and a ten will go a long way for someone.

Either way, it's very disciplined of the thief to only take that.

Despite that, something doesn't feel right. How would someone know to come to this drawer specifically? Or was it simply chance?

It's only as I'm replacing everything in the drawer that I find myself staring at the single object I know for a fact wasn't there this morning. It was the reason I emptied everything in the first place. I couldn't find it then – but here it is now, my work pass, sitting among the rest of the junk, exactly where it wasn't a few hours ago.

TEN

Dan gets in from the gym and heads straight to the fridge. His top has a V of sweat from his neck to his belly button and there's still a sheen across his forehead. It's only when he turns around, protein shaker bottle in hand, that he notices the wooden board across the pane of glass.

'What happened?' he asks.

I'm on the other side of the room, sitting on the sofa, half-watching TV but really refreshing the news sites. There have been no hit-and-run reports but also no updates on Tom Leonard. The hotel worker is still missing.

I also had a good nosey at Natasha's Instagram feed. She went to a local pub after work, where she had some sort of salad. It was both #yummy and #scrummy apparently.

'I'm not sure,' I reply. 'We might have had a break-in.'

Dan gawps at the door and then me. 'How do you mean, "might"?'

'When I got in, there was glass on the floor and the back door was unlocked. It doesn't look as if anything's been taken. I called the police but there was no one available to come out.'

'Did you say there'd been a break-in?'

'What do you *think* I said?'

Dan blinks away the remark and I suspect he knows I'm not in the mood for this. He swishes his vest, blowing a bit of air onto his saturated chest. I never know if he's going to shower at the gym or wait until he gets home. There's seemingly no pattern to his behaviour. He drops his gym fob into the kitchen drawer while still examining the board I've nailed across the window in the back-door frame. We actually have a his and hers membership. It was something he talked me into last Christmas when there was some sort of joint offer on. It ended up being our gift to each other, which saved the usual lack of imagination we show when buying gifts. I almost never use the membership he bought for me, but he's at least getting good use from his. Every time he says he's going to the gym, I think I can sense that small accusatory tone that I'm not doing the same. I'm probably imagining it. I don't know any more.

'Did you come home for lunch?' I ask.

He does sometimes – our house is only ten minutes' drive from the school – but Dan shakes his head. 'I didn't leave the school until after five,' he replies.

'I think the emergency money is gone,' I say.

Dan reopens the drawer and swishes a few things around. It's natural, I suppose, but it's still annoying. As if I could be mistaken about such an obvious thing. He does this a lot, probably without even thinking about it. He'll ask if I've seen the weather forecast for the following day and then, after I tell him what it is, I'll find him checking it anyway. He'll ask if I've emptied the dryer and then look inside to make sure I've not forgotten anything. And so on. That's him – or at least it's how he is now. He never used to be like this.

'Someone broke in and stole the money…?' Dan sounds unsure.

'I guess so. It could be Liv – we'll have to ask her. If they did take that money, there's nothing else missing. I don't know what to think.'

He nods along, apparently agreeing.

'Did you see my work pass earlier?' I ask.

'Was it in the drawer?'

I deserve that, of course.

'No,' I reply.

'I've not seen it other than that.'

He sounds breezy, as if it's not something that would concern him, and then he nods at the back door.

'It was probably kids with a football, something like that.'

'Where's the ball?'

'Perhaps they came into the garden and retrieved it?'

'What about the emergency money?'

A shrug. 'If someone broke in, why wouldn't they take the telly? Or the iPad?'

I can't answer that because he's only querying the things I've asked myself. None of what's happened in the past day makes much sense.

Dan wiggles the board I've nailed to the door and tuts. Without another word, he hurries into the garage and then he's back with a hammer and more nails. I sit and watch as he first tugs out the nails I'd hammered in and then bashes in a dozen or so of his own. He wipes his brow with his forearm, flashing the newly rediscovered muscles in his arms and shoulders. When he's done, he rocks the board back and forth once more, making sure it's firmly in place. I can't see any difference between his handiwork and mine but it's not worth arguing.

I'm not sure how our relationship got to this point because, as I watch him, I feel little other than hatred. It's a strong word; a guttural, destructive emotion – but it's hard to force away the rage.

'We'll have to get someone in to replace the glass,' Dan says.

'There's a glazier coming in the morning. I've already texted Graham to say I'm going to be late. I'll wait in for him.'

Dan bites his lip and all he manages is an, 'Oh'. There's nothing like 'good work', or 'thank you'. He has more praise for his students than he ever does for me.

When he's done putting the hammer away, Dan heads upstairs and then I hear the pipes starting to rattle as he showers. Ours is one of those houses in which everything constantly needs upgrading. We had it rewired a few years ago after Dan decided we were living in a fire hazard. He'd seen some sort of public service film at school and that was that. The plumbing system probably needs replacing as well. Sometimes, when the shower first starts up, it feels as if we're living through an earthquake. I can even predict when one pop will be replaced by a creak or a whine. It's like living in the middle of an orchestra who've never played with one another.

I find myself searching for Tom Leonard again but there are no apparent updates. I try Thomas Leonard as well, plus the place name. His name is listed on various athletic pages and then I find out he's a county-level runner. There's an interview with a local paper where he talks about entering the national championships. I find a photograph of him with his mother at the finishing line of an event, with a medal around his neck.

In the end, I have to click away but I can't help thinking how different Tyler's disappearance would be covered, if at all? If his father even bothered to report him gone? He's known to the police, so perhaps they wouldn't consider it anything unusual. I still expect him to be back when his money runs out.

I make another quick check on Natasha. She's got more than a hundred likes for the photo of her salad. On Facebook, she says she's settled on the sofa for the night with her dog, some wine and a week's worth of recorded *EastEnders* episodes.

I'm obsessed, I know.

When Dan returns downstairs, he potters around the kitchen, making himself some tea with a cold rotisserie chicken. He eats chicken almost every night, to the point where it's never worth asking him what he might want to eat, even when I'm willing to cook for everyone.

He finds his own spot on the second sofa, eating off his lap while thumbing at his phone. We continue our separate lives in the same space, existing in the solemn silence of this godforsaken room.

I go back to looking at Natasha's social media stream again, wondering what she's up to. There's nothing since the sofa update.

Dan eventually breaks the awkwardness – or perhaps enhances it – after washing up his plate. He sits back in his spot and I feel him watching me.

'Did you see Liv earlier?' he asks.

I suspect he knows the answer. She'd have texted him. 'She was getting in as I was going out,' I say.

'How did it go?'

'All right.'

He continues to watch and it's the sheer certainty of his gaze that infuriates me now. I'm certain Olivia texted him after our showdown this morning, so he already knows what happened – and yet he wants to hear it from me.

'Don't say it,' I add, keeping my tone calm and level.

'Say what?'

'I know what you're thinking – "let her be" and all that – but…'

I tail off, not sure how to finish the sentence. We've had this same argument for years.

'What did you argue about?' he asks.

I sigh: 'Tyler's missing – and Olivia blames me.'

'How come?'

'We fell out about money the other night. I told Liv I wasn't going to give her any if she was going to pass it straight on to Tyler. He ran off and that was the last anyone saw of him.'

'You told *her* that, or you told *him* that.'

I glance away from him, trying not to squirm. 'A bit of both.'

Dan screws his lips together and presses the fingers from both hands into a diamond shape. He's like a counsellor or something, pensive and too damned smart.

'You have to let her make her own mistakes,' he says.

I let him stew for a moment, wondering if he'll add something. He doesn't. He waits it out.

'Is that what you do at school?' I reply.

I'm hoping for a reaction but he's unerringly calm.

'The students at school are younger – but, yes, to a degree, we do try to let them make their own errors.'

I don't know enough about that to argue back – and we both know the truth anyway. I don't want Olivia to make the same mistakes I did. I don't want her to waste years fawning over someone with no job and no prospects, who spends all day lying around smoking weed.

I say nothing and Dan opens his hands wide.

'Stop doing that,' I snap.

'Doing what?'

'I'm not one of your students.'

Dan does this thing sometimes where he tilts his head to the side, narrows his eyes to a squint, and then snaps his neck back again. It's dismissive and makes me wither pathetically.

From nowhere, there's a tiny stab in my chest. I run my fingers across the pain, which makes it sting even more. I broke my ribs a long time ago and there are times when, regardless of what the X-rays say, I'm not sure it's completely healed.

Dan finally turns away, focusing back on his phone. 'So where is Tyler?'

'I told you – he's missing.'

'Does Liv have any idea where he might be?'

'If she did, I don't think she'd be so upset at him being gone.'

Dan lets it lie, perhaps sensing that I'm ready for a full-on row if that's what he wants. We sit in awkward silence for a bit: each of us on our phones. I'm not even doing anything, simply avoiding having to talk to my husband.

'I saw *him* earlier, by the way…'

Dan speaks airily, as if it's unimportant. At first, I think he means Tyler – but then the reality sinks in.

'Jason?' I reply.

'Yes.'

'Where?'

'He was walking past when I was leaving the house this morning.'

I continue staring at my phone's screen, not wanting to get into this. I know Jason and I will run into one another sooner or later but I didn't expect that he'd be outside the house.

'He walked past twice,' Dan adds. 'I parked along the street and watched. He got to the corner and then came back.'

'I didn't know,' I say quietly. 'I knew he was due to be paroled last week; I didn't know he'd be back here…'

There's a silence and it feels like I'm being accused of something, as if I'm sitting in a dock while a smart lawyer waits on an answer. I can't stop myself from filling it.

'How did you even recognise him?' I ask. 'It's been twenty-odd years.'

'He hasn't changed that much.'

There's a tension in the room that's so thick I can feel the tightness of breath returning once more. Dan is flexing his arm muscles, perhaps on purpose but probably not. He can't help himself.

I push myself up from the sofa and tell him I'm going out.

ELEVEN

It's dark as I stomp along the street, silently seething. I'm not even sure who I'm angry at: Dan or myself. We've known each other since school, even though we weren't together then. It wasn't long after, though. We've been married for nineteen years. Almost two decades of seeing each other more or less every day is such a long time. There are times where I can predict everything Dan is going to do or say – and I'd bet the same is true for him. It gets to the point where the individual has been replaced by the couple.

Familiarity *does* breed contempt and it's there for both of us. It didn't used to be like this but we got set in our ways. Growing older does that to people.

A dim orange glows from the street lights, shrouding the street in a gloomy, shadowed wash. There's no traffic at this time of the evening, so I cross the road at the corner with barely a glance in each direction. Our road becomes another but there's little between them, both sides lined with identikit houses and parked cars.

I stop when I reach number sixty-three, knocking on the dust-peppered white door, rather than using the adjacent bell. There's a scuffing of feet from inside and then the door swings open, leaving me staring at a man I've not seen in a very long time.

His features are silhouetted by the light behind him but everything Dan said is true: he hasn't changed that much. His nose is flat, his eyes round and far apart. There are wrinkles on his forehead, close to his temples and around his mouth – but it makes him look more rugged. I remember a boy but this is unquestionably a man.

'Jason,' I say.

'Aye…'

He stands to the side, opening the door wider for me to enter. I feel him watching me as I do and, when I get into the hallway, he speaks softly.

'Rose McNulty.'

'That's not my name any more.'

'Oh.'

'It hasn't been for a long time.'

I step around him, unbuckling my coat in the familiarity of my surroundings.

'Where's Ell?' I ask.

Jason nods towards the kitchen at the back of the house and I don't wait for him, moving along the darkened hall and hearing the front door close.

Ellie is sitting at her kitchen table staring at the disjointed pieces of a barely started jigsaw. She looks up when I enter and then glances towards the hallway. Jason hasn't followed and we wait, listening as his footsteps clump up the stairs.

'I meant to tell you,' Ellie says as I slot into the chair opposite her.

She doesn't get up but there's nothing unusual about that. She's in a set of fleecy leopard-print pyjamas; the type of cosy, warm outfit in which an entire day can be spent. In Ellie's case, it often is. Her hair is unwashed and tied back loosely into a ponytail. I doubt she's left the house today.

'It was all a bit last-minute,' she adds as Jason's footsteps become silent. 'He needs somewhere to stay for his parole and the friend he was going to live with had a few issues. It was either here or an awkward conversation with the probation officer. I didn't want to risk him having to stay inside, so…'

She tails off but it's not as if she has to explain herself to me. Not really.

'It's fine,' I reply.

'Is it really?'

'Dan said he'd seen Jason around earlier, so it's not a complete surprise. Why would I mind?'

Ellie pouts her bottom lip and then nods. She knows why I'm here. Why I'm *really* here.

'What's wrong?' she asks.

I hold both hands out, palms up to the sky. 'You name it.'

She snorts in amusement but there's nothing mean about it. Comrades on a battlefield. When all else is collapsing, what else is there to do but laugh?

'Has Olivia said anything to you?' I ask.

'About what?'

'Anything… everything. She didn't come home last night and only texted Dan late on about it. She says Tyler is missing – but it's not the first time. You know what they're like. They argue, break up, make up…' A sigh. 'She seems happy enough doing the accounting classes with you and I wondered if she ever says anything.'

Ellie's lips are pressed together and she doesn't have to say anything. I hold up a hand.

'Sorry… I shouldn't have said anything. I shouldn't put you in that position. It's not fair.'

Ellie pounces on a piece of the puzzle and slots it into place with a satisfying click. I can't remember the last time I tried a jigsaw. It must be decades.

'She always tries hard when she's here,' Ellie says without looking up. 'She's a good kid.'

'Are the classes going well?'

'Well enough. She was talking about enrolling in college to do something more advanced.'

Ellie smirks as she looks up to see my wide-eyed expression.

'She's never said anything like that to me,' I reply.

'I'm sure she will in her own time.'

There's some relief in that and, after a long day, it feels like at least some of the weight has been lifted. 'It's good she's thinking of the future,' I say.

Ellie raises her eyebrows. 'We never did.'

'…And look at us!'

She acknowledges the point – though she's right, of course. We've known each other our entire lives. We grew up a couple of streets away from each other, went to the same schools, hung out with the same people. Here we are, in our early forties, and little has changed.

Ellie must be in the same mindset as me because she suddenly sits up rigidly. 'Did you hear about the watermill?' she asks.

'What about it?'

'They're finally tearing it down next month.'

'They've been saying that for years.'

She reaches to the side, digs into a plastic recycling tub and then pulls out the local free paper. 'It's in here,' she says. 'Sounds like it's actually happening this time.'

As she finds the right page and shows me the headline and photo, there's a moment in which I feel myself slipping through time. My fingertips tingle, my mouth watering at the memories. We were all kids together – well, teenagers. We'd traipse through the woods to the abandoned watermill. It's a short distance out of town and was derelict twenty years ago. More importantly, no parents ever went there. Why would they? There was Ellie; her twin brother, Wayne; Jason, myself and – occasionally – the odd hanger-onner. Jason was a year younger than the rest of us and it was our own private play area. Ellie would climb the waterwheel while the rest of us would lay on the bank and smoke cigarettes. That was when Ellie was more active than now. Since she started doing freelance accounting from home, she rarely goes out.

We all grew out of it, of course – but there was a time when that creaky, wooden shack with a wheel on the side felt like the most important place on earth. It was certainly the centre of our worlds.

'I can't remember the last time I was there,' I say.

'Me either.'

There's a moment where it feels as if Ellie's going to say something, but she takes a breath instead – and then turns back to her puzzle.

Over the years, various companies or the council have announced plans to tear down the mill but it's never happened.

'Do you think they'll really do it this time?' I ask.

'Sounds like it.'

'I thought it would outlast all of us.'

There's a forlorn silence and – for me at least – it feels as if I'll be losing something personal. As if the memories will disappear along with the ramshackle building. I suspect Ellie feels it as well, even though we've long since moved on.

We grew up a couple of streets apart – and that's still the case, even though it is in different houses on the opposite side of North Melbury. Ellie's place is significantly bigger than the one in which Dan, Olivia and I live. She got a great deal from the children of an old couple who died. They wanted quick money and she wanted to move. There's a massive basement and attic, along with three large bedrooms. She's lived by herself for years, which is why it's something of a surprise that Jason's here now. She's always seemed happier by herself.

As Ellie reaches for another puzzle piece, she gasps and rubs the back of her neck, wincing as she touches it.

'Is that the whiplash?' I ask.

She has one eye screwed closed as she peers up but then opens it as she stretches high. 'I forget to take the painkillers,' she croaks. 'I only remember when it starts to hurt again.'

In the craziness of the past few hours, it's only now that I remember my best friend had a car crash of her own ten days ago.

Ellie pushes herself up and crosses to the cupboard above the sink, removing a small grey box and taking out a slim white disc, which she holds up.

'I couldn't swallow the first pills they gave me, so the doctor rewrote the prescription for some soluble tablets. I've got weeks and weeks' worth. I'm not sure if that's a good or bad thing.'

'Why would it be bad?'

'He must think I'm going to be in pain for a long time.'

Ellie removes a filter jug of water from the fridge, pours herself a glass, and drops the tablet inside. She asks if I want a drink and, as I say no, the pill fizzes at the bottom of her glass, sending spirals of cloudy gas into the rest of the liquid.

'I could probably kill myself ten times over,' Ellie says, taking the first sip.

'I hope you don't.'

A smirk: 'I'm joking.'

'I know.'

I *do* know – but I wish she wouldn't make light of it. Ellie's had problems in the past and, though I'm clearly no doctor, there have been times I'd have called her depressed. If not clinically, then I suppose she seemed, well… sad. After everything with Wayne, with her *twin*, I guess it's no surprise. This isolation of rarely leaving the house all feeds into that.

Ellie touches her ribs and then rubs her neck once more, before sitting back down. 'I had to pay five hundred on the excess to get the car into the garage,' she says. 'I've still got a rental to get around. I think they're going to write mine off.'

'Have you heard anything from the police?'

She starts to shake her head – and then stops herself. 'You'd think they'd have something. He was on the wrong side of the road but they keep going on about number plate cameras, lack of evidence and all that. I didn't get the number plate – I was too busy trying not to get killed. I accidentally said I wasn't even a hundred per cent sure of the colour, whether it was blue or black, so I think that's working against me.'

'Didn't any witnesses come forward after it was in the paper?'

'I'm not that lucky.'

Ellie's crash was very different from mine, or I assume it was. I'm still not too clear what happened with me. Hers happened on the High Street. Someone veered onto the wrong side of the road, she swerved to avoid a collision, mounted a kerb and cannoned into a lamp post, narrowly avoiding a smash with the front of the hairdressers' shop. The image of the street light bent horizontal was on the front page of the weekly local paper.

We've not seen one another for a week or so and talk for a while about what's been going on. It's all surface fluff, however. Even more than usual, it doesn't sound like Ellie's been out much since her accident. She got her groceries delivered this week.

As well as the accounting, she's taught herself website design. Anything that means she can be in the house. She never had any interest in maths or technology when we were at school but she's been doing these jobs for a while now. She learned much of the accounting from her father. I sometimes wonder what our teenage selves would think of us now. It was all music, ciggies and bunking off back then. Now it's white-collar jobs and mortgages.

I don't tell her about waking up in the field, or the blood. The more time passes – and I realise it's not even a full twenty-four hours yet – the more it feels like something I imagined. I remember it through a blurry haze, not clear and crisp like real life.

'We might have had a break-in,' I say, finally remembering why I came here.

Ellie looks up, concerned: 'A break-in?'

'Someone put through the window of our back door. It was unlocked but the key was still in the drawer. We don't know if anyone actually got inside.'

'Did they take anything?'

'Possibly fifty quid from the kitchen drawer but, other than that, nothing. I can't be certain they took the money, either. It might have been Liv. She hadn't got home from work when I left.'

Ellie scrunches up her face in confusion and then glances at her own back door. 'What would be the point of all that if they didn't take anything?'

'No idea. Perhaps they were distracted by a noise from next door, something like that?'

'What did the police say?'

'Not much. Gave me a crime reference number. I think it's because I said nothing had been taken. I didn't notice the money then. Dan reckons it was kids with a ball. He says he always locks the back door but I'm pretty sure *I* didn't leave it unlocked.'

Ellie raises her eyebrows, illustrating the scepticism that I had. We've talked about Dan a lot in the past few years. I wouldn't say I tell her everything – but I share a lot. It's that, or drive myself crazy.

'We might have to get the locks changed,' I add. 'I was figuring out who had keys for the house – and all I could come up with was Dan, me, Liv, the spare one in the kitchen, and you.'

Ellie glances across to her fridge. There's a small whiteboard pinned to the front with a shopping list written in neat capital letters. Next to that is a row of magnetised hooks, with keys hanging from each.

'I don't suppose someone could have used your spare key…?'

I've already said it before I've thought too much about the words. It's been in my mind since Dan said he'd seen Jason on the street. Perhaps someone simply let themselves into the house and the broken glass is there to confuse us. Nothing was taken but maybe that wasn't the aim of whoever broke in.

Ellie knows what I mean straight away. Her lips twitch as she takes a second or two to think of her response. I know she's holding back.

'You mean Jason,' she says.

'That's not what I mean,' I reply, hoping the lie isn't too obvious. Of course I mean him.

'What *do* you mean?' she asks.

'I don't know…'

Ellie could force the point, turn this into an argument, but she's too diplomatic for that. She has more patience than me. 'Are you sure there isn't another key?' she asks. 'Hidden under a flower pot or something?'

'Dan's really funny about that sort of thing. I locked myself out once and he made me wait until he was home from work. He didn't even leave early. I thought about breaking a window but didn't…'

Ellie shrugs and then winces from another twinge. It's not long after that I say I have to go. It's a little after nine and Olivia is due home from work. I wasn't joking when I said her father and I needed a word with her, even if she wasn't there to hear it.

Ellie and I hug softly – she says she's still a little fragile – and then I head back to the hallway. I'm about to open the front door when I notice the unopened letter sitting on the small table close to the exit. It's perfectly normal – white, with a plastic window – but it's the name that grabs my attention.

It's for Jason Leveson – and, even though I've now seen him for myself, the two words somehow feel more powerful. It all feels real.

Jason Leveson: A walking, talking, living, breathing reminder of the worst thing I ever did.

TWELVE

There are no further updates on Tom Leonard. The hotel worker is still missing, with no reported sightings. There are also no other reports of hit-and-runs, or killed animals on those country lanes. The blood on my car remains a mystery.

It's a few minutes after half past nine when the front door opens. I can't help but notice that Olivia is a lot quieter when entering the house if she knows her father is home. The door doesn't bang off the wall and she takes her boots off before padding into the living room in her socks.

'I'm going upstairs,' she mumbles, before turning back to the hall.

Dan and I exchange the briefest of glances and it's he who speaks. 'We need to talk to you, Liv,' he says.

She turns and looks between the two of us before dropping her bag onto the floor and lurching across to one of the breakfast bar stools. She removes a phone from her pocket and starts tapping on the screen.

'Go on then,' she says, not looking up.

'We actually need your attention,' I reply.

Olivia scowls at the pair of us. It must have been warm in the café this evening because almost all of her make-up has evaporated or rubbed away. There are a few streaky smudges towards the back of her cheeks but she looks otherwise free of cosmetics. It's unlike her – but so is wearing her glasses, and she's doing that.

'We've been trying to sit down with you for a few evenings now,' I say.

'I'm here now.'

'First of all, someone *might* have broken into the house earlier.' I nod towards the boarded-up glass behind her and Olivia turns to take it in. 'Nothing appears to have been taken,' I add, speaking quickly, fearing she'll run off to her room to check. 'I want to make sure you have your key with you.'

I don't bring up the £50 for fear she'll think I'm accusing her of something.

Olivia reaches for her bag and digs out a grubby keyring, holding it up for us to see.

'If they broke a window, why are you worrying about my key?' she asks.

'The back door was unlocked,' I reply. 'We don't know if one of us left it open by accident, or—'

'I didn't leave it open!'

'I wasn't saying you had. Like I said, we don't know if someone broke through the window and then unlocked the door somehow, or if it had been left open. Your father thinks it might have been some kids with a football who broke the glass and that the unlocked door is simply a coincidence.'

Olivia looks to Dan and then back to the door. 'But nothing's missing…?' she says.

'We don't think so.'

She starts to stand, apparently deciding this was the only thing we wanted, but then she jabs an accusing finger in my direction. 'You think this was Ty, don't you?'

'What? No.'

A lie. Obviously, I'd thought that.

'Yes you do,' she storms. 'You think he copied my key, or something. You—'

Dan cuts her off and, for once, I'm grateful for his input. 'It's not that, Liv,' he says. 'We're simply asking if you have your key with you. That's all.'

Olivia calms at her father's voice and I can't pretend it doesn't annoy me. I'm the dragon and he's the soothsayer. I breathe fire and he breathes poetry.

'Oh,' she says, suddenly unsure of herself. 'Is that it, then? Can I go?'

'No,' Dan says firmly.

There's a moment in which I think he's going to do the hard work. That he might say those difficult words. But he doesn't: he turns to me instead. Olivia follows his gaze until they're both staring, both expecting. I'm not sure why I thought this might go differently. Dan and I have known each other for too long, after all. This is precisely what I thought would happen.

'Your father and I are separating,' I say.

It's as quick as that, like ripping off a plaster in one go. Bang. Done. It doesn't even hurt.

It's like time has stopped. Dan and Olivia both continue to stare at me; him with knowing acceptance, her with wide-eyed shock. Olivia's mouth bobs open, closed and open again. She turns to her father but he's still watching me.

'You're divorcing?' Olivia replies slowly, disbelievingly. Her voice cracks midway through the sentence.

'Not yet,' I reply. 'We're going to separate first and see how things go. We've not quite figured everything out yet.'

I'm not sure what reaction I expected. Olivia is eighteen – an adult – but it was always going to be a shock when we told her. She has both hands pressed together into one giant fist, her knuckles white as she squeezes her fingers tight.

I look to Dan, hoping he'll pick things up from here, that he'll know what to say, but he's staring through me uselessly.

'What does that even mean?' Olivia's voice is pained. She cradles her knees up to her chest, somehow keeping her balance on the stool.

'We're going to try living apart for a while,' I say. 'I'm staying here, your father is—'

'Why do *you* get to stay here?'

'I, um…' I don't have a good answer, not an immediate one in any case. I stammer for a moment and then turn to the third person in the room. 'Do you want to say something, Dan?'

He jolts in his seat, as if I've just awoken him. 'Right, yes…' he says. 'We, er, decided it'd be for the best.'

I look to him and my whole body slumps. Is that it? In all the conversations we had over this, over how we'd tell Olivia, *this* is the best he can do?

'Why now?' Olivia demands.

It's clear Dan's out of this conversation, not wanting any part of it.

'We decided it was time,' I reply. 'We've not been getting on for a while and, rather than continue to make each other miserable, we thought we'd try something else.'

'If Dad's moving out, are you making me choose between you?'

'No!'

Dan and I reply at the same time – but there's no follow-up from him.

'What, then?' she demands, turning between us. 'Are you kicking me out?'

'Of course not,' I say. 'It's not that at all. Your father's going to be renting a small apartment for himself – at least for now. He's moving out in a few weeks. We've not quite figured out the date yet. It depends on a few things. There won't be room for you there, so we assumed you'd want to continue living here.'

Olivia's eyes narrow ferociously and there's a moment where I think she's going to race upstairs, grab her stuff and tell us to go to hell. There's fire in her, the same way there was in me. I was very careful to use the words 'small apartment', as opposed to 'bachelor pad', but I have my suspicions over what Dan's single life might bring.

'Oh, so that's it, is it?' Olivia spits. 'You've made all the decisions for me. I don't get a say at all.'

'We want to try to make this as easy for you as possible. Everything can continue on at the house as it has been. Your father won't be moving far – only to those new flats down by the river. You'll be able to see him more or less when you want.'

I look to Dan once more and – finally – he opens his damned mouth.

'It's for the best, Liv,' he says calmly.

I remember the first time he used that soothing voice on me. We knew one another in the way people do when they go to the same school and live in the same town. We'd nod when we passed each other in the street, or say hello if we saw each other in the same bar. Then, one evening, I was standing at the bar in the Red Lion waiting to be served. He asked if I was seeing anyone and, when I said I wasn't, he said he'd like to take me out. It's clichéd, unromantic even – but it is what it is. Our first proper date was on my twenty-first birthday. He took me out to a posh restaurant a couple of towns over. I ordered steak and chips, while he went for some Japanese thing that I couldn't pronounce then and wouldn't attempt to now. Afterwards, we went for a walk on the canal bank. It was cold and he lent me his jacket. Then, in that exact same voice he's using now, he asked if I'd like to see him again.

A little over a year later and we were married. Another year after that and Olivia was born.

She might be eighteen, but she looks so young now. Olivia's dinner-plate eyes make her look like a frightened nine- or ten-year-old, not a fully-grown adult.

'It's for the best *for you*.' Her voice begins croakily but the final two words are hissed towards the pair of us. She pushes up from the stool and grabs her bag from the floor. The spread of badges rattle into each other as she adjusts it on her back and heads for the stairs.

'Oh, and F-Y-I, Tyler is *still* missing,' she adds with venom. 'Not that either of you care.'

Stomp-stomp-stomp, plus one slammed bedroom door later and she's gone. All in all, everything went more or less as I'd expected.

THIRTEEN

- WEDNESDAY -

The house feels lonely the next morning. Dan and I are cordial with each other but there's little for us to say. We did much of our talking when we decided to separate. I know people will ask which of us first suggested it because the important thing in any break-up is who's the dumper and who's the dumpee. For the record, it genuinely was mutual. We'd argued over something stupid – me leaving a pair of shoes on the bedroom floor, if I remember rightly. He shouted, I shouted back and then we sat on the bed. He said something like, 'This isn't fun any longer, is it?' and I agreed. From there, it was easy. It was like the sun had finally come out after a long, long winter. We decided on a few things, set about figuring out what it would mean practically to separate and now we've finally told Olivia.

None of that cooperation has stopped our sniping at one another, of course. It's automatic now: a defence mechanism for me, at least.

I'm eating a bowl of bran flakes on the sofa when the doorbell sounds. Dan's pottering in the kitchen, sorting himself out some sort of healthy breakfast, but our eyes lock at the sound. It's 6.45 a.m., far earlier than any sane person would ever call round.

It's the way that Dan charges around the kitchen counter that lets me know he'd rather I didn't see who's at the door. He calls that he'll get it as he's moving but I'm much closer. By the time I'm in the hallway, there's no space for him to push past. I take my time turning the deadbolt and then pull the door open to be met by a smiling blonde in lycra. She's short, probably not even five foot, and bobbing on the heels of her trainers. I doubt she's much over twenty-one or twenty-two – if that.

I don't recognise her at first and it's only when she sticks out her hand and says, 'Alice' that I clock she works at Dan's gym. *Our* gym, I suppose – even if I rarely go. She did my induction when I went at the very beginning.

Dan had told me he was having a few personal trainer sessions but it's only now that everything is slotting together.

Alice starts to jog on the spot as Dan edges around me onto the path. He's grabbed his gym bag on the way through.

'We should get going,' he says, talking to Alice and then looking over her to me. 'I'll be going straight to school after this,' he adds.

Alice is ludicrously smiley. It's like someone's painted the grin on her face, because it doesn't slip. We shake hands and she has the smoothest skin I've ever touched – not that I routinely go around stroking people.

'We'll have to get you out one of these days,' Alice laughs – although I sense the hilarity isn't at my expense.

'Not my thing,' I reply.

'That's what everyone says. You'd be surprised how quickly that can change after a few sessions.'

'I still don't think it's for me.'

She pats her stomach. It's perfectly flat and there's a weighty thud as if she's slapping a rock. 'My brother just got back from holiday. Brought back all sorts – including *so* much chocolate. I can't stop eating the stuff. I only do this so I can eat what I want.'

Yeah, I think, *it looks like you eat whatever you want – as long as whatever you want is green and tastes of damp paper.*

Dan has all his weight on one leg and is edging towards the road, desperate to get Alice away from the house. His lack of subtlety is hilarious – which only makes me want to prolong things.

'Where did your brother go?' I ask.

'Croatia. Have you ever been?'

'No. I've seen a bit of France, Spain and Italy – the usual places. Nothing that exotic.'

'Me, either. He said it's very nice.'

Alice continues bobbing on the spot. 'Sure we can't tempt you out? If not today, then another time…?'

I put a hand across my front. 'I can't do too much. I broke my ribs when I was a teenager and it hurts if I overstretch myself.'

Alice shrugs. 'Oh well – I suppose I'll see you again.'

She waves sweetly and then turns to my husband. It's only a fraction of a second, the merest of glances, but it's unmistakeable. Dan's eyes widen slightly, his lips arching up into a glimmer of a smile. It's gone as soon as it appeared and then he swivels and Alice follows him along the path, through the gate, onto the pavement.

When the front door is closed, I give it my best middle finger. I'm not sure if it's for him or her. Probably a bit of both. It's hard not to wonder whether they're shagging. There was definitely something in the way he looked at her. He has to be twice her age but he makes a decent salary, he's in shape, he doesn't have young children to tie him down. There's a lot there that could be appealing to a certain type of young woman.

He didn't out and out lie about his personal trainer but he didn't go out of his way to make it clear he was spending time with someone who looks like Alice. I only met her today because she knocked on the door. I suspect he wanted her to wait in her car until he left the house.

It's hard to know why I care. It's not because I'm desperate to rekindle whatever it is we once had, which means I suppose it's jealousy. He's moving on and I'm not. I can't imagine there are too many twenty-something blokes out there desperate to start something with me – not that I'm looking for that anyway.

Back on the sofa and I'm starting to feel like a stalker on more than one count. Tom Leonard is still missing and there haven't been any updates in the past day. I find myself continuing on through the search results, reading articles about all sorts of Tom Leonards in case they happen to be him. Almost everything I find that relates to the correct Tom is to do with his running. There are spreadsheets of results from his club and I can't explain why I find it so compelling. I check his times from month to month, year to year, seeing how he's improved.

Then there's Natasha. Her breakfast is half a grapefruit. I've no idea how that counts as a meal but it was #awesome.

It's only when Olivia clumps down the stairs that I realise almost two hours have passed. She walks past the open door of the living room and is fully dressed, bag on her back. I call after her as she heads for the front door and get into the hallway at the same time as she's ready to leave.

'Are you all right?' I ask. We've not seen each other since the previous evening.

She turns, closing the front door slightly, though not completely. 'Fine.'

'We can talk if you want…?'

'About what?'

'Whatever you want. Your father. Me. The house. You.'

'What about Tyler?'

I clench my teeth. Of course about Tyler. He should have been the first name I mentioned. I've wasted two hours reading everything about some missing teenager I don't know, while completely ignoring the one who is seeing my daughter.

'Tyler, too,' I reply.

It's too late – and I know it. I've blown it once more.

Olivia twists back to the front door, says she has to go – and then does precisely that.

The glazier arrives at eight-thirty on the dot, exactly on time. I make him a cup of tea but, other than that, he gets on with fitting a new pane of glass into the back door. He's the perfect kind of labourer, peacefully and swiftly getting on with his work and not feeling the need to blather on endlessly about some nonsense he read in the paper yesterday. I don't know if I can manage much in the way of small talk today.

I leave him be and get back to reading Tom Leonard's race results. He's nineteen and it's perhaps no surprise that his fastest times have come in the past year. I re-read the quotes from his parents, appealing for anyone who might have seen him. There are few details about what might have happened, because no one seems to know. He left his house as usual on Monday morning but his car was found unlocked and unoccupied a couple of miles from there. Other than that: Nothing.

The blood on my windscreen is still such a vivid thought. It was the first thing I saw when I woke up this morning. Could it belong to Tom?

I open the maps app and check where he went missing, comparing it to where I found myself in that field. In a straight line, it's perhaps six or seven miles; following the roads it's nine or ten. The times still don't match up – I was at home when Tom went missing – but then it occurs to me that nobody knows *when* he disappeared. All anyone knows for sure is that he didn't arrive at work on time. A few hours later and I checked into that same hotel. Later still, I woke up in a bloodied car.

The glazier interrupts my cluttered thoughts when he tells me he's finished. He's cleaned up after himself, which must have made noise, but somehow I missed it. He writes out an invoice and says I can either pay in cash or with a card through his website. We smile and joke about how it's not like the old days any longer and then I tell him I'll pay through his site there and then. He says it's not necessary but I do it anyway and then he goes on his way, telling me we should get the locks changed.

We should, of course – except I know we won't. The only keys we've had cut are all accounted for and none of us have come up with anything that's missing. With a clear mind the morning after the night before, perhaps Dan was right. One of us accidentally left the back door unlocked and the only reason either of us noticed was because a window was broken. It might have been some kid with a ball. It feels unlikely – but unlikely isn't impossible. It's certainly more likely than me waking up in a field in the middle of nowhere.

With the house now empty again, I leave my phone to charge and finish getting ready for work. This time my work pass is in the kitchen drawer, precisely where it's supposed to be.

It's only when I'm on my way to the garage that I realise my car keys are missing.

I empty the drawer out for what feels like the twentieth time in the past day – but it's little use. The last time I used my car was for the drive back from meeting Declan yesterday – via a detour to the countryside. I walked to Ellie's and, other than that, I was home the rest of the time. There's a memory of opening the drawer and putting the car keys inside, but I can't say with absolute certainty that it was yesterday, as opposed to any of the other thousands of times I've done the same.

The keys aren't in my jacket pocket, nor my bag. I check the garage but the car is locked and I can't see them anywhere. I've spent hours on the sofa and pull off all the cushions, even going so far as to getting down on hands and knees to look underneath.

No luck.

There's a spare set – but Dan keeps them somewhere that's apparently secure and, though I assume they're in the house, I'm not sure where. I've never needed the spare set before.

I'm going to be even later for work than I thought. Bloody Natasha's going to be smugger than usual and Graham's going to kick off.

There's nothing else for it – so I call Dan. It rings and rings, plipping through to his voicemail message. It's the same as it has been for as long as I can remember.

'This is Daniel Denton. Please leave a message after the beep.'

He's clipped and formal. Perfectly perfunctory – which I suppose sums him up. It's annoying.

I hang up and try again, only to get the same notice. This time I leave a message, asking him to call me as soon as he gets it. I try Olivia – but she doesn't answer – and it's as if I'm invisible.

On the second series of checks, my pockets are as empty as they were the first time – and my bag is still full of the same largely useless stuff it always is.

The clock is unforgiving. It doesn't feel like it but, somehow, forty minutes have passed since the glazier left. It's almost half-past-ten.

I'm hot and sweating, largely from the fruitless hunt, but it's more than that. It's the frustration of questioning my own mind. It feels like I can't trust my memories. My mother went through dementia at the end. She'd ask something basic, like what I'd been up to at the weekend. I'd tell her and then, five minutes later, she'd ask again. At first, I'd say she'd already asked – but she insisted she hadn't. Her mind played tricks and I quickly learned to play along. If that meant telling her the same story four or five times in a short period, then so be it.

I'm forty-one, not that old, but this is how it feels now. Waking up in field in the middle of nowhere; losing my pass, then my keys.

Is it me?

I go to the fridge, looking for something to cool me down. I'm already reaching for the water jug when, like a mirage on the horizon, there they are. My car keys are sitting at the front of the salad drawer, nestled next to the tomatoes as if that's where they're supposed to be. I stare at them for a second, barely believing it, before sliding out the drawer and picking them up.

They're real. Chilly, of course – but real.

It almost feels as if I've willed them into being because I was so desperate to find them. It can't be true, of course. They must have been here the whole time. I did make a sandwich yesterday evening, not long after getting in – so it *could* have been me who left them there.

Who else could it have been? Olivia playing a weird joke? Dan? Why would they?

I suddenly remember I'm late, shutting the fridge and hurrying through to the garage.

I've almost finished reversing out when a car pulls up onto the road outside, blocking me in. I'm in the mood for an argument and am about to beep my horn when I notice the bright stripes along the side of the other car.

It's the police.

FOURTEEN

'Are you on your way out?'

There are two uniformed officers on the driveway as I get out of the car. The one who's spoken is the taller of the two – a typical British bobby. He stands rigid in his crisp uniform with closely cropped dark hair.

I lean on the driver's door as I reply: 'On my way to work.'

'I'm PC Heath and this is PC Harvey,' the officer says. 'Weren't you expecting us?'

My baffled look is enough to give them an answer. 'I was told you didn't have time to come out,' I reply.

The two officers turn to each other and PC Harvey shrugs. He's the smaller of the pair, with tight blond curls and doesn't have the same stiff posture of his colleague.

'It was passed to us this morning,' PC Heath says. 'We assumed you'd been told we were coming by at eleven…?'

'All I got was a crime reference number. I've cleaned up the broken glass from inside – and the glazier came this morning to replace the pane.'

PC Heath nods along as if this sort of miscommunication is perfectly normal. 'We should probably still take a statement, assuming you have time,' he says. 'We've had a few reports of youths causing disturbances in the area.'

I glance past him along the street, as if expecting to see a gang of errant young people starting a riot a few doors down. There's nothing, of course.

'What sort of disturbance?' I ask.

'Late-night noise, knock-and-runs – that sort of thing.'

It's all news to me but this is what I wanted in the first place, so it seems silly to send them away now. If Graham makes a fuss about me being even later than I said, I'll tell him the truth – that I was talking to the police.

We enter the house through the front door and then I talk the officers through everything from the previous evening. They check the back door, not that there's much to see now, and then we go through the whole rigmarole of me explaining that it doesn't look as if anything was taken. I don't bring up the money, just in case it was Olivia who took it.

I show them out to the back garden and both officers walk slowly along the length of the flower beds. Other than a few unfriendly deposits from next door's cat, there's little to see. Certainly no footprints belonging to someone who might have come over the fence. The officers ask about what's on the other side and we end up going upstairs so they are high enough to see. There's a narrow lane that skirts the back of our house, separating it from the properties beyond. The height of the respective fences on both sides means it's permanently in darkness. Through the winter, frost can sit on the ground for weeks at a time. It's a cut-through to get from one part of the estate to another, frequently used by pedestrians and cyclists to save them having to go the long way round to get to the bus stop or shops.

Some of the houses backing onto the lane have gates, allowing them to leave via the back of the house. Ours doesn't – it's one long eight-foot fence.

The officers don't say much when I tell them that Dan thought it could have been some kids coming in to retrieve a ball. It would have been a decent kick, perhaps coming from one of the gardens that back onto ours across the path. PC Heath asks if we've ever found wayward balls in the garden before and I have to admit that we haven't. We've never had issues with anything like that. Despite his mention of trouble in the area, I haven't seen any of it. The evenings are quiet and we haven't had anyone knocking and running off. Dan and I have lived here for almost as long as we've been married and we've never been burgled. The only thing I can remember is that a dead mouse was left on our doorstep a year or so ago – but we're pretty sure that was down to next door's cat.

PC Harvey takes notes while PC Heath asks the questions. It doesn't feel as if there's much I can say, let alone much they can do. I get the sense they knew it would be a waste of time before they pulled up. It's probably an excuse to get out of their office for an hour or two – and I can't blame them for that.

They give me a phone number to call if I notice anything *has* gone missing, or to report anything new.

The garage door is still open, so we leave the house that way. I get on with locking the doors that connect to the house but, when I turn, both officers are standing in the middle of the empty garage, close to the drain.

PC Harvey points at a spot on the floor and looks up to me: 'Do you know there's blood on the ground?' he asks.

FIFTEEN

There's a moment in which it feels like everything has stopped. The concrete floor rushes towards me and everything starts to swirl. It's like the rush of standing up too quickly, when it feels as if my body is no longer under my control. Mercifully, the sensation only lasts a moment, reality twisting back into view as quickly as it disappeared. There's a pain in my chest, though – not the one from my decades-old rib break, something else. It's sharp and stinging, as if I'm being stabbed.

'Blood?'

It's my voice that speaks but only on instinct.

'Right there.'

I'm not sure which of the two officers is speaking because the tingle in my chest has spread to my upper arm. Am I having a heart attack? This is how it starts, isn't it? I've seen the leaflets at the doctors.

Somehow, I move across towards the officers but it feels more like I'm drifting than walking. If they notice anything out of the ordinary, neither of the constables say so.

They're right, of course. There's a patch of dried blood exactly underneath the spot where my bonnet would usually cover.

I was certain I'd checked under the car; that I'd cleaned everything away – but here it is. A crimson stain of guilt.

'Do you have any idea why there might be blood in your garage, Mrs Denton?'

I'm still not sure who's speaking, transfixed by the floor instead. The blood is a series of spots, rather than any specific pattern. It looks like it has dripped.

'I don't think so,' I reply.

The stinging stab in my arm is clearing and so is the haze around the edges of my vision.

PC Heath clips his heels and heads off towards the driveway. 'We'll get someone over to take a sample,' he says. 'If someone did break in, it might have come from them. It's worth checking.'

He's quickly out of earshot and it's only then that I realise I should have said the blood was mine – or Dan's. Or that it was red paint for some reason. Now it's too late, I can come up with a dozen reasons to tell them to not to bother testing. I'm one of those people who is amazing *after* an emergency. Or who has a hilarious comeback a good hour after the moment has passed.

'You shouldn't worry,' I tell PC Harvey. 'I don't think anyone broke in anyway.'

'It's not a problem,' he replies. 'What we're here for.'

'But aren't these tests expensive? Don't you have tight budgets and so on? I always hear things on the news.'

This is some serious straw-clutching.

'There's been a series of break-ins on the other side of North Melbury. These are full-on burglaries, so perhaps not the same as this – but we have DNA from the perpetrator. The problem is that we don't know who it belongs to. There are no matches on the database – but we'll be able to tell if this is the same person.'

He smiles and I thank him, even though it's the last thing on my mind. What if the blood belongs to Tom Leonard? What if it belongs to someone else who's missing? Someone who's been found dead on those back country lanes? How could I possibly explain it?

How can I even explain this? I was so sure I'd cleaned the floor – but then I was certain about the location of my work pass and the car keys as well. My mind feels like one big, jumbled mess. Like the pieces to Ellie's jigsaw, all mixed up and thrown on the floor.

PC Heath walks back, his lips tight and expressionless. 'The testing team are free now,' he says.

PC Harvey answers before I can. 'That never happens. What's going on?'

His colleague shrugs and they both look to me. 'Someone can be here in half an hour,' he adds. 'Should I tell them to come now?'

I should say no – but what would that look like? I called the police to report a possible break-in. They're linking it to others across town, so I can hardly send them away. I'd look mad at best; guilty of something at worst.

'That's fine,' I reply. Except it isn't – and I have a horrible sinking feeling that it really won't be.

It is a few minutes after midday when the crime scene analyst leaves the house. He was perfectly pleasant, working by himself and scraping up the hardened flakes of blood to take away. When I ask how long it'll all take, he sighs. I'd bet it's the type of question he's asked a dozen times a day, every day.

'Anywhere from forty-eight hours to two weeks,' he replies. 'It depends what sort of priority they give it.'

'Do you have any idea whether it's a high priority…?'

'I wish I could help – but as soon as this gets to a lab, it's out of my hands.'

I'm not sure if he means literally or figuratively – but I guess the outcome is still the same.

He explains that if the blood matches someone already in the DNA Database – or a close family member – then they'll get a match and be able to identify who it belongs to. If there's no match, then it will sit on file. They might arrest someone for something unrelated in the future and, assuming a crime had been committed, would be able to charge him or her for the other offences.

I thank him and then he heads back to his car, accelerating off along the road as I watch, wondering if he has my fate in his hands.

I'm about to turn back to my car, finally ready to go to work, when a familiar face emerges from behind the postbox a few doors down. It's at the opening to the lane that runs along the back of the house and the man strides out briskly, hands in his jacket pocket. He heads towards me, watching the houses – but it's only when he sees me that he stops on the spot. He edges back towards the road, a startled, frightened animal in headlights. For a moment, I think he might rush back the way he's come but he doesn't. He presses ahead until he's at the edge of the drive.

'Hi,' Jason says.

'Are you watching the house?' I ask.

He squirms, tucking his elbows tighter into himself, his hands not leaving his jacket pockets. 'No.'

I'm not sure if being in prison should make a person better at lying – or worse. Either way, he's awful at it.

'I'm on my way to work,' I say.

'Right.'

He bobs from one foot to the other, watching me but never making full eye contact. There's a breeze that's playing with his mucky brown hair. It hasn't been washed for a day or two and is longer than it ever used to be, enough to be tucked behind his ears. He's in jeans, with a green army-style jacket and heavy leather boots.

I move towards the car, keys clearly in hand. He isn't standing directly behind the car and I could leave if I wanted – but I'd have to drive directly past him. I'm going to have to talk to him sooner or later and I suppose this isn't the worst time.

'You look good,' he says. 'All official, like.'

I'm in a suit that I've had for at least five years. It can be machine washed, which is the main reason I like it so much.

'Didn't wear many suits when I was a teenager,' I reply.

'Aye, me either.'

I remember the images from the news of Jason being hurried into a courtroom. I was twenty-one, so he was either nineteen or had just turned twenty. He was wearing a suit a couple of sizes too big. The jacket was low across his backside, the sleeves almost reaching his fingers. It was probably a charity shop job. Most of our clothes came from the local Oxfam or Heart Foundation stores in those days.

Ellie went to court every day but I never did. I'd watch the news each evening – a new thing for me – and then pore over the coverage in the papers the next morning. Also a new thing for me. I'd never bothered with news before then.

I can't remember how many days the trial lasted. It felt like weeks but was probably only two or three days. It's not like they had a lot of disputed evidence over which to argue.

'How are you?' I ask, continuing my new-found trend of asking stupid questions.

'Outside is better than inside.'

Jason glances both ways along the street and then inclines his head ever so slightly, asking for silent permission to step onto the driveway. I wave him forward and he approaches slowly, as if I'm a coiled snake who might strike. He stops when there's a metre or so between us, giving me a close-up view of his pockmarked skin. There's a scar close to his ear, zigzagging across his hairline.

'I've got to see a probation officer twice a week,' he adds. 'It'll go down to once in a few months.'

Jason crouches, tugging up the bottom of his jeans to show me the plasticky tag that's strapped around his ankle.

'I've got to be in our Ell's by nine every night. Not allowed out again 'til six.'

He hops for a moment, unbalanced on his single foot, and then settles back onto a solid standing.

'How long have you got to do that?'

'Six months if I behave.'

I'm not sure what to say, so remain silent.

'How old's your daughter?' he asks.

It's a question out of the blue. There's every reason for him to know about Olivia – Ellie would've visited him in prison over the years, and he's now living with her – but it still feels strange for him to mention something I've never told him.

'Eighteen,' I reply.

He nods slowly for a moment and then: 'Wow… that's old.'

It's not – but I know what he means. He went into prison when he was only a little older than that. He knew me as a childless teenager – and now I have a daughter the same age. There's a wistful calm between us and I know he's thinking of the things we were doing when we were that age. Ellie, Wayne, Jason and me. Us against the world.

'Is she a good kid?' he asks.

'Yes. She works at a local café in the evening. She's doing accounting lessons with Ell and might go back to college.'

A nod. 'What about your old man? He treat you well?'

For a second, I think Jason means my father – but he died when I was a child. It's only then I realise he means Dan.

'It's complicated,' I reply. 'We're sort of… separating.'

It sounds so official now I've said it out loud to someone who's more or less a stranger. Telling Olivia was talking to family; going over things with Ellie in the previous weeks was more or less discussing it with family. This is different. I'll be telling people at work next, then neighbours. It's actually happening.

Jason blinks and then quickly adds: 'Oh. He doesn't knock you about, does he?'

'Of course not. Why would you think that?'

Jason coughs an apology but it's obvious why he'd think that: he's spent two decades in prison – and it's not like his upbringing was Garden of Eden stuff before that. A person only knows what they know.

Physical violence isn't the only type of mistreatment, though. Dan's no more abusive than I am but we've been together so long that we bring out the worst in one another. This is what happens when you live with someone you can't stand. You make each other's lives a misery and, in the end, everyone loses.

Jason tugs at his jacket, glancing past me towards the house. I know what he's thinking: that this could have been him. He's wrong, but he can't know that.

'I wrote to you,' he says quietly.

'I know.'

'You never wrote back.'

'I didn't know what to say.'

He nods slowly, acceptingly, and then hits me brutally with five stinging words. 'You could have said sorry.'

'I—'

He cuts me off instantly. 'No, I didn't mean that. *I'm* the one who's sorry.'

I have to say it now. It's been twenty years in the making, words I should have said then but couldn't because it would have meant admitting my part in everything that happened.

'I'm sorry, too. I shouldn't have done that to you.'

He shrugs. 'I knew what I was getting into and then, afterwards, none of that was your fault. That was all me. You didn't set the fire.'

There's something so powerful and evocative about the word. Fire is life: it's warmth and comfort – but it's destructive and terrifying as well. It was a lesson I sure as hell learned.

When he was nineteen years old, Jason set fire to a pub, killing three people who were asleep upstairs. His legal team had little defence, other than trying to get the charges negotiated down to manslaughter. The system disagreed. He was charged and convicted of a triple murder.

Even putting aside the arguments over whether he meant to kill, the fact is that he did.

That doesn't mean it's entirely his fault.

I say nothing because I'm not sure I trust myself. I didn't drop the lighter but I'm not blameless either. I knew that then and I know it now.

Jason's eyeing the scar that hoops around my own temple. Ours almost match now. I scratch it self-consciously and he takes the hint, turning away to the street.

'Are you going with Ell tomorrow?' he asks.

It takes me a couple of seconds to remember what he's talking about – and then the true depth of my self-absorption is clear. I'd completely forgotten about tomorrow.

'Of course I am,' I reply. In my mind, I'm scrambling, trying to figure out how to tell Graham I'm going to be late once more. I'll need to invent a client or a meeting, something like that.

'Ell says the two of you visit every year…' He winces and then speaks really quickly, his words blending into one. 'Can I come, too?'

It takes me a moment to figure out what he's asked.

'I understand if you don't want me there,' he adds

'No – he was your brother, too. You should definitely come.'

'I just wanna chance to say g'bye. I never went to the funeral. Couldn't face it at the time and then, when I were ready, they wouldn't let me out on day release for the anniversary.'

'You should definitely come with us. You didn't have to ask permission.'

'I was gonna ask last night – but it looked like you were a bit shocked to see me.'

I shrug: 'Well, it has been twenty years…'

'Aye.'

He turns and steps back towards the pavement and I wonder if this is why Dan saw Jason hanging around the house. He was building up the courage to ask if he could visit his brother's grave with Ellie and me. I watch him walk off in the direction of Ellie's house. He stops to look back at me and, when he realises I'm still watching, he quickly faces forward again, ducking his head and shuffling quickly out of sight.

I sigh deeply once he's gone, unsure if this is a weight lifted, or another added. I can't believe I'd forgotten the anniversary of Wayne's death. Ellie and I visit his grave every year, yet, somehow, it had fallen from my memory. Like a lot of things recently.

Last night, I thought that Jason was a symbol of the worst thing I ever did – but he isn't. It's his brother, of course. Jason and Wayne Leveson: two brothers – and look what I did to them. Even now, look at what I've done to Dan; to myself.

Is this me?

Is this what I do?

I destroy everything and everyone around me.

SIXTEEN

'The police?'

Graham is surprised. He readjusts his tie, loosening the knot slightly and sitting up straighter in his office chair as if *I'm* the police, instead of simply mentioning them.

'We had a break-in at home yesterday,' I explain. 'The glazier patched things up first thing – which I texted you about – and then the police were a bit late. I would've called but they were busy taking statements and the like. I have to go back to the station tomorrow morning to give a few more details.'

It's a lie that comes to me on the spot but it's perfect. Who's going to argue with that?

Graham's frown softens. 'But everything's all right?'

'I was a bit shaken last night but, y'know... The police say there's been a series of break-ins in the area...'

I tail off, letting it hang there, not wanting to overdo it too much. It's not like I'm going to burst into tears and cry about the unfairness of life. He doesn't need to know that nothing was taken and it was probably Dan or I who left the back door unlocked in any case.

I can imagine Natasha along the hallway, ears pricked waiting for the sound of raised voices.

Graham shuffles through the Post-it notes on his desk, picking them up and re-sticking them until he finds the one he's after. His face is reddy-purple and it's hard to tell if it's redder than usual. He has a beetroot sort of glow at the best of times but, when he gets worked up, it looks like he's about to pop.

'Luke,' he says. 'What's going on with him?'

'I've not heard back since our aborted meeting on Monday night. He's not answering his phone or replying to texts or emails. I'm not sure what else to do. I guess he's not interested.'

Graham starts to chew on the inside of his mouth, screwing up his cheeks as he does so, as if it's something particularly gristly.

'What about this Declan from yesterday?'

'Hasn't he emailed? I thought he'd be in contact today...?'

Graham shifts his mouse around, squints at his screen and then shakes his head. 'He's not contacted me.'

I admit that I've not heard from him either – and then Graham starts drumming his fingers on the desk. I've seen this before and it's never a good sign. Graham is a salesperson's best friend while things are going well; but I've seen him turn when things aren't working out. Over the years, I've avoided many of his mood swings, maintaining enough of a sales record to be unspectacularly satisfactory. Other people take the bonuses – but other people get fired as well.

Never me.

He pushes a sheet of A4 across the desk, saying nothing but making his point. The fact he's printed it off means it has to be serious. I pick it up and scan the rows and columns. There are typos – which means Graham almost certainly created the spreadsheet himself – but that in itself tells a story. I'm in trouble.

'There's a second page,' he says, passing another sheet of paper across his desk.

I read the second and, if anything, it spells even more trouble than the first.

'What have you got to say?' Graham asks.

I take a breath and re-read the first sheet, looking for even the slimmest glimmer of hope. It's not there.

'Is there anything I should know about?' he adds.

I bristle at his words and try not to show it. Is there anything he *should* know? The obvious answer is no. My life away from the office is none of his damned business. Of course there's nothing he *should* know. There are things he *could* know – but that isn't what he asked.

The first page shows the company's sales since the beginning of the year. I'm rock-bottom – and not by a little bit. I've got a third of the sales of Mark, who's at the top; and only a little bit over half of what Claire has done. She's second from bottom. I'm the very bottom of the chasm. After me, there's zero. Natasha is only a little below Mark, the complete cow.

The second of the A4 sheets is an annual report of my sales in terms of pounds. It's steady for the first few years and then starts a slow decline until the final year – this one – which is like a lemming plunging from a cliff.

So, no, there's nothing he *should* know – but I need some way of explaining this utter shambles.

'My husband and I are separating,' I say.

It's the second time in as many minutes that I've surprised him and Graham almost falls off his seat. I'm not quite sure what he was trying to do but I think it was to appear intimidating but he leant forward at the wrong time, his elbow slipping off the desk and almost sending him head first into the keyboard. He just about catches himself and then straightens his shirt as if it never happened.

'Oh,' he replies. 'Well, I suppose I know something about that…'

'I've not told many people.'

Graham relaxes into his seat and takes a large breath. I wonder if he was going to fire me, or simply rant and rave for a bit. He's never been the best motivator and his man-management is along the lines of having a few in the pub after work alongside a tipsy 'sort it out'. Either that or a shoutathon in his office.

The red is fading from his cheeks and it feels like I've avoided the worst of the telling-off. He'd probably spent the morning building up to this, so it'll be a let-down for him.

He runs a hand across his scalp and there's a moment where I wonder if he might be about to try it on with me. Ask me out for a drink, or something. By anyone's standards, it would be fast work.

That's not it at all, though. It's wishful thinking that anyone might look at me in that way and there's an odd ambiguity that I don't want anything to happen with Graham – but I'd still appreciate that feeling of being wanted.

Graham stares off to the side at his wall of photos of himself. He takes a few seconds, probably considering his words. He slumps slightly in his chair and sighs.

'Do you need time?' he asks. 'I know I did after me and Isobel broke up.'

His sudden sadness is such a shift of direction that I'm lost for words. He's shrunk in front of me and the red in his face has faded back to flesh.

'I, um…' It's such a surprising offer that I have no idea how to respond. I think it's startled him as well.

'It's fine if you do. I didn't realise you were having problems.'

'Perhaps in the future,' I say. 'I'm okay for the moment. I know things haven't been going well this year but I'm hoping things will settle down.'

He examines me carefully and then nods slowly. 'If you're sure.'

'I think work will help take my mind off everything. It's been a complicated few months as we try to sort everything out.'

He snorts. 'At least you've got your own job. Isobel took half of everything – and she hadn't worked a day in her life. Shouldn't be allowed.'

I say nothing, not wanting to point out that running a home is a job as well. I know Graham owns a house that an estate agent would describe as 'spacious', so keeping that in a decent state would take plenty of hours.

I gently slide the chair backwards. 'I'll try calling that Declan again,' I say.

'If there's anything else I can do…'

I'm already out of the chair when it strikes me that if ever there was a time to ask a tricky question, then it's now. Graham is rarely in this forlorn a mood as it is, let alone when he's feeling sorry specifically for me.

'Can I ask something?' I say.

He nods, hard to read.

I touch the papers that I've left on his desk. 'I know this isn't the best time what with this and all…'

'Speak now or forever hold your peace.'

'It's just… with me separating from Dan… managing my money's going to be a bit different.'

His eyes narrow and then he rocks back as he realises what I'm after. 'You're asking for a raise?!'

'I know my figures are leaning the wrong way, but perhaps if I can hit some targets, we could decide on a bonus? That sort of thing. Dan's going to have his money and I'll have mine. My daughter's eighteen now, so child support isn't really in play – and then we have to figure out what to do with the house. I think—'

He holds up a hand to stop me. 'I've been through all this with Isobel,' he says. 'I don't need to hear it all again.' He bites his lip, shakes his head, but it's more in pity than annoyance. 'Look, I'll think about it. You sort your numbers out and I'll see what I can do.' He nods at the door. 'Now, for the love of God, go sell some systems.'

SEVENTEEN

Considering there was a moment where I thought I might get fired, almost negotiating a pay rise isn't a bad outcome. Perhaps I do have some sales skills remaining after all. Admittedly, I had to throw about the 'poor me' routine – but others have done far worse than that to gain a lot less. It's true as well. Money after the separation will be an issue. One of many to add to the list of my current concerns.

There's a couple of hours in the afternoon where I almost forget the whole waking-up-in-a-field-thing. I fire off a few emails to current clients that are friendly enough, making sure they're happy and so on. It's a potential minefield because, if there are problems, I'm opening myself to getting chapter and verse about it. I'd sacrifice that for being able to upgrade even one of them to a better package.

After that, I email Declan to ask if he has any further questions from our meeting yesterday – and then send a few cold emails to companies who I think might be interested in what we're selling. I search for upcoming trade conferences and forward a couple of links to Graham, suggesting that I could represent the business there.

It's all basic stuff – but it's better than the motions I've been going through over the past few weeks.

It's four o'clock when my phone buzzes with a text from Olivia.

Sry 4 overeactin last nite

At first I read it as 'over-eating' – which would be incredibly unlike her. I've worried plenty in the past over whether she could be bulimic or anorexic. There are so many stories about how hard it is for young people nowadays. It was bad enough when I was young, with the magazine photos of models and the like. But now, with social media and the way everyone's life is shared, it's so much worse for young people like Olivia. As it is, I don't think she has had any actual eating disorder, it's simply that she goes out of her way to keep herself slim. Nothing wrong with that, of course, if that's her choice.

When I do get the correct meaning, it's still out of character. Olivia isn't usually one for apologising – and certainly not to me. Her motto seems to be, 'Never apologise, never explain'. She'd make a good spy.

My thumbs feel fat as I struggle to tap out a reply. I press more than one letter at the same time and autocorrect is being as unhelpful as usual. I get there in the end.

Nothing to apologise for. Any sign of Tyler?

She replies almost instantly:

No. Was hoping u cud drive me round l8r

I ask her why and she texts to say it's because she wants to check out the places Tyler usually hangs around. She's called and texted his friends but not all of them live within walking or public transport distance of where we live. I'm not naïve and suspect this is why she apologised in the first place – but it's better than nothing. I also wonder if she asked her father first. Either way, I tell her I'll pick her up after she's finished work.

The rest of the afternoon passes with nothing in the way of new sales but little in the way of drama either. Graham does one of his tours of the office not long before leaving time, dishing out the usual array of backslaps and 'how's things?' It's his way of motivating, though I can't believe it's something he learned on one his of his weekend retreats. He lowers his voice when he gets to me, lingering for a little longer than usual as he asks if everything is all right. I tell him it is and then he replies that he's 'rooting for me', before disappearing back to his office. Even though I can't see her, I can feel Natasha glowering on the other side of the board between us and I can't pretend that I don't find it amusing.

As everyone's leaving, I wait at my desk, saying I have a few things to finish up. I'm also showing Graham I'm trying to make up some hours even if, in reality, I'm trawling the news sites hoping there's been an update on Tom Leonard.

It's definitely becoming an obsession; a largely irrational one at that. As best I can tell, there is no news. That's supposed to be good news – but it doesn't feel like that. He's been missing for three full days and I find myself searching for statistics about missing people. Somewhere around a quarter of a million people are reported missing each year. It feels so high, with almost half being under the age of twenty-one. Then I read that nearly all of those are found again and it feels like a false statistic. It's still pain and worry for someone, though. Someone like Olivia. Someone like Tom Leonard's family. I want to forget what happened – but the blood on my car had to have come from something.

The car park is empty when I get outside. I'm last to leave, so set the alarm on my way out and then make sure the door is latched into place when it clicks closed behind me. I'm always paranoid the alarm is going to have some sort of meltdown. Its screech will rip apart the local peace and I'll panic as I try to reset it, only to make things worse by getting the code wrong and ending up locked out of the system.

Not this time.

It's only a twenty-minute drive from home if the roads are clear. Roadworks can take that up to thirty or thirty-five but it could be worse.

I'm almost halfway home when I notice that the blue car behind me has been there for most of the journey. I'm not sure when it slotted in but it was there along the dual carriageway and it's still there as I head along the link road towards North Melbury.

It's not necessarily unusual – this is the main road back to the town – but there's something about the way it's keeping a steady distance that makes me edgy. It could be that simply being in a car sets my mind racing but it feels like more than that.

When I stop at a T-junction, the driver hangs back, not slotting in directly behind. When I pull away, he or she maintains the same gap between us. I don't know the make but the car is a metallic navy hatchback with tinted windows. I find myself watching the mirror more than I'm looking through the windscreen, wondering if the driver will get closer.

There's a four-way set of traffic lights at a spot where The Red Lion sits on the outskirts of town. The quickest way home is to continue straight, following the main road to the High Street and, beyond that, the sprawling estates where I live. It's where most of the traffic would head. I'm at the front of the line, watching as the disjointed stream of cars pass across the junction. There's a gap of at least a car's length between me and the blue car behind and I spend the whole time checking my mirrors, wondering if the driver is going to edge forward.

When it remains at a distance and the light turns green, I make a quick decision, turning left without indicating and then fixating on my rear-view mirror as I pull away. I tell myself it's nothing but the blue car follows, also without indicating. Aside from me, it's the only other car to do so. I speed up, zipping past the row of houses onto the country roads that now seem so intimidating. There are more overhanging trees and overgrown bushes and

I wonder what the council do with all the tax they collect. It's certainly not employing someone with a hedge trimmer.

The blue car speeds up, too, maintaining a gap that means the driver can see me at almost all times. It's only because of the twisty lanes that there are moments in which I can accelerate away, putting some distance between us.

I'm gripping the steering wheel so tightly that tiny flecks of rubber or leather are peeling away from the surface. The speed is beginning to scare me and so I try the opposite, slowing into the next series of S-bends and then remaining in a lower gear as I emerge onto a straight. The speed limit is sixty and I'm barely doing thirty. The blue car has quickly caught up. There's room enough for the driver to overtake – except he or she doesn't. The car's speed has lowered to match mine and then the driver contently sits in a couple of car lengths behind.

From questioning whether I was imagining things, I'm now certain I'm being followed. I wonder if I could call the police via Bluetooth and give them the number plate. I can just about make it out in the mirror. But what if this is nothing? I'm some crazy woman – and the driver behind is on their way home? That follows calling the police for a break-in that probably wasn't a break-in. I'll get tagged as a time-waster, or a fantasist.

I take the next right turn, which is signposted for North Melbury. I remain under the speed limit, but it makes little difference because the blue car does the same. There's mud on the road and I'm probably the only driver who has ever hoped a tractor would pull out and bobble along the road for a good few miles.

No such luck.

If the blue car genuinely is just someone on their way home, then it makes little sense for them to have come this way. I've looped around much of the town, skirting around the miles of farmland, before turning back. Whoever's behind the wheel *must* be following me. But why? And who? Could it be youths messing around? I've read stories of kids driving around too fast, terrorising other drivers on these types of back lanes, but it's always seemed a bit fanciful, or exaggerated.

There's one final T-junction and I stop precisely as I should. The blue car behind leaves its now familiar gap and so I wait. I don't indicate, simply sitting and pausing for something to happen. Perhaps another car will pass and I can tag onto the back of that until I'm back in a populated area. If not that, maybe someone will get out of the car behind and I can speed away. I wait – and continue waiting as nothing happens. Either the driver behind is the most patient person on earth, or they really are following me.

I risk a glance away from the mirror to look at the dashboard clock. It's a few minutes before six and three full minutes pass with nothing happening. I have visions of being here in an hour's time, or later when it's dark. Of a queue of traffic building up behind us as people at the back wonder who the lunatic is at the front.

There's nothing else for it. I shift the car into gear, turn right and put my foot down. The hedges and trees fizz past, blurring into one long stream of green. I'm a few hundred metres along the road when I check my mirror and see that the blue car has turned left. I squint into the mirror, leaning towards it as if that will give me a better view of something happening so far behind. It doesn't of course, but when my eyes flick back to the road, I realise I've drifted into the centre, straddling the white line. There's a car in the distance and I swerve violently back onto my own side. There's a howl of complaining tyres, a terrifying screech of machine overpowering man. The back wheels spin as the front wheels lock and by the time I pull the wheel back in the other direction, it's already too late. The car groans as it lurches into a spin. I think there's a moment where I take my hands from the wheel, possibly close my eyes, definitely scream. I don't know for sure because everything happens at once.

There's a lightning flash of leaves and tarmac, a bone-creaking thump and then, somehow, the road is directly in front of me once more. I'm at a stop as the approaching vehicle thunders past with a lingering beep of the horn.

I barely notice.

I'm not sure if the car spun in a complete circle or if I imagined the whole thing. My blouse is clinging to my arms, small pools of sweat discolouring the cream. I'm out of breath and that pain is back in my chest once more. I pinch the loose skin on the back of my hand to make sure I'm awake. To know this definitely happened. There's no sign of a blue car in my rear-view mirror and the other vehicle that was coming towards me has already disappeared into the distance. Was the blue car ever there?

It's only me on the road and, as I pinch myself once more, I can't help but wonder what's wrong with me.

EIGHTEEN

The Cosmic Café is on the furthest outskirts of North Melbury, closer to the dual carriageway than it is the town. It's a mix of a truck-stop, old-fashioned diner, and a proper English greasy spoon. It's been a fixture for longer than I've been alive, although not always under the same ownership.

It's almost nine o'clock when I pull into the car park. There are a few lorries parked in the furthest corner, shrouded in shadow, the drivers perhaps settling down for the night. There are also half a dozen cars directly outside the entrance, illuminated by the light stretching from inside. The Cosmic Café is open twenty-four-seven – which I can understand all by myself, without the need for Declan to mansplain it to me. Not only is it popular with lorry drivers and locals, it's something of a hangout for young people. It's not as if there are many places for teenagers to get out of the way of their parents in the town. If they spend any time loitering in the centre, the police get called by NIMBY locals. It wasn't that different in my day. Ellie, Wayne, Jason and I would escape to the watermill but there were plenty of people our age who opted for the Cosmic.

Olivia got a job here about six months ago. She catches the bus to start her shift for one o'clock and then takes a taxi home afterwards, paid for by the owner, Rahul.

There's a gentle buzz of voices and clinking cutlery when I enter. If it wasn't for the darkness outside, it could be any morning. The café smells of baked beans, frying eggs and sausages. I wasn't hungry before but it's hard to walk into this place and not have the insatiable urge for a fry-up.

The walls are covered with the faded record sleeves of bygone eras. Vinyl records might be making a twenty-first century comeback – but the cardboard covers here are the originals. It was decorated this way when I was Olivia's age and little has changed.

Someone calls my name and, when I turn towards the corner closest to the window, I see Rahul sitting by himself in a booth. He's originally from India, a beefy chunk of a man with a smile almost as big as his belly. He waves me across and I slot in opposite him. The red leather of the bench has long faded to a murky pink and there are small tears across the length of the seat. I'd guess this is much the way customers prefer it. There's a definite charm to this place.

'No taxi tonight,' Rahul says.

'I told Liv I'd pick her up.'

'You have any other daughters at home?'

'Huh?'

He grins. 'Your Liv's a hard worker. Good worker. Could do with another six of her.'

His smile is infectious and I find myself melting into the booth. After everything of the past couple of days, it's good to hear something positive.

The door jingles as a couple enter hand in hand. He's wearing a suit and she's in a short green dress. It's not too late, but it looks like they've been out to the theatre, something like that. Perhaps for a few drinks. His shoes are shinier than anything in the diner but they slot into a booth and grab a pair of menus. There's something wonderful about the breadth of the people who come here. There's a group of five teenagers in one of the other booths, empty milkshake glasses scattered across the table. Four or five truck drivers are sitting by themselves, reading the paper or tucking into the all-day breakfast. There are men and women; old and young; privileged and poor; white, Asian, whatever. No one worries about anyone else. It makes me proud that this tumble dryer of humanity is on the edge of my town.

'Long day?' Rahul asks.

I blink at him, wondering how he knows. It must be me, of course. Everything about me.

'Is it that obvious?' I reply.

'You work too hard. Take some time off, lay on a beach, read a book. Tell your boss Uncle Rahul said it was fine.'

He laughs and so do I. It's hard to do anything else when in Rahul's presence – as if he's carrying something infectious that automatically spreads happiness.

'I'll try that,' I tell him.

His eyebrows raise as he looks over my shoulder – and then Olivia appears at the edge of the table. She's slightly flushed, her dyed pink hair greasy and stuck to her scalp. Her sleeves are rolled up, showing off the teddy bear tattoo on her arm. At first glance, it's something sweet; a symbol of childhood innocence. On closer inspection, the teddy is clutching a knife and holding it above his own head threateningly. We've never talked about it and I haven't asked about any others. I don't think I want to know.

Olivia turns between us suspiciously.

'Have you been talking about me?'

Rahul throws his hands up, grinning from ear to ear. 'Of course. All about you. It's always about you, Livvie, my love.'

I've never heard anyone call her 'Livvie' but it's so systematically charming in the way Rahul says it.

'I checked the toilets and Tracy's logged onto the till,' Olivia says. 'Everything should be set for night shift.'

'You're too good to me, Livvie. Too good. Young girl like you should be off seeing the world, breaking the hearts of all those boys.'

She wraps her arms across her front, flattered yet embarrassed because I'm here. 'I'll see you tomorrow,' she says, before turning to me. 'Can we go?'

I use the table to push myself up, fighting and losing the battle against giving the old-woman sigh.

Olivia says nothing as we head to the car, clambering into the passenger seat and then resting her head on the window. I touch her gently on the knee and she neither flinches, nor kicks me away.

'Where would you like to go?' I ask.

'Bashington. There's that block of flats on the outskirts, near the park. D'you know where I mean?'

I tell her that I do. Bashington is the closest town to North Melbury. Our nearest rivals, if you will. There was uproar a few years back when Bashington won a Britain in Bloom commendation and we didn't. This is the sort of place in which we live.

The roads are nearly empty and, though it is largely country lanes between the two places, having someone else in the passenger seat makes everything feel more comfortable.

It's now been four full days since Tyler was last seen and I can't remember if this is the same length of time as the previous occasions when he disappeared. The last time was between Christmas and new year. He and Olivia had gone to the Red Lion at lunchtime and ended up having a row over something of which I'm not sure. I only know that much because I went to school with one of the barmaids and saw her in town a few days later. Tyler stormed out, flinging a pint glass into the wall as he went – and that was the last anyone saw of him until after Boxing Day. He was definitely back before new year but I wouldn't be sure of the actual day. All I saw of it was that Olivia was upset for a couple of days and then the clouds lifted and there were rainbows and unicorns once more.

I do worry about her mood swings, not to mention her infatuation with a young man who thinks throwing pint glasses in a pub is perfectly acceptable. That's not to mention the time he went off with another girl, or the multiple occasions he's been arrested for shoplifting. But what is there to do? If I tried to stop her seeing him, she'd rebel even more. And she's eighteen anyway. My mother used to use the 'not under my roof'-stuff on me and it only made me spend more time outside with Ellie, Wayne and Jason.

Look where that led.

Olivia hasn't spoken for almost fifteen minutes. Her head is pressed against the glass of the side window. I suspect she's dozed off, though, when I glance sideways, her eyes are open.

'I know you miss him, love.'

Her only response is a deep breath through her nose.

'Is there anything else I can do?'

'No. This is good.'

She sounds so pained that it hurts me. I want her to be small enough that I can pick her up, wrap her in a blanket and hold her tight to me.

There's a little more silence and then: 'I've set up a Facebook page.'

Olivia speaks so softly that I can barely hear her over the warm air being spewed from the vents.

'That'll do some good,' I reply, not really knowing what I'm talking about.

'It's called Find Tyler. There are some pictures of him, plus I've put down some of the places he used to go. That sort of thing. Some of his friends have shared it.'

It's a fine line between encouragement and being patronising, so I offer what I hope is a reassuring 'mmm', rather than overdoing it.

Olivia doesn't add anything to that, not speaking again until the Bashington block of flats is in sight. Despite the town's commendations for its attractiveness, this part is an ugly stain on the area. It's a ten-storey pebble-dashed mistake which the council have been talking about knocking down almost since it was built. Olivia directs me to a darkened car park and asks if I'll wait. There are no street lights, only a pair of skips and a line of overgrown trees that flail imposingly against the night sky. I'd rather go with her but don't have much of a choice. She disappears into the shadows, heading in the vague direction of the tower and I know that I don't approve of all this.

In essence, my daughter – my *teenage* daughter – hangs around with dodgy people in dodgy areas. Does that make me a bad mother for knowing about it and not stopping it; or would it make me a bad mother for *trying* to stop it and only succeeding in causing arguments that make Olivia want to move out? She could end up living somewhere like here. For now, at least there's some degree of knowing she's safe. She generally does let either Dan or me know if she's staying out but, most times, she sleeps in her own bed anyway.

The block of flats is largely in darkness, with only a handful of lights glimmering through curtains or around the gaps in blinds. From the outside, it doesn't look as if too many people live here. I've not been this close before – but it's hard to miss the blight when driving through.

I wait in the dark for a little over ten minutes before Olivia hurries back from the shadows. She's hugging her arms across her front, shivering from the chill as she slips back into the car and closes the door with a slam. A puff of breath disappears into the warming air.

There's little point in asking if she found anything because her features are taut, her gaze distant.

'Do you want me to take you somewhere else?' I ask.

She replies breathlessly. It's hard to know for certain, but I think she mentions someone named 'Peggy' – and then directs me through the roads of Bashington until asking me to stop outside a row of housing association apartments. It's an improvement on the tower block but not by much. The long terrace is grubby with years of neglect. Moss is growing between the tiles that are attached to the facias around the upper windows and there are scorch marks on the muddied lawn at the front.

Olivia opens her door, mutters that she'll be right back, and then disappears into a walkway between two terraced buildings.

A dog is barking somewhere in the distance and there is so much shadow that it's hard to see much more than the outline of the buildings. It's chilled enough that my knuckles are starting to stiffen without the heat from the vents.

Olivia returns after another ten minutes or so, her face grim. 'There's a play park round the corner,' she says. 'Can we check there?'

Her definition of 'round the corner' isn't literal and she directs me another half-mile or so through the estate until we arrive at a small playground on a patch of green next to a pub. It's a much nicer area of town, all yummy-mummies and 4x4s in the car park during the day. Olivia first checks the pub and then I spot her emerging from the door at the back. She traces the outline of the park and then sits on the swings, making a phone call before heading back into the pub and re-emerging from the front door. It's clear she thinks I didn't see her, so I don't bring it up.

'Where now?' I ask, but I get a long, mournful sigh in response.

'Can we go for food?' Olivia replies.

It's half past ten, past my bedtime, let alone time to eat – but this is the first thing we've done in a long time where it's been only the two of us.

'Where would you like to go?'

'McDonald's.'

A hint of a smile creeps onto Olivia's face. She bites her lip as if trying to force it back but it's too late. I've already seen it.

North Melbury is a relatively sleepy area – but there's a service station a little further up the dual carriageway that's open all day. Aside from The Cosmic, it's one of the few places for miles that's open late.

I set off without complaint and we have something approaching a normal conversation. It skirts all our issues, of course. Neither of us mention the impending separation and, for a few moments at least, Tyler is forgotten as well. We talk about her work and she tells me some funny stories about Rahul and her colleagues. She tells me what Ellie already has – that she's looking at possible college courses for next year. It's good to hear it from her. I don't mention that Ellie had already said something.

There's a small queue at the McDonald's drive-thru but that only extends the time I get to spend talking to my daughter as an equal. It's a glimpse of the relationship we could have. I miss her being that little girl I could smother with a blanket – but I look forward to the things she's going to do in the future. They're all parts of the same whole.

She orders two double cheeseburgers, large fries and a chocolate milkshake, plus asks for sweet chilli sauce on the side. I pay, obviously, and then any doubts she might be under-eating are shredded completely as she spends the journey home munching her way through the bag of food.

It's nearing half past eleven when I pull into the garage and park. Olivia has finished her food and is busy cleaning her fingers on a wedge of napkins.

She touches my arm before I can get out of the car, gripping me firmly until I turn to her.

'Thank you,' she says.

'You're welcome.'

Olivia closes her eyes and, when she reopens them, there are tears clinging to her lower eyelashes. 'Do you mind if I sit in here for a bit? Just to, y'know…'

She doesn't finish – but I *do* know. To have some time alone. I pass her the keys and say I'll see her in the morning.

I'm halfway up the stairs, on my way to bed, when I realise that, for the first time in a long time, I've actually enjoyed the evening. A couple of hours with my daughter that didn't involve us arguing is all it took. Perhaps it's that but, by the time my head hits the pillow, I've convinced myself that everything's going to be all right after all.

NINETEEN

- THURSDAY -

The digital clock next to the bed reads 05:53 when I'm woken by someone banging on the front door. In my bleary, confused state, I think it might be Alice. She'll be in some sort of military boot camp mode, demanding Dan get himself out of bed. He'll have to drop and give her twenty, something like that.

When I roll over, I realise Dan isn't in bed. I stumble onto the landing calling his name, but the sound of running water is coming from the bathroom where, presumably, he is having a shower.

The sound of fist on glass continues to boom through the house and then the doorbell starts ringing. It isn't one press, it's a series of endless ding-dongs melding into one as someone's thumb mashes the button outside.

I grab my dressing gown from the bannister and stumble downstairs, clinging to the rail for support and fighting a yawn. It's dark downstairs but turning on the hallway light does little for my weary eyes. The white stabs like needles into my sleep-addled brain.

Thump-thump-thump-thump-thump.

I call that I'm coming but it makes little difference, as the banging continues. I take a couple of seconds to check myself in the hall mirror, ensuring my dressing gown is actually covering what it should, and then unbolt the front door.

It isn't Alice, not that my waking mind thought it would be.

The person on the other side of the door is a man who's vaguely familiar. He has straggly grey hair with a matching overgrown beard. As soon as the door's open, he lurches towards me jabbing an accusing finger.

'You!' he rages.

I start to close the door, using it as a barrier between us.

'Don'tcha close the door on me, yer stupid bitch.'

I wonder if he's someone I once knew from school. His face is so recognisable but I have no idea who he is.

Realising he's getting nowhere, the man steps backwards off the front step, still pointing but no longer trying to get into the house. I should slam the door and lock it. Probably call the police. The only reason I don't is because it feels like I'm missing something obvious. I peep at him through the gap between door and frame, primed to slam it at any moment.

'Who are you?' I call.

'Who am *I*? You've got some nerve.'

I realise who he is at the same time as he bellows the name 'Frank' at me.

He's Tyler's father. We've met once, in the early days of when Olivia started seeing Tyler. It was around eighteen months ago when I gave Tyler a lift home. Olivia was a young seventeen then – and Tyler was twenty-one or twenty-two. I didn't know that at the time, because she told me he was seventeen. I suppose that was lie number one in what would become a series. If I'd known then, I would have shut things down straight away – and not taken her reluctance for an answer. I think Olivia might have listened to me then. In the two years since, she's become more of her own person – and significantly more stubborn in the process. There's a large part of that which is a good thing, of course. I want her to be independent and strong – but the other side is that she's independent and strong *against me*.

On the one and only time I met Frank, he was standing in the garden outside his bungalow smoking a marijuana cigarette. As

Tyler passed him and headed inside, Frank moved across to the window of the car, blowing a plume of weed smoke towards me. I don't think it was malicious, more that he was so used to smoking around other people that he didn't realise I might have a problem with it. He assumed I was some sort of social worker or off-duty police officer, bringing his lad home from whatever trouble he'd been in. It was an eye-opening experience, to say the least – but Olivia was already smitten.

Frank hasn't changed much in the past two years – but it's enough. He's dirtier, for one. There are mud stains on his faded leather jacket, more on his jeans. I can smell the alcohol on his breath even though there's a good metre and a bit between us. He hasn't shaven in days and his hair is mangling together. I think he might have slept rough, or perhaps not slept at all.

He starts to yell, aiming a kick at the flowerpot which sits next to the path. 'Where's my son?!'

'I don't know. Can you please—?'

'Don't give me that. Where is he?'

'I've not seen him.'

'He was here last. His friends told me all about *you*.'

The word 'you' is stabbing, hissed with genuine hatred.

'What about me?'

'How you're always on at him. How you think we're scroungers. How we're beneath you. I'll tell yer something, yer stuck-up bitch—'

Dan has appeared from nowhere, opening the door wider and standing at my side. He's in his pyjamas but tall and strong. I hate being a woman who needs a man to protect me – I'm not, I'm *really* not – but I can't help but feel a sense of relief that he's here.

Frank cuts himself off mid-sentence. He's never met Dan before. Perhaps he thought I was single, or that Dan might be some weedy non-threat. At the sight of someone bigger than him, he goes silent.

Dan is perfectly calm: An experienced teacher dealing with an out-of-control child: 'Do you know what time it is?'

As if the time is the most important thing here.

'I, er…'

'Look, Frank is it?'

Dan opens the door further, moving onto the step as I wedge myself in half a step behind. He offers his hand but all Frank does is stare at it.

'I'm sorry about your son,' Dan adds. 'We'll help in any way we can. It's just—'

'I don't want yer help.'

Dan slowly lowers his unshaken hand as Frank stares daggers and then thrusts another finger in my direction.

'It's *her*. She's always on at him. Thinks we're freeloaders. Thinks we're scum. I know your sort, all high and mighty. She made him run off.'

Dan stands firm but I can sense the indecision in him. The thing is, despite the venom, there's a lot of truth to what Frank's saying. I don't think he and his son are 'scum' – but 'freeloaders' is largely self-evident. Neither of them have jobs, yet they somehow find money for cigarettes, alcohol and marijuana. I'm not *always* on at Tyler himself but I do try to persuade Olivia that she'd be better off without him. Some of that will obviously get back to Tyler and, by proxy, Frank.

As I start to think about calling the police again, Olivia appears in the doorway. There's an inadvertent parting as Dan and I move to the side, surprised by her presence. Her skin is pale, almost glowing against her pink hair. She's barefooted, wearing pink hot pant shorts and a matching T-shirt.

Frank is even angrier than he was before, surging forward with a growl until Dan shoves him away.

'Where is he?' Frank snarls.

Olivia's voice is delicate. 'I wish I knew.'

'You've driven him away. You know that? *You*! All that talk of getting a job.'

It's the first I've heard of it and it's hard to suppress my surprise. Olivia has been arguing with me for months over Tyler but, away from here, when they're alone, she is also apparently trying to persuade him to get a job.

'Nag, nag, nag,' Frank continues. 'You women are all the same.'

It's Olivia who replies: 'Is that what he says about me?'

She sounds stung, damaged by the accusation. I move to step ahead of her, instinctively wanting to protect, but she pushes around me until she's in front of both Dan and me.

'Does he think I nag him?' she asks.

'You and *her*,' Frank says, nodding towards me and then turning back to Olivia. 'You're a bad influence on him. Driving him to god knows what. Don't think I don't know about you. You're—'

Dan has finally had enough. He moves around Olivia, holding one arm out and pointing towards the road with the other.

'I think you should be going,' he says.

'Oh, aye. Who's going to make me, tough guy?'

Frank takes a small step back but his shoulders are tight, fists clenched. Dan's the taller man but I'm not sure what that means any longer. I really don't want to see a fight.

A light beams out from the house on the opposite side of the road as curtains are pulled. The lace netting starts twitching and, though I can't see a face, I know this is all being watched. There'll be other neighbours, too – this is prime entertainment first thing in the morning.

'I'm going to call the police,' I say, stepping back towards the house. Olivia hasn't moved.

'You do that, darlin'. I'll tell 'em all about you.'

His words leave me frozen to the spot. There's plenty to tell – and that's only from the past two days.

'What about me?'

The smirk spreads on his face and it feels like everyone has stopped, waiting to hear what he has to say. I know it must be an idle threat, the type of thing people hurl at each other when they're arguing. But there's still that sinking feeling in my stomach, that little voice in my ear.

He knows.

'You okay, mate?'

Everyone turns to look at the newcomer standing on the pavement. The sun is starting to creep across the horizon, blending with the gloomy glow of the street light. I can't see his face but the man's hair that tells me it's Jason.

Frank turns towards the road.

'You need a hand getting home, pal?' Jason waves a hand as if to say, 'follow me'.

Frank wavers, stepping backwards and then forwards, turning between the two competing parties. The curtains are still twitching across the road.

Jason starts to walk along the path, stare fixed on Frank. He's wearing the exact same jeans and army jacket from yesterday. I wonder if this is his pattern. According to his tag, he's not allowed to leave Ellie's until six – so he must have come straight here. Does he walk past the house all day long?

There's a flicker where Jason glances away from Frank, giving me the merest of nods and then focusing back on the other man. He holds out an arm as if about offer a hug. 'C'mon. Let's go look for your lad together.'

It's like watching a charmer coax a snake from a box. Whether it's what Jason's said, or the way he's said it, Frank's fists unclench.

He turns towards away from the house and starts to walk away slowly. 'Yeah, all right. Let's do that.'

TWENTY

As soon as we're back inside, Dan locks the door. He asks Olivia if she's okay and, after a mumbled 'yeah', he disappears up the stairs without saying a word to me.

Olivia slumps against the mirror but doesn't resist when I put an arm around her and guide her into the living room. I leave her on the sofa, saying I'll put the kettle on because that is, obviously, the solution to all of life's problems.

When I return with two cups of tea, Olivia hasn't moved. Her legs are curled under herself, her head resting on the back of the sofa. She's staring aimlessly towards the corner of the room. The fact her phone isn't in her hand is the biggest indication that she's not happy. There are times where it might as well be surgically grafted to her.

'Anything I can do, love?' I ask.

She shakes her head.

I sit on the same sofa as Olivia and turn the television on, flicking through the channels until I find the repeat of a wildlife documentary. The volume is on low and there's a herd of elephants sweeping across a barren landscape. I glance to Olivia and she's twisted slightly to focus on the screen.

It's as if we've gone back in time. When Olivia was younger, she'd come down the stairs in the morning and sit watching television in her pyjamas. Our strict food-at-the-table rule soon went out the window as we let her eat cereal on the sofa. In the evenings, we'd sometimes watch cookery shows together and wildlife documentaries. Then she found mobile phones and, probably worst of all, boys.

She changed – and so did I. No longer did she eat cereal on the sofa because she didn't want breakfast. Watching a TV show when it was actually scheduled was so last century when she could stream her own clips off YouTube, or wherever.

It's a long time with neither of us speaking – but we don't need to. This is enough for me.

The peace is eventually broken by Dan bounding down the stairs and poking his head into the living room. He's confused as he glances between us – but I can't blame him for that. This is the longest Olivia and I have spent in the same room together in a fair while. Certainly, it's the longest without arguing.

'Everything okay?' he asks.

'We're fine,' I reply.

'I'm meeting my personal trainer. We're going for a 10k and then I'm heading into school. It's parents' evening tonight, so I'll be late.'

'Thank you for telling me.'

We can be forcibly polite when we want.

He hovers for a moment but then heads past with his backpack and briefcase. The door goes and then it's quiet, except for David Attenborough's soothing commentary.

'How's the Facebook page going?' I ask.

Olivia shifts position, putting her feet on the floor and then angling herself in the opposite direction. 'Okay.'

That's hardly a ringing endorsement, so I don't follow up, instead sitting quietly and enjoying the moment with my daughter.

It's a few minutes later when Olivia breaks the silence. 'Do you think he's shagging her?'

She twists to look at me and, though I can feel her gaze, I can't match it. Instinct tells me to scold her for her language but she's eighteen, not eight.

As for the question… what is there to say? Disposition makes me think my husband probably is. I saw the way he looked at Alice and there was definitely something there that's more than a trainer-client relationship. My head says no – what would Alice see in someone who's more than twenty years older than her? My heart, the part of me that once cared, hopes he isn't.

I can't say any of that, of course, so I settle for replying that I don't know.

'Is that why you're separating?' Olivia asks.

'No,' I say. 'We've been together a long time but we've grown apart. Some things don't last forever.'

Olivia takes a breath and I know what she's going to ask next. She isn't stupid. 'Did you stay together for me?'

'I'm not sure this is really the thing to talk about, Liv.'

She reaches across and touches my knee, making me turn to her. 'You can't expect me to be an adult one minute and then treat me like a kid the next.'

My daughter speaks so calmly, so reasonably, that it melts me. Despite our problems and disagreements, those fights and days we'd avoid each other, it's a moment like this that makes me believe we'll be all right in the end. I love her so much.

'True,' I reply, slowly. It takes me a second to find the words, and then: 'Honestly? We probably should have broken up ten years ago. Maybe longer.'

'Why?'

I don't know if this is an inappropriate subject but there's no going back now.

'I suppose we were never that well matched. I'd come off the back of a few things when I was a teenager and he was a slightly older man. It was only a few years but it's enough at that age.'

I've somehow missed this fact in all the arguments with Olivia over Tyler. There's a similar age gap with them as there is between Dan and I.

I gulp away the thought and then continue: 'I was infatuated with him and I suppose he liked that I did much of the chasing after he first asked me out.'

'What things had you come off the back of?' I don't reply straight away, so Olivia continues: 'Ellie told me about how you, her and her brothers would spend time over at the watermill.'

There's a second in which I'm temporarily stunned at the thought of Ellie spilling everything. The fact that my daughter might know more about me than I could ever be comfortable with.

'We'd sit on the banks if it was nice, or shelter inside if it wasn't,' I say, keeping it simple. 'Nobody bothered us. It was our little hideaway.'

When I speak of the mill, it feels more like a person than a place. It was a part of who we were as a group.

'You told me it was out of bounds,' Olivia replies. 'You said it was too dangerous.'

I snigger at that. It's hard not to. Parents make the best hypocrites. We tell our children not to lie and then spend however many years convincing them a bloke in a red suit comes down the chimney every Christmas.

'I didn't know you and Ellie talked about things like that,' I reply.

'We don't… not always. I asked what you were like at my age.'

'What did she say?'

'Not much. Just that you've been friends a long time and that you were typical teenagers. You used to go out with her twin brother.'

I nod: 'Wayne.'

'I never knew that. I didn't even know she had a twin.'

This is obviously the time to tell my daughter the thing I've kept from her throughout her life. There won't be a better moment.

Except I can't.

If I tell her about Wayne, then I have to tell her about Jason. And if I do that, then how can she ever respect me again? Why would she listen to what I have to say about anything?

'I suppose I was in with the wrong crowd,' I say.

'Ellie was the wrong crowd?'

'Not her. Just in general. I suppose that's why I've been so concerned about you and Tyler. I don't want you to repeat my mistakes.'

Olivia turns back to the screen, shifting her weight so that she's angling away from me once more. I wonder if I've lost her. It was clumsy to bring things back to her but what else could I do other than evade her questions?

'He's not as bad as you think,' she says quietly.

'I only know what I've seen. If he's better than that, then *how* is he better?'

Olivia doesn't reply but there's a big part of me that wouldn't mind being wrong. I wish she could tell me how he makes her happy, how he enhances her life. It's not as if I enjoy the arguing and fall-outs.

She doesn't defend him, though. She takes her time, and I can hear her taking a series of deep breaths before she finally asks what's been on her mind

'Was I a mistake?'

'No, Liv. Of course not.'

I shuffle across the sofa and hold her head onto my shoulder. She hugs me back, wrapping her arms around my chest and sitting with her legs across my lap.

'Your father and I got married really quickly after starting to see each other. It was only a few months – but you were *never* a mistake. We wanted a child – both of us. You were the glue that bonded us together.'

'But now you're unstuck...'

I stroke her hair, searching for the words, trying to figure out how to tell her that the issues between Dan and me are ours alone.

'There was a point where we realised we didn't need each other. Your father had his life and his interests – and I had mine. The problem is that, by then, we had a house, a mortgage, car loans, credit card payments – and so on. A marriage is so much more than saying the words. We were living separate lives but unable to do it separately. You were at school, growing up, becoming a smart and independent young woman. It wouldn't have been right to rip all that apart.'

Olivia doesn't say anything but she presses her head harder into my shoulder. We both sit and watch the wildlife show, neither of us moving. The only sound is Attenborough's calm, methodical voice seeping from the television. Thank God for Attenborough.

Eventually, Olivia disentangles herself. She's upset and there's dampness around her eyes which she wipes away.

'That's the opposite of selfish,' she says unexpectedly.

'What is?'

'The other night, I said you were separating because it was what's best for you. I thought you were being selfish – but you literally spent years making yourself unhappy so that I didn't have to be.'

It takes me a couple of seconds to respond. It's not what I expected to hear. 'Not quite,' I tell her. 'Not really. Your father and I went through the motions over the years. We made a commitment when we decided to have you and, regardless of anything since, we stuck to that.'

Olivia's eyes are ringed with tears once more. She tries to breathe but her nose is blocked, so she reaches to the table for a tissue.

Her smile is weary: 'You're going to be late for work.'

TWENTY-ONE

I'm not going to be late, of course, mainly because I've peddled Graham a load of nonsense about having a follow-up with the police. That's on the back of asking for a pay rise. I'm the worst employee going.

The thing is, I genuinely do have something more important to do today.

St Paul's Church sits on top of a hillock on the edge of town. It's ringed by a crumbling drystone wall and there's a plaque etched into the arch at the front which says how this was once the focal point of the original settlement. The grass is slightly overgrown but green and springy. I stop when I'm under the arch, turning to take in the unparalleled view below. The older I've become, the smaller North Melbury has felt. As a kid, it would take hours to get from one side to the other on foot. A trip to anywhere with bigger buildings or more people felt exotic, as if places like Ipswich or Lincoln were the epitome of adulthood and sophistication. This little town now feels like the end of everything, rather than the beginning. It's confining and empty; free of creativity and ambition. It's an island of small buildings surrounded by a sea of green. I can't believe I've spent forty years here.

Down below, the river winds its way around the mound on which the church is built. Trees flail in the breeze but, in the gaps, I can see a glimpse of the watermill and the lurid fencing that now surrounds it. I'm still staring when a hand touches my shoulder, making me jump.

'Been a while, hasn't it?'

It's Ellie, sombre and downtrodden all in black. Her hair is in a neat bun and it's all a distant cry from her usual sit-at-the-kitchen-table-look.

'A really long while,' I confirm.

Jason is standing off to the side, looking awkward in an ill-fitting suit of his own. I wonder if it's the same one he wore to court all those years ago.

A biting breeze singes across the graveyard as Ellie and I pass arm in arm through the arch. The temperature is probably a good couple of degrees cooler here than it is in the town itself. I suppose graveyards are supposed to be this cold and eerie. It doesn't feel like a place in which life could thrive.

We walk slowly because there's no rush to get to our destination in the furthest corner. The path is marked by piles of small stones that crunch as we go. The grinding, chomping noise is the soundtrack, with Jason ambling at our backs.

I ask Ellie how her ribs are feeling and she replies that she took a cocodamol before leaving the house.

'The ones the doctor gave me are too strong,' she adds. 'They knock me right out, so I got these from the pharmacist.'

'Doesn't that mean you can still feel the pain?' I reply.

Ellie is quiet for a moment before responding: 'Maybe I need that today.'

'*Pain?*'

I glance at her as we walk and there are a few seconds where all I can hear is the crunch of the stones underfoot.

'It sort of fits, doesn't it? Here I am after a car crash, hopped up on painkillers. Meanwhile, Wayne's in the ground because of his.'

A chill flitters along my spine – but it's not the wind this time. I turn back to look at Jason, wondering if he's heard what his sister said. If he has, then he doesn't react. He smiles thinly and grimly at me, continuing to trail behind. I can't read him. He's not the boy I knew.

The gravestone reads Wayne Ringo Leveson. I used to laugh at him for it, not really understanding anything other than that his mother had named him after someone who was in an ancient rock band. Jason's middle name is George. I suppose Ellie was lucky to get away without having John or Paul on her birth certificate.

It doesn't feel funny now. Every time we're here, I stare at Wayne's name and remember the way we called him Ringo because we knew it would annoy him. I often wonder what I'd say to him now.

The three of us stand solemnly to the side of the stone, not trespassing on the grave itself. It's unremarkable in its ordinariness. There are some elaborate memorials dotted around the church: crosses, mock tombs, shiny black squares rammed into the earth. Mourners have left teddies, flowers and plastic windmills to mark their losses, but Wayne's has none of that. It is straightforward: a curved stone with his name and the dates that are too close together. I think this type of stone is what he would have wanted.

I wonder if Ellie's going to say something. She normally has a few words each year – but she remains silent now, her arms behind her back, head bowed.

Jason steps forward, reaching into a pocket and pulling out a small matchbox car, which he places next to the stone.

I look to Ellie but she says nothing and then Jason slots in at my side as the three of us stand silently.

It's a long while before anyone speaks – but it's Jason who breaks the impasse.

'What d'you reckon he'd be doing nowadays?'

Ellie and I never talk of things like this. We sometimes remember the old days, the fun days, but never how things might have been in an alternate present.

Jason answers his own question: 'Probably working in a garage, I reckon. Maybe he'd even have his own place…?'

It's an uncomfortable moment. Ellie doesn't reply and, because she says nothing, neither do I. Jason somehow misses the hint.

'D'you think he'd still live here?' he adds. 'North Melbury. He was always talking about getting out.'

More silence.

'I reckon—'

'Jase!'

Ellie cuts him off. Brother and sister stare at one another for a moment, leaving me stuck in the middle, and then she turns back to the stone. There's quiet now and we're back in the pattern of what we do every year. Ellie and I stand and stare in silence. We've held hands once or twice – but not today. I have no brothers or sisters and can't imagine what it would be like to lose one. Wayne wasn't simply Ellie's brother; he was her *twin* brother. What must that be like? There was a time not long after everything happened that Ellie told me she'd felt it when Wayne died. She'd been at home, lying on her bed listening to music when she'd felt suddenly out of breath. She'd gasped and was left with an irrepressible sense of losing something. In that moment, she thought she'd forgotten to do something, but it was so much worse than that.

'I sometimes wish it was me.'

It takes a second for me to realise that I'm the one who's spoken; my lips spewing my thoughts without any filtering process. It's something I've rarely admitted – even to myself – but there have definitely been times when it's true. It was what I thought twenty-three years ago. Before Olivia. Before she saved me.

I frequently wished it were true before I had my daughter; now it's only a fleeting consideration in the darkest moments of the night.

'What do you mean?' Jason asks.

'I sometimes wish Wayne had survived the crash,' I say. 'That I'd been the one who died.'

TWENTY-TWO

23 YEARS AGO

The man's eyes are wide as he stares down at me. He's scared, possibly in shock, but then it occurs that the same is true of me. He reaches out a hand, touching my own.

'Can you speak?' he asks.

'Yeah.'

'We need to get you out of here.'

He stretches across me, muttering apologies as his head nudges into my chest. He grunts and then reels back, tugging the seat belt out from the clasp and helping me release my arm from underneath the loop.

'This probably saved you,' he says.

I mumble something back but even I'm not sure if it's a word. Everything feels blurry and uneven.

'I'm David,' the man says. 'What's your name?'

'Rose.'

'Can you lift yourself out of the seat, Rose?'

'I think so.'

He offers me his hand and I take it, even though I know I'd be all right by myself. David grips my wrist tightly and then tugs as I heave myself up and out of the passenger side of the car. He continues holding my arm, asking if I'm okay, and then supporting my lower back with an arm around my waist. I can see him sweating in the gloom and it occurs to me that he's more scared than I am. He's only a few years older than me, perhaps twenty-one or twenty-two. I wonder if we were at the same school at the same time – me in a lower year, him at the top.

'Are you sure you can breathe all right, Rose?'

His question sounds silly until I realise I can hear myself wheezing. Now he's mentioned it, I can feel it, too. Every time I breathe in, there's a grating in my chest. Somehow, I'd not noticed it in the minutes that have passed.

'I… I don't know.'

The words are raspy and sore. I have a headache as well and, when I reach up to touch my temple, there's blood. I can see it in David's face now. His eyes dart away, looking *through* me, not *at* me.

'You shouldn't speak,' he says. 'You might have broken your ribs or punctured a lung. I don't know enough, I'm afraid.'

He spins back towards the scene behind us and there's panic in his whites of his eyes. In a flash, he tugs off his hoody, pressing the material to the side of my head.

'Hold it there,' he says. 'Push it against the spot near your ear.'

I do as I'm told and there's a flash of pain that sears stars into my vision.

David helps lower me to the ground and I don't protest. The grass is dewy and soft underneath. He glances at his watch and then turns in a full circle. He's lost, unsure what to do – and it's hard to blame him for that. He offers me a smile that's far from reassuring and then stumbles off towards the carnage.

I'm on one side of the road and, on the other, there's a low stone wall. It's perhaps waist-high if I was standing – but there's not much of it left. The rocks have crumbled into dust, scattering a thin veil of ash across the verge.

That's far from the worst of it.

Wayne's car is a mangled mash of metal. The front has compacted into itself, the bonnet crumpling like a crushed, empty can.

From what I can tell, the car hit the wall and bounced backwards, spinning so that the front is now facing me. The light of the moon glitters from the shards of glass that litter the road and verge; a shimmering crystal carpet tinged with crisp curls of metal.

There's a steady crunch as David carefully treads across the glass. We must have walked over it together but I didn't notice at the time.

More light comes from the headlights of David's car beaming across the road. It's parked askew on the side of the road, his driver's door open.

David pokes his head into Wayne's car and then reels back, both hands on his head at the sight of whatever's inside. I can see his cold breath disappearing into the night and then he turns and scrunches his way back to me. His hands are in his pockets and he's shivering without his hoody. His smile is narrow and forced.

'How are you doing?' he asks.

I try to shrug – but it hurts. All of a sudden, *everything* hurts.

'You're really lucky.'

I don't feel it.

'I'm going to go and find a phone,' David says. 'I think there's a pay phone about a mile down. I don't know if I should move you, or leave you.' He tugs at his hair. 'I don't know what to do.'

David steps towards his car and then back to me, torn between us. I don't know what to do either. He glances back at Wayne's car.

'Your friend must have been going really fast,' he says. It's a statement of fact, not a question, but I nod anyway. Not much, because of the pain, but enough.

'Yes,' I croak. 'Fast.'

TWENTY-THREE

Jason steps towards me, his boots crunching on the stones of the cemetery path. For a moment, I'm back on the side of the road with David treading over the splintered windscreen. I still think of David sometimes, wondering what happened to him. The papers called him a hero and he was to me. I wrote him a letter, thanking him for saving me. I'm not sure if he ever got it because I never had his actual address. I gave it to the police officer who'd taken all my statements and she said she'd make sure he got it. If she did get it to him, then he never wrote back. He wasn't someone who'd gone to my school, not even a local resident. He'd been visiting a penpal girlfriend he'd met through a letter-writing club at his university. He was driving home when he'd stumbled across the horror movie at the side of the road. It's no wonder he was scared. I used to think about whether he carried on the next day as if all was normal, or if he had similar nightmares to me. They offered me therapy and perhaps he had the same suggestion. He might have taken them up on the offer.

I wish I had.

I said no at the time because asking for help would have admitted there was a problem. Sometimes, in the darkest moments, I see David's wide eyes staring across me. His eyelashes are long, his pupils expanding and contracting in the gloom of those early hours. He's an angel I'd never met before and haven't seen since.

Something touches my lower back and I wince away. Jason withdraws his hand and apologises but I say it's not him.

'It's not your fault,' Jason says. 'You weren't the one driving too fast.'

I stare down at Wayne Ringo Leveson and shrug. Twenty-three years and there are times I can remember it like it was a moment ago. The memory is as sharp as the shards of glass that littered the road.

'Watching someone do something bad or reckless isn't the same as doing it yourself,' Jason says.

'Isn't it?'

'I know a bit about this.'

'So do I.'

'Not like me.'

Jason touches my lower back again and I don't stop him this time. It's comforting. Ellie stands unmovingly, staring at her twin's headstone.

'Culpability,' I say. 'That's what they call it. There's a degree of culpability to everything. The law says that there are some crimes where bystanders are as culpable as the individual who actually commits the act.'

'Not with this. You didn't know what would happen because he was driving too fast. People break speed limits all the time. It wasn't a premeditated thing.'

He sounds so unlike himself, or unlike the Jason I knew. The Jason of before would've never known the phrase 'premeditated', let alone used it.

'It was his pride and joy,' Jason says.

'What was?'

'His car. You remember? He spent all his money on it. Begged, borrowed, probably stole. We'd go bin-dipping at the back of the MOT garage in case they chucked anything out that was useful. That's why I reckon he'd have had his own garage now. He'd still have a side project; probably restoring some old sports car, something like that. He'd have bought the chassis and then rebuilt the rest himself.'

It's an awkward silence now. I don't know what to say and Ellie clearly doesn't want to hear this type of thing. Her shoulders have slumped as she stares down at the grave. Jason finally seems to realise he's at risk of upsetting his sister as he takes a small step away and stops talking.

The situation is starting to feel uncomfortable. Ellie and I only usually spend a couple of minutes here and then walk away. She's laid flowers in the past but I think it was more that she felt that's what she should do, rather than anything Wayne might have wanted. The matchbox car Jason has left is something far more apt than either of us have ever managed – and we've been doing this for more than twenty years.

Ellie turns and fixes me in her gaze. Her eyes are grey but bright. 'Do you remember it?' she asks.

'The funeral?'

A shake of the head. 'The crash.'

I blink, not sure she's ever asked me this. Nobody's asked me this in a long time. I start to say something and then stop myself, stumbling over nonsensical syllables. 'Not really,' I manage.

'You must remember something?'

'Only flashes. Like photographs but not the full set of moving images.'

'Do you remember David?'

The mention of the name is so surprising that I actually stagger. It's the gentlest of wobbles, a flinch in my knees, barely noticeable. It's partly because I was thinking of him moments ago and it's as if Ellie has read my mind – but it's also because I'm stunned she remembers his name.

'David…?'

I say it like a question, mainly because of the shock.

'The man who pulled you out of the car.'

'I know… I just… I'm surprised you remember his name.'

Ellie shrugs. 'You talked about him enough.'

That's true. I'd elevated him to this mythical figure as if he actually *was* an angel, instead of someone in the right place at the right time. Or the wrong place at the wrong time.

'Of course I remember him,' I reply. 'I wrote to him but he never wrote back.'

Ellie nods slowly, as if it's her memory too. She stares off into the distance, lost among row after row of this morbidness.

'I remember the hospital,' I add. 'Mum was at my bedside saying she'd never let me get in another car.'

'You were eighteen.'

'I know. I don't think anyone was thinking straight. They didn't want to let me out for the funeral.'

'But you came…'

A nod. 'My mum was carrying around this airbag thing in case I hyperventilated.'

Ellie stands, listening for a moment, but then she loops her arm into mine and starts to walk back towards the arch at the front of the church. Jason trails a few steps behind.

When we get to the exit, I stop, asking Ellie if I can have a minute alone with her brother. She looks between us but doesn't ask why, turning and walking off towards the car park.

I leave it a moment, taking a step until we're completely out of the graveyard. 'Was everything all right this morning?' I ask.

Jason's hands are in his pockets, his shoulders arched forward and angular, like a bird on a perch. 'Aye.'

'Thank you for helping.'

'No problem.'

I should ask him if he's been walking past the house regularly; probably ask him to stop – but it's not the time.

He motions towards the car park. 'I've gotta meet my probation officer,' he says. 'Can't be late.' He steps away and then turns back. 'You shouldn't say you'd rather it was you who died. It's a sort of karma, isn't it? I believe that. I saw it in prison. People get what they deserve.'

Jason pierces me with his stare and I'm frozen to the spot. It's only for a moment but, for the first time in a very long time, I remember that I was once scared of him. Scared of what he could do and the way he looked at me.

As quickly as it started, it's over. He puts his hands back into his pockets, turns, and walks away.

TWENTY-FOUR

Tom Leonard has been found.

That little voice has been niggling at me for days, saying the only place he'd be discovered was in a ditch because I'd killed him. But that's not true. He wasn't found in a ditch and he's not dead. The police force for the area has posted a short article saying that he is 'safe and well' and 'reunited with his family'.

At least it wasn't his blood that was on my bonnet. I keep searching for his name and find that a few news sites have covered the update, more or less verbatim from the police release.

The replies are predictably vicious.

'Wot a waste of taxpayer money.'

'If the tossers gonna kill himself why dont he just do it?'

And so on.

There are a couple of replies along the lines of, 'So glad he's safe' – but they're the minority.

I'm on the work computer, shielded from view because of the dividers between the desks. I check over my shoulder anyway and then log in to Facebook. There was a time when it had been blocked from our network – but the lads on the other side of the office complained that some of the companies with whom they were dealing had Facebook pages they needed to access. It sounded suspiciously like nonsense – but Graham went for it and unblocked all social media.

I find Olivia's page and scroll through her recent posts. It's only recently that she accepted my friend request, for which I don't really blame her. When I was her age, the last thing I'd have wanted was my mother checking up on me.

She has more than five hundred friends, which always surprises me because it's rare she mentions anyone other than Tyler. I keep scrolling and clicking until I find the page she's set up for Find Tyler.

The truth is, I rarely post on Facebook and predominantly use it to spy on other people. I feel a bit better about myself when I can see that someone down the road, or an old school acquaintance, is in the middle of self-inflicted drama. There's someone named Julie who lives a couple of streets over. We met at the swimming pool one time and had a coffee. That's enough to become friends online. Her daughter was only fifteen when she got pregnant and I couldn't help but think that at least things weren't that bad with Olivia. It's reassuring that there is always someone in a shoddier situation than me; that I'm not the *worst* parent out there.

I'd never admit to that, of course.

There is a downside of living vicariously through others, though – and that's when somebody's clearly having a better time. Of course, some are smart enough to make it look as if every day is better than the last. It's the game Natasha plays with the endless selfies and pictures of nights out and celebrations. From the outside, her life is never-ending joy but even I've heard her arguing with people on the phone. Nobody's life is that perfect. I know that – but I still feel that twinge of envy when I see photos of some friend who's off in the south of France, or living it up in some American diner. I'd love to see the emerald lakes of Canada, or spend weeks drinking by a pool in the Med. Dan and I have had holidays, of course, but, because of his teaching job, everything is planned with meticulous monotony. Never anything during term time; never anywhere he might run into a student. He prefers quiet, modest affairs. Perhaps I did, too, at one point. I suppose that if a life is spent comparing it to others', there will only ever be one winner.

The Find Tyler page has fifty-one members and the only major posts have been left by Olivia. The most recent one from this morning is a slight rewording of the one before. Olivia says that Tyler was last seen on our road at a little after nine o'clock on Saturday night. She lists a few places that he hangs around and asks if anyone's seen him. There's a photo of him that I've never seen before. It's striking because he's so… well… *attractive*. He's in a park, wearing skinny jeans, no top and a leather jacket. His skin is pasty – but he is British, after all. He's staring into the distance like a model in a catalogue or a rock star on an album cover. I find myself staring, wondering how the young man with the filthy black hair and no job can be the same person.

I scroll to the comments and immediately wish I hadn't. The very first one reads, 'I hope he's dead'. The name is 'John Smith', but when I click his profile, there are no other details. I assume he's one of the trolls who leave offensive remarks on memorial pages for dead kids or fundraising pages for someone with cancer. There's always someone who can't help themselves – and I know Olivia will see it sooner or later.

After hunting through the page for a couple of minutes, it's clear that nobody's admitting to knowing very much and all the work has been done by Olivia.

There isn't much else to see so, through habit, I have a quick look at Natasha's page. She went for a jog this morning. #winning #crushedit

Having wasted a decent chunk of time, I get back to work. There's been no enquiry from Declan, let alone an offer, so I send him the standard email asking if there's anything else I can help with.

There's still nothing from Luke, either. After getting me out to the hotel for no apparent reason, it seems pretty clear he, or I suppose she, never existed. It's all a bit odd. I wonder if it was a rival from another company trying to waste my time – or, of course, a rival from the other side of the desk.

#cow

Other than that, things are picking up. One of my clients has renewed for a further two years and they seem happy to pay an increased fee. I've even received an email thanking me for providing such good assistance over the past twelve months.

I forward the invoice request onto Graham and there's a moment where it feels as if the cloud is lifting. The memory of that field is fading, Tom Leonard is safe and well, Olivia and I are getting on, the separation is finally going to happen. As awful as it sounds, I always feel better in the days after the anniversary of Wayne's death. After visiting his grave each year, it feels like a new start – even more so this year.

There is a worry about Jason, though. The fact he seems to be stalking the house is bad enough – but there was something about the way he said 'people get what they deserve' that left me cold. Was he talking about himself? Someone else?

Me?

He was released from prison a little over a week ago and it's only since then that odd things have been happening. He could have got hold of the key for our house via Ellie and let himself in. Perhaps he smashed the window as a diversion in case someone noticed things had been moved around? Perhaps something *is* missing – but we haven't noticed yet?

He might've found out I was staying in the hotel and then…

I remember his ankle tag. He has to stay at Ellie's overnight and I presume there's some sort of monitoring to make sure that happens.

It doesn't make sense – but then little of what's happened in the previous few days does. How did I end up in that field? Was I drunk? Did I drive drunk? I've never done that. Never, ever. I wouldn't. Not after what happened to Wayne.

And then there's Tyler, whom I keep forgetting. My daughter's boyfriend who's been missing for five days.

I spend the rest of the afternoon following up an overdue payment, chasing down a new lead and then arranging an appointment for next week. I also help Claire pick a hotel for a conference she's attending next month.

It doesn't sound like much – and I suppose it isn't – but this is the reality of my day-to-day job. This normality feels good.

My journey home is mercifully uneventful. There is no blue car following and, even if there had have been, there's a calmness that I've not felt for days. It feels like a different person who overreacted and raced along those country roads.

It's when I park in the garage and the door closes behind me that the apprehension starts to creep into my stomach once more. When I get into the house, I call out Olivia's name but there's no reply. I even shout for Dan, despite knowing he has a parents' evening. The house is empty but it's hard to forget walking in through the double doors and sensing that something wasn't quite right.

I check the back door but there's no glass on the floor this time. After that, I make a point of putting my work pass, car keys and house keys in the drawer of miscellaneous things. After closing the drawer, I reopen it to double-check they're still there.

All is well.

Then the doorbell sounds.

I'm nervous at first, assuming it's Frank back to start shouting again. There's no Dan this time, and I can't be lucky enough to have Jason walking past a second time – unless he really is stalking the house.

I edge towards the hall, wondering if I could get away with pretending there's nobody in. The garage doors shield my car and there's no reason to assume the house is occupied. I slip along the hallway wall until I'm close enough to the peephole.

It's not Frank – it's Mr Rawley from across the road. Mr Curtain-Twitcher. I open the door but not too far. Don't want him to think there's an open invitation.

We exchange a few niceties – the weather's getting cold, his grandkids are growing fast, the usual – and then it's on to business.

'I was just making sure everything was all right after…'

He tails away but I'm not letting him off that easily. Whatever I say will be halfway around the town before I've closed the front door.

'After what…?' I reply.

'After, um…' he swirls a hand. 'After this morning.'

'This morning…?'

Even if I do say so myself, I'm doing an amazing job of appearing clueless.

'The, erm, incident on your driveway…'

'Ohhhhh, right… I didn't know you'd noticed anything.'

He squirms awkwardly on the spot, which is perhaps a little harsh. I'm bad enough at living through other people but he's in his seventies. If it wasn't for the neighbourhood watch programme and a bit of day-to-day gossip, he'd not have much going. This will be his highlight of the month.

'It *was* a bit a loud,' he replies. 'I was about to call the police.' He hesitates and then jumps back in: 'On your behalf, of course. Didn't want things getting out of hand.'

'No, you're right. Thanks for keeping an eye out. Good job it didn't come to that.'

'Your man seemed very angry.'

'He's not my man but, well… yes. Sorry about the noise. I hope it didn't wake you. If it's any consolation, he *did* wake me.'

Mr Rawley says he's up at half past five every morning – 'have been since 1973', he adds, without specifying what happened in the year that made him start getting up so early.

I put a hand on the door, signalling that the conversation might be over, when Mr Rawley takes a half-step forward: 'So, um… who was he?'

Things are awkward now. I don't particularly want everyone on the street gossiping about me and, more importantly, about

Olivia. But I also don't want to fall out with the bloke across the road. He's a nice man, even if his life is a little empty.

Whenever I'm asked that clichéd survey question, 'What's your greatest fear?' I always reply 'spiders', simply because it sounds good. In truth, I don't particularly mind spiders, nor any creepy-crawlies. My greatest fear is what's in front of me right now. It's growing old and lonely. It's being ill and having no one who cares. It's waking up in the morning and not knowing what to do with myself.

'My daughter's boyfriend is missing,' I reply. 'That was his father. He's upset about his son, obviously – and he was wondering if we knew anything.'

'Oh… well that's a turn-up.'

At first I think he says 'turnip' and it takes me a second or two to figure it out.

He continues: 'Is there anything I can do?'

'Probably not. Her boyfriend's name is Tyler. The last place he was seen was on our road on Saturday night. Sometime around nine o'clock. He's got longish black hair and is usually wearing a leather jacket.'

'Oh… him. I've seen him around a few times with your Olivia.'

'Did you see anything on Saturday?'

Mr Rawley pouts out a bottom lip and glances upwards. 'I don't think so… I can ask around some of the neighbours if you want. Perhaps help put up a few posters…?'

I wonder why I never thought of that. Olivia's grown up in the digital age. Her first thought is always going to be social media and the internet – but knocking on a few doors on the street should have been the first thing to do.

'That's really kind of you,' I say. 'I think I'll do that with Olivia, though.'

'Of course. Is there anything else I can do?'

I'm about to say 'no' when another thing that should have been obvious occurs to me.

'Someone broke a window at the back of our house on Tuesday,'
I reply. 'It might have been nothing but I was wondering if you
saw anyone hanging around…?'

Mr Rawley scratches his head, as if the movement of his fingers
might nudge the grey cells along. 'Tuesday,' he mutters to himself.
'Tuesday… Tuesday…'

'It would have been between about midday and six.'

I'm half expecting him to bring up Jason – the bloke in the
military jacket – but he starts to shake his head.

'Tuesday's the day that I'm at bridge in the afternoon.'

'Right.'

'I did see your Dan on the way out, though.'

I've almost started to close the door when this stops me still.
'You saw Dan on Tuesday?'

'Right. I was getting into my car to head to bridge club. I waved
but I don't think he saw me.'

'This was in the morning…?'

A shake of the head: 'Lunchtime.' He clearly sees the confusion
in my face, adding: 'Everything's all right, isn't it?'

'Of course, yes.'

'He was doing his running – with all the tight clothes and that.
I don't know how he does it.'

'He's marathon training,' I reply.

Mr Rawley starts to back away as he looks at his watch. He
mentions something about 'having to get back' and then we go
through the motions of saying goodbye. It's never simple. I tell
him to say hi to his children for me; he says he'll ask around about
Tyler 'just in case'. We each hope the other has a good evening.
He reminds me it's supposed to be cold tomorrow – and finally,
mercifully, that's that.

I close the door and then press back against it, trying to remember precisely what happened on Tuesday. It takes a moment for
the memory to come – but I know I'm right. After he'd noticed

the broken glass on the floor, I asked Dan if he'd been home for lunch. He specifically said he didn't leave school until after five.

Why would he lie?

TWENTY-FIVE

The more I think over things, the more something about my husband doesn't seem quite right. When I awoke in my car in that field in the early hours of Tuesday, his text was already waiting for me. He told me to call anytime. I went along with that because I was confused – but, in retrospect, it was an odd thing to do. He had to be up early for school and, though he'd texted primarily about Olivia not coming home, when we spoke, it never felt as if he was overly concerned for her. I wasn't, either. I assumed she was staying over with a friend, or Tyler. Not only that, when I called at three in the morning, he answered straight away. If he'd been sleeping, it would have taken a few rings. He'd have sounded disorientated.

It was almost as if he'd been waiting for my call.

When the police came around, they found blood on the garage floor – except I'm certain I cleaned everything away. I washed what was on the car, letting it all run into the drain, and then checked the surrounding area and the ground in case I'd missed anything. I even scrubbed a few extra spots around the garage that were likely oil. It was about as clean as it's ever been. I've been doubting myself in recent days but how could I have overlooked something so obvious?

Then there are the smaller things – my missing work pass that magically reappeared where I'd left it; my car keys turning up in the fridge; the £50 that might or might not have vanished. I know I'm not the person I was when I was half my age. Remembering a name is occasionally a challenge. I make lists of things I have to do because, if I don't, there's a pretty good chance something will slip my mind. I know there's a chance I might have put my keys in the fridge for some reason. Perhaps I'd gone to put them away and then wanted a drink and got mixed up. Things like that *do* happen – but with everything else going on, it's one more odd occurrence.

Then there's the fact that, assuming Mr Rawley is correct about his days, Dan was home when he told me he wasn't – on the very day that the glass in the back door was smashed. When I thought someone might have broken in. What reason could Dan have for not admitting he'd popped home at lunch? It might have helped narrow down a time for whatever happened with the glass. Unless, for some reason, he was the person who broke it.

As ever, the internet gives me an answer quickly enough. I can barely remember what life was like without it.

It's called gaslighting and I find myself scrolling with increasing horror through the stories of various women. For whatever reason – and I could be looking in the wrong place – it always seems to be women who are the victims. That's not to say the other party is always a husband or boyfriend; there are a terrifying number of accounts where a parent is the manipulator.

Gaslighting is making someone think they're going mad. It's moving someone else's things and then denying it, making them question where they left it. It's saying something and then claiming it never happened. It's doing something like leaving a light on and then asking the other person why *they* left the light on. It's a collection of small things that grow and grow until the victim is convinced they're losing their mind.

I continue to look through the sites and eventually stumble across one with a checklist that would indicate possible gaslighting.

Q1: Are you constantly second-guessing yourself?

It feels like a light bulb going off, because the obvious answer is yes. Everything in the past few days feels exactly like that.

Q2: Do you frequently ask yourself if you're overly sensitive?

This is more complicated but I could say yes. There's the incident in which I was certain I was being followed by a car, for instance.

Q3: Do you find yourself withholding information from friends and family?

This is unquestionably true – but is that somebody else's fault? I've not told anyone about waking up in that field because I'm afraid of the trouble it might put me in.

I keep reading through the list but each corresponding question leaves me less sure. I definitely don't 'make excuses for a partner's behaviour to friends and family' because there's no need.

It also says that this type of behaviour would have likely been going on over a lengthy period of time but I can't with any conscience claim that's the case. Dan and I have had our problems but it was never about these sorts of things. At its core, it was a lack of compatibility.

That first question still feels as if it's been written for me, however.

On another website, there's an article that says gaslighting is often down to clingy husbands or wives; boyfriends or girlfriends, who are desperate to make their partner remain with them.

That doesn't ring true, either. Dan and I are separating. We've spoken about it for a while and now it's happening. Why would he want to convince me that I'm having some sort of breakdown?

And then it dawns on me.

It's about this. The house, the road on which we live, the handful of mutual friends we have, the social standing of him being a deputy headteacher.

When we get divorced, there's a stigma. It's not what it might have been in decades gone by – but society is obsessed by winners and losers. If I remain in the house with Olivia, then, to an outsider, it looks like I win. If he can convince me I'm losing the plot, then perhaps I'd concede I'm not able to look after a house of this size. I wouldn't be able to manage the bills, the maintenance and so on. Perhaps it'd be better if *I* moved out.

Could it be that?

I put the laptop down, telling myself it's ridiculous. I've known him half my life. We've been married most of that time; we have an adult daughter. But then I realise I'm second-guessing myself once more. It's question one all over again.

I don't know details of things like how Dan could've arranged for me to wake up in that field, but perhaps the method can be figured out when I discover if it is something to do with Dan.

The drawers on Dan's side of the bed feel like a good place to start. At first I decide I'm looking for other things of mine he might have hidden, though I have no real idea what I'm expecting to find. It quickly becomes apparent that there's nothing other than socks, underwear, our passports, his birth certificate, some old photographs of Olivia, deodorant, ties… boring, usual things.

I check under the mattress and the bed itself. I look in the wardrobe where he keeps his suits and the drawers where his other clothes are stored.

Nothing unusual.

Our downstairs is a cluttered mess of a design. The kitchen and the living room are more or less the same room – but there's a separate area that was billed as a 'guest room' back when we bought it. We've turned it into a junk room, containing everything from

Olivia's old toys to a bike I never ride to various electrical items we never use. There are old TVs, an outdated stereo, a DVD player, and so on. The only reason I ever go in there is to get the vacuum, which is too big to store anywhere else.

This time when I enter, I move the vacuum to one side and take in everything else. It would be an easy room in which to hide something, largely because it would be in plain sight. I'd never go out of my way to come in here.

I still can't find anything incriminating, though. There are all sorts of old letters, bills and bank statements in a box and I stop to read some of the correspondence. There are some of Olivia's old school reports and I suppose the signs were always there. 'Knows her own mind', 'impressive creativity but often unwilling to listen to others' ideas', 'frequently reluctant to put her hand up, even when she knows the answer' – and so on. It was Olivia then and it's still her now.

More than an hour has passed when I realise I've achieved nothing other than feeling a little silly.

Except, if this *is* something to do with Dan – and I'm not convinced it is – why would he keep any evidence at home? He could keep anything at work, though he shares an office with another deputy head, so perhaps that's unlikely. The other option is much more of a possibility.

He'd keep it in his locker at the gym.

TWENTY-SIX

It's the first time in a long time that the his and hers gym membership is going to come in handy. Up until now, it's largely been a 'his' membership.

Dan might have misplaced his pass but mine has been in the top drawer on my side of the bed for months. I grab that, stuff some barely used gym gear into a bag and set off.

The gym is only fifteen minutes from the house in the car. It's on the way towards the dual carriageway, off on a little estate of its own. It's been custom-built in an anonymous warehouse-type building and sticks out because of the complete lack of anything anywhere near it. There were the typical petitions against it originally, with some claiming it would be an eyesore, or cause huge traffic problems, and so on. As soon as it was actually built, everyone stopped whingeing.

After entering the gym, I approach the access gates wondering if it might beep and lock me out for lack of visits. I had the initial tour and induction six months ago but, after that, I've only been twice – both times to use the pool.

There was no need to worry because the barrier retracts into the wall and allows me to enter. The gym feels busy, with men and women bustling around the entranceway and heading up the stairs into a glass-fronted studio above. I always assume everyone else will be stick-thin gym bunnies or ripped Greek gods – but the truth is that there's a bit of everything here. There is a bloke wondering around topless, showing off bulging arms that look like they might pop at any moment – but there are also those with normal, slightly overweight physiques, like mine.

It smells of sweat and cleaning fluid, the two battling each other to see which gets to win. I stop and look at the sign, trying to remember where everything is. I've had the tour, tried the equipment, been given the hard sell about personal training and so on – but that was months ago.

After waving away a staff member by insisting I'm fine, I head for the women's changing rooms. I can't really have a poke-around in my regular clothes. The floor is wet, with half a dozen bright yellow signs littered around, spelling out the obvious. I figure there's more chance of someone falling over a sign than there is of them slipping on the damp floor. In other news, coffee is hot, packets of peanuts will contain nuts, and some people are idiots.

The changing rooms are empty aside from an old woman in a one-piece swimming costume at the far end. She says 'hello' and then heads off to the showers.

My gym shorts feel tighter than I remember and the top isn't that much better. I damp my hair and forehead to at least make it look like I've been doing something and then stretch for little reason other than it feels like the thing to do. There's instant pain in my chest. It's the same dull ache that's always there, the one that goes all the way back to the car crash when I was eighteen. It's not an excuse that physical exertion makes the old injury hurt but I have played it up over the years. There was a parents' and children's sports day at Olivia's school when she was eight or nine and I got out of it by saying my ribs were too painful. I knew I'd be awful at whatever sports they had lined up and didn't want to embarrass myself, let alone her. All the other parents at least pretended to enjoy it – but I didn't see much fun in grown adults falling flat on their face during a sack race.

I've also used it with Dan. In the early days, we'd go out at weekends and hike over moors and through forests. I never enjoyed it. For me, it was traipsing through mud and rain for five hours for no reason other than that there was a bit of a view at the end. On some days, there wasn't even a view – just low clouds and large patches of mud. I did it anyway at first but then I started using my ribs as a reason why I couldn't go any longer. We moved to shorter weekend walks and then, after a while, not even that. It wasn't my thing and I suppose it was hard for Dan to enjoy anything with me lagging behind and complaining. We never really replaced it with anything else, other than the odd pub lunch.

I know I'm not an angel when it comes to the reasons why we're separating.

There *is* a gentle pain in my ribs but I don't think it's enough to stop me being active. There's also a niggle at the back of my mind that perhaps it is a mental thing now. Whenever I have to do anything physical, I pre-empt the stabbing sensation because I expect it to be there.

It doesn't feel that bad now I'm here. It's more the *idea* of the gym that seems intimidating than it is the actuality.

There's a moment where I start to think that perhaps I'll come here regularly. I could take some classes, or go for a swim now and then. There's a coffee shop that overlooks the pool, so perhaps Ellie and I could make a morning of it. Olivia might even be interested. It would be nice to find something we could do as mother and daughter – especially now it feels like we're getting on better. Tyler would have to show up first, of course.

I won't, of course. As soon as I leave, that'll be that. I'll forget this feeling and fall into my old ways. I know myself too well.

There are lockers in these changing rooms, the standard types with keys that are strapped to a person's wrist or ankle. But one of the major selling points for the his and hers memberships was that it gave complimentary access to a permanent locker area. This was important to Dan because it meant he didn't have to carry so much with him at the start of every day. With his papers and case for school, plus gym kit, shoes and the like, it all added up. He wanted to be able to leave things here.

I head back into the reception area and then follow the signs for the permanent lockers. It's along a corridor plastered with posters advertising various classes and small-scale sporting competitions. There's an element that makes it feel like being back at school: the jammed-in drawing pins, the curled corners on the pages.

The locker room is at the furthest end of the corridor, lit only by a dim yellow bulb, far away from the outside world. There a plastic box to the side of the door with a red LED glowing in the gloom. I can just about make out the sign pinned to the door: 'This room is for annual members ONLY'.

I press my fob to the plastic box, the LED changes to orange and then, after a teasing half-second, back to red. Like the hotel room keys that never work first time. I try again but the same thing happens, then a third time with no luck.

A woman is a little along the corridor wearing the red polo shirt that indicates staff. She's about to head into a room but stops when she notices me.

She asks if everything's all right – but in a tone that makes it pretty clear she thinks I'm a would-be thief.

'My fob's stopped working,' I say, speaking with a confidence I don't feel.

The woman strides along the corridor towards me and I try the fob again, only to get the same red-orange-red denial. There have been times where I'd swear the traffic lights at pop-up roadworks have the same sequence.

'You do have to be an annual member to have access to this room,' she says sternly, as if my eyes are somehow unable to read the sign directly in front of my face.

'I am.'

'You'll have to go to reception in that case.'

It almost goes without saying that there's a queue. Of course there is. Some bloke is saying that the chocolate machine has stolen his pound coin. I get the annoyance but, from the way he's banging on about the injustice, anyone would think he's been defrauded of his entire savings account. You're in a bloody gym, mate. Forget the chocolate.

Next up is a woman who says there's a 'funny smell' in the toilets. I'm not sure what else she expects. She should try ours at work after Graham's spent half-hour in there. Then there's another woman who's asking if anyone's handed in a pair of shoes to lost property.

By the time I get to the front, I've almost forgotten why I'm there. The poor bloke at the counter has the look of a man who didn't think he'd signed up for this. I tell him my fob's not working for the locker room and then he asks for my name as he taps away on a computer keyboard.

'It might be under my husband's name,' I add. 'We joined together.'

He frowns when he looks up. 'I can't give you access to your husband's locker, Mrs Denton.'

'It's not his locker – not entirely. Both our fobs have always worked. It's only today mine has stopped.'

His eyes narrow but he doesn't openly question me. The line continues to grow behind as well.

'My swimming costume is in there,' I add.

He looks from me to the computer and then back again. I don't think he's convinced. 'There are some security questions,' he replies with the hint of a sigh.

'Okay.'

He starts to go through the list – but I know Dan's date of birth, postcode and mother's maiden name. With all that cleared, he takes my fob, presses it onto some panel connected to the computer, and then removes it. I feel a bit guilty when he apologises for the inconvenience considering I never had access in the first place – but thank him and then head back along the murky corridor.

This time the light blinks from red to orange to green and the door clicks. I push inside and walk into an empty room that's lined on all four sides with rows of grey lockers. There's a wooden bench in the centre of the room, a bin next to the door, and that's it. Some of the lockers have been personalised with stickers and fridge magnets but most are plain and unidentifiable in any way other than a small number in the top right corner. There are no old-fashioned keys on wristbands here – everything is locked by the same type of plastic pad that secures the main door. That leaves a series of unrelenting red dots arranged in straight lines, like the eyes of a neatly ordered group of horror-movie monsters.

I have no idea which one is Dan's, so do the only thing I can. I move from locker to locker pressing my fob to each of them, hoping for a green light.

Visions engulf me of being caught and having to explain myself, or being in here for hours with no luck. I barely have time to second-guess my motivation this time. I'm only at the fifth locker when the light winks green and the door opens itself. I figure this is a moment of truth. If I find stinking socks and a pair of shorts, then my imagination has been overdoing it. If I find some of my things that should be at home, then perhaps all this weirdness *is* down to my husband.

There's a gym bag that's filled with, among other things, socks, underpants, tracksuit bottoms and two long-sleeved tops. There's a scuffed pair of trainers at the back of the locker and a photo of Olivia taped to the back of the door. It's all very normal and I can't pretend I'm not disappointed.

Perhaps that's the wrong word.

I'm disappointed that there are things I can't explain. But, more than that, I'm relieved.

I'm about to close the locker when I spot the crumpled Sainsbury's bag in the far corner. There's no light and I almost missed it. I have to stretch to reach and, when I tug on the bag, it's quickly clear that something heavy is inside. The contents clank off the metal of the locker as I pull the bag forward, almost dropping it before grabbing it at the second attempt.

It's really heavy.

I unwrap the bag and realise a second carrier bag is inside the first. Like the trick present on Christmas morning.

Inside that second bag is something that's definitely not a Christmas present, however. I remove the contents, weighing it in my hands, staring at it disbelievingly. Of all the things I might have expected to find, this would have been close to last.

It's a gun.

TWENTY-SEVEN

I've never held a gun before. I've seen them on television in crime shows, marvelling at how everyone is such a bad shot. I suppose if people were *good* shots, that would be the end of the show. I've watched the odd Olympic event if Britain has a chance of a medal… and that's it.

Even from that, I know there's something not quite right about this weapon. It's shaped like a pistol and has a trigger like a regular gun, but it's dark blue with a plasticky feel. It's only when I turn it over in my hands that I see the words 'Taser Pulse' etched onto the barrel.

It's not a gun that shoots bullet, it's a taser. I've heard the word, of course – mainly in relation to the police. I think someone might have been tasered to death by accident a few years ago but never paid much attention. I switch it from one hand to the other, surprised at how heavy it is. If real guns are like this, perhaps that's why everyone is such a bad shot on TV.

There's a clunk from along the hallway and I'm suddenly aware of how this would look to anyone who might walk in. I put the gun down on the edge of the locker so I can push it inside quickly if anyone does come in. I pause for a moment, waiting for silence from the corridor, and then take out my phone. I take a series of photos from various angles and then wrap the gun back into the bags. After that, I return everything else to the locker and click it closed.

I sit on the bench to steady myself. My hands are damp with sweat and I feel light-headed. Like most Brits, guns aren't a part of my life. I've never shot one, never been threatened with one, never dreamed of needing one. It's another world, one of which I do not want to be a part.

I'm so worked up as I exit the gym that I realise I'm still in my makeshift disguise – and that my bag is in one of the regular lockers. I have to turn around and re-enter through the barriers, keeping my head down with embarrassment in case anyone noticed me leaving moments before.

My mind races as I'm changing. Why would Dan have the weapon? Does the taser work? Does it need to be charged? What would it do to a person? Could it kill someone?

At first I wonder why Dan would keep it at the gym – but the answer's obvious. He couldn't risk the house, car or school in case someone else stumbled across it.

Is it his?

Is it illegal?

Even in the darkest moments of arguing with Dan, I'd never have suspected something like this. The fact it's my *husband* who's concealing a weapon is barely conceivable. My deputy headteacher husband, whom I've known for more than twenty years.

I barely think about what I'm doing as I drive home. A horrible thought begins to grow. It's obvious but the only reason to have a taser or stun gun is to stun someone. To subdue them. Could Dan have used it to incapacitate Tyler for some reason? The only reason I have to think that is the timing. I wouldn't say they get on – but Dan does stand up for him to a degree. Or, at least, he says we should let Olivia make her own choices, her own mistakes. He's never had an issue with Tyler in the way I have, so could he really have done this?

Very little makes sense and I'm already driving along our road when I realise I'm almost home. That's when I spot the police car parked outside the house.

TWENTY-EIGHT

When I get into the living room, Olivia is sitting on one sofa with a pair of police officers on the other. She's made them a cup of a tea each and, at least on first impressions, it looks like it's all very friendly. Everyone is leaning back in their respective seats.

These are different officers than the ones who visited about the smashed window. There's a man and a woman, each in uniform, both with their hats on their laps. The man introduces himself as PC O'Neill. He's greying but has the type of reassuring look that works for a police officer. I suppose Dan has it, too. A mix of authority and kindness blended together. He'll probably raise his voice at some point but at least there'll be a reason for it. The female is PC Marks. She's younger and has a friendly smile with big, round eyes. The type of look that's perfect for giving bad news.

Which is why it's such a relief when her first words are: 'Sorry, Mrs Denton. I hope we didn't worry you. There's nothing to be concerned about.'

I don't know if I look flustered – but I feel it. I keep thinking of the taser in Dan's locker.

'It's about Tyler Lambert,' she adds. 'We were hoping to have a few words with yourself, your husband and your daughter.'

'Oh…'

It was always going to happen, of course. Tyler's been gone for five days and, though it's not the first time, there had to be a point where someone decided to involve the police. Given I've heard that Frank finds a lot of things that have fallen from lorries – not to mention his smoking preferences – I wouldn't be convinced he'd made the call. I wonder if it was Olivia.

'My husband's at work,' I say. 'His name's Dan. He's a deputy head and he has a parents' evening tonight. I don't know what time he'll be back.'

It's PC O'Neill who cuts in before his colleague can reply: 'We can make a start with you,' he says.

'Do I need to come to the station?' I ask.

'Not necessarily. If you're comfortable, we can talk here. We're a lot more informal than people tend to think.'

He has a kind smile, which reminds me of Dan's. Not too broad, not overdone. There's almost a shyness about it, but, without words, it says, 'I understand'. The problem is that I've seen that a lot in my marriage. I'm not sure if Dan *does* understand or, more importantly, if he cares.

And it's that which makes me edgy about PC O'Neill. Now more than ever, I associate this smile with mistrust.

I'm slow to respond, not completely sure what to say. I eventually settle for a weak, 'Okay.'

The two officers have stood to greet me but PC Marks makes a movement towards the stairs. 'Did you say you had some photographs we could look at, Olivia…?'

My daughter watches me for a moment and then gets the none-too-subtle hint. She pushes up from the sofa and leads the constable to the stairs.

We listen to their creaky ascent and, after the bedroom door closes, PC O'Neill speaks up: 'Your daughter makes a superb cup of tea,' he says.

It's so out of the blue that I can't do anything other than laugh. 'That's if you can get her to make one. I don't suppose you can convince her to clean her room, can you…?'

He laughs this time. 'I'm not sure our resources quite stretch to that.'

'I thought that's what ASBOs were for…?'

The constable settles onto the sofa and I sit on the other. He takes out a small notepad, resting it on his knee. His hat is now abandoned on the coffee table, next to his colleague's.

'We've spoken to Mr Lambert,' he says, 'and he insists the reason his son is missing is because of some sort of argument between the two of you.'

'That's ridiculous,' I snap back. 'Tyler's gone missing before.'

A nod: 'Your daughter has filled us in on that – but I believe he's never been gone for five days…?'

'I don't know.'

He gives me that knowing smile again. Parents united and all that.

'Tell me about the argument.'

His pencil is poised over the pad. It's a small gesture but it doesn't feel like it. It's a long time since I've given any sort of statement to the police – even if he is calling it informal. It's not the same as telling them about a broken window; it feels as if I'm under investigation myself. What if it *was* the argument that made Tyler disappear? Does that make it my fault?

'We've never really got on,' I say.

'Tyler Lambert and yourself?'

'Right.'

'How long has he been seeing your daughter?'

It takes me a second. 'Eighteen months, something like that. I don't know – I think he was seeing her before I knew about it. Back when she was seventeen. He's five years older than her.'

PC O'Neill scratches something onto his pad but I suspect he already knows this if he's spoken to Tyler's father and Olivia. There's nothing illegal going on, even if it doesn't feel right to me.

'Is it the age gap of which you don't approve?'

'In part.'

He smiles calmly. 'I have a daughter myself. Not quite Olivia's age – but she's getting there.'

It's irrelevant, of course. Dan does this – linking happenings to something he's seen or dealt with at school. I suppose there's no specific reason to be suspicious. It's how people think, how they talk. One person's experience is aligned to their own. I do it. The problem is that, with my confusion and now suspicion, I'm not sure who I trust. Is he saying this to try to trick me, or is it a genuine parent-to-parent interaction?

'You've got all this to come,' I reply meekly.

He tilts his head, conceding the point. 'What else is it that you don't approve of?'

'Tyler doesn't have a job and it doesn't seem like he wants one. Olivia works really hard for a low wage – and then uses part of her money to buy things for him. I don't think many parents would approve of that.'

PC O'Neill is tight-lipped. 'And is that what you argued about on Saturday?'

'I suppose. It wasn't really an argument, not like that. I asked how the job hunting was going and he took it the wrong way.'

There's a pause, and then: 'Which way was he meant to take it?'

I snort at that. 'Well, yes. Okay. He took it the exact way it was meant. Either way, he stormed off, slamming the door behind him. It's not like I knew he wouldn't be seen again.'

There's a scratch of pencil on pad and then the officer looks up to me. 'Is this the main reason why you don't get on?'

'Do any mothers get on with their daughter's unemployed boyfriends?'

'Good point.'

PC O'Neill pushes back into the sofa, wiggling his backside, making himself more comfortable. 'How is your daughter's relationship with Mr Lambert?'

It feels strange to hear that. *Mr Lambert.* It makes Tyler sound like a grown-up. He is, of course, but it never seems that he acts like it.

'You're better asking her,' I reply.

'We are – but I think your input would be useful as well.'

I shrug, wishing I had the cup of tea he had. I could do with it right now. 'Olivia and Tyler break up and make up,' I say. 'They fall out over things all the time. I've stopped asking Olivia about what's going on between them. Sometimes he disappears for a weekend but he always comes back.'

'Any idea where he disappears to?'

'You'd have to ask Olivia. I have no idea.'

Something new goes on the pad and I wonder if he's written 'no idea'.

'Olivia's set up a Facebook page,' I add. 'It's called Find Tyler. I don't think she's having much luck.'

'She showed us.'

'Oh.'

'Do you know much about your daughter's friends?'

I puff out a long breath. 'I used to when she was at school. There were birthday parties and trips out in the summer. I'd hire a van and drive them off to the zoo, or a few of us mums would carpool. Then Olivia hit about fourteen and that was that. She stopped talking about what was going at school, or about her friends. She was out a lot, or using her phone to message them. I know hardly anything about her friends now.'

'Do you know much of what she gets up to in her free time?'

'She works evening shifts at the Cosmic Café and I pick her up every now and then. The owner pays for her taxi other times. Sometimes she says she's staying out with Tyler.'

'But you don't know what they get up to?'

I shrug. 'They're eighteen. What am I supposed to do?'

'I'm not criticising.'

I stare at the floor and it feels like he is. All of this reeks of reckless mother. The opinion pieces almost write themselves. I'll be in the *Daily Mail*; some privileged wife of an MP banging on about how I'm a terrible example of twenty-first-century parenting.

'Tyler smokes weed,' I say, looking to push the blame for all this back onto him. 'He smells of it a lot and I've caught him with cannabis a couple of times.'

I expect a response, not quite a leap-off-the-sofa, call-for-the-riot-squad-reaction, but something. Instead, PC O'Neill calmly adds a few words to his pad.

'Do you know if there are harder drugs involved?'

His question takes me by surprise, not because I haven't asked myself the same thing, but because it's so unruffled.

'I hope not.'

'Have you seen any signs?'

'I mean… I… don't know. I suppose I'm not sure what to look for. Liv's moody – but she's a teenager. I was moody at her age. Dan's a deputy head. He's trained with this sort of thing. I think he'd have noticed.'

He seems to accept this answer but I feel like asking him what I could do. Should I go through Olivia's room, looking for evidence? And evidence of what? That would only make our relationship worse, regardless of whether I found anything. Even if I did find something, what then? An ultimatum? It's us or Tyler? I don't know who or what she'd choose.

'I don't think my daughter's on drugs,' I say. 'I know she's not. She drinks – but everyone does at eighteen. I don't think she smokes, not cigarettes anyway. I don't think she's that different from any other teenager.'

'What about Tyler?'

'I…' I stop myself, not quite trusting my own words, before telling him I don't know. 'You'll have to ask Olivia,' I add, aware I'm beginning to sound like a parrot.

We go over a few details, mainly relating to timings. He asks if there's anything else I can think of and I mention the broken glass that might have been a break-in. We examine the door together and he says he'll check the details in the file.

We're still standing in the kitchen when he nods towards the back door. 'Do you suspect this was Tyler?' he asks.

'It crossed my mind.'

'But nothing's missing?'

'There might have been a bit of money. Neither Dan or myself can remember everything that was in there. We checked the important things – passports, expensive goods, that sort of thing. Nothing obvious has gone.'

PC O'Neill writes that on the pad and then pockets it, along with his pencil.

'Do you think you'll find him?' I ask.

'I'd like to think so. Most missing people turn up themselves.'

'What about those who've been missing for five days?'

'I don't know the specific stats…'

'But what do you think?'

He glances towards the stairs, willing an interruption that doesn't come. The gesture says more than words and it's probably only at this moment where I realise how serious this all is. I've expected Tyler to return at any point. Olivia would be overjoyed and everything would continue as they have. That now seems naïve.

I wonder if I should tell the officer about the taser in my husband's gym locker. Could it be relevant? I want to say no – but I'm unsure about so many things at the moment. If I *do* say something, there's no turning back. It's a can of worms I can't reseal.

'You shouldn't read anything into this,' PC O'Neill says, 'and please don't take offence, but I do need to ask about your whereabouts for the past few days.'

'Oh…'

'It's perfectly normal procedure.'

'You don't think—'

'I don't think anything – but I have to ask. I'm sure you understand why…?'

I can't reply that, no, I don't understand. I'm sure there'll be a load of police double-speak – 'ruling out of inquiries' and the like – but the only reason to ask is if there's a nugget of suspicion about me, however small.

'I've been at work during the day,' I say, 'then here in the evenings. Nowhere special. My friend Ellie's down the road.'

The officer doesn't write anything down but he nods acceptingly.

'And that's since Saturday…?' he asks.

The thing is, I *know* I had nothing to do with Tyler going missing – but I also know how easy my schedule will be to check. If I lie, I'll be found out – and then it'll look bad. The problem is that I can't tell the truth, not all of it.

'I was in a hotel on Monday night,' I reply. 'It was for work. I can give you the name if you want…?'

He waves a hand as if it doesn't matter, but takes out his pad and notes the name anyway.

'When did you get back?' he asks.

It's perfectly innocent, of course. A normal question – but how can I tell him I woke up in a field?

'Early on Tuesday,' I reply. Not a lie.

We're interrupted by movement from the stairs. My daughter's timing has never been better as, moments later, Olivia and PC Marks appear in the living room. There's a momentary glance between constables and then PC O'Neill says he thinks that's all for now.

I see them to the door, full of thank yous and needless apologies. It's the British way. They head along the drive and sit in the car chatting. It takes about a minute for me to realise I'm staring.

I close the door and take a breath, wondering what counts as lying to the police.

Is omission a lie?

Is keeping information back something that can get a person in trouble?

Because, if it is, then I could really have a problem.

What I didn't tell PC O'Neill is that, after Luke did his no-show on Monday night, I spent at least part of the night at that hotel with another man.

TWENTY-NINE

Olivia is sitting by herself on the sofa when I head back into the living room. She's staring aimlessly towards the wall, her body present but her mind elsewhere.

'I'm worried about him,' she says quietly. It's haunting: a crumbling, vulnerable tone bereft by angst.

'At least the police are involved now,' I reply. 'They'll be able to get a proper search going.'

'I suppose.'

'What did they ask you about?'

'Not much. Where he hangs around, who his friends are. That sort of thing.'

She asks me to take her to work, so I do. It's a near silent journey and I know my daughter well enough – know *myself* well enough – to realise that it's not the time to push this. After leaving her at the front of the Cosmic Café, Olivia thanks me and then heads inside solemnly. I doubt even Rahul can cheer her up today.

Back at home by myself and I quickly find out that stun guns – or taser pulses, as Dan's weapon is called – are illegal in the UK. There's not even a grey area when it comes to civilians. I thought there might be some sort of low-wattage version allowed – but the law seems clear enough. Or Google, to be more precise. It's an offence to possess a stun gun, let alone use it. It's illegal to buy and sell – which means there's nowhere in the country that Dan could have bought it from legitimately. It's not even a trivial offence. Under the firearms act, someone in possession of a stun gun can go to prison for five years.

I find myself staring off into nothingness, much like Olivia earlier in the evening.

Five years.

Why would Dan risk something like this for *five years* in prison?

There's a chance he might have confiscated it from a student. Perhaps he was concerned that reporting the find to the authorities would ruin the youngster's life? He used some discretion, gave the student a stern warning and then… hid the gun in his gym locker…?

It's *possible*. Highly implausible but possible.

I find the exact model of stun gun online, pictures and all, and it seems readily available in a handful of Eastern European countries. It can be imported from the United States as well. It would be a brave person who ordered and then sat back waiting for Royal Mail to deliver. There'd be every chance it would be the police knocking, rather than a cheery postman.

So where did it come from?

Dan gets home a little before half past nine. He's flustered and seems tired. We make small talk over our respective days but there's more of a distance than before – and that's saying something. There's a massive part of me that wants to ask him outright what's going on but the words never quite seem to form. I'm not sure where to start.

Hey, by the way, I was snooping in your gym locker earlier and I was just wondering what's going on with the highly illegal weapon you're storing in there?

Ahead of the separation, we're at an uneasy truce. If I accuse him of gaslighting, or admit to my own snooping, that's it. There's no going back. If I'm wrong, I'm the paranoid, unhinged spurned wife. If I'm right, what then? Can I prove anything before he gets rid of any evidence?

For Olivia's sake, I need him. He's her father and I have to be sure before I make any accusations.

The only thing I feel some degree of certainty over is that I'm not in danger. I've known Dan for more than twenty years. I've rarely seen him angry, let alone violent. That's one of the things that annoys me the most. I might raise my voice, shout, scream, throw around an insult or two. He'll sit there calmly listening to it all and then reply with perfect composure. It's infuriating. I always seem like the deranged one.

Despite that, he must sense something isn't as it should be. He asks if everything is okay and I palm him off by saying the police were round to ask about Tyler. I say they need to talk to him at some point and that I passed on his mobile number. I watch for a reaction but there's nothing except an accepting nod. He asks if I have the details of the investigating officer – and says he'll call tomorrow. All very straightforward. No drama.

Being in the house alone with him doesn't feel quite right, so I say I'm going to nip to Ellie's for an hour. It's late – but he doesn't object. He replies that he's got a little bit of work to finish and that he'll probably be in bed by the time I return. This is how we've been for months… years. He does his thing, I do mine. Occasionally we cross over but not really.

I text Ellie, telling her to put the kettle on, and then set off along the street. Her house is only five minutes but I walk more slowly than usual, looking for things on the route that I take for granted. This journey is the last one Tyler apparently made and I find myself noticing the cut-throughs I'd normally pass without hesitation.

There's surprisingly few places he could have deviated from the route back to the High Street. One of the cut-throughs loops back to the furthest end of our road and then there is the row of houses that leads to the crossing before I get to Ellie's road. The junction is the first place he could realistically have strayed onto a different path. One road leads to the High Street, one to our house, one towards Ellie's, and the final one towards the dual carriageway.

I stop and look up at the lamp posts, checking for CCTV. It's everywhere in the cities – but not here. North Melbury is too small, too inconsequential. There's almost no late-night trouble. Major news stories are a noisy cockerel waking people up on a Sunday, or the weather forecast for the summer fete. I can't remember anyone going missing around here.

Ellie opens the door herself when I knock. She's in a different set of pyjamas from the other day, along with fluffy bunny slippers. She says hello but then groans when she turns, stopping to rub her breastbone.

She leads me through the hall into the kitchen and slumps into a seat at the table. 'Forgot my painkillers again,' she says.

'You should set an alarm on your phone to remind you.'

She starts to shake her head and then catches herself. 'I've never really liked taking pills and other medicines. You know what Ma was like.'

I do know what her mother was like – but had largely forgotten. Ellie's mum was always taking something, be it a miracle youth potion she'd seen on television, or some homeopathic nonsense she'd been sold along with the drum of snake oil. I'm not sure what she was hoping to achieve – but it didn't do much good in the end.

'Jason's in bed,' Ellie says.

'I was here to see you.'

'Sure it's not to get away from Dan?'

The smile is knowing. She can see right through me.

'A little from column A…'

I laugh and cross to the kettle, asking Ellie if she wants a tea. She says there's wine in the fridge if I fancy it – but my mind is muddy enough. Alcohol is the last thing I want.

Ellie is still working on her jigsaw but it's not that much further along than it was when I saw it last. She has got the straight pieces along the sides all in place. The box is on the table, leaning against the wall with a photo of a canal. It's a night scene, lights streaming down from windows above as a narrow boat drifts along serenely. I think it's probably Venice but I'm not sure and have never been. It's beautiful and, wherever it is, I wish I could see it for myself.

'How's Olivia?' Ellie asks. 'She cancelled our accounting session earlier.'

'Did she? I didn't know. The police were over to talk to us about Tyler – so it was probably because of that.'

I empty the recently boiled kettle into two mugs and then realise I haven't answered the question.

'She's upset,' I say. 'It's been five days since he was last seen and it's gone a bit beyond his usual disappearing acts.'

'What do you think?'

I return to the table and cradle the mug until the heat makes my fingers tingle. 'I don't know. I assumed he'd be back by now. I don't know enough about him to know what might have happened. I told them about his cannabis, so perhaps they think he owed money, something like that…' I tail off and run a hand through my hair, tugging at a knot that has appeared. 'If it *is* drugs, I hope Liv isn't involved.'

Ellie touches my wrist. 'I'm sure she's not.'

'I feel like an awful mother. I don't know how it's come to this.'

When I look up, Ellie is tight-lipped and I realise my mistake. She can't have children. Her mother died of ovarian cancer and Ellie had hers removed as a precaution. Olivia called her 'Auntie Ellie' for years – but that's as close as Ellie got to a child of her own.

'Sorry,' I say.

She blinks and, for a moment, she's no longer in the room. She breathes and then the moment has gone and she tells me it's fine. I know it's not. I'm usually careful with what I say around Ellie but I'm shattered from the past few days.

'Liv was talking about the mill,' I say lightly, trying to make it sound like a joke. 'I didn't know you were telling her our secrets…?'

Ellie bats it away with a wave of her hand. 'It sort of… came out. She was saying how you didn't like Tyler and I told her it wasn't that straightforward. I said we used to get up to all sorts when we were her age and that you were concerned. I hope you don't mind. I was trying to help.'

She doesn't look up, reaching for a piece of the puzzle instead and slotting it into place. I guess there's nothing wrong with what she told Olivia.

'It's like the boy who cried wolf,' I say. 'Liv and Tyler break up and there's a week of devastation, then it's all fine again. I don't know if I believe he's missing in the sense that people go missing. He might be at some hippy weed festival in a field somewhere.'

Ellie winks: 'Sounds like fun.'

'Not at our age.'

'Speak for yourself.'

It's good to talk about this. A small part of that weight is finally shifting. 'I've got a feeling he'll waltz back into everyone's lives in a day or three as if nothing's wrong.'

I've been looking at the puzzle, trying to see if I can help. Rather unhelpfully, all the water pieces look the same – which I guess is the point. I glance up and realise Ellie is staring at me.

'What?' I ask.

'Can I say something?'

'I think we've known each other long enough for that.'

She bites her lip. 'It's just… you don't seem massively concerned.'

'About what?'

'Tyler.'

As always, she's seen right through me. I spoke to the police; I've tried to say the right thing to Olivia… but it's forced. None of it is real. I glance off to the fridge, the wall, the window. Not making eye contact.

'Does that make me a horrible person?' I ask.

A shrug. 'You tell me.'

It takes me a few seconds to find the words. 'It's not like I wish he was dead or anything. It would just be nice if he sort of… sodded off and left Liv alone.'

'He's done the sodding off part.'

I'm not sure if she's joking: I'm playing with my hair again but catch myself this time. It's the type of thing that annoys me when other people do it, so I stop. There's a bump from upstairs – Jason, presumably – and we both stop for a moment.

'I hope Tyler's safe,' I reply. 'I honestly do… but I kind of wish he was with another girl. Something like that. It'll turn out he's got someone else pregnant and she's busy having the kid. Something big that will make Liv walk away.'

I realise what I've said but it's already too late. More children talk.

Ellie doesn't seem to mind this time. She's back to the puzzle. 'You got work tomorrow?'

It's a tactful – and timely – change of subject. I tell her I do and then we're uncharacteristically silent for a minute or two. I slot a piece into the puzzle and then accidentally knock another onto the floor, before retrieving it.

'Can I tell you something?' I say. It's me who's fumbling this time.

Ellie looks up from the table and we lock eyes for a moment. 'Of course.'

I take a breath and can't keep the eye contact. There's so much I could tell her. So much I *want* to tell her.

'I lied to the police.'

The words hang between us like a knife on a rope swinging back and forth. Something dangerous that could go either way. I can't believe I've said it.

'Not lied,' I say. 'I didn't tell them something. Kept it back. I don't know if that's lying.'

'About what?'

'They were asking about Tyler, about how we argued over his lack of job and Olivia's money. They asked where I'd been since Saturday. I told them I was in a hotel on Monday night, it's just…'

I tail off, wishing I'd said nothing. It's too late now, of course. Ellie edges forward a minuscule amount, hanging on my words.

The memory wasn't clear at first. In the aftermath of waking up in that field, everything was blurred and hazy. It's not soap opera amnesia in that I've suddenly remembered everything I'd forgotten, but the pictures have sharpened and smoothed.

'I was with another man,' I say.

Nothing happens for a moment. It feels real now I've said it out loud. I've sort of known it since waking up in that field – but knowing and admitting it to myself are two different things.

When it comes to separation, to Dan's possible infidelity – which is based on nothing other than the way he looked at Alice – I've been able to take a high ground. But after the night in the hotel, there's a part of me, perhaps a big part, that wonders if I'm the bad person here. Perhaps it's not a fifty-fifty thing in that Dan and I were never matched. Perhaps he's a perfectly loving husband and father – and it's me who's destroyed everything. That's who I am and what I do.

'Wow,' Ellie says.

'Maybe not *with* another man,' I add quickly. 'Not like that. I don't remember everything… I remember bits…'

Ellie takes a second or two to reply, picking her words. 'Does Dan know?'

'No.' I pause and glance towards the hall, wondering if I heard a creak from the stairs. 'I'm not sure Dan would care.'

'So what have you done wrong?'

'It's not much of an example for Liv, is it? We're separating and trying to do it amicably. Irreconcilable differences is one thing; adultery is something else entirely.'

Ellie has a gulp of tea and then clanks the mug back onto the table. She walks around me very deliberately and pulls the kitchen door closed with a quiet click. Perhaps the creak from the stair wasn't in my imagination.

'How did it happen?' she asks.

I don't want to talk about it – but can hardly back away now.

'I was at the hotel to meet a client but he didn't show up. He texted to say he was running late and then that he couldn't make it at all. I was waiting in the bar. One drink became two and then I got talking to this guy. He bought me another drink and then I insisted on buying him one. One thing led to another and then we went upstairs…'

Ellie is silent for a moment but then she reaches across the table and grips my hand. The veins in her fingers are a vibrant blue but the skin is smooth. An accountant, not a builder.

'Did the police ask if you were alone in the hotel?'

'No.'

'So you didn't lie. You're clear with them – and, for Dan, you're separating. The only reason you're still living together is because it's taken time for him to find a flat. If it wasn't for that, you'd be apart anyway. If he meets someone else – or you do – then that's fine.'

It sounds logical and reasonable. It *is* a matter of timing. If Dan had found a flat more quickly, we would be living apart already. We've not discussed precisely what the separation means, although there's an understanding that it's a prelude to divorce. Neither of us believe we'll spend a month apart and suddenly fall for each other all over again. So, with that, why would either of us have a problem with the other having a relationship with someone else? Living together now is about timing and the divorce will be paperwork. Emotionally, we're already separate.

The problem is that this is about more than that. It all is. I woke up in a field in a car drenched with blood. I have no idea if that's connected to the man at the hotel, or, indeed, what happened after we went up to my room.

I want to tell Ellie this as well – except I can't. It feels like a secret only for me.

There's no chance to elaborate anyway because my phone starts ringing. Olivia's name flashes – which is unusual because she rarely calls. It's all texts, emojis and acronyms I don't understand. I have to google them to figure out what it all means.

'Hi,' I say.

Olivia's voice quivers as she replies.

'I need you,' she says. 'I need you now.'

THIRTY

Olivia is pacing the living room when I get home. As I enter, she thrusts her phone into my hand with an imploring, '*Look*!'

She's showing me the Find Tyler Facebook page but the font is too small for me to make out much.

When I tell her this, she jabs the screen. 'The picture!'

I squint at a grainy image that looks like one of the dodgy CCTV images police put out all the time. It's been zoomed to such a degree that most of the definition has gone.

'It's Tyler,' she says.

I twist the phone to view the image diagonally. It is definitely a person. Whoever it is has longish, shaggy hair and is wearing dark clothes. He might have a goatee – but it could be a scarf. I'm not even sure it's a 'he'. The goatee might be a shadow.

'It's from an hour ago,' Olivia says. 'Someone uploaded it onto the Find Tyler page. He's in Bashington.'

I move the phone further away and then closer, trying to see what Olivia's seeing.

'Is this the only photo?' I ask.

'One's enough. It's him. The poster said they saw him at that statue thing in the town centre.'

I look at the name of the person who uploaded the photo – Sam Jones – but it means nothing to me. Olivia doesn't know him or her, either. The profile photo is of a tree.

'Can you drive me?' Olivia asks. 'We've gotta go now or he'll be gone.'

'It's getting on for eleven.'

'Exactly – that's why we've got to go now. If he's sleeping rough, he'll be bedding down.'

'What did your father say?'

Olivia is a bundle of frustrated energy. She tugs at her short hair and strides across the room and back again. 'He has to be up early…'

That means he said no.

I tell her I'll drive her to Bashington and know deep down exactly why. The photo could be of anyone and I'm not convinced we'll find Tyler there, so it isn't for that. Part of it is because I know Liv will worry all night otherwise. She might even try to make her own way there. The biggest reason is that Dan said no. I don't know if he has been trying to make me doubt myself and I don't know why he has a stun gun in his locker – but I *do* know this is me getting one over on him with our daughter.

It's pathetic and childish. A game of brinksmanship – but that's what we've come to, after all. Perhaps I *am* the baddie in all of this. For now, I don't care. I grab my car keys and, moments later, we're on the road.

The light from Olivia's phone in the passenger seat is a constant in the corner of my eye as we follow the street lights out of North Melbury until we reach the darkened lanes on the outskirts of town. The stars are out tonight and the moon is so much brighter than when I was waking up in the field. There's little fear of these roads with Olivia at my side.

'Any other comments on the picture?' I ask.

'No.'

'Any updates? New photos?'

'No.'

I want to tell her not to get her hopes up, that the blurry mess could be anyone, but there's little point.

'Did you try messaging Sam Jones?' I ask.

'I'm not stupid.'

'I know, Liv. I'm only asking.'

'Well I did – and they've not got back to me.'

'Do you know a Sam Jones?'

'No.'

I leave it there, more certain than before that this is a wild goose chase with no goose – and that we're probably only one more question away from an argument that will undo any of the good work between us from the past couple of days.

It's a silent drive the rest of the way, though Olivia's phone screen never dims. Bashington is as unremarkable as North Melbury; both typical British towns that run on gossip, tea, summer fetes, suspicion of the young and, *whisper it quietly*, anyone who doesn't look quite British enough. Most of the shops are closed after five o'clock and all day on Sundays. That's why it's no surprise that the town centre is empty when we arrive. Everyone's always complaining about the lack of parking spaces – another telltale sign that people have little to do – but it's no problem on this occasion. I park next to the obelisk in the square and switch off the engine.

'Where do you want to start?' I ask.

Olivia is out of the car and doesn't reply. By the time I'm out and around her side, she's already off along a lane that has darkened shops on both sides. She's ducking to peer into the shadows and criss-crossing to the doorways in case any bodies are shadowed by the murk. I say nothing, pulling my coat tighter and following.

We're almost at the end of the street when she makes a small squeak and darts into a covered archway. It's only a moment until I catch up but, when I do, she's crouching over a man in a sleeping bag who's using a crammed bin bag for a pillow. Even before he rolls over, it's obvious that it's not Tyler. His hair is greyer and he's a bag of bones. Olivia makes him jump by touching his arm. He growls at her, a startled wolf protecting cubs as she leaps away, apologising and saying she thought he was someone else. He eyes her – and then me – with understandable suspicion as he cradles his pillow filled with what are likely his only possessions. He shouts something along the lines of 'get out of it' – but the words are slurred and barely understandable. The sentiment is clear.

This time I don't allow Olivia to walk ahead, gripping her wrist like she's a child until she relents and remains by my side. We reach the end of one street and double around to follow the parallel one.

Olivia says nothing but she's shivering. I offer my coat but she dismisses me with a rapid shake of the head.

There are two more homeless people on the next street but we continue with only a squint in their direction. It's awful but what am I supposed to do? Drive them home to ours for the night?

Olivia's pace starts to quicken as we arrive back at the car. A man is hurrying past, hands in pockets, likely on the way home from the pub – and she calls him over, showing him the photo on her phone and asking if he's seen anything. He looks back and shakes his head before carrying on.

We try the main High Street and then a final row of shops near to the river – but there's no sign of Tyler. It's close to midnight and Olivia catches me checking my watch as we head back to the car.

'It could be someone playing a trick,' I say.

I half expect a fiery response, though it doesn't come. Instead, Olivia replies with a solemn whisper: 'I know.'

'I saw the comment left on the page earlier.'

No reply.

'How many have you been getting like that?'

Olivia takes my hand and squeezes her fingers into mine. I can't remember the last time she did this. She rests her head momentarily on my shoulder as we continue to walk slowly.

'A few,' she says.

'C'mon,' I tell her. 'Let's get you home.'

THIRTY-ONE

- FRIDAY -

I wait at the top of the stairs and watch Olivia go into her room. I want to follow her in, read her a story and tuck her into bed like the old days but I don't know that many happy endings nowadays. There's a shuffling as she gets undressed and then quiet. I don't know if she's settled down to sleep – but I hope so. I suspect she's on her phone, refreshing her Find Tyler page in case there's an update.

Our room is directly ahead. Dan will be asleep and I doubt he's stirred much since we left. He's always been something of a heavy sleeper – all the more reason why it's so odd he answered my phone call in the early hours of Tuesday.

I'm touching the handle to enter when I change my mind. I'm not sure what I think of him and his secrets and, though there isn't fear at being in the same house as him, I don't want to share a bed.

It's not the first time I've slept in the spare room – we've had more than our share of flouncy arguments – but it's the first time in about a year. On the last occasion, it was because Dan cleaned the kitchen counter after I'd already done it. It sounds like nothing and, to a large degree, it is. But there was something about the way he did it, the extra small circles he made with the cloth as if I wasn't capable of doing it properly myself. I shouted, he did his usual thing of remaining calm and speaking to me *reeeeeeaaaallllly slllllooooooowwwwwwwly* – and there's little that infuriates me more.

He knows it, of course, which is why he does it. In the end, I slept in the spare room for a night, we barely talked the next day, and then we got back to normal by living around one another.

The spare room has a double bed that's permanently made, largely because nobody ever sleeps in here. When Olivia was younger and had her friends over for the night, they'd double and triple up across the two rooms. Before that, Dan's mother had a night or two here while she was still alive. We had the odd friend after dinner parties back when we were trying to be sophisticated – but it's been empty almost every night since we moved in.

I don't bother going into our room to fetch nightclothes, instead slipping under the covers in my underwear. The mattress is softer than what I usually sleep on; the pillows harder, sheets stiffer. It's comfortable, though; more so because I'm on my own. I close my eyes and hug the covers tight under my chin. I even say a silent prayer to a god in whom I don't believe, hoping Tyler's back sometime soon. At least things might start to get back to normal.

Dan is in the kitchen when I head downstairs in the morning. He's in his gym kit, eating a bowl of porridge while standing at the counter. He's reading something on his phone but glances up as I cross the living room. He says the kettle has just boiled but doesn't mention anything about our sleeping arrangements from the previous night.

Even without separate rooms, this is our routine for the morning. One of us boils the kettle, making sure there's enough water for both of us. Other than that, we do our own things. If either of us stops boiling the kettle, it really is the end of days.

I should ask him about the stun gun... about my keys in the fridge... about why he was still up in the early hours of Tuesday... but I don't.

Dan asks if I heard Olivia moving around in the night and I say I didn't. I remember nothing after my head hit the pillow. He says she was up and about through the night, going to the bathroom and back a couple of times. I say I'll let her sleep before popping some bread into the toaster.

I notice Dan watching but his gaze instantly flickers away. He's been off carbs for a few months now. Bread, pasta, rice and potatoes are evil, so I tend to make meals for myself and Olivia – if she wants anything – while he'll drink protein shakes and buy rotisserie chickens.

The toaster pops just as there's a knock at the door. Dan moves way too quickly for me this time. He mutters a sharp, 'see you later', and then he's gone.

I watch through the net curtain in the living room window as he and Alice stroll along the path. Dan glances back to the house but I'm pretty sure he can't see me. Alice is in yoga pants that are so tight, she might as well not be wearing them. I'm not sure if she is a natural blonde or if it's bleached but she has it in a ponytail today and is bouncing on her heels athletically as she walks. She slaps him playfully on the shoulder as they get to the end of the drive, before both getting into Dan's car. I continue watching until he's pulled away and disappeared behind next door's hedge.

It's hard to resist, so I creep up the stairs quietly, avoiding number seven from the bottom because it squeaks. With the greatest of care, I nudge open Olivia's door, standing in the frame and watching. She's wrapped herself in the bedclothes but there's a pillow on the floor, along with what looks like half her wardrobe. A single leg juts out at an angle, showing off a zigzagging tattoo that loops around her lower thigh. I think this is a new one. Her toenails are a shiny black, but the rest of her is cocooned in the covers, her chest rising and falling oh so slowly as she sleeps.

Olivia has never been one of those teenagers who sleeps all day. We usually see each other in the morning, even if she doesn't say much. She seems even more vulnerable when I watch her like this.

I close the door and then, when back downstairs, check the Find Tyler Facebook page. The photo from last night is still there – but, even on the laptop with its bigger screen, it's hard to make anything clearly. It *could* be Tyler but it could be pretty much anyone. There are no new comments or posts, so I close the site and then check Natasha's page. She had a home-made fruit salad for breakfast, which is #winning.

Old habits. Hers and mine.

That done, I get ready for work.

Natasha went out with her boyfriend for dinner last night. I know this because she's telling Claire in intricate detail about seemingly every moment of it. He dressed up in a suit; she popped to Tanfastic after work. He got his back waxed last weekend; she's thinking about hair extensions. He ordered a mixed grill – a sure sign of a classy place; she had the mushroom burger. He was drinking John Smith's; she had a 'cheeky' few glasses of rosé. He got up to wee *three* times; she lost an earring somewhere. Only a cheap one, though.

Pulling off my own ears seems something of an overreaction and I'm not sure this would count as mitigating circumstances were I to burn the entire building down in an effort to make her stop. It doesn't sound as if Claire's that interested. There's the odd 'yeah' and 'right' but, other than that, it's a one-way barrage of vacuous vapidity.

Still, I'm the one who spends my time poring over her online updates, so what does that make me?

It's a merciful respite when Graham walks into the main office. He heads straight for me, crouching and whispering so that only I can hear. 'I need a word.'

He stands straighter, raising an eyebrow and then heading back towards his own office. Everyone has gone silent, watching as I stand and follow. It's rare that Graham leaves his office during the day, rarer still he comes and talks to me directly. Something's definitely not right.

When I get to his office, he's already behind his desk.

'Close the door,' he says grimly.

I do and then take the seat on the opposite side of his desk.

'You met a potential client named Declan on Tuesday,' he says.

'Yes.'

'Tell me about it.'

'Has he put in an order?'

Graham glances away towards his monitor and then rests both hands on the desk, fingers splayed. He breathes in heavily through his nose.

'Not exactly,' he says. 'There's been a complaint.'

THIRTY-TWO

I laugh because it's got to be a joke. 'A complaint? What would anyone have to complain about?'

Graham doesn't join in and it's then that I realise he's serious. 'I don't understand,' I say.

'What happened when you met Mr Irons on Tuesday?'

'Declan? Not much. We… er…'

I strain to remember but it was an unremarkable twenty minutes in among a ludicrously eventful four days. The journey took a lot longer than the meeting.

'We met at this industrial estate,' I say. 'You gave me the address. It was this little office on a rank of three or four. There wasn't much inside and the other offices were empty. We were the only two people there.'

Graham scribbles something on a Post-it note that I can't see. 'And…?'

'And what? There's nothing to tell. He told me about his business, I told him about our services, that was more or less it. He sounded interested and I thought he'd be in contact to haggle prices or put in an order. We swapped business cards and I left.'

'That's it…?'

I hold my hands out. 'I don't know what you want me to say.'

Graham takes another breath, his hulking chest rising high and falling.

'Mr Irons tells a slightly different tale.'

'What has he said?'

He nods at his monitor, even though I can't see what's on it. 'He claims you propositioned him.'

The room spins, first one way and then another. Graham zooms out of view and then back into it.

'Are you all right?' he asks.

'I, um…'

'Do you want some water?'

He doesn't wait for an answer, clambering around his desk and disappearing into the hallway. He's back moments later, pressing a plastic cup into my hand. The liquid is icy through the plastic, stinging the tips of my fingers. I force myself to drink anyway but it's like swallowing a razor. It's so cold that I gag on the final few drops, spluttering and patting myself on the chest until it clears.

'You okay?' Graham asks.

He's back in his swivel chair on the other side of the desk.

'Rose?'

It's the sound of my name that brings me back. Nothing like this has ever happened before. I didn't pass out… but it was as if I'd frozen.

'I'm all right,' I reply gingerly.

'Can we continue?'

'Yes. I, um… I don't know what he means by propositioned.'

'He says you offered him a lower price in return for what he calls "some mutual fun".'

Graham reads the last three words from his screen.

'That's nonsense,' I reply, although my attempt to remain calm is failing. I'm a mix of confusion and fury.

'I'm going to have to read some things you might not want to hear…' Graham looks up to me over invisible glasses. He's nervous.

'Fine.'

'He says you told him you could, "teach him a thing or two" and that you could "make a regular thing of it".'

Graham leafs through the papers on his desk and passes me a page. By the time I've finished, I'm shaking.

Graham,

I have thought long and hard over whether or not I should send this email over the past few days. After agonising with my conscience, I have decided that it would be a disservice to you if I did nothing.

Further to our correspondence from late last week, I was delighted when we arranged a time for your salesperson to explain how our companies could work together. Unfortunately, what transpired on Tuesday afternoon is not anything to do with the way I do business.

Upon our initial meeting and introducing herself, your salesperson, Rose Denton, touched my bicep, remarking that it was 'the best bulge I've seen all day'. Despite the inappropriateness of the comment, I continued with the meeting, hoping we would at least talk business.

In fairness, we did discuss the ways in which your services could help my company grow, however the professional nature was not to last.

After mentioning a price, Ms Denton again touched my bicep, remarked that she could 'teach me a thing or two'. She added that if we 'make a regular thing of it', she would be able to offer a better price. When I replied that I had a girlfriend, she responded by saying that it was 'only a bit of mutual fun'.

Needless to say, I did not take her up on the offer. I have no idea if this is a one-off occurrence, or something that happens regularly but, as one employer and director to another, I thought you would want to know.

Despite this, I have not ruled out working with you in future. However, as I'm sure you'll understand, I would much rather do business directly with you. Please call if you wish. I have not mentioned prices here because I was unclear whether Ms Denton was quoting officially, or speaking out of turn. If the lower end of what she quoted is correct, I believe we could still do business.

Declan signs off with his name and phone number but that's it. I read the email twice but it's so different from my own memory – from what *actually* happened – that it's like he's writing about a different person. I stare at my name – Rose Denton, Ms Denton – and it's me. But it's another me. No. It's *not* me.

'I didn't do this,' I say.

Graham takes the page and scans it himself.

'I was a professional,' I add. 'If anything, he was the strange one. We shook hands at the end and he held on for a little too long.'

'You never said anything.'

And this is the problem. Of course I never said anything because, to a degree, this sort of behaviour *is* normal. Small instances like this – a touch on the arm or thigh, a hand on the nape of a person's back – happen all the time. And to whom would I report it? Graham propositioned me himself while we were away at that conference *and* we were both married.

'It didn't feel like much at the time,' I say, hating myself for it. Perhaps if I mentioned this sort of thing every time it happened, it would stop happening. 'This isn't true,' I add. 'Almost none of it. We talked business, we swapped business cards, he said he'd be in contact and that was it.'

'So nothing untoward occurred?'

'No!'

'I have to ask.'

He says that as if he really does. As if he's giving a political grilling, not talking to someone who's worked for him for more than a decade.

'No,' I repeat, more firmly this time. The confusion is becoming full-on anger.

Graham presses back into his chair, the damning page of lies in his hand. He scans it once more and purses his lips.

'He's doing this for a lower price,' I say. 'It's in the final line. If you call him, he'll quote something below what I said and claim that was the special rate. He told me it was a small business and his office was empty. I bet he can't really afford it.'

Graham finally puts the page down.

'It *would* be a new client for you…'

I stare at him and it takes me a second to get the words out: 'Are you joking?'

'Do I look like I am?'

He definitely doesn't. His eyebrows are arched down, meeting in the middle. He's not an attractive frowner.

I know what he's going to say a moment before says it. He glances away from me towards the door and then spins a quarter-turn in his chair so that he can admire the photos of himself on the wall. I follow his gaze, focusing on a sign that reads: 'ATTACK EACH DAY'. This is, presumably, the type of meaningless bilge he learns on his weekend retreats. If attacking each day means spending hours at a time alone in an office, then he's nailed it.

'I'm going to have to stop you seeing clients,' he says. There's a brief pause and then he adds: 'Temporarily.'

'How temporarily?'

'I actually *have* called Mr Irons. He mentioned contacting the ombudsman with the complaint…'

'Did he ask about a discount?'

Graham doesn't answer, which is as good as a big, fat 'yes'. Of course he did.

'Did he *actually* contact the ombudsman, or just mention it?'

Graham shakes his head. 'I can't risk it. I'm sure it'll all go away in a week or so.'

'You mean after you've agreed to his price. You know that's blackmail.'

He doesn't react. 'You can continue to work from your desk, use the phones, and so on.'

'What's the point? If I set up any leads, someone else will end up getting the sale.'

He throws both hands up, palms to the ceiling. 'It is what it is. Leave it with me. I hope it'll all be sorted soon enough.'

I stand a little too abruptly, knocking the chair over. I should storm out, slam a few doors, tell him what I really think of him.

But I don't.

With Dan and me separating, I need this job more than ever. I'll have bills to pay, food to buy. Olivia doesn't make much to contribute and I don't want her money anyway. Dan might pay his part of the mortgage but we've not got that far yet. I don't know what's going to happen – and being unemployed would only make things worse.

I only realise I'm clenching my fists when I feel the nail on my index finger pierces the skin of my palm.

I don't call Graham an arsehole and I don't slam the door. I *do* pick up the chair and put it back into place. I'm about to stomp out when Graham stops me by saying my name.

'What?' I reply.

'Don't even think about contacting Mr Irons,' he says firmly.

'I wasn't—'

'I mean it. If you so much as text him, I'll have to fire you. I can't risk him complaining to the ombudsman.'

I try to think of a smart comeback but don't have one. I say nothing, spinning and walking out before returning to my desk. My palm isn't bleeding but there's a small pink slice in the base of my thumb from where I pinched it.

Natasha has mercifully stopped wittering on about her night out but I dig out a pair of earphones, plug them into my phone and find something to drown out any future noise anyway.

The rest of the day ticks along with typical humiliation. Claire asks me at one point if everything's okay – but she's the only person who talks to me. Graham doesn't leave his office. All of that is fine by me as I sit and stew. I wonder if the others are talking about me. Laughing about me. It's the way things go in offices. One person knows and then everyone does. Natasha's going to love this when she finds out. Innocent or not, I'll never live this down for as long as I work here.

When I'm sure no one is watching, I register for a couple of jobs websites, though it isn't encouraging. Part of the problem of living where we do is that there isn't a lot of industry here. Most of the work is city-based, so there aren't many jobs to begin with. For the ones that do exist, the company bosses all know one another. It's a golf-playing private club and to work for one, I'd need a decent reference from another.

Beyond that, there's so much effort involved. The last time I put together a CV, it was based on one I'd created for school. I've let all the career stuff slip and I'd have to start from scratch.

The end of the day cannot come fast enough and, for the first time in a while, I'm literally counting down the minutes. I'm the first out the door when it's time to go but I've not even got to my car by the time the next problem has arisen.

Jason is sitting on my bonnet, casually swinging his legs and smoking a cigarette. He looks up, spotting me and giving a small wave. That happens at precisely the same time as Natasha and Claire leave the office. They stop and Natasha whispers something to Claire I don't catch. I'm caught in the middle, with little I can do other than hurry to my car.

'How did you know where I work?' I hiss.

Jason shrugs and flicks the cigarette butt towards a drain. 'Ell told me. I came on the bus, then walked for a bit.'

'What are you doing here?'

'I've been thinking things over since the cemetery.' He stumbles, stops, and starts again. 'Since *before* then. Since, well... ever.'

'Thinking over what?'

'When I got nicked all those years ago.'

'What about it?'

'I was wondering...' He stops, scratches his neck and then fiddles with the sleeve of his army jacket. He takes a breath and looks directly at me. 'I guess I was wondering if you were pregnant with my kid.'

THIRTY-THREE

I stare at Jason and it's like being back in Graham's office all over again. That feeling of dizziness; the confusion, the anger.

'What are you talking about?'

I'm shouting but it's too late now. Graham is leaving the office but he stops and stares across the car park to us. I can feel him questioning me. He knows I'm separating from my husband, that I'm accused of propositioning a client – and now I'm shouting at a strange man in his car park. I'm falling apart. Perhaps this is why I've been confined to my desk? Maybe he actually believes Declan.

Jason seems unaware of anyone other than me: 'I was thinking that you and I, well, y'know and then, well—'

'Get in the car.'

I unlock it and Jason does as he's told, slotting into the passenger seat as I start the engine. His clothes reek of stale cigarettes, like the smell that clings to walls and carpets and never quite goes. It reminds me of being young and there's comfort there – even though I haven't smoked in more than twenty years.

He clears his throat but has only got out the words, 'I think' when I shush him.

'We'll talk in a bit,' I say.

I keep an eye on the rear-view mirror as I drive. There's no particular logic behind it but I don't want to be heading in the same direction as any of my colleagues. I don't want to be stopped at traffic lights when Natasha or someone else pulls up alongside me and gets a good look at who's in the passenger seat. There's little chance anyone would know him – but that's not the point. This is my workplace and I can't have it crossing over with home. I've got too much going on as it is.

I drive with little direction, taking turns without much thought, not knowing where I might be going. I suppose it's fate when I realise what we're close to. There's a turn-off that becomes a narrow lane and then a dirt track. When it's rained heavily, it's impassable in anything less than a 4x4. A wet autumn will see leaves stick to the mud and then more dirt compacting on top. Nobody bothers to clear it because there's little here. For now, there is only a thin, dry carpet of dirt. We bump over that and then rattle over a cattle grid, even though I've never seen cows in the area. Eventually, I pull onto a patch of tarmac that has long since been abandoned. The cracks splinter in all directions, plants and weeds sprouting through the gaps. The trees hang low on all four sides, turning daylight into something close to night.

The engine is switched off and we sit facing front. I can't bring myself to look at him.

'You shouldn't have come to my work,' I say.

'I know, Rosie – but it's been eating me up.'

'Don't call me that.'

Rosie is what Wayne used to call me and then Jason copied him. It's a teenage nickname that isn't who I am any more. Ellie only ever used my actual name and no one's called me Rosie in decades.

Jason is chastened and goes silent, so I speak next: 'Why do you think I was pregnant? *When* do you think I was pregnant? I don't know what you're talking about.'

He unclips his seat belt and wriggles to free his jacket from underneath his backside. 'Before now, the last time I saw you was five or six months before the fire. We didn't use a johnny or anything…'

He's right – but I hadn't thought of what we did in that detail for a long time. I remembered the sex, of course – not because it was anything special, more because I regret everything about it. I've been fixated on the act, while he's seemingly spent a little over twenty years going over the specifics.

'Is that what you've been thinking about all this time?' I say.

Jason takes a few seconds to answer. I've probably embarrassed him. I don't want to know for sure but there's a good chance he hasn't been with a woman in all this time. It's no wonder he'd fixate on a precise instance.

'Even when I was on remand,' he says. 'I guess I thought…'

'Why would you think I was pregnant?'

A shrug: 'Because I didn't see you at all. Not in court, not in prison. I wondered if it's cos you were hiding something.'

'You thought I was hiding a *baby*?'

Another shrug. 'Or an abortion.'

For the second time today, I can't quite process what I'm hearing. It's like being told stories about someone else.

'None of that happened,' I say. 'None of it. It's all in your head, Jase. I didn't visit you in prison because I'd moved on. I'd started seeing Dan by the time you were in court. We got married a year after that. I've only ever been pregnant once – and that was with my daughter eighteen years ago. When I conceived her, I was already married and you were in prison.'

I twist in my seat, fighting against the seat belt and then unclipping it so I can turn properly. I want to see his face, to know that this delusion he's had is exactly that.

I press it because I need to see that he gets it: 'Do you understand what I'm saying, Jason?'

He nods solemnly, his Adam's apple bobbing. It looks like he's going to cry but I know I can't offer the assurance or comfort that he needs.

The car suddenly feels warm and the windows are starting to steam. I open my door and offer the best condolence I can with a firm 'come on'.

Jason follows my lead and we start walking through the trees, following the barely there trail that we used to know so well when we were teenagers. It's overgrown now, with leafy bushes and fallen trees invading the path. We continue on anyway, crunching our way around the blockages where necessary.

The babble of the river quickly becomes a thunder and it's not long before I can see the water as well as hear it. The trail starts to follow the river, widening out until we reach a clearing that's ringed with mossy low shrubs. For the first time in a long time, I can see the watermill on the edge of the bank. It's ringed by a six-foot chicken wire fence that's covered with red and yellow 'keep out' signs. The building itself is like a shrunken lighthouse, with a circular base that has a dome on top. Attached to the side is the waterwheel. A century or more ago, it was used to grind grains. I'm sure it was repaired and replaced over the years but, by the time we were teenagers, it was our hideaway. There's a large, rotting wooden circle that looks as if it could disintegrate at any moment. I can't see if any of the actual paddles are still intact. It would have once been majestic but now it's a crumbling mix of nails, screws, hooks and wood.

A chill licks along my spine that isn't because of the cold.

Jason and I stop in the clearing, listening to the roar of the river as we stare towards our old playground.

'Ellie says it's coming down soon,' I say.

'I can't believe it's still here.'

It's hard to hear much over the water, so we cut back towards the woods, finding shelter under the canopy of a sprawling oak. The watermill sits on the edge of my vision in the same way it does my thoughts.

'I'm sorry,' Jason says.

There's sincerity in what he says and that only makes me feel guiltier for my part in everything.

'I should've visited you,' I reply. 'Or written back at the very least. It wasn't fair.'

He shrugs. It's not like he can disagree.

'I couldn't face you,' I add. 'I was immature and stupid. Still getting over Wayne and the crash.'

Jason nods. He must know this is true. He's had twenty years to think about it.

'I was the rebound...'

He somehow makes it sound like a statement of fact and a question at the same time.

'Yes.'

The rustle of the woods and the ripple of the river take over our conversation for a moment as the wind whips venomously through the trees. It feels like nature itself is listening in.

'I didn't plan it like that,' I add. 'It's not like I woke up one morning and thought I'd replace one brother with the other. It just happened.'

We should have had this conversation all those years ago but some things only become apparent with time. Age changes people. It gives context and experience. Sometimes that's for the better, sometimes not.

'I think I knew that,' Jason replies. 'I wanted to be with you when you were seeing Wayne – and then, when you weren't… I let it happen. I—'

'Don't.'

He's about to say something else but stops in the middle of a word. I can't think of Wayne at the moment. It's too much.

'You went on hunger strike,' I say.

He's quiet for a moment and takes a few paces off towards the next tree, where he picks at a shard of loose bark. He'd rather not talk about it – but I could say the same.

'Did you want to kill yourself?' I ask.

'No.' He sighs and then quickly adds, 'Yes… Maybe… I don't know. I was messed up back then. They were going to let me die.'

'But you changed your mind?'

'I guess.'

He reaches out to take my hand but I pull away and shake my head. He reels back, embarrassed. He says sorry but I say there's no need. We stand awkwardly for a few moments and then I spot a tree stump on the edge of the clearing. The felled trunk stretches off into the woods, with moss and leaves clumping and growing, giving it a new lease of life. I cross the soft ground and then sit on the stump. Jason follows, sitting on the other side so that we're back to back. I lean against him and he presses against me so that we're supporting one another's weight.

'Was it because of me?' I ask.

'What?'

'The fire, the trouble… was that all because we broke up?'

I feel his chest rising through his back. 'What do you want me to say?'

'That it's not my fault.'

He says nothing. One second. Two. Three. It's enough.

I slump forward a little, holding my head in my hands. It's not news, I suppose. My boyfriend died and I rebounded onto his brother, who'd always had a crush on me. When I realised what I was doing and broke it off, he went off the rails – and ended up behind bars. Among all that, my best friend is their sister.

I've known for a long time how much of a mess that all is. With Jason in prison, I've been able to suppress it, to forget my own role in it all. It's far more difficult to do that now. I sometimes think that what I did to Jason was the worst thing I ever did. I *knew* he had a crush on me. I was older and *I* let it happen.

'I should've said no to you,' I say. 'The problem was that, after that first time, it was already too late. You were never going to be your brother. We were always going to break up.'

'We didn't have to.'

'We did. You'd always remind me of him.'

There's a cough that might be a sob. All of this is long overdue. It should have been said back then. The truth is, Jason and I never had anything in common. It's not like we ever went out for meals, or cosy Sunday drives. We had no money. It was all cheap fags and booze. Everything between was physical. It made the pain of what happened with Wayne go away… even if it never lasted for long.

Jason's not speaking but I can feel his spine rubbing against mine as he bobs up and down.

'I didn't think Ellie would ever talk to me again,' I say. 'She didn't for a while. She was so angry at us – and then, after you were arrested, she started again.'

'She had nobody else. You were like sisters. Of course she turned to you.'

He's right – but she is *actually* his sister and he's had to make do with sporadic visits while Ellie and I have carried on as normal without him.

'Sorry.'

It's the only word I can say. I mean it but it doesn't feel like enough.

'Don't be. No one forced me to set fire to that pub.'

I feel his back tense, so stand and turn, looking down as his body straightens. His fists are balled tightly.

'What?' I say.

He doesn't turn. 'Sometimes I think about all the years I've lost.'

Perhaps it's not what he says but the way he says it. There's bubbling fury in his voice. A volcano that's hissing and fizzing, ready to blow. He practically spits the words and, for a moment, a ripple of fear surges through me. Nobody knows we're here and there's likely no one anyone near us. My guilt has put me in this position and now I'm stuck. A vein in Jason's neck bulges as he continues to squeeze his hands into coiled fists.

Can it be a coincidence that Jason's release has coincided with that morning I woke up in a field? With things going missing or being moved in the house? Perhaps it's not Dan at all, perhaps it's Jason – although it still wouldn't explain the stun gun in Dan's locker.

'You've got to stop hanging around the house,' I say.

He doesn't turn. 'Okay.'

'I'll give you my phone number. If you want to talk, or if you need to ask something, call me. Or text. Everyone texts nowadays. The world's different than it was when we were kids.'

He nods, still not turning around.

I take a step back towards the path, asking if he's coming. For a moment, I think he's going to stay where he is – but he doesn't. He stands, head bowed, hands in pockets and traipses with me back to the car.

I wanted his forgiveness, but the truth is, with or without it, I don't forgive myself. I swapped one brother for another – and that's one of those things a person simply doesn't do.

And then there's what I did to Wayne.

THIRTY-FOUR

- SATURDAY -

The bed in the spare room is so comfortable that I have no idea why I didn't start sleeping in here months or years before. I suppose it was the stigma of separate bedrooms – but it's fantastic. I wrap myself around the pillow: one arm under, one over, then spread out and close my eyes. There are no errant limbs crossing the invisible no man's land along the centre of the bed. No invading forces to repel. No grunts and snores in the middle of the night – or, if there are, they belong to me and nobody else cares. It's a whole new world. Why did anyone ever decide that couples needed to sleep – actually *sleep* – together?

I expect to dream of Dan and Jason, of unexplained guns, of steering wheels, blood, cloudy nights and shadowed fields. It's only when I wake up the next morning that I realise hours have passed. My arm is dead from barely moving but the fuzz has cleared from my thoughts and I finally feel alert.

I shower, dress and head downstairs. Dan is on the sofa and snaps the laptop lid closed as I cross to the kitchen. Not much point in asking what he was looking at.

'I can move out in two weeks,' he says.

His words stop me dead, still a pace or two from the kettle.

'Sorry?'

'Two weeks,' he repeats. 'I got an email from the landlord overnight. The old tenants are moving out early because they're buying a place. One minute the sale was on, then it was off, now it's back on again. You know what these things can be like: nothing happens for months and then it's all go.'

I quickly recompose myself, or attempt to give that impression at least. I touch the side of the kettle and it's warm, so I start to make myself a cup of tea.

'That's a bit quicker than we thought,' I say.

'True – but that's not a problem, is it?'

'No, but I suppose we've not really talked everything through in regards to money and the house…'

Dan waits as I fill the mug with water, drop a teabag in and then give it a swish and a squeeze with a spoon. Traditionalists would blow a gasket at the spoon usage.

I perch on the second sofa, cradling the mug for warmth. After all the talking, it finally feels as if this is happening.

'I'd hope we can agree that it's better to do this without lawyers,' Dan says. 'The minute we involve them, any money will get soaked up. We're both adults, after all.'

The way he says it makes it sound like an implication that *he's* the adult and *his* plan is the grown-up thing to do. Anything else would be childish.

I let it go.

'That sounds like a good place to start,' I reply.

'We've each got our own cars, so no reason to change anything about that…'

He pauses for a moment but I agree.

When it's clear I'm fine with the suggestion, he asks if there's anything in particular that I want.

I look around the room, taking in the television, the phone docks, the appliances in the kitchen. I'd not thought of it much before but it's quickly apparent that this is all just stuff. In the end, none of it matters. Possessions can be replaced and it's people who matter.

'Olivia's box,' I reply. 'That's all.'

He nods. There's a small plastic crate under our bed that is a chronicle of Olivia's life. It has a couple of her baby teeth, for which the tooth fairy gave her a pound a piece. Inflation these days. There is some of her hair, photos, school reports, paintings, handprints from when she was a baby. I kept her first pair of shoes, which are small enough to wear as finger-warmers. She wrote a couple of letters to Santa when she was young that I still have; another to Jesus. Olivia was sporty when she was little – and she was part of the first-ever girl's football team at her school. I've got the team photo and a report from the local paper. She was third in a handwriting competition and I have her entry for that. There are swimming certificates, running certificates, computer proficiency test results – and so many more odds and ends.

When things have been bad between Olivia and I, when we've not spoken for days, I'll go through the box and remind myself of better times.

'I'd never want to take that from you,' Dan replies. 'Are you sure there's nothing else?'

'Not really. What about you? Is there anything else you particularly want?'

'The iPad.'

'Take it.'

'Oh.'

He reels back a little, perhaps surprised there's no argument.

'I don't need any furniture,' he says. 'Not yet anyway. The flat is fully furnished. Perhaps in six months or so, depending on how things go. IKEA's cheap enough, so I can go there if need be. It's not like we've ever done extravagant.'

I more or less knew that already, so say nothing.

Dan is in his running gear but it doesn't work with the way a deputy headteacher sits. He has his knees crossed and swaps them so they're crossed the other way. It all looks a bit odd, like a drunken giraffe trying to perch on the floor. It's like he has too many limbs. He shuffles uncomfortably before zeroing his attention in on me.

'I suppose the biggest issue is the house…'

'Right.'

'I know you'd rather stay here – and obviously that's good for Liv. But I guess she won't be living here forever. After that, it's a big place for one person…'

'I don't want to sell it.'

He nods officiously, expecting this. 'I was thinking we could have it valued and then split the total. Obviously, some of our joint savings will cover whatever's owed.'

'You want to take all of our savings?'

I want him to turn away, to feel awkward, but he doesn't. He continues to stare. 'Only to offset part of the house's value.'

'But there's no way my half of our savings is going to cover half the value of the house. I'll end up owing you tens of thousands.'

He still won't relent and turn away. 'We could remortgage. Or *you* could remortgage. We'll put the house into your name, get the lump sum to pay me off and then the house is all yours.'

It sounds so matter-of-fact. Not a discussion but a decision made. I realise it is precisely that. He's thought all this through without me and now he's presenting it.

He's right, of course. There's no easy way out of this. If I want to continue living here, I'm going to have to buy his share. I don't have the money for that, so I'll have to remortgage. I'll be back at the place I was years ago – working month to month to pay off a house. By the time that's done, I'll be ready to retire. Some life, huh?

'What about Olivia?' I ask.

'She can continue to live here, obviously.'

'I mean as an inheritance. If we're her parents, wouldn't we want to leave her the house eventually? If it's all mine, then what are you contributing?'

He bites his lip, uncrosses his knees and pushes back onto the sofa. It's so satisfying to have stumped him – although I do wonder how our daughter's future has completely escaped him.

'Perhaps we can figure something out once we have a valuation,' he says.

'Figure *what* out?'

'I don't know… perhaps split the house three ways. I'll gift you Olivia's share, and then you buy out my share.'

'You don't need to gift *me* anything. She's *our* daughter. You're doing this for her.'

He chews on the inside of his mouth and it feels like we're about to argue. He'll say I know what he meant, I'll say I know *exactly* what he meant. He'll ask what I mean by that. I'll reply that he always puts himself ahead of anyone else, including our daughter. And then it'll explode. He'll storm out, I'll sit and stew. We won't talk tonight or tomorrow – and then, at some point next week, we'll start again with trying to figure it all out. We've been in similar positions so many times before.

Dan pushes himself up from the sofa and smooths down his vest. 'I've got to go,' he says. 'I'll be at the gym for a couple of hours, then I'm doing lunch. I'll be back this afternoon. We can talk about this again later or tomorrow. I'll have a think and you can do the same. Perhaps we'll come up with a better idea? I'm not adverse to anything.'

He doesn't elaborate on what 'doing lunch' means. On whether he's by himself, or with someone else. And, if he's with someone, then who. I hate the way he says it anyway. You don't 'do' lunch, you eat lunch.

It's not lunch that's the real problem, of course. I'm going to be in someone's debt for decades – if not Dan's then the bank's. I'm stuck. Not only that, he's right: Olivia will be leaving soon and I'll be alone. Perhaps I *should* let the house be sold. I can hold on until Olivia's found somewhere of her own, then we can sell and split the money. I'll use my half to have a midlife crisis. I can travel and explore and… stop imagining such fantasy nonsense.

I won't do any of that.

Dan's already in the hall when I call him back from the living room. He pokes his head around the door frame, surprised at the interruption to his routine.

'You all right?' he asks.

'Work are organising this group bonding thing at the end of the month,' I say.

'Okay…?'

'They're talking about going shooting. I think it's clay pigeons, something like that. I don't know. Someone else mentioned going to a range so we can be indoors. I was wondering if you know much about it.'

He steps back into the room. His head is tilted, his eyebrows dipped in bemusement. We never talk about things like this. 'Much about what?'

'Guns. Shooting. Things like that.'

He frowns and then holds his hands up. 'You know I don't. I didn't know it was your sort of thing.'

'It's probably not. I guess I was wondering if you've ever shot anything…?'

It's as subtle as a sledgehammer – but I can't think of a better way of asking him about the stun gun in his locker. I could ask him outright – but then I'd be admitting my own snooping.

His body language doesn't shift. He continues to stand with a straight back, features unmoving.

'When would I have shot a gun?' he asks.

'I don't know. I was only asking.'

'I'm the wrong person to ask.' He glances to his watch. 'Was that all?'

I tell him it is and then he spins on his heels. The front door clicks closed and I listen as his car engine starts to grumble.

All these years and I never realised how good a poker player my husband is. My question was hardly waterboarding, but he didn't crack at all. If it wasn't for the fact I'd seen the gun in his locker, I'd swear it didn't exist. I know it was a *taser* in his locker, but it's still a weapon. I'm sure he would have still reacted to the word, 'gun'. He's also left me in a position where I either have to ask him directly about it, forget about it, or do something unpredictable, like tell the police.

I'm still thinking that over when there's the sound of a key scratching against the lock. By the time I get into the hallway, Dan is back inside.

'Forget something?' I ask – but he shakes his head and holds the front door wider.

Behind him are constables O'Neill and Marks. PC Marks' friendly smile seems a long way away as she shares her colleague's grim look.

It seems obvious why.

'You've found Tyler…?' I say.

I expect forbidding acceptance. Something awful has happened to him and I'm going to have to break the news to poor Liv.

PC O'Neill shakes his head. 'I'm afraid not. Can we come in?'

He looks between Dan and I, but neither of us protest. Dan holds the door open and the officers wipe their feet before stepping into the hall. We all move through to the living room and I close the door, pointing upwards and telling them that Olivia is sleeping.

The officers exchange a quick glance. 'We might have to speak to her,' PC O'Neill says.

'Why?'

'I believe there was a possible break-in here a few days ago…?'

'Right.'

'There was a blood sample taken from your garage…?'

It's clear he knows the answers to these questions and I again confirm he's correct.

He takes a breath and, in that moment, I know what he's about to say. My knee wobbles but I hold onto the back of the sofa, maintaining some degree of control.

'We've got the results back on the blood,' PC O'Neill says. 'It belongs to Tyler Lambert.'

THIRTY-FIVE

I stare from one officer to the other, expecting some sort of follow-up. I'm not simply holding onto the back of the sofa for support any longer, it's the only thing holding me up. My legs are jelly.

I killed Tyler.

Me.

Not Dan with that stun gun; not Jason with his cryptic remarks about people getting what they deserve. Not Frank going after his own son for whatever reason.

None of them.

It was me.

When I woke up in that field in the early hours of Tuesday, Tyler's blood was on my car.

'Are you okay?'

It's PC Marks who speaks. She's calm, using that measured tone that public service workers like police officers, doctors and nurses can pull off so well. Dan does it, too. For a long time, I believed it was because someone genuinely cared. After the arguments with Dan, the passive aggression and the breakdown of our relationship, I've become confused about it all. I've wondered if that tone is an act. I'm muddled at whether strangers really do care.

'Surprised, I suppose,' I manage.

PC O'Neill responds this time, asking to talk to Olivia.

Dan seems a little bemused and I can't read him. I'm not sure how but I make my way to the stairs without my knees giving way. There was a second after they confirmed it was Tyler's blood in which I assumed they knew everything. They were here to arrest me and it was game over. As it is, it's not even me they want to talk to. It should have been obvious. The clearest reason for his blood to be in our garage isn't because I hit him with a car, it's because he spends time at the house with Olivia. At some point, they were in the garage and he cut himself. Simple.

I forget about the creaky stair and wince as the screech echoes through the house. I push open Olivia's door and whisper 'Liv' through the darkness. She's a groaning mass of bedcovers as she asks the time. I reply that the police want to speak to her and she sits up so quickly that it makes me jump backwards. Like a scene from *The Exorcist*.

'Have they found him?'

'No.'

There's a pause as she wriggles against the sheets, fumbling her legs over the side of the bed. 'He's not…?'

'They don't know,' I reply. 'They're not here to say he's dead. They only want to talk to you.'

She says she'll be right down and so I turn on the light and close the door for her, heading back downstairs to sit awkwardly with the officers. Dan's on one of the sofas making small talk, out of place in his running shorts compared to their uniforms and my regular clothes. There's nowhere for me to sit other than next to him and it feels so weird. We're husband and wife, yet we haven't sat by one another in years. It's always on separate sofas, or across from each other if we end up going out for a meal with mutual friends. I'm paranoid that the police must notice our awkwardness. He's in one corner, me in the other. It's like either or both of us have a contagious disease that the other is trying to avoid. If the constables do see it, then they say nothing. Instead we talk about weather and roadworks. About plans for the weekend and what's on telly tonight. The usual. I play the part well enough, or think I do; my stomach is doing cartwheels.

It takes around five minutes for Olivia to come downstairs. She's in jeans and a T-shirt. Her hair is unwashed, the pink dull and faded. She still has bedhead. I ask if she wants my spot on the sofa but she's already plonked herself cross-legged on the carpet in front of the officers as they explain about finding a patch of Tyler's blood in our garage.

Olivia turns to look at her father and me and it's clear she has no idea what's being talked about.

'How do you know it's his blood?' she asks.

'The sample from your garage was tested and compared to the DNA database,' PC O'Neill says. 'Mr Lambert is in there because of his shoplifting convictions. It's a one hundred per cent match.'

He waits for another question and, when it doesn't come, adds: 'Do you have any idea how Tyler's blood could be in your garage?'

I look to Dan and then Olivia, hoping somebody other than me might answer.

Dan's the first one to speak with an odd-sounding, 'I'm not at home much.'

It's true, but it's a strange way to answer the question. I think he realises it because he then offers a prompting, 'Liv…?'

'No,' she says. 'We never went in the garage.'

This is bad. This is *really* bad.

PC Marks writes on a pad while PC O'Neill leans forward. 'You *never* went in the garage?' he asks. 'Not once?'

Olivia shrugs. 'Why would we? None of my stuff's in there. I never go in there, let alone Tyler.'

'Is he interested in cars at all?'

'He couldn't care less.'

'Have you ever left the house through the garage?'

'That's what the front door's for.'

She replies clinically and it's good to know it isn't only me she can make sound like a fool.

PC O'Neill is unmoved. 'Is there any chance he could have gone in there by himself. When you weren't around, perhaps?'

'Like when?'

'I don't know. That's what I'm asking.'

There's frustration in her voice when she replies. That annoyance that other people don't see Tyler as she does. I've heard it so many times myself. 'No. He wouldn't go in there without me.'

The constable holds her in a firm gaze for a moment and then nods.

There's a silence in which I can't help but think of all the quotes from television. Things like, 'It's always someone close to the victim'. It sounds like a cliché but it's probably true. Do they suspect Dan? Me? Olivia? Is that what this is about?

'That does leave us in rather a quandary,' PC O'Neill says.

'Why?' Olivia replies.

'Because if he never went into the garage, then how did his blood get in there?'

'I…' Olivia stops herself and then starts to rock. She can't answer because she doesn't know.

Dan's voice cuts across everything. 'Perhaps we should get a lawyer…?'

I turn to stare at him and then I realise that everyone's doing the same. Olivia's the first to question him.

'Why?'

'Because there are questions that none of us seem able to answer.'

I turn from him to a gaping Liv to a pair of officers with unreadable straight faces. Is Dan right? Are we really suspects and this casual visit is anything but? Does he believe Olivia's not being entirely truthful? Does he suspect me? Or is it guilt on his behalf? He used the stun gun on Tyler for whatever reason and now he's scrambling to cover himself?

'I haven't done anything wrong, Dad.'

Olivia's stung and the air is suddenly thick, like a smoggy August day before a thunderstorm.

'I'm not saying you have—'

'So why do I need a lawyer?'

'It's complicated, love. I'm not saying—'

She spins back to the officers: 'Ask me whatever you want. I want you to find him.'

Dan shuts up but there's a big part of me that thinks he probably knows what he's talking about. If the officers suspect Olivia for whatever reason, then she could talk herself into trouble even is she's done nothing. Not only that, the blood might have come from *my* car. *I* should be the suspect.

I don't know what to do, so I end up doing nothing.

And then Olivia proves how much smarter than me she is by saying something that hadn't crossed my mind.

'Do you think Tyler broke in?' she asks. 'You think he got in through the back door, cut himself somehow and then bled in the garage?'

Sometimes I can be so thick-headed. PC Marks shifts in her seat and it's obvious that's what they think. Why didn't I come up with that? The answer's obvious. Not only am I paranoid about Dan and his intentions but I'm convinced I did something awful on the night I woke up in the field.

It's PC O'Neill who answers. 'That's a possibility we're examining,' he says.

Classic police speak. It's up there with 'proceeding in a northerly direction'.

'Have you noticed anything missing?' he adds.

Everyone's looking at Olivia and she must feel it because she hugs herself a little tighter, shrinking under the attention. The thing with Olivia is that, deep down, we really do share a lot of the same traits. I was happy with my own small group of friends when I was her age, never caring for the approval of adults. She's like that, too – except her look is her shield.

It took me a long time to realise that I picked the wrong battles with her. Her hair's pink now – and it's fine. But I was furious when she dyed it black the first time. It seems so silly now and I don't remember why I cared. I told her to wash it out but she refused. It was permanent, so I don't even know why I was arguing. When she turned it silver, I said she was blessed with youth; that older people do all they can to *not* have hair that colour. I wish I'd simply told her that it suited her. I made a fuss over tattoos, over too much make-up, the piercings. In the end, none of that matters. She's still the vulnerable, shy, introverted kid inside. All of the other stuff is the way she wants to portray herself. The hair colour, the piercings, the tattoos are about confidence. She likes those things, so it gives her self-assurance. That is then projected to everyone else. It's a good thing, and yet I tried to make it negative. I made it about me instead of about her.

I never understood that until it was too late.

The wrong battles were fought and lost. When it came to the right battle – Tyler – Oliva was too far gone to care for my opinion. And why should she? I'd been wrong about all those other things.

That confidence she portrays through her look is evaporating now as she pulls at the metal bar that pierces her right ear in two places.

'I'm not missing anything,' she says.

PC O'Neill looks up to me.

'There was fifty pounds in the kitchen drawer,' I say. 'Or, I *think* there was. It's been there forever – emergency money. It's gone now. That's the only thing I've noticed.'

Dan says he thinks there was money in the drawer, adding that he's not noticed anything else missing.

The constable focuses back on Olivia. 'Do you know of any reason why Tyler might have been in the house?'

'No.'

'Or the garage specifically?'

'No.'

'Did he have a key?'

'No.'

We go around in circles for a while. The officers clarify some information from the last time they were here, but there's no getting over that Olivia insists Tyler wouldn't have been in the garage. She asks if they have any idea where he might be and they tell her they've checked his debit card use and mobile phone records, plus the small amount of local CCTV footage, all to no avail. They're not as brutally direct as they could be but the message is clear – they have no idea what happened to him.

They do say the quality of photos received from Frank weren't great and ask Olivia if she has anything better. She scrolls through her phone with practised ease, her thumbs a blur until she twists the screen to show them a selection of images. The officers ask her to email the pictures to them, which she does in about two seconds.

They seem in no hurry to leave and it's PC Marks who picks up the conversation, asking if there's anything particular by which Tyler can be identified. 'Does he have any tattoos, for instance,' she says. 'We've gone through this with his father but figured you might have a better idea.'

'He's got the letters TY tattooed on his chest,' Olivia replies. She pats her left side, pointing out the spot as the officer makes a note.

'Anything else?' PC Marks asks.

'No other tattoos but he always wears his tags,' Olivia adds.

'Tags?'

'Dog tags. I bought them for his birthday last year. He was really into army stuff at the time.'

'Is there anything distinctive about it? A logo? Something like that?'

'It has T-Y on one side and O-D on the other.' She pauses and then quickly adds: 'Olivia Denton.'

PC Marks nods. We all got it, but her initials are unfortunate when it comes to a gift for her boyfriend, who may or may not be into drugs.

'Do you have a picture?'

She does, of course. Olivia flicks through her phone, finding another photo and emailing that to the officer as well. Now that she's mentioned it, I remember the small rectangle of silver attached to a chain that Tyler always seemed to be wearing. I didn't know Olivia bought it for him. He played with it absent-mindedly and, though it's really annoying, there were bigger things to be frustrated about when it comes to Tyler.

The officers check a couple of other things with Olivia but I'm not listening. I've done my best to avoid the inevitable, to try to forget waking up in that field, but it's obvious what I have to do. It was apparent before and even more so now.

I need to find out what happened in the Grand Ol' Royal Hotel.

THIRTY-SIX

After the police leave, Dan heads off to the gym for the second time. On this occasion, he doesn't return with the police after a minute. Olivia has an afternoon shift at the café. She says she'll be fine and I get the sense she wants to be by herself. I don't blame her.

With no weekend work appointments because of my suspension, I have two whole days with nothing to do.

I plot a drive to the hotel, making sure to follow something close to the route by which I returned in the early hours of Tuesday morning. It's a brighter day, crisp with a blue sky and a low sun. Perhaps it's that, or maybe it's something within me, but the country lanes don't hold the fear they did just days ago. I pass the spot where I spoke to the farmer and pull onto the side, craning to stare towards the field. The hole is still in the hedge, as are the tyre tracks veering from the road across the verge. I should continue on but stop the engine and get out. If the farmer from the other day were to return, he'd no doubt have some questions about why I'm here again – but there's a part of me that feels drawn here. I walk along the verge, knowing I've already done this in the dark and the light. There are weeds and nettles; grass and small shrubs.

No blood.

No trace that there was anything, or anyone, out of the ordinary other than me.

I get back in the car and don't stop again, following the route to the dual carriageway and then back onto more leafy lanes as I go around Leamington Spa. The roads are wider here, with large houses and long driveways interspersed with signs for farms.

The Grand Ol' Royal is one of those hotels that has taken an age-old building and pushed it into the twenty-first century. There are business meeting rooms, wedding packages, a spa, two pools, and any number of other amenities. The board at the front is advertising a wedding fair for next weekend and a kids' fun day for the one after that. There's a long driveway lined with vast lush lawns on either side. A pair of gardeners are up ladders on the far side, trimming the hedge with a sheet underneath. All this is familiar so far. There are fountains on either side of the drive as I near the hotel itself and then I follow the signs to the car park at the side.

It's packed.

There are arrows for the 'Martin' wedding party pointing in one direction and another for the 'James' marriage directing people the other way. There's no space in the main car park, so I continue following the gravel until I find a spot in the furthest corner, shielded from the sun by the shadow of the hedge.

The hotel lobby is a vast expanse of extravagance. Lord knows how I persuaded Graham to let me put a night here on expenses. The floor is an echoing, solid marble, with dual staircases winding up on either side. The whole area is full of people milling around in suits and fancy dresses. High heels click-clack on the floor and there's a staccato chatter of people talking over each other.

The line to check in is a good dozen couples long, each with small suitcases or bags at their feet. There's no point in waiting for someone at the reception desk – and I'm not sure that's the best thing to do anyway. Instead, I do what everyone else is doing – mingle. I'm not as fancily dressed as most but I'm smart enough in a work skirt and top. I certainly don't stand out.

Weddings are a great place for freeloaders to get away with it because a vast majority of the guests only vaguely know everyone else anyway. I don't involve myself in anyone else's conversation but I listen in to plenty. I'm hoping to jog my memory of what happened on Monday night but, aside from the check-in desk, the lobby brings back nothing.

As for the reception desk, I remember checking in because my keycard didn't work the first time and I had to return to get it reprogrammed. There was no line then – but it doesn't do much to help me recall what happened.

I follow the hall to the lifts, where there is a bank of three. It's the noise that brings back the memories. There's a steady *ding-ding-ding* as the elevators slot into place and then set off again. Like being in a seaside arcade. On quiet days, when the noise echoes through the corridors, it must drive the staff bonkers.

The hall leads to a sign that directs people to ground-floor rooms to the left and the bar to the right. I head towards the bar. The floor is still an echoing marble, with vast paintings on the walls, showing Britain's green and pleasant land.

It's here that something starts to buzz at the back of my mind. There's a painting of a ship being battered by the wind a little offshore. A lighthouse is in the background but its beam is searing in the opposite direction. It's fuzzy and unclear, like a dream I can barely remember, but I know this painting. I walked past it and stopped to look at some point.

Further on and the bar is more like a bank converted to a fancy wine bar than it is any sort of traditional country pub. The ceiling is high, making everything echo more than usual and there are floor-to-ceiling windows that show off the lavish lawns beyond. There's a small chapel-like hut in the centre, where some of the wedding guests are starting to gather.

More still are mingling in the bar, of course. It's more relaxed here; jackets on the backs of chairs, handbags strewn on tables.

I order myself a sparkling water so that I can at least fit in with everyone else who has a drink in hand. The barman is young and slim in a tight waistcoat. He's friendly but busy, drifting from one person to the next, multitasking with dazzling ease.

With no other ideas, I do a lap of the room. There's a small dance floor in the corner but the rest of the space is filled with tables and chairs. Everything is familiar but it's unclear and muddied in my mind. As if someone has told me about this place, rather than I've been here before.

It's only when I stop and check the menu that I have another spark of familiarity. I drank here – but I ate here as well. The tortellini is described as 'delicious filled rings of handmade pasta' and I know I laughed at that when I read it days before. The beef burger is 'luxurious minced rump in a toasted brioche bun, with ripened plum tomatoes, leafy lettuce and chipped potatoes on the side'.

Chipped potatoes? They're called chips.

It goes on and on. A hungry punter can't order rice, but they can get 'gently simmered granules of wholegrain Arborio'. A pizza has, 'a hand-milled wholemeal base, with seasonally sourced sundried tomato sauce'.

Someone, somewhere has a lot of time on their hands.

It's only reading this menu when it dawns on me that I laughed about this with the man I met.

Stephen.

His name had escaped me until now but it suddenly appears in my mind as if the letters have been painted there. How did I forget? We laughed at the salad with its 'lovingly shredded lettuce', saying how there would be a frustrated poet sitting in the kitchen delicately tearing leaves while Spandau Ballet played in the background.

It's only now that I realise how little I remember. It sounds obvious but I've assumed all week that the last thing I could recall was being in my room and settling down to sleep. I *do* remember that – but only as a flash. There's an enormous gap before that.

I remember drinking at the bar, then eating at a table by the window. Stephen and I could see the outline of the chapel through the dark but couldn't quite make out what it was. I had the tortellini and Stephen ordered the risotto. Both meals took a long time to arrive but we only noticed because the waiter mentioned it. The time had flown as we'd chatted and laughed. We returned to the bar for another drink, we headed for the lifts – which I came to remember – and then… I don't know. I'm back in the room, with that flash of the tight sheets – but that's it. In between the bar and bed, there must be at least an hour that I can't remember.

The tables are a little too close to each other but I weave between them until I'm at the bar once more. I take a stool this time, sitting and closing my eyes.

Listening. Breathing.

The hum of voices provides a constant buzz alongside the clinking of glasses and the scratch of cutlery. There's a low undercurrent of innocuous, inoffensive elevator music. It's nothing memorable as such – but I feel myself drifting back to the other night. It's the same melody; gentle and pleasant, like being rocked to sleep.

'You all right?'

I jump, opening my eyes and momentarily disorientated as someone touches me on the arm. I wince away, taking in a man in an ill-fitting suit. He's older than me, perhaps early fifties, with his top button undone and his tie loose.

'Steady on, love,' he says.

'I, um…'

'You were wobbling there.' He nods at my glass of water. 'Bit too much of the hard stuff?'

'Something like that.'

He swigs from a pint of dark amber liquid. 'Gotta pace yourself on days like this. Long night ahead.'

The man laughs at his own joke, though from the way he's rocking on the stool, his pace seems to be going hard and going early.

'Which wedding are you with?' he asks.

I hold up my left hand, showing my wedding ring. The only reason I still wear it is that it's too difficult to take off. I've tried washing-up liquid with dental floss but it's stuck hard. Ellie told me something about putting a hand in a tray of ice and having a go but I've not got around to it.

'I'm here with my husband,' I reply.

He grunts something I don't catch and then adds, 'Right you are then', before shuffling to the other side of his stool.

Through the window, I can see one of the wedding parties beginning to form by the chapel. The groom and best man are making nervous small talk with the registrar at the front as the trussed-up guests try to figure out where they're going to be sitting.

I take that as a sign and head back through to reception, which is decidedly emptier than it was before. A lone bellboy is busy wheeling various cases up and down the floor, the wheels creating something close to an atomic boom. I dodge around him and head to reception, where the queue has disappeared to nothingness. A twenty-something man in a sharp grey suit is busy typing on a keyboard but looks up and smiles with practised charm when I approach the desk.

I get the full-on 'madam' treatment, before I explain that I stayed here on Monday night.

'I made friends with someone in the bar,' I say. 'Another guest. He left behind his petrol station loyalty card but I didn't realise until it was too late. His name's Stephen. I was hoping you might be able to help me track him.'

The receptionist has one of those smirks that has a barely concealed 'get stuffed' directly behind it. He smiles as he explains that he can't do anything, throwing around words like 'privacy' and 'data protection' liberally.

'Is there no way you can check?' I say. 'I'm only asking for a name, perhaps a telephone number…'

A shake of the head. 'Sorry, Ma'am.'

'Just his name?'

'I wish I could.'

I bet he does.

I dig into my bag and remove my purse, delving around for a scruffy folded-up twenty. 'I don't suppose this would help, would it?'

His name badge reads Peter and his eyes narrow as he takes in the allure of the purple paper. He checks over his shoulder and then snatches the note away. He types something into the computer and then frowns.

'What did you say his name was?'

'Stephen.'

'There wasn't anyone here called Stephen staying on Monday.'

He twists the monitor so I can see. There's a list that's sorted by first name which jumps straight from Sonia Somethingorother to Terry Thingamabob. No Stephen, regardless of the spelling. No Steves, either.

'Do you want me to check another name?' he asks, the data protection act seemingly long forgotten.

I shuffle on the spot, trying to think. He definitely said his name was Stephen. He even said 'with a P-H' when I asked about the spelling. I'd forgotten but the memory is now as clear as if it had just happened.

'I suppose he could have checked in on a different day…?'

'This is a list of everyone staying here on Monday, regardless of which day they checked in. Was he definitely a guest here?'

I remember that, too. He said he was on the third floor. I didn't ask about a room number but he told me he had a good view of the gardens.

'Is there CCTV I could check?'

His smile loosens at this. 'I really *don't* have access to that.'

A woman appears a little behind, wielding one of those massive cases that somehow still count as hand luggage. It's the type of bag someone spends half an hour trying to shove into an overhead bin on a plane as everyone's waiting to take off. She hefts it along in front of her with an enormous sigh.

The receptionist glances to her and then gives me his best *get stuffed* smile. It's even better than last time and, on this occasion, I take the hint.

THIRTY-SEVEN

I'm a little lost on what to do as I crunch across the car park. I have more knowledge than I did this morning – of the man I was with nights ago – but I have no idea how I might track him down. I can picture his face, the rash of dark black stubble peppering his cheeks and chin, plus the matching glossy dark hair which was that perfect length of smart but not quite shaggy. He had thick eyebrows but clearly waxed or did something similar to keep them tidy. His eyes were dark brown, a little set back, with that smouldering stare that makes a person feel as if they're the only one who matters.

In my mind, he was one of those handsome young guys who create a start-up company and make millions right away. Either that, or an aspiring actor. He was handsome, funny and, better than all that, he actually wanted to talk to me.

I'm most of the way back to the car when I spot a young man struggling to do up a pair of cufflinks as he hurries in the opposite direction. He's wearing the same black trousers and maroon staff waistcoat as the other men at the hotel. We're almost past each other when our eyes lock and there's a moment of recognition. He's someone I've met before and I can see that he knows me, too. He has freckles and short red hair but is otherwise unremarkable.

I reach out a hand towards him and say hello.

He stops and turns until we're facing each other.

'I know you, don't I…?' I say.

His gaze darts away towards the hotel as he mutters a brisk, 'Don't think so.'

He takes half a step but I reach out and catch his arm. I don't grip tight, just enough to stop him. His name badge reads 'Gavin'.

'I was here on Monday night,' I say. 'I was in the bar. You were here, too.'

He shrugs. 'I work here.'

'Right… but you *do* recognise me, don't you?'

A smirk drifts momentarily across Gavin's lips before he conceals it by scratching his nose. 'I served you drinks,' he says. 'I'm running late. Sorry. I've got to go.'

I stop him once more. 'Sorry, I'm not a nutter… I mean, I know a nutter would say that, but I'm honestly not. I'm trying to remember someone I was with on Monday. We were both in the bar together. Can you help me?'

'Who?'

'His name was Stephen. He had dark hair, stubble, about six foot and a bit.'

Gavin nods dismissively but I've dealt with young people who don't tell the entire truth way too often to miss the nose scratch.

'I've gotta go,' he says.

'Please. It's really important. I wouldn't ask otherwise.'

He bounces from one foot to the other; me on one side, the hotel on the other. 'Ah, forget it,' he says, angling towards me. 'I'm late anyway. Another ten minutes won't matter.'

Gavin digs into an inside pocket and pulls out a pre-made roll-up with a lighter. 'You smoke?' he asks.

'No.'

He doesn't add anything as he sticks the cigarette in his mouth and lights it before nodding towards a hedge. 'I'm going to have to hide behind there,' he says. 'I'm on a second warning for smoking on company property. You coming?'

I follow him past my car and around a corner until we're tucked into a hidden alcove where one hedge meets another. The area must be permanently in shadow because the ground is damp. There's also a telltale collection of cigarette ends dumped in the mud.

'What do you wanna know?' Gavin asks.

'I suppose what you remember.'

'About you?'

'I guess.'

He inhales from the cigarette and puffs out a plume that spirals high over the hedge. 'You were in by yourself,' he says. 'I was on night shift in the bar and Jimbo had called in sick so I was by myself. At first I figured you were one of those career types who spend the evening getting steadily plastered. Anyway, you were a drink or two in when this bloke sidled up and sat next to you.'

'Stephen?'

'I guess so. You were getting on like a house on fire. Went off to the window for dinner, then came back to the bar. You were *so* pissed. I served you three wines and you were gone. I thought you must have spent the afternoon on the lash.'

'I hadn't had anything to drink before I got to the hotel.'

'Well you were pretty much off your head – and I only served you three glasses.'

He clearly doesn't believe me and gives a *suit yourself* shrug. I'd bet he sees this type of thing regularly: people in suits and business wear away from home and the office getting lashed on expenses.

'Alcohol hits me hard,' I reply.

It's not exactly a lie – but it normally takes more than three glasses of wine to get me going. I don't want to interrupt his flow by arguing over how much I drank. He seems clear enough I only had three.

He snorts. 'You're not wrong on that.'

'What else happened after we came back to the bar after eating?'

That smirk returns for another brief appearance before he catches himself. 'Not much.'

'But something did…?'

Gavin is smoking quickly and has almost got through his rollie. He switches it from his right hand to his left, gulping down the smoke and breathing it out again.

'You went to the toilet,' he says.

I have no memory of that but I tell him I remember anyway.

'I had a chat with your bloke,' Gavin adds.

'What about?'

Another puff and the cigarette has gone. He drops it to the ground and mashes it in with the others. 'Well, no offence, but I asked him what the deal was. He was, like, twenty-odd. Some gym guy. A model type. And you… well…'

He tails off but the point is savagely clear.

'You can say it,' I reply.

'Right, well, I ask him why some fit young guy would be chatting up an older woman. I thought he might have a type, y'know? Like some dudes are into black chicks, or Indian girls. Some blokes like 'em young, or whatever. I asked if he went for the MILFy-types.'

'I'm a MILFy-type?'

He shrugs. 'Not *my* type, but, y'know, some guys are up for anything. I have a mate who's into furries. You know what that is?'

'I honestly don't want to know.'

Gavin bats a hand. 'Anyway, I asked him what the deal was and he smiled and said, "What do you think?".'

I stare at him, confused. 'I don't get it.'

Gavin sighs and then rubs his thumb across his forefinger and middle finger. The universal sign for money. Like some dodgy market trader trying to get something cash-in-hand.

'I still don't understand.'

Gavin steps around me and moves towards the car park. 'I dunno what to tell you. That's what he told me.'

It takes a second for the penny to drop. 'He told you he was talking to me for money?'

Gavin rocks back and laughs. 'Aye, *talking* for money. That's a new one. I thought you might be some rich divorcee who got a big settlement. Flashing the cash and gash. All that.'

He's already another step away when I tell him I don't have any money.

He looks back over his shoulder and laughs. 'Whatever. I've gotta get to work. Have a good day, an' that.'

THIRTY-EIGHT

I'm on the way home thinking over the conversation with Gavin by the secret smoking corner. None of it makes sense. Stephen was *paid* to talk to me? It makes no sense.

Gavin's snidey giggle about *talking* for money is true. Who pays someone to *talk* to them at a bar for an hour or two?

I've only gone a couple of miles when I pull into a layby and turn the engine off. My brain is hurting from trying to force the memories. It would explain why Stephen chose to speak to me instead of the smattering of other people in the bar. It now fits why I found him so charming and why he seemingly thought the same of me. I wondered those same things at the time, suspecting that perhaps he had a thing for older women.

In all honesty, I didn't care. He was young, handsome, intelligent and charismatic. I've not had anyone like that pay attention to me in a long time. I'm not sure about 'MILFy' but there was a big part of me that hoped he *did* have a thing for older women. It was exciting, making me feel important and wanted.

I now remember a really clear thought from the time. We were sitting at the table by the window, looking out over towards what I know now is a chapel. We were trying to figure out what it was, speculating that it might be an elaborate shed for a demanding gardener. It doesn't sound like much now but, at the time, it was hilarious. I turned to him and took in this beautiful man and thought, *why should all the skinny gym girls have all the fun?*

It crossed my mind that I would be cheating on Dan. I've never been with another man since marrying him, despite the way we've argued in recent years. We had already agreed to separate and I wondered if this counted as adultery. I was still wearing my wedding ring, yet Stephen either didn't pick up on it, or didn't care.

My relationship with Dan in recent times has very much been something like don't ask, don't tell. He's had weekends away at teaching conferences, nights away for courses. More recently, he's been at the gym a lot; or he's *said* he's at the gym a lot. I've considered that he might be doing his own thing with another woman – or wom*en* – but I've never asked because I didn't particularly want to know. Without the truth, the illusion of our marriage could continue for Olivia; with it, everything might come tumbling down.

I thought about all of that in the moment by the window with Stephen – and I decided that if he wanted me, then I wanted him.

But I don't remember much after moving from the table back to the bar with him. It's only vague flashes after that. After waking up in my car, I assumed I'd been drinking – but Gavin says I only had three glasses of wine. That sounds about right. Two or three is my limit nowadays, especially when I'm out.

There is a blurry flash of the lifts, that jackpot machine dinging which I found hilarious for no reason. I was leaning on Stephen as I giggled myself stupid and then… we were in my room. Another smoggy memory of him lowering me onto the bed. He was telling me I was fine. The sheets were tucked hard and he lowered me down. I leaned in, kissing him on the neck, feeling that prickle of stubble against my lips. He said something like 'that's nice' and then… I was in the car in that field.

But none of it was real. Stephen was *paid* to be with me.

So who paid him? It wasn't me.

And was he *paid* to sleep with me?

If he was, then I'm almost certain he didn't. Perhaps it was because I was too drunk, perhaps he changed his mind. I'm sure I'd know if we'd done that and am about as convinced as I can be that we didn't. It didn't stop me wanting to. It didn't stop me kissing his neck, or spending the night flirting.

Googling male escorts is an eye-opener. There is so much bare flesh on display that I could've accidentally clicked onto an advert for a butcher's shop. I narrow things down to this area and find a couple of online agencies advertising 'male company'. I never realised there was such demand for this sort of thing and it all looks so official. On most sites, there are price lists and a phone number to call. On the first site, there is a 'companion' page, with half-naked photos of twenty or so men. Their heads have all been cropped out but each man has a good dozen professional pictures.

It feels creepy but I'm not sure what else to do, other than scroll through the images. As people say: it's hard work but somebody has to do it.

There's nothing that seems familiar on the first two sites – but that's hardly a surprise. I don't hang around with many bronzed, muscled gym-goers.

It's on the third site where I find myself staring at one of the photos. I'd clicked past it and have to go back, eyeing the spiky tattoo on the man's upper arm. It's the type of tribal markings that are sometimes on display at the beach or the pool. The sort of thing appropriated from Pacific Islanders without context or care.

This man is a little different from many of the others. He doesn't have the thick chiselled muscles, nor the bloated upper body. He's tall and lean, with definition but nothing over the top. His torso is waxed smooth in a couple of the photos and he's wearing a suit in some others.

I return to the tattoo photo and stare. It seems familiar and yet I don't remember seeing one like it up close before.

None of the companions have been given names, they're anonymous bodies categorised under various search terms, such as hair colour and body type. There is a button at the bottom, which reads: 'To book, click here'.

I do precisely that – and then I'm left open-mouthed at the result.

You have selected STEPHEN. To continue with your booking, call now

There is a phone number but no other contact details. My heart flutters as I hover a thumb over the button to call. Calling an escort agency isn't the type of thing I'd ever thought I'd do. Should I? Stephen must know that I wasn't the one who hired him and I can't imagine he'll tell me over the phone who paid him. Why would he?

I suppose there's only one way I'm going to be able to talk to him properly…

As I press the button to make the call, I close my eyes and hold the phone to my ear. It rings once, twice, before it's answered.

It's a woman's voice, though it's hard to judge the age. She sounds officious and organised.

'Hello,' she says. 'Can I help?'

'Oh… I was hoping to talk to Stephen. I might've got the wrong number.'

'This is the right number. I take Stephen's bookings for him. How can I assist you?'

She's calm and it sounds as if she's done this a lot. It dawns on me that she'll be the person who takes *all* the bookings from the site – not only Stephen's. She will get a cut of whatever they make and it's probably her who organised the professional photos. As with the stun gun, I have no idea if this is legal. This is all a new world to me.

'Oh…' I'm stumbling still off guard from hearing a woman's voice. 'I was hoping to book a meeting with him. I, um… not a meeting. Sorry, wrong word.'

She sounds warm, as if she's heard all this before. 'It's okay, my love. I know what you mean. When were you thinking?'

'Today…?'

'I'm afraid Stephen's all booked up for today. I do have some lovely other options you might be interested in?'

'No. I really wanted Stephen. When is he next free?'

There is a brief pause and I can hear my heart thundering through the silence.

'Stephen has some time tomorrow,' the voice says.

'Okay, that's good.'

'Where would you like to meet?'

'I've not really thought about it. Where do people normally meet?'

I'm stumbling over my words like a nervous child about to go on stage for a Christmas nativity.

The woman remains perfectly calm. 'Some prefer a public place like a restaurant,' she says. 'It depends what you're after. Sometimes it's more private, like a hotel room.'

She lets that hang but it doesn't take a genius to figure out what is being implied.

'A restaurant,' I say. 'I'm only looking for company, not for, erm…'

'That's absolutely fine, my love. Do you know which restaurant?'

The only one I know in this area is at the hotel – and I can hardly suggest there, not if either Peter is on reception or Gavin's at the bar.

'I don't know the area well,' I reply. 'I'm here on business. Can you suggest somewhere?'

'Of course. What type of food do you like?'

If I was being honest, I'd say chips from the chippy but that's not the best of ideas. I tell her Italian instead because it's neutral enough. 'Somewhere quiet,' I add.

The woman says she knows the perfect place and asks for a time. I ask if an afternoon is fine, assuming it won't be, but it's starting to sound like anything is doable.

We set the time for four o'clock at some place named Marco's. She asks if I need directions but I say I have maps on my phone. I can barely remember the time when everything was atlases with curled corners tucked into a car door.

'Are there any other requirements?' she asks.

'Like what?'

'Any specific outfit you might want? Aftershave? We can accommodate many things…'

'Just normal,' I reply, not knowing what to say.

'We can do normal.'

There's an awkward pause because there's only one thing left to discuss. It's her who brings it up. 'Have you seen the rates on our site?'

'Yes.'

'And how long were you looking for?'

'An hour… no, two.' I take a breath. 'How do I pay?'

'You can pay with cash placed in an envelope at the start of the appointment, or via credit card. It will appear as something discreet on your statement.'

'I'll pay cash.'

I hear the faint tapping of a keyboard in the background but it doesn't stop the woman's flow. She sounds cheerier now. 'We're all booked in that case. Do you mind if I take your name?'

There's a split second in which I panic. I'd somehow not realised that she hadn't asked for my name until now. I've started to say 'Rose' when it occurs to me that I've already told Stephen my real name. There's no point in making him suspicious.

'Olivia,' I say. The first name that popped into my head.

I feel terrible straight away, even more so when the woman repeats it back to me.

'In that case,' she adds, 'Stephen will see you tomorrow.'

I hang up and then finally open my eyes. The brightness of the sky burns green and pink stars into my eyes. I can't afford five hundred pounds but I'm going to have to find it somehow.

The bar at the top of my phone is blinking red. My first mobile phone had a battery that would probably still have charge all these years on if I'd not chucked it out. Luckily, there's a cable in my glovebox precisely for scenarios such as this. It was a birthday present, which sums up how much Dan and I have enjoyed our recent celebrations.

I unclip my seat belt and stretch across the gearstick, fumbling in the glovebox until I reach…

Something that isn't a charging cable. Something far more ominous.

It's a chain with a rectangle piece of silver attached to a clasp. The letters TY are engraved on one side; OD on the other.

Tyler and Olivia.

I stare at it, chasing the rough shape of the links with my fingers. It's real, precisely as Olivia described to the police. Her birthday present to her boyfriend.

Tyler's dog tag.

THIRTY-NINE

I did it. I killed Tyler.

I must have done. There was blood on my car, blood in the garage. Something happened that perhaps Stephen can help me remember. Or, maybe, he's part of what happened for a reason I don't yet understand.

Unless I *didn't* do it.

Someone paid for Stephen to spend time with me that night – and the same person did something to Tyler. I'm being set up.

Unless I *did* do it.

Tyler was in my car. I don't understand how or why – but he was. There was a struggle and he was run over. His blood ended up on the car and, consequently, the garage.

Unless I *didn't* do it…

I have no idea what to think and there are far too many gaps in my memory to know much of anything. Could Tyler have been a hundred miles from home at the same hotel as me? Or could Dan, Jason or someone else have planted the dog tag in my glovebox? Or did Tyler break into the house and somehow leave it in my car himself?

I've thought this whole time that Tyler had either run off, or got himself into trouble with someone he shouldn't. But perhaps it's not about him at all? Perhaps it's about me? Jason, Dan or someone else has done something to him to get to me.

Or that's all ego and narcissism because of course it's nothing to do with me.

The truth is that I have no idea. Everything is a mess.

I've not been in the glovebox all week, so the chain could have been in there for days. Equally, it might have been placed in there more recently. Today? Yesterday? It's chilling to think that the police have been in the house. If they'd asked to search the garage and my car, I'd have said it was fine. If *they'd* found Tyler's necklace, I would've had no way to explain it. The blood was pooled under where my car would be parked. I'd be prime suspect. It's only through luck that I'm not.

I'm riddled with that ambivalence as I drive home. There are moments in which I'm convinced this is all down to me; others where I'm convinced that I'm a victim.

It's early evening when I pull into the garage and, instead of returning Tyler's dog tag to the glovebox, I bury it at the bottom of my bag. The house is empty anyway; Olivia at work or with friends; Dan is who knows where. I certainly have no idea. I've not received any texts and there are no notes on the kitchen counter or fridge.

With the house to myself, I figure I should hide the chain somewhere safer than my bag. It's not beyond the realms of possibility that the police might want to search here at some point, so indoors is out of the question. I have visions of digging in parks or throwing it in a pond – but it's too much. I'm already out of my comfort zone, doing things I'd never have pictured myself doing.

There's an all-weather plastic storage crate at the back of the house secured with a padlock. The lawnmower is inside, along with a selection of scuffed tools. Neither Dan nor I have ever been much for gardening. It all seems like hard work, especially as the grass, weeds and everything else always grows back so quickly. There have been times when it's like Dan and I are playing a game of chicken with one another. I don't want to mow the grass and neither does he, so we wait until it's so long it can't be ignored. One of us will eventually crack, huffing and puffing about having to do it.

The trowel is caked with dried mud, the tip rounded and blunt. I peep through the back door to make sure nobody has returned home and then carefully tread my way around the edge of the lawn until I'm at the flower bed that runs the length of the fence. It's scruffy and untended, with wiry shoots of green mixing in among the actual plants. There are two small wooden crosses, one with the name 'Bertie' scratched into the wood. He was Olivia's hamster when she was eight or nine but only survived for eighteen months before she came down to feed him one morning and found him dead in his cage. She cried for an entire weekend and it was her first experience of death. I cried, too – not for Bertie, more for her. Something like that closes the door on youthful innocence and it can never be opened again. Olivia had lost more than a hamster.

The second cross is for Lizzie, a lizard that Olivia kept for a couple of years after Bertie died. She did everything right, with the heat lamps and other expensive equipment – but Lizzie succumbed to nature in much the same way that Bertie did. Olivia didn't cry that time. She buried the creature herself and then asked if we could get rid of the vivarium. She didn't want a replacement and that was the last pet we owned.

I kneel and dig in the spot where Lizzie is buried, carefully mounding the dirt at the side. It's not long until I hit the plastic ice cream tub in which the lizard was laid to rest. As coffins go, a square of plastic with 'Wall's Neapolitan' isn't the most dignified way to end up. The tub hasn't degraded at all, though the white is imprinted with a brown sludge. I don't bother removing the lid, placing the tub on the side as I continue to dig the hole underneath.

My upper arms are burning, my fingers rigid like an old arthritic's when I decide I've gone deep enough. If the garden was to be excavated in its entirety, the dog tag will be found – but the chances seem slim.

I drop the necklace to the bottom of the pit and then start to refill the hole. There is a thick layer of mud, then the ice cream tub – and then I carefully pat down the final mounds, being as careful as I can to keep the surface in a similar style to the rest of the flower bed. I do the final few bits with my hands, rearranging the green shoots into clumps until it's impossible to tell by eye that anything has moved. I clean much of the mud from the trowel, leaving just enough so that it's not obvious it's been used recently, and then return it to the storage locker.

It's only when I'm about to step back into the house when it hits me what I've done. If washing the car was tampering with evidence, then this is literally burying it. I didn't outright lie to the police but I kept at least one important detail back. This is what guilty people do; hiding and obfuscating.

The only justification I have is that I'm scared of what I might have done. I'm frightened by the gaps in my memory, of the thoughts that I might not be able to trust those around me.

Who *am* I?

When I get inside, I wash my hands and arms, then clean my shoes. I dry the soles with a towel and put them on the rack near the front door. I might be a guilty hit-and-runner, an evidence tamperer and liar – but at least I don't have dirty shoes in the house. After that I scrub the filth out from under my fingernails and finally take a spot on the sofa with the laptop, as if nothing has happened.

Natasha's Saturday was spent walking her dog/rat, then she had her nails done, ate some leaves for lunch and she is currently #chilling with her 'babez', who I assume is her boyfriend. I wish I could stop checking up on her but I'm too far gone. The first thing I do when I go online. I scoff at her life but mine is worse. I pull myself away from the gloom and look at the Find Tyler page. There haven't been any posts in a day.

I'm busy fiddling around on the internet, achieving nothing, learning nothing, when I realise that spending hundreds of pounds on a male escort will leave a paper trail somewhere. Dan and I share a bank account, which is also linked to a pair of credit cards. I suspect this won't last much longer – but, for now, our salaries each drop into the same place.

It takes me a good ten minutes to find the security gadget needed to log on and another couple more to remember my password. It's not exactly a forensic money trail created by some boffin at revenue and customs but I click through the login screens until I'm looking at our credit card balance.

And there it is – a £1,000 debit paid to DBA Enterprises last Sunday. I stare at the line, clicking back and then forward again, wondering if I've somehow misread it. There are the regular debits – home insurance, a couple of bills – and then, completely out of step with everything else is a payment for a thousand pounds.

The payment is linked to Dan's card but he hasn't once mentioned spending so much money on one thing. Even during the times at which we've been at one another's throats, we've never done anything like this. We've bought furniture, cars and holidays – but always as joint decisions.

I search the internet for DBA Enterprises but there's almost nothing – and then I remember the woman on the phone from the agency telling me I could book on a card and it would 'appear as something discreet on your statement'. The company name is certainly inconspicuous and it's only the amount that's noticeable.

Did Dan pay for Stephen to seduce me?

If he did, then using our joint credit card seems so stupid, so simplistic. Except that I never check the accounts. It took me long enough to find the log on device and then I could barely remember my password. We don't get paper statements and I'd have no reason to check unless I was suspicious. He knows this because it's always him who questions small things on statements.

I return to the escort website and it's right there on the price list. Two hours costs £500 but five hours is £1,000. I suppose that's close to the length of time we were with each other at the hotel.

Did Dan set me up so that the impending divorce would be about infidelity rather than a breakdown to the relationship? Would that get him a better deal? More sympathy from Olivia and our friends?

I stare at the figure on the screen with no idea what to think. If it was Dan who booked Stephen, then what about everything else? The car, the field, the blood? Tyler? The stun gun? Even the smaller things like missing keys? Is this an elaborate plot to frame me? Or to confuse me to the point of questioning my own sanity?

If it's that, then he's really pulling off a masterstroke.

I log out of internet banking, snap the laptop lid closed and head upstairs to the spare room. I don't trust Dan but I barely trust myself. The only thing I can hope is that I get some answers from Stephen.

FORTY

- SUNDAY -

Dan never bothered me in the spare room when he got in last night. He didn't even check I was there. It was only Olivia who knocked quietly and then entered. I told her I had a headache and she perched on the end of the bed asking if I wanted painkillers or water. I told her I was okay and then she replied that work had been fine but that she was going to bed early as well. It looked like she'd been crying but there wasn't much I could say to help. I didn't trust myself to say much of anything, not when it came to Tyler in any case.

The next morning, I head downstairs to the living room before Dan is up. I check the banking website once more but nothing has changed. When he comes downstairs, Dan is already dressed in jeans and a sweatshirt.

'No gym today?' I ask.

He heads to the fridge but grimaces slightly, annoyed at my apparent intrusion. 'No.'

'What are you up to?'

It's innocuous enough but not really the type of thing we go out of our way to ask one another nowadays.

'Car boot sale,' he replies. 'I'm going to look for a few things for the new apartment.'

It sounds suspiciously like nonsense. We went to a few Sunday morning car boot sales when we were younger and not as well off – but that would be more than a decade ago. Dan said his apartment was furnished and, for the few things he might need, why buy second-hand?

As with all the other things, I don't question him.

He says he's having breakfast first and I reply that I'm going to pop to Ellie's for a while. Dan barely acknowledges this and certainly doesn't ask if I want to go with him.

I check on Olivia, but she's out of it, head buried under a pillow, her body rising and falling gently as she sleeps. After that, I put on some warmer clothes and a coat and then half-jog along the street until I'm outside Ellie's. I phone her from outside, rather than knocking on the door, not wanting Jason to answer.

Ellie is in a dressing gown and slippers when she answers the door. She yawns twice and asks what I'm doing up at this time on a Sunday.

'I need to borrow your car,' I reply.

'It was banged up, remember. The insurance company took it.'

'But you have a rental…?'

'Yes.'

'Can I borrow that?'

'Why?'

I want to tell her about the credit card statement and Dan's obvious made-up story about the car boot sale but don't have time. I don't feel like sharing at this time, either.

'I can't say,' I reply. 'Please trust me.'

Ellie fights back another yawn but then she breaks into a smile. I feel it, too. There's that hint of the old days, of mischief and mayhem. She nips back into the house for a moment and then returns with a key and fob, before pointing to a maroon Ford on the opposite side of the road.

'That one,' she says. 'Please don't crash it.'

'I won't.'

It takes me a moment or two to figure out where everything is. I bunny-hop away from the kerb but, once I've got it, the car turns out to be a smooth drive. I glide along the road, across the junction, and then slot into a spot next to the postbox at the end of our road. I dig into my coat pocket and retrieve the beanie hat, bundling up my hair and pulling the hat down over my ears. I've got a view of the entire street and so sit and wait.

Barely two minutes have passed when Dan's BMW cruises from our driveway. It's so big considering he's the only one who uses it. I doubt the back seats have ever had anything on them other than the odd bag or file.

I try to remember what I've seen and heard about following someone else in a car. It's something like keeping two cars in between – except there is no other traffic. All I can do is maintain a distance and hope he doesn't stare into his rear-view mirror too closely.

One thing that's certainly true of my husband is that he's a good driver. He's predictable, maintaining a steady speed within the limit and signalling his turns early. Even though I don't know what I'm doing in terms of following him, his competence as a driver makes it easy.

I trail him out of the town, following the main road to the dual carriageway where there is a little more traffic. It's easier to keep a distance yet still see him, and so I sit in a couple of hundred metres behind and wait for him to make a move.

I'm not quite sure *why* I'm following him, other than that his car boot story seemed so obviously a lie. I suppose it feels like I'm doing something – and something is better than nothing. This is proactive.

It's only another ten minutes or so until Dan signals to leave the dual carriageway. I do the same and by the time I'm pulling up to a roundabout he's already taking a left. The lack of traffic lights makes it easy to maintain a distance without making things too obvious.

I'm feeling like a right smart-arse until I see the sign for the GIANT boot sale. The first sign says two miles, then one, then half. Dan continues on the same route until he slows, indicates and takes the turn into a field.

He was telling the truth.

It's too late for me to do anything other than continue. A line of cars is following one another into the field, stopping at the gate to pass two quid for parking into the hand of some lad who looks about fourteen. I end up delaying the queue by delving through my bag and purse until I find a fiver. The teenager sighs as only teenagers can, as if me giving him a note has ruined his entire day. He scrabbles around in a money belt and passes me back four fifty pence pieces and five twenties. The stroppy little sod.

I follow the line of traffic as a pair of bored lads in wellies point me towards a second field as if they're directing a plane in to land. There are three cars between mine and Dan's and only one way to go. Another pair of lads directs Dan into a parking spot halfway along a long row of cars. I grin to myself as he holds up the line by stopping to reverse in, rather than going head-first like everyone else. It's such a Dan thing to do. The instructions are simple enough as I copy the other drivers, parking parallel to Dan with the same three cars between us.

People are clambering out of the vehicles but I slide down, staring through the lined-up windows to where Dan remains in the driver's seat of his car. He's on his phone, texting or using the internet, seemingly oblivious to everyone around him.

I was so certain he was lying about coming here that it's hard not to wonder what else I'm wrong about.

The couples and families from the cars between have long since disappeared off to the main part of the boot sale when Dan finally opens his door. I scrunch down in the driver's seat of Ellie's rental car, giving myself the merest slit through which to watch him. My husband is grinning to himself about something, phone still in hand as he strides off towards the main gate.

I gently open the door, slithering out like a snake – albeit an older one with a dodgy back. I might have been wrong about Dan coming here – but I'm not ready to let things go quite yet. I crouch on my heels, watching through the windows of strangers' cars, until I'm sure my husband is far enough ahead that he won't look back. With that, I lock the car, pull my hat down low, and then set off after him.

If I'd known I was *actually* coming to a car boot sale, I would have worn better shoes. The ground is soft, though not quite a full-on mud pit. I'm in flats but they're thin and I've only gone a few steps when there's a squelch and the earth oozes over the top of my feet, into the shoe itself.

As I pass through the main gate, the smell of barbeque drifts across from a burger van where a line has already formed. There's an enormous bouncy castle in the distance, with an attached inflatable slide. On the other side of the gate is the traditional meat man, bellowing on about how he's not going to sell a dozen steaks together. Oh, no. This bloke wangs fifteen into a plain white carrier bag and asks for twenty quid with a thump of the gavel. The punters are lapping it up, practically charging the van with their wallets aloft.

Dan has ignored all of that. He's bounding along the central aisle, not bothering to look at any of the stalls. He's always walked too fast for me, surging ahead and then turning back with disdain as if I'm the problem for walking too slowly. 'I'm going as fast as I can,' I'd say – but he'd never accept that. He was never going too fast; I was always going too slow.

I'm practically at a jog in an attempt to follow as he disappears into the depth of the market. It's only his bright green jacket that gives me any chance of keeping an eye on him. He disappears around a corner and, by the time I get there, his green coat is storming around another.

The pace at which he's travelling makes it clear that he knows where he's going. When I get to the next corner, he's in the distance, weaving between shoppers and browsers with impressive ease. He's always been impatient, often walking away from shops or restaurants simply because there's a queue. He never suffered fools, either.

We're towards the furthest reaches of the field now, with a hedge at the end of the aisle instead of more stalls. I'm still at a jog when I realise Dan has slowed almost to a stop. The stalls are further apart, with regular people selling from a car, as opposed to professional traders.

I'm still a good distance from him but it's quickly apparent why Dan is here – and why he's stopped. One of the final stalls is selling exercise gear. There are yoga balls and mats, small weights, stretch bands, and protein shakers.

I edge forward slowly, closing the gap because Dan is moving even slower. My first thought is that they've arranged this but that changes immediately when I see the look on Alice's face after she spots him. She's in her tight yoga gear, a bright figure-hugging pink and blue lycra against the gloom of the field. The smile is initially painted on as she tries to attract customers but, as soon as Alice sees Dan, her expression slips. She's confused and definitely not expecting him. I drift off to a stall selling second-hand clothes, flicking through the items on a rail and using it to shield myself from Dan and Alice.

He steps towards her, arms wide for a hug. She accepts it, but only leaning forward with the top half of her body. I'm too far away to hear what's being said but her body language gives away that her opening line is something like, 'What are you doing here?'

Dan is all smiles and charm – but she's like a wall. He speaks for a few seconds and she replies with one- or two-word answers. I move to a second rack of clothes, still watching, fascinated at seeing someone I thought I knew so well in an alien situation.

And then I get it. Dan's smitten with her.

For Alice, the cheery pleasantness is part of the job. If her clients book more sessions, she makes more money. That's how she pays her bills. It's her job to put on that front. Dan has misread everything. What Alice sees as drumming up repeat business, Dan has misconstrued as flirting.

Oh, God.

I'm cringing as I watch them. It's like the geeky kid trying to ask out the most popular girl in school. Ellie and I used to gossip and giggle about this type of thing when we were young teenagers. This type of tittle-tattle was our lives before we discovered cigarettes and alcohol.

Alice's arms are folded across her front and, every time Dan takes a half-step forward, she takes one back. She's smiling but, even from this distance, I can see that it's not real. She isn't enjoying this at all.

Dan is oblivious. He's leaning forward, doing that thing where he talks with his hands like an excited octopus. They do a strange semicircle around her stall, Dan taking small steps forward as she takes larger steps back. It's like an elaborate performance dance piece and so terrible to watch.

It takes a good five minutes but Dan eventually seems to take the hint that she's not interested in whatever he has to say. They do the relieved goodbye wave that people do when they're grateful an encounter is over, and then Dan turns on his heels. I duck behind the original rail of clothes but he's not looking anywhere other than the path in front of him. He's frowning, confused, unsure what's just happened.

I watch him go, striding at the same pace as before in the direction we came.

It's perhaps the last thing I expected but there's a part of me that feels sorry for him. Here we are, half our lives gone, neither of us apparently knowing what's next. He was convinced he'd caught the eye of a gorgeous young woman. Who wouldn't be flattered? Perhaps he still thinks that's the case? It's not love, perhaps not even lust, but crushes can come from nowhere. Suddenly, a perfectly sane and settled person can be fourteen again, insides churning at the thought of somebody else's attention.

I watch my husband disappear into the distance, not bothering to try to keep up this time. Then I remember the thousand pounds on our credit card statement – and everything else that's been going on. It doesn't feel so innocent any longer.

FORTY-ONE

Stephen is already sitting at the restaurant table when he realises who I am. I approach quickly and he starts to stand with an awkward 'oh', but I'm moving too fast. Before he can step away, I take his wrist and squeeze.

'Sit,' I say.

Seeing his face up close makes my memory of the other night so much clearer. He's not quite the image of perfection I'd convinced myself he was. There's a spot under his chin and the hint of wrinkles around his eyes – but he's still good-looking. He's got dark designer stubble and his hair is thick and swept back as if he's on a cliff-top photoshoot.

'Do you want to make a scene?' I ask quietly.

The restaurant is far from full but Stephen glances around at the meagre number of patrons and retakes his seat.

The person from the agency who I spoke to on the phone chose well. Marco's is a nice place. It's all high ceilings, bright lights, potted plants and gentle music. I imagine it's the type of place with a wine cellar, or where companies will book the whole place out for a Christmas party.

Stephen is looking anywhere but at me. I was ten minutes late, wanting to make sure he was in place so that he couldn't spot me early and disappear.

Before either of us can say anything else, the waiter has swooped, filling glasses with water. He has a Mediterranean accent that sounds a little exaggerated and says he'll be back shortly for drinks orders.

I sip the water, waiting for Stephen's attention.

He stares at a spot towards the door, doing all he can to avoid my stare.

'You were far chattier the other night,' I say.

'Yeah, um… I think I should probably go.'

'I think you should stay.'

He doesn't move, so I reach into my bag and remove the envelope, pushing it across the table. 'That's your five hundred,' I say. 'Count it if you want.'

Stephen reaches for the envelope instinctively but withdraws his hand without picking it up.

'My daily limit at the cash machine is three hundred,' I tell him. 'I had to split it between my credit and debit cards. It's all there.'

'You should keep it. I've got to go.'

He starts to stand but I grab his wrist once more, squeezing harder this time. 'Sit down and listen to me.'

The woman two tables away has noticed something's happening and is starting to stare. Stephen flashes her a toothy grin to let her know all is well and then he slips back onto the chair. He's in a slim-fit suit, with a skinny tie and glimmering cufflinks. It's a bit overdressed for an afternoon in this Italian – but I'm not fussed if he stands out.

'What do you want?' he asks.

The waiter arrives before I answer and I order a sparkling water. Stephen says he's fine with the standard table water and the server scuttles off once more, clicking his heels as he goes. That's his *actual* heels. He's wearing a pair of Cubans, adding at least half an inch to his height.

I have a large sip of my own table water, taking my time.

'I think you know what I want,' I reply.

Stephen's fiddling with his cufflinks, spinning the crystal stud one way and then the other. It's far too shiny to be a real diamond. He says nothing.

'Is Stephen your real name?' I ask.

'What do you think?'

'I think it's probably a work name.'

He shrugs.

'You get paid to spend time with women.'

Stephen undoes the cufflink entirely, dropping the two pieces into his jacket pocket. He wriggles his shoulders and slips the jacket off before starting to roll up his shirt sleeve.

'You spent most of an evening with me and yet I never paid you,' I say. 'That means you either did it out of the kindness of your heart, or someone else paid you.'

He undoes the other cufflink, puts that into his pocket and rolls up the second sleeve. That done he presses his forearms onto the table, interlinks his fingers and leans forward.

'That's private,' he says.

'Are you joking?'

'Does it sound like I am?'

He stares at me now and there's little trace of the flirty stare I so remember. He's not angry; he's cornered and doesn't know what to do. He's older than I thought; older than his profile claims. There's no way he's twenty-four, he has to be at least thirty. The creases around his lips are the giveaway.

'How can it be private?' I say. 'I thought you were interested in talking to me. I thought we had a fun evening. If I'd known you were being paid—'

He cuts me off: 'Then what? What would have been different? All of that still happened. Why does it matter?'

'It matters to me.'

He holds up both hands. 'How? Explain it. Is music better if you get into a gig for free? Is a meal better if someone else pays?

The experience is still the same. If you enjoyed something, then what does it matter about the other stuff?'

I start to reply but realise that I don't have an answer. I'm not convinced it's the same thing and yet there's an element of his argument that's unquestionably true. The parts of the evening I remember *were* good.

He shows no joy at leaving me speechless and I get the sense he's argued this point in the past. Probably to friends, possibly to girlfriends. Maybe even his parents.

Before either of us can say anything else, the waiter hustles over with glass of fizzy water for me. He asks if we've had a chance to look at the menu but I tell him I think we need more time.

I wait until he's well out of earshot and then lean forward, speaking firmly but quietly. 'You conned your way into my bedroom.'

His eyes widen: 'Now you *are* joking.'

'Why would I be joking?'

He stares, his perfectly manicured eyebrow twitching: 'Don't you remember?'

'Remember what?'

'That evening.'

'Flashes – that's all. I remember eating by the window and then going back to the bar. I remember the lifts kept dinging while we were waiting to go upstairs. You lowered me onto the bed in my room. That's it. I think I drank too much.'

He leans in slightly and then presses away again. It's like he's trying to read my mind, to make sure I'm not lying.

'What?' I ask.

'I really should go.'

I end up banging the table with my palm. It's louder than I meant and the three or four couples dotted around the restaurant all stop to look. The envelope of money remains untouched on the table.

'You owe me an explanation,' I hiss.

Stephen glances around and sighs. The other sets of eyes slowly shift back to their own tables. Of course, it's at this minute that the waiter reappears, full of a thin-lipped smile.

'Have we had a chance to examine the menu yet?' he asks.

'Can I have the spaghetti bolognaise,' I ask.

I've not looked at the menu but spaghetti has to be a solid bet in an Italian.

The waiter smiles and makes a note on a pad before turning to Stephen: 'And you, Sir?'

He sighs again but doesn't touch the menu.

'Order something,' I say.

The waiter turns between us and there's a moment in which it feels like we're all looking to each other. He knows something odd is going on but can't delve into what. Instead, he asks if we need another minute.

'No,' I tell him firmly and then turn back to Stephen, repeating that he should order something.

'Lasagne,' Stephen says. He hasn't looked at the menu either.

'Very well, Sir.'

The waiter collects both unopened menus and does a very good impression of someone who has witnessed a perfectly normal occurrence.

'Who paid you?' I ask.

'I don't know.'

'Come on. That's rubbish.'

'It's really not.'

'So how was it set up?'

'It's private.'

Stephen squirms like a kid on a church pew and I realise that the confidence is all a shield. He's immature, probably broke. This is one of the few things he has going for him.

'This was off the books, wasn't it?'

I'm not sure how I know but Stephen gives enough of an answer by wriggling even more.

'I'm going to call your boss,' I say. 'That woman from the website. Ask her if she knows you were working for someone else on Monday night.'

'Don't!'

He hisses the reply and then glances over his shoulder to make sure he's not being overheard. '*Please* don't,' he says, far more quietly.

'So tell me.'

He sighs again, checks around to make sure nobody can hear and then lowers his voice so that I can barely catch the words. 'It was all on email,' he says.

'How did someone get your email? I thought it was done through a website?'

'It is… well, it usually is. I've got two mobiles – one for work, one for me. I've also got a few email addresses. Sometimes I give my actual number or email to a client.'

'The person who contacted you is a former client?'

He bites his lip and shakes his head: 'I've been doing this for years. At first it was just the odd woman but then I started telling people they could pass it onto their friends. I probably get half a dozen emails a week from people I've never met. My details have been passed on so many times over that it's not really a secret any longer.'

'What does that mean?'

Stephen presses back and runs a hand through his hair. He glances across to the waiter, who is perched on a stool at the bar, pretending not to watch us. He's well out of earshot.

'It means I often meet women who've not gone through the agency,' Stephen says. 'They say they got my email or phone number from a friend and I take it at that.'

'You make more money if you arrange things yourself…?'

'Obviously.'

I don't know enough about the industry to know how things work but it sounds genuine enough. I have another sip of water, taking a couple of seconds to think it over.

'Who emailed you asking you to meet me in the hotel?'

'I don't remember.'

'I don't believe you.'

He's unrolling his sleeves now: 'It's the truth.'

'How much were you paid?'

'Doesn't matter.'

'*How* were you paid?'

'PayPal.'

'Is DBA Enterprises something to do with you?'

He looks at me blankly and pouts a lip. 'Should it be?'

I try to look for any sort of tic to say he might be lying – but there's nothing. I'm not convinced I know when someone's telling the truth anyway. I couldn't spot the truth from my own husband a few hours ago. Just because Stephen doesn't know DBA Enterprises, it doesn't mean the thousand pounds that left Dan's credit card wasn't funnelled through some other account before being sent via PayPal to him. That's low on my priorities for now.

'What happened in the hotel?' I ask.

Stephen bites his lip and frowns. He seems confused. 'We ate, we talked and we drank.'

'Then what?'

'We didn't sleep together.'

I was almost certain of that anyway but breathe out in relief. I might tamper with evidence but I'm not an adulterer. Bully for me. 'You were still in my room, though…?' I say. 'You helped me into bed.'

'I made sure you were safe.'

The word stings. I start to say something and then stop myself. 'Safe from what?'

His eye twitches as he realises he's said too much.

'What did you do?' I ask.

He rubs his forehead and squeezes his eyes closed tight. As I watch him, an ominous creeping sensation starts to ripple through me. The dawning realisation of something I should have figured out before.

'I only had three drinks,' I say. 'You spiked me, didn't you?'

Stephen doesn't reply, instead screwing up his lips and chewing on them. His allure has long gone and he looks like a man whose life is crumbling in front of him.

'What was it?' I ask.

'I don't know.'

'Come off it.'

'I really don't.'

'So how did you get it? Why did you do it? Were you going to rob me?'

He shakes his head. 'It was all in the email,' he replies.

It takes me a moment to understand what he's said.

'Someone emailed you asking to spike my drink?'

It's barely there but he nods. He glances to the waiter again but nobody has moved. No one can hear us. 'They wanted me to befriend you and then slip something into your drink. They said it would be funny – that you'd find it hilarious.'

'*Hilarious*? Are you joking?'

'I wish…'

He can't look at me – but the same is true of me. I can't stand the sight of him. It feels like I've been invaded.

'I thought you didn't know the person who paid you?' I say.

'I don't.'

'So how did you get the pill or whatever it was you put in my drink? Do you have that sort of thing lying around?'

Stephen is barely moving. His head is in his hands and he's staring at the tablecloth. 'I got it in the post,' he says. 'They said they'd send it and it arrived a day later. They said it would dissolve in a drink and it did.'

'What was it?'

'I don't know. Probably Rohypnol, something like that.'

'You put *Rohypnol* in my drink and thought that was fine…?!'

I'm on the verge of shouting but also on the brink of not caring. He shushes me and I've never been closer to hitting someone in the face. I've never been violent, never had those urges and yet my fists are clenched. The whole of my upper body is coiled. I'm not sure how but I manage not to shout or lash out.

Stephen must see the fury in me because he leans in again, his voice low and pleading. 'They said it was a joke. That you'd think it was funny. They said you prank each other all the time. I wasn't going to do it, but…'

'But what?'

He shrugs, not needing to say he did it for the money. He's either an idiot, dangerous, or both. Someone sent him a pill in the post which could have been anything. It could have poisoned me but he slipped it into my drink anyway because of the pay-off. I can barely comprehend it – but, if I'm honest, when it comes to money, people have done far worse things for what would likely be far less. Junkies have mugged and killed for pound coins. Pensioners have had their houses burgled while they sleep for the contents of their purses and wallets.

'Why'd you need the money so badly?' I ask.

'Do you care?'

'Perhaps.'

With all sense of decorum gone, he wipes his nose the back of his hand and cleans it on his trousers. 'Online poker,' he says. 'I spent over a hundred grand last year. I'm constantly moving money between three credit cards just to pay rent.'

He's right that I don't care – but at least I have a degree of understanding.

As if reading my mind, he glances to the envelope on the table but doesn't reach for it.

'Is there anything you won't do for money?' I ask.

He's past caring as well. 'Not much.'

'How much were you paid for me?'

There's no delaying this time. He answers straight away: 'A grand.'

I wish I could be surprised but I'm not. I wonder how Dan got hold of Stephen's details, or how he knew about Stephen's financial problems. It could have been luck, or perhaps Dan cruised a host of websites and tried multiple people before stumbling across Stephen. Perhaps someone turned his request down but gave him Stephen's email address and said to try him instead. I'm not sure it matters. It's the here and now that counts.

'What did you do after taking me to my room?' I ask.

'Put you to bed.'

'And…?'

'And I left you. The email said to put the door on the latch so they could walk in. It said they were going to surprise you.'

There's something terrifyingly creepy about the way he says it. He must have known how vulnerable I'd be. I was left on a bed, barely conscious, with the door unlocked. Anyone could have walked in.

It's hard to contain my emotion. I'm scared of what might have been and I'm so furious that I have to grip the arms of my chair to stop myself shaking. I can barely get the words out.

'What was the name on the email?' I hiss.

He shakes his head. 'I don't remember.'

'I still don't believe you.'

He looks around, hoping the waiter will save him. Either that or a meteor.

No such luck.

'You've still got the email, haven't you?'

He swallows and rolls his eyes. I know I'm right. Without me having to ask, he digs into his pocket and pulls out a phone. He shields the screen with one hand, scrolling with the other and then re-pocketing it.

'What was the name?'

He shakes his head but I push the envelope across the table towards him. He takes his time, looking for the absent waiter, then to me, and then he picks up the money. He folds the envelope without checking the amount and pockets it.

'Tyler,' he says. 'The name on the email was Tyler Lambert.'

FORTY-TWO

I'm driving back to North Melbury, fingers trembling on the steering wheel and barely able to concentrate. Cars flash past me as I stick to the slower lanes, only focusing on the strip of tarmac directly in front. I'm so angry, so scarred, that I shouldn't be driving. I know that – but I want to be home.

I should call the police. I know that. Stephen is almost certainly not his real name but, whoever he is, he's a danger to women. I figure I'll call the agency and tell them Stephen's working on the side. It's not as much as I should do but it's something. If I call the police, there'll be too much to explain.

As for Tyler, my first thought is that there's no way he'd have a spare thousand pounds lying around. Except, I don't know much about him. Perhaps he deals drugs and has plenty of cash – it's just that he likes using Olivia to pay for things anyway. He has shoplifting convictions but perhaps there are many more crimes of which he's guilty, where he hasn't been caught. He might burgle houses, or rob shops and sell what he steals. It's possible he'd have the money to set me up.

It *could* be straightforward: Tyler arranged this, I found out in my hazy drug-addled state, somehow ran him over, left him dying in a ditch somewhere and then woke up in that field. I'm not sure why he hasn't been found but everything else makes sense.

Sort of.

It takes me a good twenty minutes to realise that none of those assumptions have to be true. It would take me five minutes to go onto the internet and set up an email address in Tyler's name. It *might* have been him – but this is no more proof than I had before.

All it does show is that whoever set me up knew Tyler's name and which hotel I was staying in. And when.

Off the top of my head, that's Dan, Olivia and Graham from work. Graham's a stretch because I've only mentioned Tyler's name to him once when he said he'd seen Olivia outside the Cosmic Café with 'some kid who looks like he's homeless'.

It's not only those three, though. Other people at work could easily have found out in which hotel I was staying – and then discovered Tyler's name by looking at Olivia's Facebook page. As could anyone else.

Once the hotel had been booked, I pinned the details to the fridge in case of an emergency. Tyler could have seen it there before he disappeared. Ellie hasn't visited the house in a while – but she has a key. Jason was released from prison a few days before all this happened – but he could have used her key and got into our house.

And then there's the fact that any of those people could have passed the information onto anyone else.

To a degree, I'm no closer to knowing who set all this up – except for the thousand pounds that was paid from Dan's credit card. I've seen first-hand that he has something between a crush and an infatuation with Alice, so perhaps his long game is a divorce from me; while still being able to keep the house, Olivia's affections, and everything else. It feels long-winded and ridiculously drawn out but it's not beyond comprehension – especially if part of that long game is to frame me for whatever has happened to Tyler. If the police had searched the garage, I would have been in serious trouble. Everything happened shortly after I argued with Tyler and we've been at odds for months. That's motive. Blood on my car and his chain in my glovebox is some degree of proof. Perhaps that would have been enough to charge me? If I was charged, let alone convicted, that's Dan's out.

It still doesn't feel quite right.

This is a man I've known and lived with for two decades, someone with whom I have a child. It's hard to believe this could be him – but then he does have a stun gun in his gym locker. And it wasn't that long ago Stephen was telling me he'd do more or less anything for money. People do strange things at the promise of cash.

I suppose the talk with Stephen has cleared up one thing. After Stephen left me, whoever paid him entered my hotel room and then got me out to my car while I was barely conscious. Perhaps that person stayed in the hotel as well, or maybe they simply walked in and headed up the stairs without pausing. Looking confident is half the battle in situations like that. Staff aren't going to challenge someone who walks up to a hotel room like they belong. The person might have used the fire escape to get me out and avoid being seen. Or maybe they simply held me up, smiling at any members of staff who passed, making a joke of it by saying, 'One too many', or something like that. Once I was outside, they drove my car out to that field and then put me in the driver's seat.

I still have no idea what went on with the blood on the bonnet, nor if this is what happened. It's still a mess.

Somewhere in all this, Tyler *is* involved. I can't know whether it was really him who emailed Stephen but his blood was on my car and his dog tag inside. He's also missing, so did he do all this and then disappear; or has someone kidnapped him to get to me?

There is someone else who might be able to help. Someone else who has helped make my life miserable in the past week. Before I contact him, I'll have to do a bit of non-literal digging.

FORTY-THREE

- MONDAY -

The spare room is starting to feel like my own bedroom. I make the bed each morning and then return each night. There's a lock on the spare room door and I click it into place each night, just in case. Neither Dan or Olivia mention me sleeping in there and I don't bring it up either.

I have a mini lie-in the next morning and, by the time I get downstairs, Dan has already left for the gym or school. Olivia is up, though – which is quite the surprise. I only need one hand to count the number of times she's beaten me downstairs this year.

She's on the sofa eating a yoghurt; something I've forbidden her to do in the past after a spillage a few years ago. I say nothing, clicking on the kettle and then slotting onto the other sofa.

'How are you holding up?' I ask.

Olivia looks so tired. She peers up with ringed eyes and an aimless stare.

'Empty,' she replies. 'I feel empty. I'm doing all the things I normally do – I go to work, I message my friends, I go out, I stay in, I've got a class with Ellie later. I do everything the same – but it's all empty without Ty. I used to tell him about all these things. I know you don't like him but he'd listen. Now I don't have anyone to talk to.'

I think about Tyler and how he might be involved in everything that's happened to me in the past few days. How his name was on the email to Stephen. I can't reconcile it all.

I could say, 'You have me' – but it's not right. It's not the same thing. Those mothers and daughters who share everything are weird. It's not supposed to be like that.

Olivia puts the yoghurt pot on the side table and then slumps back further onto the sofa. 'I just want to know what happened to him.'

I cross and sit next to her, putting an arm around her shoulders. 'I know, honey.'

Olivia lets me hug her for a second or two but then shrugs away. She mutters an apology and then pushes herself up and stretches. 'I've got to have a shower and get dressed,' she says. 'I'm at Ellie's for accounting class in a bit – and then I have work after that.'

She puts her rubbish in the kitchen bin and then yawns her way into the hallway before disappearing up the stairs.

I wish I knew what to say but what is there? The not knowing is awful. It would be awful if he was dead – but at least she'd know. For now, Olivia doesn't know whether to mourn or to keep searching. She's stuck in limbo. So am I, though for different reasons. At the centre of it all, seemingly, is Tyler.

With the living room empty, I do at least get a chance to do the rest of the googling from last night. It's surprisingly easy, probably ominously so, to find the information I need. I spend a bit of time learning the names and places, making sure it's clear in my mind before putting the laptop away.

I text Graham, telling him I'm not feeling well, and then say goodbye to Olivia before heading to my car. The journey is straightforward enough and I spend the time repeating back to myself the names I need.

When I reach my destination, there's nobody there. I park outside and go to the window, pressing my hands to shield the glare. All the lights are off inside, which is quite the annoyance. I'd worked myself up for a big showdown and now there's nobody around.

I head back to the car and go for a drive. When my stomach starts grumbling, I realise I haven't eaten in almost a day. I left the restaurant before my spaghetti arrived, didn't eat when I got home yesterday evening, and didn't have breakfast this morning.

Luckily, I passed a roadside café a mile or so back. I drive there and pull into a car park rammed with vans and lorries. The smell of sausage and bacon is almost overpowering and I've not even left the car. By the time I get inside, I'm practically drooling. The air is thick with grease and there's a fizz of frying food hissing across the chattering voices. I'm in my work clothes, drastically out of place against the backdrop of truckers and men in overalls.

I still don't care.

I head to the counter and order a full English. The manager gives me a sideways look. 'You sure? It's a lot of food…'

'I think I can handle it.'

I pay and then find an empty table. There are newspapers scattered around and I pick one up, flicking through to the Sudoku and finding a pen in my bag.

It feels good to be doing something that isn't thinking about conspiracies. Nobody knows me here; nobody cares who I am. For the first time in what feels like a really long time, I actually relax.

The food arrives after a few minutes – and the guy behind the till was right about it being a lot of food. It's only now I spot that there's a half-English on the menu – but it's too late. The plate is loaded with a good half-tin of beans, half a dozen rashers of bacon, five sausages, four slices of black pudding, three tomatoes, three fried eggs, two turtle doves and a partridge in a pear tree.

Maybe not those last two things.

I take my time, both with the puzzle page of the paper and my food. The manager comes around with a pot of coffee and asks if I want more, which I do. He asks how the food's going and I tell him it's one of the greatest meals I've ever had. I'm not even lying.

An hour has passed when I stand to leave. My stomach is bloated and I dread to think what the bathroom scales would think of it all. My clothes feel too tight but it's a bit late now. I'd not even noticed him, but the bloke on the adjacent table points to my empty plate and gives a thumbs-up. I laugh and he congratulates me as if I've achieved something worthwhile. It's so satisfying to enjoy an interaction with someone and not doubt their motives.

Which is a far cry from what I have to do next.

Declan is inside his office when I pull up outside for the second time. Graham told me I'd be fired for even texting him, so I figure I might as well go out in blaze of glory. As I get out of my car and step onto the kerb, I spot Declan through the window. He sees me at the same time and rushes to the door, probably to lock it. I get there first and push my way inside, standing defiantly in front of him as he steps away.

'You're not supposed to be here,' he says. He's in the same suit from the other day and there's not so much lustre about him this time. Perhaps it's because I'm not trying to sell him something, but I suspect it's more because he's so shocked to see me.

'I'm not going anywhere,' I reply.

'I'll call your boss.'

'Do it. I quit this morning.'

I didn't – but Declan doesn't know that and it's the one thing he holds over me. He knows it, too. His eyes dart both ways but there's no way out. I'm standing in front of the only door and it's only us in the office. The back of the room is still filled with boxes but largely empty otherwise. I have a feeling it'll always be like this.

'I'll call the police then,' he says. 'You're trespassing.'

'Please do call the police. I'll tell them how you made up lies about me and tried to defraud my company. It should make an interesting story.'

Declan's worried now. It's all bluster on my part but it's starting to dawn on him that he might not have thought all this through.

Just as I'm beginning to feel confident, my phone rings. It's instinct to pull it from the pocket on the front of my bag. It's Ellie and I almost press to answer – except that I can't talk to her in front of Declan, and I really need to get this over with.

I press reject – and then turn back to him.

'Your girlfriend is called Nicole,' I say. 'You got engaged about six weeks ago while on holiday in Spain.'

'How do you know that?'

'I've got Nicole's phone number and I'm going to call her to say how you tried it on with me. You can make things up – and so can I.'

Declan has stopped backing away. He's now staring curiously, eyebrows dipped. 'Even if you did have her phone number, she'll never believe you.'

'Maybe not. You know her better than me. But do you think she'll completely dismiss it? Or do you think she might have the tiniest inkling of doubt? She might tell me to get lost – but every time you leave the house, she'll wonder what you're doing and who you're with.'

My phone rings again but I ignore it. Declan glances to my bag and then back to me.

'She won't believe you,' he repeats.

'I'll take that chance. What have I got to lose?'

He gulps and I know I've got him. Confidence is the thing. It took a full English and a thumbs-up from a stranger but I feel like a rock star. A fat, bloated one – but a rock star nonetheless.

'What do you want?' he asks.

'Who put you up to it?'

Whatever he expected, it wasn't that. His neck cranes back a little. 'What?'

'Someone put you up to all this. Who was it?'

Declan starts to shake his head slowly. 'I don't know what you're on about.'

We stare at each other for a moment, seemingly both a little off guard. With everything that's gone wrong in the past week, I've linked it all together. Stephen was put up to doing something for money and I thought Declan had been as well.

Trust is such an important part of a person's life. It's intrinsic to someone's well-being that the people in his or her life can be relied upon. Over the past week, I've viewed almost everyone with suspicion. It's only Olivia who has escaped that. When that trust goes, everything becomes a conspiracy. But I can see in Declan that the timing of his complaint is a coincidence that made everything worse. Graham might have given Declan's details to Natasha or Claire – and the complaint would have come about either of them. This was a dodgy scheme to try to get a discount for a struggling business. Nothing more. As with Stephen, it's all about the money.

It's almost disappointing.

'You're going to call Graham,' I tell him. 'And you're going to say that your complaint about me was all a misunderstanding. Got it?'

Declan doesn't seem to know what to do. He steps forward and then back, pivoting and turning to the side, glancing towards the exposed wires on the wall. His teeth are clenched and I can almost see the cogs whirring in his mind as he tries to figure out the best thing to do.

'I thought you'd quit.'

'Who says I didn't?'

'So why should you care if I withdraw the complaint?'

'Because I *do* care. Because it's my reputation and I've worked with those people for a long time. Because the way people see me is more important than you getting a few quid.'

He glances past me, through the window towards the car park. I check over my shoulder but there's no one there. When I turn back, he's taken a stride towards me. For the first time since I got here, there's a flicker of fear. Declan is bigger than me, stronger, and we're on our own. This part of the trading estate is new and empty. Anything could happen.

'If I make the call, what then?' he asks.

'What do you mean?'

'What happens to me?'

'*Nothing* happens to you. That's the end of it.'

His nose twitches as if there's a bad smell in the room. 'What do you want me to say?'

'That you've thought things over and that you think there was a misunderstanding. No harm done but you think it's best for all involved if you do business elsewhere.'

He's thinking it over. I'm in a hole but he could be, too. I don't actually have his girlfriend's phone number; all I have is a name. There are photos of Declan and Nicole across Facebook. He's not willing to take the chance.

'Fine,' he replies. 'I'll do it now.'

I listen as he does precisely that. It's a short, awkward phone call. I can't hear Graham's half of the conversation but I can imagine him joining some dots back in the office. Declan has to repeat the 'misunderstanding' line three times and I suspect it's clear to all involved that 'misunderstanding' is a poorly concealed version of 'made it up'.

By the time Declan ends the call, I already have the door open. He shouts after me, asking if the deal's still on. I don't reply. This tawdry deal *is* on, seeing as I couldn't call Nicole even if I wanted to.

I'm back in the driver's seat when my phone rings. It's Graham, perhaps ready to apologise without *actually* having to apologise. He's not one for admitting mistakes, so he'll phrase it in a way that makes it sound like he's a victim somehow. He might even go for the 'misunderstanding' line as well. I should probably take the call and tell him I quit, that I'll find another job somewhere.

Perhaps the guilt will kick in and he'll offer me the pay rise I very much don't deserve.

I ignore the call anyway and it goes into the missed calls list along with the two from Ellie. I press to return her call and Ellie answers on the second ring.

'I was starting to worry,' she says without a hint of hello. She sounds rushed.

'What's wrong?' I reply.

'Did Liv call you?'

'No.'

It's only the length of time it takes to breathe but there's a pause from the other end of the line. In that moment, my chest tightens and it feels like I can't get all the air I need.

'She ran off halfway through accounting class,' Ellie says.

'Why?'

'She got a call from Tyler and said she had to go meet him.'

FORTY-FOUR

I stumble over my words because so many thoughts collide at once. Tyler's back? Olivia's gone? Is she in danger?

'Did you hear me?' Ellie asks.

'Yeah… I… when did she leave?'

'About a minute before I called you the first time.'

That was a good fifteen minutes ago, when I was busy with Declan. I should've answered the damn phone.

'Where did she go?'

'Well that's the weird part?'

'What is?'

Ellie sounds unsure of herself. 'She said she was going to the watermill.'

'The mill? Why?'

'I don't know. She was speaking really quickly. I was trying to keep up. I offered her a lift but she was already half out the door. She didn't look like she was thinking straight. I think she was going to call a taxi. I don't know.'

Ellie doesn't have anything else to add but that's not surprising considering it sounds like everything happened in a matter of seconds.

I hang up and try calling Olivia. There's no reply, so I leave a message asking her to call, and then phone her again. Still no answer, so I text, telling her to *please* call.

If she was getting a taxi, she'd be at the mill in a matter of minutes. If only I'd answered my phone.

I think about calling Dan – she is his daughter too – but he'll be at school and, besides, I don't trust him.

Who do I trust? When the confusion and obfuscation is shunted away, is there anyone I have faith in? Maybe.

I race away from the trading estate, trying to think if there's a quicker way to get to the mill. The very fact it's on a river means there isn't. There are bridges a few miles up and downstream on either side – and then one road in and out. The only way to get there is the long way.

The alleged voice assistant on my phone seems to have had a meltdown because, whenever I say 'Call Olivia', the voice chirps back 'Did you say, "All you live here"?'. I give up after the third attempt and try something else.

It takes me almost forty minutes until I bump across the dried mud on the road and pull into the empty weed-ridden expanse of tarmac that was once a car park. A taxi might have dropped Olivia off, but there are no vehicles parked here now.

The breeze has whipped up a light mix of dust and dirt that flits across the crumbling lot at ankle-height. I try calling Olivia once more, without the useless voice assistant this time, but there's no answer. I try Ellie to let her know where I am but she isn't answering either.

I follow the once familiar trail into the woods, heading towards the rush of the river and then tracing the route towards the mill. When we were young, this route had been walked bare. It was dry and dusty in the summer, like walking on concrete. Ellie, Wayne, Jason and I didn't visit as much in winter, partly because the mud could reach knee-height in places but also because the mill itself was so cold. There was never any heating and a lot of the joy was lost when we'd have to traipse out here in coats, scarves and wellington boots. That's not to say we never came. If ever it snowed, we'd meet on the street and then race here to build snowmen, hurl snowballs, and try to walk across the semi-frozen river. This area felt like more of a home than our respective houses ever did. We grew up here as a foursome. Sometimes we'd allow others into our circle but they never lasted long. It was always us four against the world.

Then there were three and then two.

I get to the fence surrounding the mill and stop, looking for anything out of the ordinary. I'm not sure what I was expecting but there is no sign of Olivia or Tyler. The fence is taller than me and much of it is covered with the bright 'keep out' signs that only ever serve as an invitation to see what's beyond. The rest of the fence is made up of tight rings of thick metal, which makes it easy enough to see what's on the other side – not that there's much. The mill is a run-down shell of its former self. Weeds and plants have started to grow around the base and the window frames, climbing and entwining into the rotting wood and brickwork.

'Liv?'

Her name echoes around the empty space, bouncing from the trees and mill until it sounds like there are half a dozen people calling her name.

There's no reply.

I phone Ellie again, wanting to double-check she was definitely right about the mill. Could Olivia have said something else that sounds like it? She was off to a hill, or something like that?

No answer.

I try Olivia's number next, not really expecting her to pick up. She doesn't and I'm about to hang up when I realise the ringing I can hear through my phone's speaker isn't the only sound. There's a gentle distant-sounding chirp of a tinny rock song. I muffle my own phone, leaving it to ring as I walk closer to the fence, trying to figure out where the music is coming from.

I'm almost sure it's emanating from the mill itself – but then it stops. The call has dropped, so I hang up and try again. Perhaps it's because the wind changes or it might be because I'm listening for it properly, but I can hear the tune clearly now. There's the grinding of guitar strings and then a thump-thump-thump of drums. I vaguely recognise the song but couldn't place it.

It's definitely coming from inside the mill.

'Olivia?'

Her name bounces around the woods once more without reply. I follow the line of the fence from riverbank to riverbank as it loops around the outside of the mill. It's too steep for me to climb – and the metal looks sharp and dangerous in any case. I could wade out into the river and walk around the fence to the other side – but the current is surging, the water smashing into the rocks, and that's probably the least appealing option. It might be fine but there's every chance I could be half a mile downstream before I know what's happened.

'Tyler?'

His name reverberates with no response, moments before the wind fizzes louder, stealing the word and sending it far away.

If Olivia's phone is inside the mill, then she must have got through, over or around the fence somehow. I can't believe she went around the outside, but she might have got a boost from Tyler to get over. That doesn't explain how he'd have got in. If he'd tried climbing, his hands would have been scratched bare.

I follow the route once more, this time pushing on the fence every metre or so, hoping for give. I've not gone far when I spot a patch where the wire has been snipped neatly. From anywhere other than directly next to it, the fence looks intact, but with the merest of pushes, one section separates from the other and opens like a cat flap.

It seems simple but the sharp edges of the fence rake my forearms as soon I push inside. There's blood instantly, thick and dark red, dripping onto the grass and my shoe. The pain stabs as if I'm still being gouged and it doesn't help when I take a moment to prod and poke the skin. It's opened me up like a burnt pasty and is a good millimetre or two deep. When I clench my fist, the blood oozes, trickling along my hand and again running onto the ground.

I swear under my breath, digging into a pocket for a tissue and clamping it onto my arm.

'Liv?'

No answer.

I take a couple of steps towards the mill and then freeze as an overwhelming sense of trepidation hits. It's almost as if I've walked into a wall. It's there but it's not. For a moment, it feels as if something has touched my shoulder but, when I spin, there's nobody there. Only the wind. Only the woods. Only the rampaging rush of water.

I'm being watched.

I can't know that for sure – the windows of the mill are boarded up and there's no one visible around the treeline – but there's a prickling at the base of my neck that's almost overpowering.

'Liv?'

I take a step forward and then another, moving slowly towards what used to be the front door. It's boarded up – but then it always was. When we first came here, it was nailed into place but Jason and Wayne brought a pair of hammers to take care of that. We'd leave the board in place and then move it to one side when we needed. It would have been fixed in the decades since but this is always the type of place where no entry and keep out signs feel optional.

The board is thick wood but it's only leaning against the door frame, with nothing holding it in place. Like the old days. I nudge it aside, sliding into the mill for the first time in more than twenty years. I can't remember the last time I was here for sure but suspect it was before Wayne died.

The inside of the mill is almost entirely dark. The electrics never worked when we used to visit and certainly wouldn't have been fixed since. Thin tendrils of light creep through gaps between boards and there's one large spotlight in the middle of the floor beaming down through what must be a broken window high above.

'Liv? Tyler?'

My voice echoes again but nobody moves, nobody answers. I take out my phone once more and the window of white almost blinds me against the shadows. I call Olivia one more time, waiting the second or two it takes to connect until something on the far side of the mill flashes to life. The almost familiar tune blares as Olivia's phone screen blinks on and off.

I set off towards it, the worn soles of my shoes slaloming on the sawdust and dirt. Olivia's phone has been abandoned on the floor. The screen is cracked like a spider's web from numerous drops and accidents. She's asked Dan and me to buy her a new one in the past but we always say that if she can't look after this one, then how can we expect her to look after a brand-new one.

It seems so silly now.

As I crouch and reach for Olivia's phone, there's a scuffing scramble of feet from behind. I turn but it's already too late. Something, some*one*, is upon me – and then it all goes black.

FORTY-FIVE

There's blood on my windscreen.

It's in the corner, a few speckled spots and then a thicker pool towards the bottom.

This is definitely a dream. There can't be any question about that. There's a hazy grey around the edges of my vision; that blinking, fuzzy sense that everything in front of me is a bewildering construct of my imagination.

Only this time, it *is* a dream.

My mouth is parched and I cluck my tongue trying to catch my breath. When I open my eyes, there is blood but it's not on a windscreen; it's on my arm. The scratch from the fence has started to dry, leaving a gloopy mound that is neither solid nor liquid. Like paint drying on the can's lid.

It takes me a few seconds to realise I'm still in the mill. I'm leaning against a wall with the dampness of the flaking plaster soaking through my top. There's a thin shaft beaming down from above, giving me barely enough light to see the slice along my arm. The back of my head hurts close to my ear and, when I touch it, there's more sticky blood there.

I pull myself to my feet, calling Olivia's name. There's no reply and I reach for my phone – except it's no longer in my pocket.

Aside from the bump on my head and slight dizziness, I don't feel too bad. It's then that I notice the gentle undercurrent of moaning and realise it isn't coming from me; there's someone else here.

Another limp shaft of light is illuminating the corner of the mill and there's a lump there, which, from a distance, looks like a discarded bin bag. It's only as I take a few steps closer that I see the shape bobbing up and down with each intake of breath. Every exhalation brings a husky groan.

I take a few steps towards the shape, wary that someone has very recently bashed me in the back of the head.

'Liv?'

I hiss the name, hoping she'll roll over – but it's not her. The shape does twist, blinking into the light. His face is so much narrower than the last time I saw it, hair straggly and unkempt. One of his eyes has swollen and closed, like a boxer who's been on the end of a hiding.

'Tyler…?'

He moans an acknowledgement, rolling around until I can see that his hands are bound in front of him. I hurry towards him and kneel. He reels his head back, like a puppy frightened of being kicked. It surprises even me but there's definitely relief at seeing him alive.

'It's Rose,' I say. 'Liv's mum. It's me.'

I can barely see him but his one good eye squints through the shadow with an ominous gleam. His hands are bound with some sort of plastic cord; perhaps a washing line. The knots are tight and small and I have no chance of getting a fingernail inside.

His voice is husky and dry: 'Water.'

'I don't have any on me,' I reply. 'We'll get you outside to my car.'

He starts to croak something but is interrupted by a third voice from behind me, 'You won't.'

It's a woman's voice but hard to place. Vaguely familiar but like she's trying an accent. I spin but there's nobody there, only the shadows.

'Who's that?'

There's the creak of a floorboard but the echo is so loud that I can't figure out from which direction it comes. I'm literally backed into a corner. Tyler is at my side, still trying to croak something.

The voice echoes around the empty mill: 'You did it, didn't you?'

'Did what?'

'The car.'

Whoever it is knows about me waking up in the field… although I'm not sure what that means. There's another footstep and another rasp of ancient wood.

'What about the car?' I reply.

Two more footsteps and Tyler ekes out the word, 'Don't'.

'Don't what?' I ask.

It's the woman's voice who answers: 'He means, "don't come any closer". I think he's missing a "please" from the beginning. He's been saying that word a lot this week.'

'Liv?' My voice echoes once more.

There's silence… and then: 'Oh, she's here. She's not feeling well.'

Another squeak of rotting wood booms around the mill.

'What have you done to her?'

A silhouette fills the spotlight in the middle of the floor. It's only the legs at first, then the lower torso, then arms. I think it's a trick of the light at first but it isn't. One of the shadowed hands is clutching a knife. The razor point is clear, even through the gloom.

'Not much,' the voice says, though the accent has gone. There's no disguise any longer. No point. 'Not yet,' it adds.

Another step and then the figure is fully in the light.

FORTY-SIX

'*Ellie?*'

The figure relaxes slightly and it's unquestionably her. She's wearing wellington boots, jeans and a slim-fit coat. Aside from the graveyard, I've not seen her in anything other than nightclothes for weeks. Her hair is tied back into a tight ponytail. I've seen her more days than not for almost all my life.

'It took you long enough,' she says.

'I don't understand…'

'Neither did I. It took me *years* to get it. *Decades*. But the truth was right in front of me the whole time.'

'What truth?'

Ellie says nothing but I know. Deep down, I always feared this day. Not Tyler, not Olivia, not Dan, not Jason – but Ellie. I've hurt people over the years but probably no one more than her. My biggest fear all this time was the truth.

'Tell me,' Ellie demands.

'Tell you what?'

'Tell me how my brother died. Tell me how my *twin* died.'

'You know.'

Ellie huffs a furious breath. I can't see her clearly enough, but I know her teeth are bared, like a wolf, primed and dangerous. 'I know the story,' she says. 'Everyone does. Wayne was driving too fast and he killed himself. Almost killed you. A selfish and stupid act; that's what the coroner called it. Selfish and stupid.'

'Ell—'

'And what about Jason? You broke his heart and watched him go off the rails. You heard he was on hunger strike and wouldn't visit. He almost killed himself to see you – but that still wasn't enough.'

'I didn't mean—'

'And yet, somehow, we're friends. How does that work?'

'I never meant for that to happen with Jason. We were kids. I wish I'd done things differently.'

Ellie walks in a small circle around the spotlight, scuffing her feet. The knife is ever-present in her shadow. Tyler shuffles himself into a sitting position, moaning with pain. Each of his breaths grates and catches in his throat. I'm not tied up, I could do something – rush Ellie – except she said Olivia is somewhere around here and I believe her.

'My own car accident was an experience,' Ellie says. 'Completely out of the blue – but it opened my eyes. Pain's an odd thing. When they told me I'd cracked three ribs, I couldn't believe it. Three cracked ribs and I can barely feel a thing. They said the adrenaline might be hiding the pain and gave me painkillers anyway – but it's never really hurt. The whiplash was a bitch, though.'

She rubs her neck to illustrate the point.

'*You* broke your ribs in the crash with Wayne,' she adds. 'You still feel it now and again. You've told me that.'

'Right.'

'But Wayne didn't.'

Oh, no.

I suddenly get it. I get more or less everything.

'I was driving,' Ellie says, 'and I cracked my ribs on the steering wheel. So, if Wayne was driving, how come you broke your ribs and he didn't?'

There's an answer, something obvious – except I can't think of anything. My mind is blank.

'Say it,' Ellie demands.

FORTY-SEVEN

23 YEARS AGO

Wayne is sitting on the bonnet of his car, tossing the keys from one hand to the other.

'No way,' he says.

I press myself up against him, running my nails along his chest. I dig them into his T-shirt just enough so that he can feel it and a grin creeps onto his face.

'Pleeeeeeease,' I beg. 'Please let me drive.'

'No.'

There's something particularly gorgeous about him today. He's been working on his car most of the day and, because of the heat of the day and the fact he never drinks enough water, the muscles in his arms are bulging. He's really become a man.

'I'll make it up to you,' I purr.

The grin grows wider. 'How?'

'You know…'

He glances past me towards the dusty, deserted car park outside the mill. His is the only vehicle here. After spending the day with his car, I finally persuaded him to bring me out here. Just us this time. No Ellie or Jason to disturb us. Nobody else from the town was around either, not even a nosey dog-walker. It felt like the world was ours and ours alone.

He glances up to the sky but only for a moment. His eyes are for me. 'It's getting dark,' he says.

'So let's get going. I'll be really careful.'

'You've not passed your test yet.'

I press against him again, lips level, barely a couple of centimetres between us. 'No one's going to stop us. I do know *how* to drive. It was that stupid examiner who spoiled things. You know that.'

I've cracked him now. I can see it in his smirk.

I press the car keys out of his hand and peck him gently on the nose before pushing my lips hard onto his. I've been trying to get Wayne to let me drive his pride and joy for weeks but he says no to everyone. This is a victory. This means he loves me.

I have to shunt the driver's seat forward so I can reach the pedals.

Wayne fusses by telling me about how fourth gear sticks sometimes. 'You need to shove it hard,' he says.

'Whatever.'

'Not "whatever". Listen to me.'

'I am!'

I almost stall the car on the way out of the car park but blame it on a sticky first gear and try again. The engine purrs powerfully and beautifully. It's much better than being behind the wheel of the instructor's car. He complains if I get out of third gear but this is real freedom. The vibration of the engine surges up through the bodywork of the car, making the driver's seat hum with thunderous power.

'Good, innit?' Wayne says from the passenger seat.

I turn out of the lane that leads to the mill, moving onto the windy country roads. Wayne scolds me for not indicating but it's not as if there are any cars near. Whenever I push harder on the pedal, the engine roars its approval. I can feel Wayne watching from the passenger seat, not quite approving as I accelerate out of a bend. It's only when the tyres skid across a loose coating of gravel that he speaks up.

'Slow down,' he says.

'I know what I'm doing.'

'You've not passed your test yet.'

'I know how to drive.'

I slow for the next bend but forget one turn leads into a second. At the last moment, as the black and white chevrons blare large in front, I brake and then make the car lurch by going straight from third to first.

Wayne is thrown forward in his seat and then turns to stare in disapproval: 'What are you doing?'

'It's the car.'

'You're going too fast.'

'No I'm not.'

I take the next bend far more carefully but the steering wheel is stiff. I wouldn't admit it to Wayne, but it almost feels as if it is fighting against me whenever I try to turn it at lower speeds.

There are a couple more bends and then, finally, a long straight. This is the bit I've been looking forward to. As Wayne said, I have to ram the gearstick into fourth, but, when I ease onto the accelerator, the entire machine pulsates with power. The vibrations start under my feet, rippling up through the seat until it feels as the car and I are one and the same. It's beautiful.

Wayne is saying something but the engine is so loud that I can't hear him. It'll be something about my speed, about slowing down. Not yet, though. I've been waiting for this. This is what living is all about. I don't think he gets that sometimes. He's never waded out across the river when it's flowing at its fastest. He hasn't run the paddles of the waterwheel, trying to get to the top. Ellie has. Jason has. I have. Not Wayne. He sees the danger; we see opportunity and fun.

Faster still. The hedges blur, the tarmac tears.

More, please. Give me more.

FORTY-EIGHT

'Say it.'

Ellie demands I speak for a second time. Her voice is firm and calm – but it's that unruffled tone that terrifies me. This is the teenage Ellie, the one who'd lead the way clambering up the paddles outside, trying to get to the top of the waterwheel. She's mellowed over the years because that's what time does to people. What was once important gradually becomes just another thing.

Except Ellie lost a brother, a *twin* brother. How can that ever become 'just another thing'?

'I was driving.'

My words are almost lost to the sound of the river outside. Nothing happens for a moment.

It was so long ago that there are times where I've convinced myself it's not true. The reality is that Wayne was driving. Everyone knows that. It happened. It's only when I let my mind wander that the truth appears.

'Louder.'

I shout this time, finally saying what I should have done so many years ago. 'I was driving.'

As if to confirm it, the scar around my temple throbs and there's a stabbing pain in my ribs. I was never the same after the crash and I suppose the physical changes pale compared to everything else.

'Louder.'

'I WAS DRIVING!'

The only other sounds are the river and the gentle wheeze of Tyler trying to breathe at my side. Ellie takes a step forward, her silhouette swelling in the spotlight.

'That car was his pride and joy,' she says.

'Yes.'

'He was a sensible driver.'

'Yes.'

'I'd been in the car with him, we all had. He was careful. He didn't speed. He didn't like taking risks.'

'I know.'

'So why would *he* have been showing off? You were driving.'

'Yes.'

The way she spells it out now is so matter-of-fact, so obvious, that I can't believe nobody ever questioned things.

'You switched places,' she adds. 'You belted yourself into the passenger seat and put him behind the wheel. You dragged his *dead* body into the driver's seat after *you* killed him.'

I'm silent at that. I haven't thought about those moments in a long time.

Actually, that's not true. It's strange in that I seem to *always* think about it and yet it's a memory that sits behind other thoughts. It's like a fingernail; always there and yet hardly noticeable.

'I didn't mean to,' I say.

'Tell me what you did.'

'Ell—'

'Tell me!'

'Where's Olivia?'

'Tell me, or I swear to God...'

She doesn't finish the sentence but she doesn't need to. What choice do I have? I can see what she has done to Tyler.

'Why him?' she asks.

'I don't know what you mean.'

'Why did he die and you survive?'

Ellie is choked, the words sticking in her throat.

'I don't know,' I reply. 'Luck. That's all I can say. I remember opening my eyes. My chest and eye hurt but I felt okay. Then I looked across and saw him in the passenger seat and he… wasn't. I don't have a better explanation. When I said at the graveyard that I sometimes wish it was me who died, I meant it.'

'What happened then?'

Tyler wobbles, his head lolling to the side. I try to prop him up but Ellie hisses for me to leave him. All I can do is lean him against the wall.

'I didn't plan it,' I say. 'It was impulse… instinct to move him. After I'd done it, I was going to put him back but then I heard the other car pulling in.'

'Your Angel David?'

I shiver at the memory. 'Right. There was no turning back. I wanted to tell people but it was too late. It was Wayne's car and he was in the driving seat. Everyone assumed he was driving.'

'You *made* them assume.'

'I know. I'm sorry.'

The shadow of the knife rises and, though she's across the floor, there's a moment in which I think Ellie is going to leap forward. Even over the noise of the river, I hear her take a breath. Her silhouette hulks larger and then softens.

'It wasn't enough for you, was it?' she says.

'What wasn't?'

'You couldn't stop at ruining one of my brothers, you had to have the other.'

There's a lump in my throat. Self-serving, I know. How can I feel sorry for myself after what I did? She's right to hate me.

'I didn't plan that,' I say.

'You knew Jason adored you.'

'Yes.'

'And you led him on.'

'I…'

I stumble, because I don't have the words – and she wouldn't want to hear them anyway. I *didn't* lead Jason on as such but I didn't discourage him. Of course I knew he had a thing for me. Everyone did. The kids at school knew. Wayne knew. Ellie knew. He was a couple of years below us but he'd follow his brother and sister around to spend time with me. If I lay on the riverbank, he'd lay at my side. If I tried to wade into the river, he'd follow. When we were fourteen or fifteen and he was eighteen months younger, it was funny to see what he'd do for me. By the time I was nineteen and he'd recently turned eighteen, things were different. It definitely wasn't funny any longer.

'I shouldn't have let it happen,' I say.

'But you did – and then you broke his heart.'

'I was young, Ell. *We* were young. I didn't know what would happen after I broke up with him. I'm sorry.'

'Oh, you will be.'

She spits her reply with righteous fury.

'What do you mean?'

'You took my brother – my broth*ers* – and I'm going to take your daughter.'

I scramble to my feet. The sawdust and sand scuffs underneath. My knees wobble because I've been sitting on them for too long.

'Stay where you are,' Ellie says.

'Where's Liv?'

'Sleeping. She had a rather strong sedative with her can of Coke during her accounting lesson. You know I can't have children. I was doing all that for *your* daughter after what you'd done to me?'

She's right. How can I ever justify it?

'I never meant for everything to happen,' I say.

'But you never spoke up about it, did you? You let everyone believe Wayne was driving when it was you. It took me crashing my own car to realise.'

'I'm sorry.'

'Stop saying that!' She speaks through clenched teeth. 'It's always about you, isn't it? You're obsessed with yourself; always whining about your husband. You know the problem isn't Dan, don't you? It's you.'

Her words hurt because they scratch at my darkest fears. She's only saying what I've laid awake thinking about. Life is so easy when everything's an injustice. If it's someone else's fault, then every day is a challenge to prove a point. Without that, a person can only wallow in failure.

'I don't know how he put up with you this long,' Ellie adds. 'And then, after everything you have – a successful, smart husband; a daughter – after all that, you're getting a divorce! It's always, *always*, about you.'

I don't argue. She's right. How many conversations have we had about her problems over the years? I've accepted that she lives alone, never asking if she craves more. We haven't had a conversation about whether she wants to have children, or how the removal of her ovaries has affected her life. I wondered if she was falling into depression because she rarely left the house – but I never actually asked and I didn't offer to go places with her. It *is* always about me. I scoff at someone like Natasha for the mundanity of her life – but mine is a constant invented drama. All the arguments with Dan and Olivia over nothing – and for what?

'What are you going to do?' I ask, not sure I want the answer.

Ellie replies with mortifying calm: 'I'll tell the police Olivia has been confiding in me during our classes. She was scared of what her mum might do. Her dad's leaving and her mum fears she can't afford to be by herself. Her mother's been arguing with her boyfriend and making threats. She's been saying, "we'll always have each other", and things like that.'

It's more or less true.

'People love to believe others are crazy,' Ellie adds. 'They say, "You're mad", "You're mental", "You're not right in the head" – all that. Look at how erratic you've been all week. Not hard to believe you're going off the rails.'

There's a horrible, creeping realisation that she's right. What's going to happen if the police talk to Peter the receptionist, or Stephen? Or Graham from work? Or Declan? Or Dan himself? All of them will confirm how unpredictable I've been. There's a pattern. I presume Ellie's orchestrated much of it but that won't matter.

'What are you going to do?' I ask again.

'Wait and see.'

'Is Liv here?'

'Wouldn't you like to know?'

Tyler mumbles something and I turn to look at him as he slides to the floor. I want to help but I'm not sure what I can do.

'What did you do to him?' I ask.

'He was a late addition. Bit of an accident, really. He's dropped around a couple of times to pick up Liv after her class. Always seemed like a good kid to me – not that you thought so. You always see the worst in people. He was stomping down the road looking angry the other night. I asked if he was all right and he said you'd been on at him. I asked if he wanted a smoke or drink back at mine. Quick couple of dissolvable painkillers in his beer and out he went. I told you they knock me right out. They did the same for him.' She pauses and I can imagine her licking her lips. '...And Liv.'

She said Olivia was sleeping and I can only hope it's true and nothing more. I wonder if I can get to Ellie, perhaps wrestle the knife away. The moment I take a step forward, the sandy dust crunches underfoot.

Ellie tells me to stop and I do. Any movements I make are a giveaway. I'm stuck in the corner next to Tyler until she decides otherwise.

'Have you had Tyler here the whole time?' I ask.

'Course not. He was in my basement most of the time. Heavier than he looks, mind. Getting him up the stairs and into the rental car was hard work.'

'That's how you got his blood?'

'Obviously. For a while I hoped the police might latch on. Find the blood on your car, then I realised you'd done a good job cleaning. Had to leave a little more.'

I suppose that explains the little things around the house. Keys being moved, a faked break-in, the missing money. All little bits and pieces to keep me on edge. Ellie waited for me to leave the house and then used her keys to get in and out.

'I told Tyler I'd kill Olivia if he tried to escape,' Ellie says. 'He really does care for her. He's been as good as gold all week. I guess the sedatives help, but still… Good job the doctor was so happy to dish out the prescription. I was only turning it on a bit to try to get a whiplash claim in. Didn't realise he'd give me more drugs than a Colombian war lord.'

'What did you mean when you said you were going to take Liv?'

'What do you think?'

'She's not dead…?'

Ellie lets it hang, taking a while to reply. '*I'm* not going to do anything,' she says. '*You've* already done it. Going off the rails, remember? Erratic. Unpredictable.'

It suddenly dawns properly that it's her aim to pin on me whatever she has planned for Olivia and Tyler.

I shiver, my words trembling as well: 'People won't believe I did any of this.'

'*Really*? Not even after Olivia texts her father to say you've been acting really weird? That she's worried about what you might do? Not after your many arguments with Tyler? All the rows with Dan? The blood in the garage? You don't think that perhaps there's a speck of blood you might have missed in your car? Did you find his chain? After all that, you don't think people will believe you could do any of this…?'

She's right. She was right before that people are desperate to believe others are mad and she's right about this. I've left a trail of destruction around me for seven days and it's all too easy to believe I've lost it.

'Were you at the hotel?' I ask.

'I didn't think you'd make it so easy. Simply enough to invent Luke and set up an email and website. Suggest a hotel. Took me less than an hour. Keeping track of mobile phones was a nuisance, though. I almost texted you from the wrong one. After that, it wasn't hard to persuade someone to slip something into your drink. Expensive but easy. There was something cathartic about driving you out to the middle of nowhere and then dragging you into the driver's seat. The whole time, I was thinking about how you'd done exactly that to my brother. I wondered if it might trigger some memories. A bit of guilt for once. Perhaps you'd own up to your own actions, instead of blaming others?'

I'm silent but I slide myself forward a couple of steps without raising my feet. It's the only way I can manage to move without making a noise. I can only see Ellie's shadow but, if she's in the dark, that means she can't see much of me either.

'What I didn't expect,' she adds, 'is that you'd be suspicious of so many other people. You're so self-centred. It's been hilarious watching you this week. You even ran over wanting to borrow my car. What is *wrong* with you?'

I suppose she has me there. Something *is* wrong with me. There has to be. I leave carnage in my wake. Look at Dan. He's intelligent with a good job. We've created a talented, smart young woman in Olivia – and yet I've spent years arguing with both of them.

'Why go through all the effort?' I ask. 'The hotel, the car, the house, Tyler…'

'Because I wanted you to feel a fraction of the confusion, the *anger*, the pain, I've had of being by myself for twenty years – all because of you.'

Ellie's shouting now, drowning out the roar of the river with the snarl of her voice.

'You can't know what it's like to have a twin, to share a womb, and have that ripped away. At least you'll get to feel some of that now.'

'Where's Olivia?'

Ellie has crescendoed to a peak of fury but when she speaks next, she's measured once more – and terrifyingly direct. 'She's already dead.'

FORTY-NINE

It doesn't sound real. I've heard what Ellie said but she speaks with such disdain that I can't take it in.

'She's… dead?'

'Drowned in the river outside by a jealous parent. What a tragedy.'

'No…'

'See for yourself.'

It takes a second or two for my legs to move. They're heavy with fatigue and the burden of everything I've done.

As well as the front door, the watermill has a second that leads almost onto the river itself. It opens onto a wooden platform adjacent to the waterwheel. All of that was rotting twenty years ago.

Ellie disappears into the shadows, allowing me to stagger my way to the far wall. I can make out the door because of a faint rim of light around the edge. It's held in place by a flimsy hook and I'm blinded as the white-grey of the sky pours inside. I'm squinting as I clumsily fumble my way onto the platform. The wood is soft and springy, like a trampoline. The combination of that and the dazzling light leaves me on my knees, crawling towards the waterwheel.

Decades back, we'd run along the platform and leap onto the wheel, trying to scramble up as the water drove the paddles in the opposite direction. Like trying to walk up an escalator that's going down.

I turn in a semicircle, looking at the water for any sign of Olivia. She's not here.

Except… there's a dark shape next to the waterwheel… *under* the waterwheel. At first I think it might be a flapping piece of plastic or rubber – but then I recognise Olivia's leather jacket. I hurl myself flat onto the edge of the platform, trying to scoop my arms around her as the torrent surges into me. Olivia is face-down, held in place by a piece of the same washing line rope with which Tyler is tied. It's strung across two hooks embedded in the wheel. There are many other hooks and nails protruding from the sodden wood and, as I reach for Olivia, something slices into my other arm. At least I'll have matching scars.

I unhook the rope and, for a terrifying second, Olivia drops limply under the surface of the water. The only reason she isn't carried away is that she catches on the paddle board itself. It takes all my effort to get an arm underneath her and then yank her clear of the river. I fall backwards onto the platform with her on top of me.

She's a mass of ruffled pink hair and sodden, torn black clothes. When I turn Olivia over, her eyes are closed, her skin waxy and grey. My only hope is that she was somehow able to breathe in the air pocket under the paddles of the wheel, rather than being dragged completely under by the river flow. I say her name but there's no response. Her chest isn't rising.

'Shame…'

I glance backwards towards Ellie, who has emerged onto the platform. Tyler is at her feet, slumped and seemingly unconscious.

'How long was she under?!'

I'm shouting but get no response. We were talking inside for a good while and I have no idea how long I was unconscious before that. I turn back to Olivia, pushing down hard in the centre of her chest, pumping five times and then pressing my ear to her lips. I'm hoping for a miracle.

'You drowned your own daughter,' Ellie says. 'Then you drowned her boyfriend.'

I pump five more times on Olivia's chest. 'No.'

'People will believe it.'

I risk another glance and Ellie is closer to me, knife in her hand. Five more pumps. Olivia's not moving.

'I figured I could get rid of your body somewhere in the woods,' Ellie says. 'Let someone discover poor Liv and Tyler in the river. Let everyone make up their own minds about you. They'll probably assume you're on the run. Either that or killed yourself and floated downstream. Doesn't matter which.'

Five more pumps and then I stand and spin. Ellie is a couple of steps away, the knife tight in her grip, the blade angled towards me. I ball my fists, trying not to shiver.

'*Really?*' Ellie's laughing. 'When have you ever been a fighter?'

And then Olivia coughs.

FIFTY

It's a beautiful sound.

I spin back to Olivia and she rolls onto her side, spitting water onto the platform. She would have swallowed so much water but must have found the air pocket. I drop to my knees, cradling her head as she groans and continues to spit up nastiness. I want to stay with her but there's a creak from behind and I turn quickly, rising to face the advancing Ellie.

'Stay away,' I hiss.

I felt defeated before, perhaps deserving of whatever happened to me. But Olivia doesn't warrant this, and neither does Tyler. Ellie's face is twisted with wrath, the knife raised. She lunges towards me, but it's hard to get a sound footing on the saturated wood and she slips. It's not enough to send her tumbling but plenty to telegraph her move. I step to the side, which only makes her angrier. This time, I don't wait for her. I hurl myself at Ellie's midriff, throwing an arm around her in a rugby tackle. I slip but my momentum is enough to send us both flying.

Something hurts... lots of things hurt. I have scratches along both arms, the thumping at the back of my head, the old rib injury. For a moment, everything is spinning but I blink it away as we slide towards the water. Ellie is thrashing and fighting but I'm on top... or think I am. The moment I try to stabilise myself, my knee sinks into the plasticine-like mush of wood. That shifting of weight is enough for Ellie to ram an elbow into my side, which is quickly followed by a second that connects with the spot where I broke my ribs all those years ago.

I see stars for a second as everything swirls. There's blood in my mouth, more drooling across my eyelid. When I open my eyes, Ellie is on top, knees straddled across my chest, pinning my elbows to the floor. She's foaming at the mouth, eyes frenzied.

She raises the knife with both hands, sacrifice-style.

'Goodbye, Rosie.'

I close my eyes, anticipating...

And then the weight lifts.

I open my eyes, feeling the sting of the light. The shadow of an angel is standing over me. Big and strong David. Always my saviour.

I blink.

It's not David. There's an army jacket and scruffy boots.

Jason.

He's torn the knife from Ellie's hand and hurls it into the river as she aims a slap towards him. He deftly steps away, somehow making it easy to balance on this sponge.

'No,' he says.

Ellie flings herself at him but he holds onto her wrists with poise and control.

'This is for you! For us!'

Ellie is howling, practically spitting in her brother's face, but he doesn't react.

'She was driving. She killed Wayne. It was always her. Look what she's done to us.'

Everything is hazy, like watching through greaseproof paper. I might imagine it, but I'm sure Jason glances to me. He doesn't speak, doesn't do anything other than offer the briefest of glimpses, but in that moment he tells me that's he's always known. Ellie might have been taken in by me switching seats in the car, but never Jason. He knew I killed his brother and yet he willingly started a relationship with me anyway. I'm hardly blameless but this is why he went off the rails. I may have broken his heart – but he'd already betrayed his flesh and blood.

'I don't want this,' Jason says.

Ellie flaps and tries to fight but Jason is far stronger than she is. My head flops back as pain surges through me. I wonder if Ellie has broken my ribs again, or if the blow to my head did more damage than I thought. I want to open my eyes and watch what's happening, to see how it ends, but it hurts so much. I want to cradle Olivia, to make sure she's safe. My last thought before everything goes black is to wonder whether this is a dream. Perhaps there is no Jason at all. No angel. Not this time. Ellie stabbed me and it's all over.

FIFTY-ONE

The lights are so bright that it feels like I'm burning. It's either the fiery brimstone of hell, or the pearly gates of heaven. Except it's neither, of course it's not.

'Hi…'

Dan.

His voice is soft and kindly and I feel something – him – stroking the back of my hand. For a moment, I'm twenty-one and in love – and then I sit up so quickly that my head spins.

'Liv!'

'She's safe,' Dan says.

I'm in a bed, surrounded by a blinding white.

'You're in hospital,' Dan says. 'You both are. She's a couple of rooms down. Tyler's here, too. Everyone's fine.'

'But Ellie—'

'I know. Everyone knows. The police are looking for her.'

A hazy grey still taints everything around me. When I turn slightly to see what else is in the room, it's like I'm seeing everything in slow motion.

It's as if he's read my thoughts as Dan says: 'You're on some pretty strong medication. You're supposed to be sleeping.'

'Ellie got away?'

I think Dan nods. It's hard to tell. Everything is swaying. 'Jason saved you but, yes. You're safe here.'

'I want to see Liv.'

'I don't think—'

I don't wait for him to say no, pushing myself up and trying to free my legs from the tightly tucked sheets. Dan tries to stop me but he doesn't get much choice when I slump into him, using his hard body to hold me up. It's been such a long time since we touched in any way that I've forgotten how well we fit together. My head slots into his shoulder as he supports my weight.

'The doctor said—'

'Please,' I say. 'Please take me to her.'

Dan stops protesting but he's practically dragging me as we head out of the room into an equally white corridor. I think I close my eyes because the next thing I know, I'm at the side of another hospital bed in another white room. So much white.

Olivia is sleeping, her chest rising and falling slowly and rhythmically. Her hair is tufty and dirty, some of it plastered to her forehead. I feel like such a fool for all those arguments over hair colour, tattoos and who knows what else.

'She's safe,' I whisper.

There's no reply and, for a moment, I wonder if I've actually spoken. Perhaps I only thought the words. It's all very confusing.

'Yes,' Dan says.

'She'll be okay?'

'Yes.'

'What about Tyler?'

Dan lowers me into a chair and then stands at my side, hand on my shoulder. I grip his fingers and, for the time in years, there's reassurance there.

'He's stable at a different end of the hospital. His dad's with him but it sounds like he's going to be okay. Liv's been asking for him in between sleeping. They had to give her something to calm her but she will be fine.'

I want to wake her, to hear her voice and say I'm sorry. I know I can't, though. It's not all about me.

'Why'd you call him?' Dan asks, unexpectedly.

'Who?'

'Jason.'

It's only now that Dan brings it up that I remember. When I was in the car and the stupid voice assistant on my phone couldn't call Olivia, I was trying to think of who I trusted. I'd doubted Jason, suspected him of being in on whatever was happening to me, but then I'd remembered our shared history. The times we had before and after Wayne died. And for once, I ignored the self-doubt and I called him, saying I was on my way to the mill because Olivia was there. I didn't know I was walking into a trap but figured he might be able to help if Tyler was a problem.

'Why not me?' Dan adds.

'Because...' I screw my eyes closed, partly because my head hurts less when it's dark but mainly because I don't want Dan to look at me. 'Because I've been doubting myself,' I say. 'Doubting everyone.'

'Including me?'

'Yes.'

'Why? I know we're separating but it's all been amicable. I know we're not in love but I didn't think we were enemies.'

That word stings. *Enemies*. I didn't think Ellie was an enemy, either.

'A lot's happened,' I say.

'Like what?'

I tell him about the hotel, Stephen, waking up in the field, being told by Mr Rawley that Dan was home on the day the house was broken into and everything else I can remember. He listens without reply and then, when I'm done, he squeezes my shoulder gently.

'Our neighbour is wrong,' he says. 'I wasn't home on that day. He must have been mistaken.'

I believe him. Mr Rawley from over the road has always been a nosey so-and-so. There's every chance he got the wrong day.

'There's more,' I say.

'Go on.'

I open my eyes and glance to Olivia. She's still asleep, chest rising methodically.

'Not here,' I say.

I take a moment to watch Olivia's chest rise and fall, to convince myself she's safe. Dan's at my side and then he steers me away. I remember little of the corridor or journey but the next thing I know, he's tucking me into my bed and making sure I'm comfortable. He sits at my side, saying nothing, though I can sense him anticipating. He's not questioned any of what happened so far, taking it in his stride.

'I went to the gym,' I say. 'I opened your locker.'

'Oh.'

This time I wait. Dan clears his throat.

'Did you tell anyone?' he asks quietly.

'No.'

'The stun gun belongs to Alice's brother. He brought it back from holiday, not knowing it was illegal. I have no idea how he got it through airport security. Alice had it her gym bag. She was going to hand it in to the police but that's technically an offence. I said I'd do it as a favour. Figured being a deputy headteacher would go in my favour. I'd say I found it in a hedge, something like that. It's gone now.'

I think of seeing Dan trail after Alice at the car boot and that twinge of sorrow I felt for him. I feel it now, too. Stronger this time. Perhaps he's in love with her? If he is, it's not reciprocated. The poor sod. No wonder he said he'd do that for her.

'DBA Enterprises,' I say.

'Who?'

'The credit card.'

'Oh…' He raises his eyebrows in surprise. 'That's the leasing company for my new apartment. I thought I told you? I had to pay a deposit. That's okay, isn't it?'

Of course it is. It makes perfect sense.

'Where's Jason?' I ask.

'With the police, last I heard. They're waiting to talk to you, Tyler and Liv. I think he's the only one in a decent state. I don't know for sure.'

I sigh with relief and regret.

Dan's hand reaches under the covers until it meets mine. He locks his fingers into me and squeezes gently. Neither of us speak because we don't need to. We're still breaking up – we both know it. Nothing has solved the underlying problems of our marriage – but at least we have trust. Our beautiful daughter is along the hallway and we owe it to her to be her parents.

'She'll be fine,' Dan says, reading my mind.

We've got many conversations to have in the days to come – and I've got some serious explaining to do, not only to him but probably the police as well. For now, I can think only of Olivia.

'Yes,' I agree. 'She'll be fine.'

FIFTY-TWO

A second police car pulls up outside Rose's house to join the first. A pair of officers get out and head inside, joining the two already in there.

I wonder what they're doing. Wonder what Rose has told them, not to mention my traitorous brother. My house is out of bounds – more police – but the time will come when Rosie, Dan and Olivia are all back here. A time when they think they're safe.

That's when I'll return. I'll be ready the next time. I owe it to myself and I owe it to Wayne. I waited more than twenty years for this, so what's a few months more?

Be seeing you around, Rosie. Be seeing you around.

A LETTER FROM KERRY

Writing books is a weird thing. I can't speak for other authors but, with me, there's a part of everything I write that is a window into who I am as a person. Many of the things I find funny are right there in my characters. Things that frustrate and annoy me will also annoy my characters. If you've read a few of my books and liked them, we'll probably get on. If you hated them, well, we probably won't.

There's also another side – because an author *isn't* his or her characters. It's easy to think that something like a character's politics are a direct reflection of the author's views – but, if that was true, every crime writer would be a secret murderer.

There is this line that's hard to define where part of a character comes from the creator but another part is pure fiction. I write a crime series with a character named Jessica and get asked all the time about how much of me is in her. The answer is that there's a lot of me in her... but, simultaneously, we're also opposites. I doubt we'd get on.

As I've got older, I think I increasingly try to write about characters to whom odd things tend to happen. The character makes the plot, rather than the plot makes the character. I completely realise that this is polarising. An author can write a chapter in which the only thing that happens is that two characters talk to one another. One reader will say, 'Well, nothing happened there.' Another will say, 'I love how those characters developed.' It's all about perception.

The reason I say all that is because my wife will read this book and this letter. The first time she reads these words will be after she's finished the book. Perhaps more than any thriller I've written before, there is a lot in here about relationships.

The entire backdrop to *Last Night* is that Rose's relationship is falling apart. While that's happening, it just so happens that something strange is also going on in her life.

I've been married to my wife for nearly ten years and I suppose there is a part of me in this book. There are the tiny inconsequential things about a partner that can drive a person absolutely mad, while, at the same time, there's an awareness that none of it really matters. There was a side of me that enjoyed taking these thoughts of marital break-up to the extreme. Art and life are not the same thing – but they're not completely different, either.

So, anyway. Hi, Louise. I don't want a divorce, I think you're awesome, but, for the love of all that is holy: STOP LEAVING SO MUCH CRAP ON THE FLOOR.

Whew. It feels cathartic to get that out.

As for literally everyone else, I do hope you enjoyed the book. Please leave a review on your platform of choice. I genuinely appreciate every review... except the one-stars that say 'not read yet'. At least give it five stars and say you've not got round to it!

Feel free to email me through *kerrywilkinson.com* - or to tweet me via *@kerrywk*. I try to respond to everything I receive.

Thanks for reading.

Kerry
February 2018